THE SONS OF
THE FALCON

DAVID GARNETT

MACMILLAN

SBN 333 13578 4

First published 1972 by
MACMILLAN LONDON LTD
London and Basingstoke
Associated companies in New York Toronto
Dublin Melbourne Johannesburg & Madras

Printed in Great Britain by
NORTHUMBERLAND PRESS LIMITED
Gateshead

TO

AGNES MAGRUDER PHILLIPS

CHAPTER ONE

At that point the defile through the mountains ran east and west, so that it was lighted up by the rising and the setting sun, but towards midday the shadows grew and only the northern face of the cliff was in sunlight, except at one place where the mountains stood back a mile apart, the river divided and between the two swirling torrents stood the island rock on which the Sons of the Falcon had built their fortress home several centuries before – with a few flat-topped houses of their retainers around it, the whole forming a typical aoul or fortified village of Transcaucasia.

The fortress itself was a pele tower of the kind that is found in most border countries: a square stone tower rising above the castellated wall which enclosed the living house, the stables, sheep pen and byres and the great courtyard, the fortified gate of which was open during the day, but locked and barred against marauders at night.

Every morning it was misty before dawn, with swirls of vapour rising from the river. Then the sun broke through and in ten minutes the defile was clear. After that the gate was opened, the bars of the sheep pen slid back and two of the girls drove the goats and the sheep upstream to pasture, and Malik, who was a renegade Kurd, saddled his pony and with his gun slung over his shoulder, mounted and picked his way down to the river, which he crossed at the ford, and then rode past the four great arable fields which constituted the estate; from there he trotted away down the river to the point where one could see an approaching friend or foe from five miles away. Up the defile and on the other side of the mountain pass, were Turks and Kurds and Tatars and Persians in whose towns and aouls muezzins called out from minarets, instead of bells pealing from belfries with conical steeples. At one time raiding parties used to come fairly often over the pass and down the river in the hopes of carrying off sheep and horses and a girl or two. But the bitter defence of the Caucasus against the Russians had led to a temporary peace between the Sons of the Falcon and their Moslem enemies, and at the time this story opens, Shamyl, the greatest of Moslem guerrilla leaders, was a prisoner in Russia and the Moslems were broken. The danger since then was from fellow-Christians downstream, in particular from the younger branch of their own family, who disputed the leadership of the clan and laid claim to its chief treasure – the wonder-working icon of Saint Anne.

The younger branch of the Sons of the Falcon, called the Solutz or Sultzi, had moved down the river to a stronghold beyond the town from which it exacted tribute from passing merchants and protection money from the inhabitants. Desperate men had joined it, and under the leadership of Ziklauri, their chief, it numbered some fifty armed men as well as a dozen boys who were learning the trade of bandits. The elder branch was weaker in fighting men: not more than eighteen with five boys, as yet untried. The head of the clan was Prince Gurgen, aged seventy-nine. His first wife had given him three sons, all of whom had been killed in the family feud, his second wife had given him two sons, Valeri and Djamlet, and two daughters. His third wife, Anastasia, one son, now five years old, and that was all. He had also an illegitimate daughter, Iriné, who had been brought up with his other children. During daylight hours the watch downstream was always kept – at midday a lad relieved Malik.

The four fields were divided as follows: one of rye, one of barley, one of potatoes, cabbages, melons and the women's gardens, and one of white flowering opium poppies, which were the only crop grown for sale. Besides the fields there was a straggling orchard along the river with apples, apricots, quinces, plums, damsons, peaches and a few almonds.

Before dawn, while it was still almost dark, old Nina had milked the goats and carried the wooden, or birchbark, buckets to the dairy, where she ruled as queen, making the kefir and yoghourt and setting bowls of milk to curdle for cheese, or to skim to make butter.

Later her mistress, Anastasia, would appear, a tall pale young woman of twenty-six with her son Vasso, five years old, and who was, it seemed, likely to be her only child, for she had had three miscarriages since his birth. She was a very handsome, proud and fierce woman, and she would sometimes flare up and answer her old husband back in front of them all, and defy him. He had only taken the whip to her twice in the seven years during which they had been married, and the second time she had thrown a knife at him. The circumstances of her marriage were these: she was the daughter of Grigori, a cousin and loyal clansman of Prince Gurgen. As a young man Grigori had left the Castle and gone to live with the Circassians, or Tcherkesses, far to the north-west in the mountains looking on to the Black Sea. The Circassians were mostly Muslims and were hostile to Russia with whom they waged an intermittent war. But the difference in religion had not prevented Grigori from marrying a Circassian beauty of high rank. She had given him two daughters. The eldest was Anastasia, her sister Tamar was ten years younger, and her mother died shortly after her birth.

Soon after his wife's death, Grigori returned to the town where he lived peaceably for another six years, when one day he was murdered in a brawl, not of his own seeking, by one of the Solutz. Prince Gurgen's second wife had died shortly before Grigori's murder, and the Prince had solved the problem of who was to look after his kinsman's orphan girls by marrying Anastasia and providing a home for Tamar.

It was for Tamar's sake that Anastasia had accepted the Prince's proposal, though there was really no alternative, as she did not know how to return to her mother's family, and had no reason to think that they would have welcomed her and her sister, if she had.

At the time of her sister's marriage, Tamar was a child of nine. She grew up as a wild creature, keeping out of the way of the Prince and Nina as much as she could. The only person she loved in the Castle, besides her sister, was Valeri, the Prince's eldest son, who was invariably kind to her and would take her to carry his tackle when he went fishing in the river. To her he was something superhuman – almost a god. Besides Valeri her chief companions were some of the boys of her own age.

The day on which this story opens in late autumn was a great occasion, but its details had exasperated the Prince because they had not been arranged as he would have had them. His second son, Djamlet, was marrying the daughter of the Archpriest Paphnuty and would be bringing his bride back to the Castle after the ceremony.

Valeri, Djamlet's elder brother, had not gone to the wedding because Katerina, the bride, had first been offered to him by the matchmaker and he had refused to marry her, so he felt that his presence might be embarrassing. The Prince had refused to go because he thought that the marriage should have been celebrated in the Castle – but Katerina had insisted that it should take place in the Cathedral in the town. Thus the young woman's wishes had overcome the express orders of the Head of the Family. Prince Gurgen was furious – but nevertheless he had to put a good face on it. Great preparations had been made, and were still being made for the reception of the happy pair. Carpets had been taken off the walls and beaten, rooms swept, the floor of the great hall washed, dark corners dusted for the first time in ten years. Iriné, the Prince's illegitimate daughter, had been deprived of her bedroom in the tower and made to share that of her young half-sisters Elisso and Salomé. Nina was icing a cake, and Salomé was whipping cream in the kitchen.

Valeri, who disliked the fuss and bustle that was going on, decided to absent himself until the hour of his brother's return. First, going to the larder, he helped himself to some slices of raw ham, half a loaf of rye bread, some apples and a copper pot to boil water for tea. With these and his Martini rifle, he walked across the yard to the stables. To his surprise Tamar was there standing inside the door. She had been waiting for him.

'What are you doing here?' he asked. Then as she did not reply, he said laughing: 'Keeping out of the way, I suppose, in case Nina gives you some household chore.' He had guessed right, for Tamar looked embarrassed and blushed.

'I am playing truant too,' he added to put her at her ease.

'Where are you going, Valeri?' she asked.

'I thought I would ride up to the lake and see if I can round up that Kabarda mare and bring her home. She must be due to foal any day now. It is autumn and she must come down for the winter.'

'Can I come with you?' asked Tamar.

Valeri was carrying his saddle and threw it over the back of his Arab mare. He was surprised at her asking.

'Come on then, if you want to. I'm taking some food. We'll eat it at the far end of the lake.'

Tamar looked at him gratefully. She could hardly believe her good fortune. What she had most hoped for had come to pass. Anastasia had given her the job of embroidering Katerina's name on the towels for her room. She had done one, and then rebelled and had run out to the stable. 'Hurry up and saddle your pony,' said Valeri without offering to help. Tamar was terrified of being caught by Anastasia or Nina before she could get away. However all went well. Three minutes later Valeri led out his mare and mounted,

Tamar climbed on her pony and followed him out of the yard. They rode down and through the ford and then took the track by the river which led up to the lake and the pass beyond.

They followed the river, winding in and out of huge boulders that had fallen from the sides of the cliff beside them. But after some miles the track left the river and there was a steep ascent up the side of the gorge, the path winding up between the rock wall and a swelling bank of slippery silver grey shale. Above them was the blue sky, opposite on the other side, naked white birch trees shining in the sun and scattering their golden leaves. Between them were interspersed black shadows of rocks and caves where no rays penetrated. As they climbed, the roar of water came louder and louder until it was deafening, and they rode out close to where the river spilled itself from the lake over a wall of rock and fell in a cascade, sheer for a hundred feet, into the gorge below.

Tamar dismounted, and while Valeri waited, holding her pony, she ran to the edge and even took a few steps along the rock wall which held back the deep waters of the lake. On her right the waterfall, white and deafening, on her left the waters of the lake, deep and motionless, until suddenly they were snatched away in a race that was like green glass at the lip in front of her and suddenly broke into a blindingly white vertical column falling, falling. She turned and picked her way back to her pony, and Valeri looked at her, noticing, as though for the first time, that she was a beautiful, slender girl, that her light brown hair was luxuriant, that her blue eyes were shining with excitement and her cheeks red, and that her nose was straight and not too large or too small. A regular Circassian beauty: much more of a Circassian than Anastasia, he thought.

Tamar was shouting at him, trying to tell him that he must go and look at the waterfall, but he shook his head, so she mounted her pony and they went on.

An hour later Tamar was collecting dry driftwood along the high-watermark of the lake, while Valeri was blowing a spark he had struck into the tinder which would light their fire. He had built it between two smooth flat boulders on which they could sit comfortably. When the fire was burning, he hung the copper pot, full of water from the lake, over it and as soon as it boiled, sprinkled in shreds of brick tea. They had only one cup between them and passed it from one to the other after each drink. The air was chilly, but they were warm with riding, and Tamar heaped more driftwood on to the fire until their faces were almost scorching. The tea was smoky and delicious.

After each swallow of tea and during her bites of bread and apple Tamar looked at Valeri and around her. The lake was sparkling in the sunlight and on the far side of it, rose up the thickly wooded slopes of the river valley, above which towered the snow peaks, outlined against a sky which seemed a deeper blue where they touched it.

Neither man nor girl spoke. Occasionally Valeri picked up a flat stone and sent it skimming in ducks and drakes across the surface of the lake, but Tamar only watched and did not imitate him.

He was unhappy about his brother's marriage – not that Djamlet should marry – that was splendid – but because he knew that Katerina was a managing woman who admired everything Russian. He expected that she would be jealous of Anastasia, treat her contemptuously and, in any quarrel, side with his father against her. She would probably try and stir up trouble between his father and himself. He had seen how she flattered the Archpriest and managed him and had little doubt that she would try the same methods on the old Prince and that they would be successful.

He did not dream of revealing such thoughts to a child like Tamar, and he soon put them aside to enjoy the beauty of the present moment.

Then Tamar went off to pull in a big log from farther

along the shore and came back very excited, as she had noticed some fresh horse-droppings and guessed that the mare he had come to look for was not far off. She was right, for presently Valeri's mare gave a piercingly loud whinny which was answered from farther off and, by the time they had finished eating their apples, the mare anxious for company, but shy of it after long months of loneliness, had approached to where their mounts were hobbled. Beside her there was running a foal which would not be more than two days old.

Though they had been silent before, the sight of this long-legged little creature – a curious skewbald – with its fresh velvet skin and curly frizzed-up tail, brought a burst of excited talk from both of them. The mare, though attracted to them and the other horses, was nervous, and when Valeri rose and approached her gently, she threw up her head, raised her tail and would have run off, if he had not turned his back on her. He walked to his hobbled mare, picked a coiled halter from the saddle tree, and gave it to Tamar.

'Take this and see if you can trap the foal.'

Tamar waited until the foal was back beside its mother, twisting his head under her, to pull at the little black milk-bag, and then she approached very gently, but instead of trying to hold the foal, she slid her hand over the mare's mane and held her by it just long enough to swing the halter over her nose and head. Then she had her.

'Well done,' said Valeri.

Tamar would have liked to have stayed by the lake until evening, but Valeri looking at the sun, said: 'We must get back now. We have to change into our best clothes and be there to welcome Djamlet and his bride.'

For Tamar the thought of the newly-married pair was dis-agreeable. She did not like Djamlet, who treated her with con-tempt, and she felt instinctively that any change at the Castle would be for the worse. She hated the squabbles that went on between Iriné, who was clever but a little crazy, and her two younger half-sisters. She hated being a woman and being expected to please men, and was happiest when she was with horses and the stable boys and, above all, the rare times when she was with Valeri. But the gloomy thoughts about girls and women and marriage were dispelled by the problem of getting mare and foal down the steep little path and down to the river.

Tamar dismounted and held her pony and the mare by the halter, while Valeri rode down the steepest part of the path alone, his mare feeling her way gingerly, so as not to slip or start a landslide of stones and scree. When he got to the bottom, he tied up his riding mare and climbed back on foot. Then he took the mother by the halter and led her down very slowly while the foal hesitated, ran a little way, stopped and finally went after them. Tamar followed slowly on her pony, keeping well back, for fear of startling the foal. Once or twice when the wild little creature ventured on to the bank of shale and she saw bits beginning to slide under his hoofs, she thought that he was done for and would be carried away in a slide into the abyss below. But each time he sprang to the rock wall in time. At last they were all safely down, and then, suddenly, Valeri was saying to her:

'I did not like to say anything before, because I thought that the little colt was quite likely to go over the edge and break his neck, but would you like to have him for your own?' Tamar stared and he went on: 'His mother is a pure bred Kabarda from the Lov stud, but he looks as though he might have the lines of his sire, Djamlet's Arab stallion. The cross may turn out well.'

Tamar could scarcely believe that she was being given the foal. To have a horse of her own was an almost unimaginable bliss. She had literally no possessions except a silver ring that had belonged to her mother.

'Do you mean that you are *giving* me the foal, to be really my own?' she asked and then ran up to him as he sat, a splendid mounted figure, and caught his hand from the bridle and kissed it.

Valeri looked at her shining eyes and saw that she was overcome with gratitude. He pulled his hand away and laughed – 'I am so glad you are pleased to have him. When he is weaned you will have to look after him and, in two years, break him to the saddle. He'll have to be castrated I suppose.'

Valeri had really given her the foal because it was a colt. Had it been a filly, he would have kept her to breed from. He was touched by Tamar's pleasure at the gift and was glad that he had thought of it. She was a charming girl and he had enjoyed her companionship. He did not guess that the reason for her shining eyes was not simply the gift of the colt, or that even without his present, it would have been the happiest day of her life because she had spent it with him.

They got back in time not to be late for the arrival of the bridal pair, or to attract attention.

The Castle had never looked more impressive. The stone floor of the great hall had been scrubbed, its unplastered walls were hung with newly beaten and brushed Kelim and Bokhara carpets.

Prince Gurgen, who had made a nuisance of himself in the morning, had taken a nap and then had spent two hours in the inner chamber where he slept with his young wife, dyeing and trimming his beard, waxing his moustaches, washing his hands, scenting his face and neck, cleaning the dirt from his ears and from under his finger nails, oiling and combing his hair which Nina had dyed and washed the day before, and then putting on a clean embroidered linen shirt, and dressing himself in his best black velvet trousers, tucked into high boots of Russia leather, a sleeveless waistcoat, a Persian silk cummerbund, the swordbelt with his big sabre and, to balance it, a pistol with an enamelled butt and burnished silver triggerguard was thrust at his right hip, and his favourite kinjal, or dagger, in its silver sheath chased with gold, made and inscribed by Mourtagale the most famous swordsmith in the Caucasus.

He was a fussy man, obsessed by a sense of his duty and of dedication to his position, which was one not of particular grandeur, in the sense of riches, but of surpassing glory as one chosen by God as Head of that hierarchy that he had ordained for the proper subordination of mankind in that obscure and well-nigh inaccessible valley.

After his toilet, reeking of jasmine, he spent a full hour upon his knees praying in front of the icon of Saint Anne.

In the past she had achieved miracles. She had intervened in person, a hundred years ago, when the Castle had been besieged for weeks by Tatars and the supplies of food and gunpowder had run out, with a cloudburst.

The river had risen in flood, and the tents of the Tatars and their horses had been swept away, and by the time the river had subsided the remnants of the horde had abandoned the siege. Prince Gurgen had made sure that they would never run out of gunpowder and bullets again, however long the siege. The Castle was amply provisioned also and could hold out against everything except artillery. The holy wonder-working icon was little more than a miniature. The mother of the Virgin was represented with black hair rippling in abundant tresses, which were held in place by her halo. But her most astonishing features were her eyes. They were brilliant light blue and seemed alive. The picture was painted on a thick slab of cedar wood, honeycombed with wormholes at the back and measuring not more than three by two and a half inches. This little panel was set in an immense surround of silver gilt which in its turn was doubly framed in silver and in a yellow wood, probably cypress.

The old man knelt on a hassock in the tiny chapel where the lamp burned eternally in front of Saint Anne. His knees hurt him. Occasionally he lifted his head and saw her strange eyes fixed upon him. Then he bent again and prayed: his prayer was that his son Djamlet might have many, many male children.

But when he rose at last, after crossing himself three times, and had walked slowly to the other side of the hall, a doubt had come into his mind and he turned to seek Valeri, his eldest son, and went up and said to him: 'My son you are twenty-five. You are making trouble for the future by not taking a wife. You have let your brother get ahead of you, and if his wife is a good breeder, by the time you have a son, his cousin will be older and will take the leadership in their sports, though he will not have the inheritance. That was how the trouble with the Sultzi arose; pray God it is not repeated.'

'I may never marry, I shall not marry without love,' said Valeri.

His father spat and turned aside trembling with anger. Before he spoke, the boy Tengiz appeared and said: 'Malik is riding back here with Irakli, My Lord.'

Prince Gurgen whirled round and ran up the steps of the tower, like a young man, to the look-out point. A moment or two later he came down the spiral stairs, his sabre clanking on each of the steps. He looked very stern. The appearance of Irakli, Djamlet's servant, in advance of his master and of his bride was unexpected. Already it seemed to the old Prince that something in connection with his son's marriage must have gone wrong. As Malik and Irakli rode their ponies through the fields and then across the ford, Prince Gurgen and his household crowded into the doorway to await them.

Malik rode into the courtyard, swung himself off his pony, throwing the reins over the iron hook and walked swiftly up to the group. The boy Irakli hung back behind.

Then Malik drew himself up and saluted the Prince ceremonially and said: 'The lad brings word that your son, the knight Djamlet was shot before his wedding, while he

18

was standing at the church door and that he has died.' There was a long silence.

'Boy, come and tell me your story,' said Gurgen in a voice that was firm but not unkind.

Irakli looked terrified and might have run like a scared animal, but Malik caught him and threw him forward. He fell on his knees before his master.

'Tell me from the beginning. I will not harm you,' said Gurgen gently, and there was something strange and terrifying in the unaccustomed softness of his voice. Irakli suddenly spoke up clear and shrill.

'It was the morning of the wedding. My master had slept at the house of the Armenian Gulerian, whose son Avetis was to be his best man. They both wore their best clothes with nosegays of white flowers, but they did not wear swords or pistols because they were going into the house of God. I went with my master, and with Avetis were his sister and his brother-in-law. They went into the Cathedral, but my master waited at the door for the bride. Then she and her father drove up in a tarantass and they alighted, and he gave her his arm and led her into the Cathedral. My master and Avetis were following, when a shot rang out and my master fell. Everyone ran into the church and I ran with them. But I turned in the doorway and I saw that my master was struggling on the ground, so I ran back and caught hold of his hands and dragged him into the porch, and then others came and lifted him and carried him into a side chapel, and a priest came and sealed him with the Holy Oil and then he was dead.

'Seeing that he was dead and that the clergy were in charge of his body, I thought I should get back with the news as fast as I could. I did not dare go out of the Cathedral door where the Solutz, men of our blood, were gathered, so I went into the cloister and through the priests' house and ran back to the Gulerian house where my pony was stabled. There was nobody but old Ephraim there: everyone else had gone to the wedding, so I saddled my pony and rode round the town to avoid the market place, which was full of armed men of the Solutz. I was in two minds about bringing my master's stallion, but he was rather fresh that morning, and I thought he might make trouble and delay me.'

'Did you see who fired the shot?' asked Gurgen.

'No. But there was a group of four armed young men, two of them sons of their chief, Ziklauri, who rode up while the bride was alighting from the tarantass. My master was shot by one of them. They were about fifteen yards away, by the cross, and all of them still in the saddle. My master and all of us were watching the bride and did not notice them until the shot was fired and he fell and we all ran into the Cathedral, lest they shoot again. But I saw them watching, while I dragged my master into the porch, and they were all men of the Solutz, of our blood.'

'You did well to bring the news at once.' Prince Gurgen took hold of the boy's arm and raised him up.

'He is tired, poor boy. Take him and care for him.'

Irakli was sobbing and kissing the Prince's hands. Anastasia and Valeri led him away. Malik stood motionless waiting for orders.

'Arm all the men in case of an attack. After this they might think to surprise us when we are expecting the wedding party. Send Surbat down to watch the road, and tell him to ride back at once if he sees anything moving.'

In the evening all the animals were driven into the courtyard and then carefully penned; the great gate was barred and torches put in readiness to illuminate the area outside the wall in case the enemy should attempt a night attack.

After the practical, the spiritual. The Prince summoned all his household to pray and intercede with Saint Anne for the punishment of the murderer of Djamlet. The prayers went on for a long time. At the end the Prince said: 'I hereby promise that when the time is ripe, I shall take the

Treasure of our House, the wonder-working Saint Anne to a service at my son's grave.'

The party was beginning to disperse when Iriné said in a voice that everyone could hear: 'Saint Anne has to be taken to the grave so that she can be quite sure that Djamlet really *was* murdered, and didn't just run off, leaving the Archpriest's daughter at the church door, so as not to have to marry her.'

As usual, when Iriné made these remarks, no one appeared to hear except Salomé, who turned scarlet, trying to stop her hysteric laughter and finally had to run out of the hall and up the steps of the tower so that she should not be heard.

It was impossible for any of them to go to the funeral. The Sultzi would respect them at the graveside and in the presence of the corpse, but they would be on the look-out and might ambush them on the way there, or on the way back.

The winter passed with the usual excitements of hunting and shooting. Malik rode down a wolf that had been forced into the open fields by the hounds and shot it from the saddle. Prince Gurgen shot an elk, and Valeri speared a wild boar which charged him after it had been cornered by the huntsmen and the hounds.

Christmas came and passed as usual. Presents made by the girls were handed round and trinkets given to them. Vasso was given toys, which he trod on, and a wooden sword, made by Malik, which he loved and took to bed with him. There was a service in front of the icon of Saint Anne and a feast at which Nina got drunk and had to be helped out of the hall by Anastasia and the girls.

Early in the New Year there was a diversion. Strangers were sighted coming up the track. They proved to be a Persian and his wife, riding on ponies with two mules carrying heavy loads. Everyone came out to look and greet them as they rode through the great gate into the yard. The

Persian was a short man with thick hair escaping from under the round Astrakhan cap which he wore. He had a fine forehead and a merry, confident smile as he looked about him, greeting everyone. Then he dismounted and walked up to Prince Gurgen, who was standing in the doorway of the hall, and bowed to him with affable dignity.

'I have come, at this bad season, to seek shelter with you, Prince. I am a master silversmith and worker in precious metals and jewels. If you will give me lodging until I can cross into Persia, I will work for you and you will not be the loser,' he said.

'What crime have you committed that makes you come at this time of the year, when no man would travel unless he were driven to it?' asked the Prince.

'That is true enough,' replied the Persian. 'I was working in Tiflis, where I was ordered to make a set of silver spoons for a Russian General's wife. But the General would not pay me, nor return the spoons. I went to a lawyer, but before my case was heard, the Governor of Tiflis sent a policeman who told me to leave the town, or I should be arrested for not having a permit to work there. And that I should be flogged or put in prison. So I left the town. But when the General heard that I had made a complaint to the court, he sent some Cossacks to beat me. I was warned of their coming and escaped, and I think they will not follow me here.

Prince Gurgen smiled and asked: 'What is your name, silversmith?'

'Mustapha Sasun,' replied the man.

'Well, Mustapha Sasun, I will put you up willingly and you can work for me but, unlike the Russian General, I will pay you for your work. But if your story isn't true, I shall throw you out.'

'Quite right, too,' said the Persian. 'Now may I show you some of my work?'

But while this dialogue was going on, Mustapha's wife

was already unpacking her bundles and asking Nina where they would be lodged. 'There must be a lock on the door, as my husband deals in valuables.'

'You are making yourself at home before it is settled whether you are to stay,' said Nina.

'Oh, I can see that you are good people with kind hearts. And anyway there is nowhere else for us to go. You have either got to lodge us and feed us, or drown us in the river. That's all the choice you've got,' said the woman, at which Malik and all the men standing around burst out laughing.

For the next month or two there was more laughter in the Castle than ever before because of the outspoken Persian woman, whose name was Kamela. Nobody had ever been so free-spoken. Once when she came across the Prince and Anastasia quarrelling in the yard, instead of hurrying away and pretending not to hear, she drew near to listen and watch. Then, when the Prince turned on her angrily, she said: 'You are a lucky man, Prince. If you had married me, I should have given you a time of it. I shouldn't have been as patient as that poor girl. Trust me.'

At that the Prince burst out laughing, and even Anastasia could not help smiling, and the quarrel, whatever it may have been about, was forgotten. The Prince sometimes said to Anastasia afterwards: 'After all, my dear, I was lucky not to marry the Tinker's wife!'

Kamela was no beauty, as she had lost several front teeth and had a nasty scar on one cheek. Yet she behaved as though she were a handsome woman, and perhaps she may once have been.

One day the Prince, meaning to humour her, said: 'A fine woman like you . . .' only to get the reply: 'You are an awful old lecher. Five years ago, before I lost my teeth, I should have been smacking your face three times a day to make you keep your hands off me.'

Prince Gurgen was delighted.

If the silversmith's wife kept them amused, he himself

charmed everyone. He had set up his little charcoal forge in an outhouse next to the smithy and was constantly at work and yet always pleased to see anyone who looked in. All were fascinated by his little crucibles of clay, in which he melted silver in his little furnace and by the skill with which he hammered silver over moulds of pitch. The blacksmith used to come and squat in his room, watching him for hours. They became close friends. Mustapha Sasun was an artist who made designs of birds and fish and flowers, inlaying them in one metal upon another. He made, without its being commissioned, but as a present, a silver platter with VASSO SON OF THE FALCON engraved round the rim and a falcon engraved in the centre, and gave it to the little boy casually, without telling the Prince or Anastasia. Prince Gurgen ordered him to make a set of silver spoons and forks, in the modern style, and several silver bowls. Sasun was delighted and was never so happy as when he was working. The difficulty was that, once all the Maria Theresa dollars in Prince Gurgen's secret hoard had been melted down, there was no metal to make them of.

In this dilemma the Prince asked Malik to go to the town and negotiate the sale of last year's opium crop and buy silver.

'If you send me, I shall not return,' said Malik.

'You won't go?' asked the Prince incredulously.

'I would never refuse to obey your orders, Prince. If you order me to go, I shall go. But I shall not return, and you will lose whatever valuables I am entrusted with.'

The Prince did not pursue the matter with Malik, but explained the difficulty to Mustapha.

'That is quite simple. My wife will go if you give her a letter to Gulerian, authorising her to sell the opium and asking him to pay in dollars, or silver roubles. The rouble is not such pure silver as the Maria Theresa dollar, but Gulerian may not be able to lay his hands on a sufficient number of dollars.'

Kamela herself made light of the commission. The Prince who had been made angry by Malik's refusal, did not tell him of the project, but asked Valeri to accompany Kamela with three armed men. They escorted her until they were almost in sight of the town. Then, with the sacks of opium loaded on two donkeys with bundles of firewood on top, and dressed as a gypsy, she went into the town, attracting no attention and delivered the opium to Gulerian, handing him the letter which Mustapha had written and the Prince had signed with his signet. She took delivery of the dollars, hidden in two sacks, one of bran and the other of rye flour and rejoined her escort without interference from the Sultzi, or the Russians, who were becoming more troublesome every month.

When she came back, Kamela greeted the Prince with: 'You never saw such a fool as I am, Prince. I meant to buy myself a sable shuba with some of that silver but I forgot, until I was halfway back. Well, remember you owe it me.'

From that time on, it was her constant joke. 'When are you giving me those sables, Prince?'

Everyone laughed just as she did, but the old Prince did not appreciate it. He hated above all things to be thought mean. No doubt he was indebted to the woman – but a sable shuba was absurd. When Kamela saw that he took her words half-seriously, she went into fits of laughter. But this did not reassure the old man, to whom sables were not a laughing matter. Listening to these exchanges made Anastasia chuckle and Nina double up.

'I've never known anyone like you. Our dear Prince more than half believes that he owes you a sable shuba,' she said wiping her eyes.

Lent came and went, and at last the set of spoons and forks, each engraved with a tiny falcon, were finished; the pass was open after the spring floods, and Mustapha and Kamela loaded their mules, mounted their ponies and rode away, leaving a duller community at the Castle.

Because the Prince had sheltered him, housed him and fed him, Mustapha charged him less than half price for his work, and Kamela said nothing about the sable shuba until she was riding out of the yard, when she shouted back at the Prince:

'I shall come back for my shuba. I shall need it next winter – not till then.'

'I'm really cross with myself. I let those good people go away almost empty-handed,' Prince Gurgen said soon afterwards to Anastasia.

The weeks passed and, early in the summer, Prince Gurgen called Valeri to him and said:

'My son, I need not remind you that you are expected to avenge your brother. You can take your time. No one expects an immediate stroke. In fact it might be better for you to marry a nice healthy girl first. No doubt the Archpriest would be pleased if you took Djamlet's place. Katerina will bring a good dowry. But this time we'll have the marriage here. In front of Saint Anne. It was the girl's vanity, wanting to show off in front of her friends in her wedding dress, that lost me my son. Once is enough; you must make that a condition.'

Valeri bowed deeply, but made no reply. There had been little in common between the brothers, and their characters were as unlike as they were in looks. Valeri took after his mother who came from a family which claimed to be descended from the Crusaders. He had light brown hair, red cheeks, blue eyes and a white skin, and he grew to be tall, broad-chested and physically very strong. Djamlet had been like his father: a small swarthy man, his hair growing low on his forehead and almost jet black. He had had hazel green eyes. But while Prince Gurgen had the character of a spoilt child, there was something mysterious and hidden in that of his younger son. Valeri had never liked him and had thought him ambitious, jealous, selfish and a tell-tale. Then there had been that incident, which he would have thought little of, but which Malik had taken very seriously. Indeed Malik had, Valeri realised afterwards, saved his life on that occasion. But the fact that Valeri had not liked his brother, was, he knew, quite irrelevant to the fact that it was his duty to avenge his murder. His chief feeling, when he had heard of it, was disgust. It was nasty, unpleasant, disgusting; he had no wish to be mixed up in that sort of thing. If he had to kill the murderer, now known to be Ziklauri's youngest son, Lazar, he would do it openly, in fair fight. Unfortunately, however, fair fights were not the custom of the country. If he had tried to explain what he felt, his father would think him mad.

Next morning he said to Anastasia: 'My father is sending me to the town. I am going tomorrow. Can I have my best shirt?'

He made this request because Anastasia had made the shirt herself. It was of pale green linen – a Mohammedan's colour – but embroidered with traditional Georgian patterns in gold and silver thread. It was because of this delicate embroidery that she always washed it herself after Valeri had worn it. The shirt was the thing he most treasured in the world – more even than the signed Damascus sabre made by Ali Ben Ezra that had belonged to his grandfather.

Next morning Anastasia came to the little room where Valeri slept at the top of the tower. He was standing, stripped to the waist, and had just put on a pair of clean white cotton drawers. She was not embarrassed by seeing him wearing so little, but walked up to him so that she was almost touching him.

'Here is your shirt,' she said looking into his eyes. He turned away as he took it out of her hands. Anastasia laid her fingers on his wrist and, at her touch, he turned to look at her. Her face was very close to his.

'Do not avenge Djamlet,' she said in a whisper.

'My father sends me on that errand.'

'And to get married.'

'I shall not do that,' said Valeri.

'You should marry.'

'You must know that that is impossible,' he said.

'How should I know?' she whispered.

Valeri looked at her almost angrily. 'You understand the reason. I must not say more.'

Anastasia dropped her eyes. She was silent for a moment, and then whispered with ferocity: 'Do not avenge Djamlet. It is senseless. It goes on for ever.'

'My father...' he began.

'Disobey him. He would destroy us all.'

'But honour...' said Valeri.

Anastasia interrupted him. 'There is no honour in war. Only murder. The Russians have driven my mother's people out of their lands. They have stolen their farms and orchards. They herded my people by the sea coast where they died of plague. Those that would not submit have been led by my uncles and the Prince into Turkey. A whole people robbed and destroyed ... unutterable cruelty ... And you glory in fighting and talk of honour ... I spit on your honour.' And without another word, Anastasia glided away. Valeri pulled on the shirt she had brought him. Then he dressed himself, as though for his wedding, in his very finest clothes. He wore dark maroon velvet trousers tucked into high Russia leather boots with gilded spurs, a white waistcoat covered with silver braid open down the front, a high-waisted long-skirted chokha, or Circassian coat with silver mounted pockets for cartridges on the chest, over which he wore his sword belt, with his Damascus sabre in its green morocco scabbard, and on the other side a double-barrelled Russian pistol, made by Demidoff himself, and a straight kinjal in a scabbard of white shagreen. Valeri ate a full meal, for he might not be able to stop to eat again till evening. He was taking Irakli with him as his servant. When he had eaten, he joined the household in prayer, and Anastasia, Iriné, Tamar and the two girls sang the hymns: *Depart in Peace* and *Thy Ways are Inscrutable*. His father signed him with the cross, he put on his tall papakha of white baby lamb. His father then kissed him three times and said with tears suddenly running down his cheeks: 'God and Saint Anne bless your errand and preserve you.'

Valeri replied in a firm voice: 'His ways are inscrutable.' Then he swung into the saddle, touched his grey mare with his heels and rode out of the courtyard with Irakli on his pony behind him.

He did not notice Tamar standing by the yard gate. She burst into tears because he had not said good-bye or looked at her.

As he rode Valeri was deep in thought; reflecting that Anastasia had never before spoken to him so openly in defiance of his father – and that he had told her that he would never bring a wife to the castle, because he loved her. And he began to think what his life would be if he married the Archpriest's daughter as his father wished. He saw clearly how his young bride would hate Anastasia, how she would side with Gurgen and would try to seduce him, and how quickly the old man would respond to the girl's sympathy and overtures – and how at night the two couples would separate – each of the four sleeping with a partner for whom there was no love – or actual hate. It was not romantic devotion for Anastasia that kept him from marriage – it was clear sight. His appetites were normal. It was just bad luck that kept him living under the Castle roof with Anastasia, whom he had loved ever since she first came to the Castle when he was a boy of eighteen. No, he would not marry. That was the first irrevocable act of disobedience. The second act, not to avenge his brother, was more doubtful and since it did not depend entirely upon himself, more difficult. For if the Sultzi were to try and ambush him, he would fight back. Anastasia had asked him not to avenge Djamlet; she had said that it was senseless and that the feud would go on for ever. When she said that, it was of her little son Vasso, that she was thinking. She cared for Valeri; she would lose her most devoted friend in the Castle if he were killed. But it was of little Vasso's inheritance that she was thinking: if Djamlet were not avenged, the boy might grow up free of the feud. She was right, of course, when she said that Gurgen would destroy them all. But that did not absolve him from his duty and from the laws of honour. It was as well that it did not depend entirely upon himself. He would not seek out a quarrel: he would wait for the Sultzi to attack him and he might not have to wait long. In a mile or two the cliffs closed in, within gunshot of the river and the mule track along which he was riding. Some of them might be waiting there on the off-chance that someone from the Castle would come along. Then the idea came to him that perhaps he was committing the worst sin: that which Saint Paul had thundered against – that of being a Laodicean – neither hot nor cold. A brave man would either obey the laws of honour and avenge his brother, or go into the church so as to avoid committing a murder. If he wished to have no part in the feud, he could turn monk. That was the only way in which he could do what Anastasia had asked him and give Vasso a chance to grow into a man without the hereditary curse hanging over him. Turn monk! With his Martini-Peabody rifle across his saddle bow and his sabre by his side, he made a fine-looking monk! Well, he could not decide. He would go through the town, avoiding no man, armed but uttering no challenges. The Sultzi would learn that he was there. If they came after him, he would fight. If they did not, he would go to the monastery and put his case of conscience to the Archimandrite.

It was impossible for two men to ride along the mule track abreast until the river left the mountains and the defile opened out into the foothills, which sloped down towards the plain. The town was built upon the terraces overlooking the high river gorge.

Valeri rode ahead, holding his rifle across the pommel of his saddle. His eyes scanned every rock that came in sight as the track turned and twisted. He noted the birds that flew up, proving that no enemy was hiding by the rocks from which they sprang. Twice he had to ford the river, as the track came to an end and continued on the far side. Irakli, riding behind him, called out once, and he waited for the boy to overtake him.

'It is my turn to go forward. If there is an ambush I shall see them,' he said.

'There has to be someone to ride home with the news,' replied Valeri.

'I shall not do that. I could not carry such news twice. If you are killed, I shall do my best to avenge you before I fall,' said Irakli. He was armed with two old flintlock pistols that had been converted to percussion caps. They were in holsters strapped to his pony's saddle.

Soon after midday they halted where a cataract fell from the rocky wall and ran down a pebbled stream into the river, at that point, far below. They dismounted, let their horses drink and crop the fresh grass by the stream, and ate a slice of cold mutton and drank a bottle of cold tea. Then they remounted and rode on into the town. There had been no ambush, and they met no armed men of the Sultzi in the streets, or in the market place, or near the Cathedral. Valeri dismounted and went into the inn. There were none of the Sultzi there. He had shown himself everywhere, so he re-mounted and with Irakli riding twenty paces behind him to cover him, took the road to the monastery.

As in all the monasteries of the Holy Orthodox Church, its spiritual head was a Bishop. Valeri was, however, unable to consult him on his case of conscience and would have to put it to the Archimandrite, the administrative head, for the Bishop was a dying man who had not spoken to a layman in his diocese for the last five years. When he was last seen in public, he was an emaciated skeleton: a skeleton which could move, but only in spasmodic jerks like a puppet twitched by invisible wires, some of them broken. His powers of speech had become blurred and almost unintelligible. His eyes alone showed that he understood the horror of his position. They shone out from deep sockets in his skull with extraordinary brilliance. In his look no emotion could be read but horror: love, charity, compassion, forgiveness, all human tenderness had been burned out and fear alone remained. For if his punishment on earth for a few sins of the flesh was so appalling, how much more terrible must be those awaiting him when he came for judgement, and had to account for how he had exercised his position as vicar of God?

For the last two years the Bishop had become totally paralysed and lay supine, only able to swallow enough nourishment to stay alive. He was tended by a team of eight monks who never left his bedside, night or day, and fed him at intervals on tiny cups of fermented mares' milk sweetened with honey specially sent from Greece and occasional spoonfuls of champagne.

For the prolongation of the Bishop's life was essential for the Archimandrite, as when he died the Exarch of Tiflis would appoint a new Bishop and would choose a strong man, able to sweep clean.

Irakli dismounted and rang the bell. Valeri waited, sitting on his horse. No one had followed them. When the porter opened the judas in the door and looked through, Irakli said: 'My Lord Valeri, Son of the Falcon, desires to speak with the Archimandrite Hagystiarchos.'

The porter closed the judas and went away. After a time he came back, threw open the big door and said: 'My Lord is welcome.'

Valeri dismounted and walked in and Irakli led the two horses round the back of the building to the stables.

Hagystiarchos was a small, very hairy and very dirty man, with a long grey and black beard and hair distinctly grey in colour, with long locks framing his face, falling on to his chest and more long greasy locks covering his shoulders. Through the forest of hair, a pair of black eyes like Kalimata olives darted quick glances at Valeri's face and at his arms and fine clothes.

'What would you, my son?' he asked, as Valeri remained silent, after making the Archimandrite a deep bow.

'I have come to consult you, Holy Father.'

'Come with me to where we can speak privately,' said the Archimandrite. Valeri removed his high white papakha, dipped his finger in holy water, signed himself three times with the cross, and followed Hagystiarchos through the inner doorway and across the cloister, along a corridor and into a small cell, which smelt of incense, excrement and dirty linen, and was furnished with a narrow bed and a stool. On the bare stone walls hung a crucifix with the body of Christ made of ivory and the cross of solid gold. The Archimandrite sat down on the bed and told Valeri to sit on the stool.

'I have come into the town at my father's orders because my brother Djamlet was killed standing at the door of the Cathedral by one of the Sultzi, while his bride was walking into the porch on the arm of her father, the Archpriest Paphnuty.'

'Why have you come to me?' asked the Archimandrite.

'My father has told me to marry the girl, if her father so wishes. But I shall not do so. I shall not marry anyone.'

'Have you a mistress?'

'No, my Lord. I have no mistress. But at present I shun marriage.'

Hagystiarchos smiled. 'Is it on this subject that you have come to consult me?' He was obviously amused.

'No. I need no advice as to marriage.'

'The girl is rather conceited, I am told. A young woman who likes her own way. But she is respectable and rich and I am assured that she is a virgin.'

33

'It is not because of her that I abjure marriage,' said Valeri.

'Well, what is it?'

'I came to ask your advice on another matter.'

'Prince Gurgen laid other duties on you besides marriage, perhaps?' asked the Archimandrite.

Valeri nodded. After a little while he said: 'Duties. In the Old Testament it is written: "An eye for an eye." In the New: "Do no murder."' There was a silence. Valeri went on: 'As you see I have come armed into this town. Any of the Sultzi could have shot me as I rode here, any man hiding behind a rock. But, if he had missed, he would have paid for it with his life. I rode round the town. I rode round the market place and I went into the inn, and if any man had challenged me, I would have shot him dead. When I leave you, I shall go to the place where my brother was killed and pray for him. I shall go into the chapel where he died, and I shall pray there. I shall go to his tomb and pray there. I shall go again to the inn and show myself there and in the market place. And if any man attacks me, I hope that I shall kill him. But I will not seek a quarrel. I shall show myself where they know that they can find me. But I will not lie in wait to murder a man who does not suspect danger, as one of them murdered my brother Djamlet.'

The Archimandrite said nothing, and Valeri continued with ardour: 'I used to believe that I would grow up to be a great warrior and a true Christian, to fight against the dragon like the patron saint of our country, Saint George. But the scales have dropped from my eyes. I see that with this endless feud it is not possible. And rather than kill men in cold blood and commit abominations like the murder of my brother, rather than that I choose to be a true Christian, at whatever the cost to my pride and to my heritage.'

The Archimandrite stared at him in astonishment, unable to believe his ears. 'And when you have said those prayers and shown yourself publicly in those places, and, if no man attacks you, what will you do then?' he asked with evident curiosity.

'If you, my Lord and Father in God, give me permission, I will return here and hang up my arms like one of the knights of olden time, and become one of the brethren under your rule.'

Hagystiarchos was astonished. 'You are not hoping to play a trick on your enemies, are you, my son?'

It was Valeri's turn to be astonished. 'A trick? I do not understand what you mean.'

'A trick to exact an eye for an eye while in the habit of a monk, who would not be suspected, and to run back here afterwards to take sanctuary?'

Valeri rose from the stool. 'I swear by the sacrament...'

'And by the wonder-working image of Saint Anne, the mother of the Blessed Virgin, also?' asked the Archimandrite, with a cunning smile.

'Yes, by the image of Saint Anne in my father's castle, and by my own honour, I swear that I would never commit such treachery and such a sin, under the cover of a monkish habit.' And Valeri glared angrily at the hairy Greek who was smiling, indeed laughing at him.

'Well, I believe you, though what you say surprises me. Well, on account of that wonder-working icon of Saint Anne you will be made welcome, if you return from exhibiting yourself where your enemies can find you. You will be accepted as a novice for a year and, if and when the time comes for you to take the vows, we shall know each other better. You understand that, as a novice, you will be free to leave us whenever you wish, but in that case we will not take you back.' The Archimandrite Hagystiarchos stood up and held out a very dirty paw with very black, long, broken fingernails. Valeri bent over it and kissed the ring he wore, noticing as he did so that the Abbot's yellow wrist and forearm were covered in black hair stiff with grease.

Before becoming Archimandrite in this faraway monastery of the Georgian Church, Hagystiarchos had been a Bishop in the Greek Orthodox Church. He had, however, been unfrocked after a scandal about money, and, after ten years of expiation as a monk at the top of the mountain of Meteora, where provisions are hauled up and down in baskets, he had been sent as a missionary to Armenia and thence had run away to Georgia, had entered the ancient Georgian monastery, had become the Archimandrite's secretary and, after his unexpected death, his successor.

Hagystiarchos believed in devils and had frequently been in close contact with them. They usually assumed the forms of beautiful youths, occasionally of girls or young children. He could tell a devil immediately by the feel of its skin and by the luxuriant beauty of sparkling eyes, flashing teeth and glossy or windblown hair. Devils assumed the graces of youth and airs of innocence. Hagystiarchos would not have understood the phrase 'the flesh *and* the devil' since for him flesh and devil were one, and it was only by degrading the flesh that the Christian could hope to win a victory, however temporary, over Satan.

He did not enjoy the company of others. He preferred solitude, though he could tolerate the presence of the very old, the diseased, the ugly and deformed, and idiots and the insane. In an earlier age he would have been a hermit, and he had all the qualities in which hermits excel: wrath, holiness, secret visions and filth.

He was particularly ill-suited to be the head of a monastery, as he hated communal life and had no conception of the arrangements necessary for administration. Thus all practical affairs, except the religious services (if they qualify as such), were left to the Bursar and the Farm Bailiff. With neither would he have any communication for months, and he only saw them when they were present at mass.

At intervals there would be a trial of strength between the Archimandrite and the Bursar in which the former was by no means always victorious. The greatest of these was over the bath-house. As is well known, monks and nuns are enjoined never to strip naked when they go to the bath, their usual attire being a loose woollen gown, like a long nightdress, with cotton drawers worn underneath. It was reported to the Archimandrite by his spies that this rule was being infringed, and that some of the monks removed their cotton drawers while in the bath and put on a clean dry pair after it. Hagystiarchos issued a strict instruction that this dangerous practice, which he believed had been winked at by the Bursar, was to cease. It was obeyed. Elated by this victory, Hagystiarchos ordered the bath-house to be closed, but three days after his order had been carried out, his spies reported that the Bursar had opened a new, traditional steam bath-house in an old fruit store, which was technically under the control of the Farm Bailiff, and that he had sanctioned a bathing pool in the river, where he allowed monks to splash about together in the heats of summer, after the day's work in the fields was done.

When the Archimandrite forbade this practice, the Bursar challenged him to find an authority in the monastic rules, or the Scriptures, forbidding it, and this Hagystiarchos was unable to do, since he could barely make out familiar passages in the Divine Office and only just sign his own name. For this reason the Bursar was victorious and what was worse became popular, for, with few exceptions, the monks did not enjoy being dirty, though many had lice in their hair.

Hagystiarchos had never washed any part of his person except his hands. In this he knew that he was following the example of many of the Saints and of the early Christians, who regarded the Roman habit of going to the baths with as much abhorrence as they did the naked bodies of Apollo, Aphrodite and other gods and goddesses of antiquity.

But in spite of keeping to the strictest rules, in spite of mortifying the flesh, both his own and whenever possible that of other men, Hagystiarchos had never known happi-

37

ness. The nearest to it that he had enjoyed was a sense of triumph, of gratified vanity, or satisfied vengeance. His spirit had never known peace or contentment, because he was always afraid. There was nothing in the outside visible world: not a bird in a tree, or the sun at noonday, or the stars at night, that he did not fear. All things that could be seen, heard, touched, smelt or tasted were there to entrap him. And if the external world terrified him, how much more did the thoughts, dreams and visions which assailed him and which he could not ignore by shutting his eyes, holding his nose, putting his fingers in his ears and clamping his jaws.

Only by total inactivity of mind and body was it possible, for a little while, not to incur the wrath of God.

Valeri made his tour of the town and its cemetery without incident and entered the monastery. Young Irakli was sent back riding his master's grey mare, carrying his precious Martini rifle bought from the Turks, and leading Djamlet's stallion – a journey filled with incident – to deliver the news that Valeri had abjured the world and entered the monastery. Prince Gurgen received it with less philosophy than he had taken that of the assassination of his second son.

The monastery was an enormous grey building built of stone: a miniature city in itself. There was a church at the east end with many courtyards leading one from another, a cloister overlooking the river gorge, a vast kitchen and dining hall, a laundry, a smithy, and stables and byres for animals with various workshops, for the monks grew their own food, worked their own farm, wove cloth and made their own clothes. All the outdoor work was under the direction of the Farm Bailiff, a Pole who had worked in several countries before coming to the Caucasus. After him in importance was the Bursar, who was responsible for the kitchens, dormitories and general condition of the monastery. He had not said a friendly word to the Archimandrite for three years.

Valeri knew nothing of all this hierarchy and only learned the details of it after he had been in the monastery for several weeks. At first he was simply given a cell, with a box in which to keep his belongings, a stool on which to sit and a board on which to lie. Also his clothes: two pairs of cotton drawers, a cassock, a rope girdle, sandals for his feet and a brass crucifix to hang round his neck. When he had dressed himself in these garments and packed away his grand clothes in the box, he hung up his sabre below the holy icon of Saint George, and decided to find a really good hiding place for his pistol – for, if he failed in his vocation as a monk, he might have need of it. Shutting the door behind him, he went into the corridor and along it until he came to a stone staircase, turning on itself, which led him down to the great refectory with its plain wooden tables, each with its pair of wooden benches, and only at the top table, set crosswise on the dais, were there chairs with backs to them for the Archimandrite and the officers of the monastery.

One of these officers, a man of between forty and fifty, at once approached him. He was small with a wide mouth, continually open in a grin, or spasm of noisy laughter. He had the high cheekbones of the Kalmuk, merry brown eyes and a nose that in spite of being small, stuck out and gave him a look of perpetual impudence.

'So you have come to teach us to repay evil with good and to persuade us that there is some relevance in the teaching of Christ after all. I welcome you my Lord Valeri, Son of the Falcon.' And to Valeri's amazement the little man seized his hand and kissed it.

'I am in charge of the muniment room and of the Holy Books. My name is Foma Ilyitch, and, if you care to become my pupil and learn calligraphy and the art of illumination, I shall be glad to have you as my assistant.'

Valeri paused and replied cautiously: 'You do me great honour, my Lord Foma.'

'None of that,' said Brother Foma laughing. 'I am not a Lord like you. I am a bastard: half Russian and half Kirghiz. My father was a Russian music master and my mother a Kirghiz woman who cured him of the pox and of consumption and other diseases, by sweating them out of him in steam baths and by feeding him on koumiss, which is, as you know, fermented mares' milk. She succeeded and in the process I was born. My father was a kind-hearted man and sent me to learn my letters in Tiflis. After that I had the good luck to travel, to learn languages and to see the world. I have lived in London, Paris, Rome, Florence, Venice.... But I don't want to bore you, though no doubt I shall, if you accept my offer.'

There was a pause, and then Brother Foma continued: 'All the same it wouldn't be a bad idea for you to become my assistant. You wouldn't have to go out into the fields and do farm work and expose yourself as a target for your cousins to practise at. Why put them into temptation?'

What Brother Foma said was true enough and, after a little thought, Valeri accepted his offer. That evening after Vespers and a simple meal of a glass of buttermilk and a bowl of millet kasha, he went to bed in the dormitory where the four other novices slept. They snored, cried out in their sleep, and got into each others' beds, and there were bugs. Next morning he sought out the Bursar and asked to be allowed to sleep in his cell, alone and undisturbed. His request was granted, and after that he saw little of his companions, except Brother Foma. That morning he began work in the library and was set to learn the two alphabets, the modern and the ancient Georgian, and then those of several languages of which he knew nothing. Latin, Greek, and Slavonic were the first essentials. Hebrew, Armenian and Coptic would come later. Each letter had its sound, and Valeri found himself at school for the first time. He had to learn three languages at once as well as the arts of reading and writing in them. Foma did not seem to think that this was asking too much and was always laughing at his pupil's mistakes.

Perhaps Valeri would have found this discouraging if Foma Ilyitch had not laughed at everyone and everything. Soon the freedom of his conversation and his ribald mockery became an education and a delight to Valeri. The little Kirghiz bastard challenged everything – and Valeri found himself agreeing with his heretical views on subjects which he himself had always accepted, and would never have thought of questioning.

'We are all equally God's creatures, and surely He, having created us, would not favour one of us, in order to be unfair to another?' said Foma.

'I agree. We are all equal in the sight of God,' said Valeri.

'In that case special prayers to God are cheating. Just like a child trying to get in first by telling tales on his brothers and sisters. Do you like the child who does that? Would you favour him if you were God?'

This question meant more to Valeri than Brother Foma suspected. In fact he would not have asked it, if he had realised that it brought Djamlet, as he had been, back into Valeri's mind. He crossed himself and said: 'His ways are inscrutable.'

'Don't repeat stuff and nonsense like that to me. When you say that, what you really mean is that you are afraid of using your reason and judgement. That is to say that you are frightened of thinking.'

'How dare you say that I am frightened of thinking?' Valeri blazed out.

'There you go. How dare I speak to Lord Valeri like that?' sneered Foma.

'I didn't mean that. Only I don't think I am afraid.'

'Well, you are. You believe that we are all equal in God's eyes, and at the same time you believe in the wonder-working icon of Saint Anne and that she protects your family while you keep her icon in your Castle.'

'I have always prayed to her. She was the mother of the

41

Blessed Virgin and you know she saved our Castle from being burned by the Tatars. There is no doubt about that.'

'I'll discuss the Tatars later on. But you pray to Saint Anne and you believe that she answers your prayers, don't you?'

'I hope that she does, if I find favour in her sight,' said Valeri.

'Well, you must see that there is a contradiction in your beliefs. I call special prayers said to her cheating if they are granted to you because you are a princely family and happen to own her icon, and trying to cheat if the prayers are not answered. You Sons of the Falcon are simply trying to get a pull over other, poorer, people by family influence. All that side of religion disgusts me. What's more I don't believe it works. I should despise Jesus Christ if He let His sense of justice be influenced by His grandmother. There is no sign that He paid special attention to her wishes in the gospels.'

Valeri could not forget this conversation. For, terrible as it was, what Brother Foma had said was obviously true. Indeed that was what made it terrible – and it was only terrible if he were, as Brother Foma had said, afraid. It was against all Valeri's instincts to feel fear. He was a proud, predatory animal, and the notion that he was afraid disgusted him. Why should he fear truth, when he was not afraid of the wild boar that had charged him trying to rip him up with its gleaming tusks? And he knew that he would have knelt calmly and held the boar spear level, even if he had known that the animal were going to be the victor in their combat. So, whatever the truth, he would never be afraid of it. As he made this decision he suddenly wanted to shout with joy. He felt that he had changed: that he was a new man entering into a new world.

And surely, if he was to be a really religious man, truth mattered? Surely that was what religion was really about? To a monk truth should be like honour to a warrior. And to live up to either, courage was needed. Then, as he lay upon his plank bed in his cell, he decided that truth and honour were really the same thing. He would explain it to Brother Foma in the morning. But somehow his explanation failed. Brother Foma was unconvinced. 'I know about truth, because I believe that things are either true or not true and that has nothing to do with us, or what we believe. It's absolute. But I don't know about honour; I don't think that there is an absolute honour, is there? Each man, or each age of history, has its own. And that ought to be true of women too, oughtn't it?'

Valeri was puzzled. He would have to think about it, but he liked his own idea.

Another day Foma laughed and said: 'Everyone loves cheating. I indulge in it. I got my job here by cheating. It was before I had taught myself Greek. I knew that the only languages that our dear Archimandrite can speak correctly are Turkish and Demotic Greek and Georgian. So I learned a long passage from the Greek Testament by heart, and when he asked me if I knew Greek, I recited it to him – though I didn't know which words meant what. And then I recited it to him in Slavonic and then in Latin and finally in Armenian, which I didn't know a word of – but neither did he. Oh, I love cheating our old renegade Turk! I believe that our Archimandrite had a Turkish father and a Greek mother, and was a bastard like myself. I expect I am just as bad as everyone else in the sight of God, only I don't like telling lies and pulling long faces – it's so boring.'

Another day he said: 'What's the use of all this pretence? You can't deceive God, can you? So it's better not to try. I've got enough sins to answer for, without hypocrisy.'

'What sins have you got, Brother Foma?' asked Valeri.

'Sodomy, drunkenness, malice, uncharitableness, pride of heart and above all, doubts about God and everything written in the Testaments and the Gospels.'

'Do you have doubts about Holy Writ?' asked Valeri astonished.

Brother Foma nodded.

'I don't believe in Job. I don't think God would have treated him so shamefully. Then I don't believe that God would have turned Lot's wife into a pillar of salt, knowing that it would inevitably make him sleep with his daughters, which He had forbidden and which is at variance with His Commandments. And I don't believe in the Fall of Man, Eve and the apple and original sin. So you see I'm not a true believer. And it's all or nothing. I can't face nothing ... and I can't swallow everything. There it is – I'm in a fix.' He paused, and Valeri waited expectantly. Presently Brother Foma went on : 'I believe in God. But I don't believe in the Scriptures. All the men I have known have told lies – lies about everything; have lied about themselves and have lied to themselves, and they usually end by believing the lies they have invented. And all they say about God and Jesus and the Virgin Mary is lies. And all the stories of the Saints and their miracles and holy relics are lies. Even the devils are just made-up stories.'

'But what *do* you believe?' asked Valeri.

'I believe the world is a good place. I worship the beauty of God's trees and His flowers and His stars in the sky, and I wonder. I am full of wonder. I marvel. And I don't know why men and women fight and quarrel and live in dirt and why they all love telling each other lies and believing in things which could not be true.'

'Have you ever wanted to get married?' asked Valeri.

'Of course. But I never met a woman I could love, who would marry me. And I have been afraid of living like other men who get drunk and beat their wives and shout at their children. So I took shelter in this monastery. And I'm all right here.'

'Does the Archimandrite know about your heresies?' asked Valeri.

'No, I am very careful to tell lies to him,' said Foma and went into fits of laughter.

Another day he said to Valeri : 'You must learn Greek and

Latin, too. There are all sorts of things written in those two languages which are worth everything in the Scriptures put together. It's extraordinary. You see they are worth reading for their own sake, which the Scriptures very seldom are. People read Holy Writ because it's about God and the prophets, but Greek and Latin are about what men feel. They are the languages of poetry and of love. I was in love with a Turk once. Such a fine man. But that story is for another occasion ...' In such fashion Brother Foma Ilyitch chattered on, while Valeri learned to write a few simple words in Greek, and afterwards the same word in Latin and in Slavonic. Foma had a poor opinion of Slavonic. 'It's just old-fashioned Russian, and there's nothing written in it except the Scriptures, which we have enough of anyway, and the lives and miracles of a few lousy saints.'

However he conceded later: 'You'll have to learn modern Russian well, because they are coming into the country fast, and they are enlisting the Tcherkesses into their Army, those that didn't run off into Turkey to escape from them, and all the other tribes too. They don't care whether they're Muslim or Christian so long as they are ready to kill other men. The day when the Sons of the Falcon ruled the roost is over. You know that, without my telling you. Well, come on: repeat your lesson in Greek.'

At other times Foma would tell Valeri about his travels and the people he had known in foreign countries.

'I was a sort of secretary, valet and nursemaid to a young Russian count who was making a tour of Europe and staying a few months in each of the countries we visited. We lived in grand style, wasting money which he had got by cutting down marvellous forests. But it enabled me to see the Duke of Wellington and Garibaldi with my own eyes, though I never spoke a word to either. I was the humble secretary. But I did make a friend of the most gifted poet and writer and the most adorable companion you can imagine – a Frenchman called Gérard de Nerval. And I was able to see the great collections of pictures in Florence and Rome and Venice, to learn French well and a smattering of Italian and, most important of all, to pick up other men's ideas, which I have been mumbling over ever since, until I sometimes believe that I have thought of them for myself.

'But after I got back to Russia I had a bit of bad luck: I opened my mouth in the wrong company, and I was lucky to be able to take refuge here. It was either being a monk or Siberia, or perhaps even the Schlüsselburg with solitary confinement for life.

'There is no need for me to pity myself. The life isn't too bad, and I've formed a fine library with lots of books for which I should be beaten to death if anybody here could read them. The only drawback is that there is no one interesting. I talk to the Bursar sometimes: he's a nice honest man, but I sometimes feel desperate to meet someone with an idea in his head. And the world is full of them. Young men, poets, scientists, writers. There they are in France, in England, even in Italy, and now they are turning up in Russia – but I'm getting old and am cooped up mumbling imbecile church services in a forgotten language. Sometimes I think I shall explode.'

Valeri did not repay these confidences. It was impossible for him to explain his feelings for Anastasia. And everything stemmed from them. It was because of Anastasia that he was unable to please his father by getting married. It was because of her wishes that he had decided not to avenge Djamlet – even at the expense of his personal honour and of being stigmatised as a coward by all the men he had known since childhood, and who had believed in him. But since he could say nothing about himself to Foma without explaining about Anastasia – and he could not speak of her to this merry, sceptical, older man, he said nothing.

It was early spring, almost a year after he had entered the monastery, and one day Valeri was tempted to go out of doors instead of straining his eyes at the task of illuminating a manuscript. It occurred to him that he could go and pray at his brother's grave: not because he had ever loved Djamlet, nor because after all that Foma had said, that he believed that God would listen to his prayer ... No, it was because it was the first day of spring. The river was already in flood with snowbroth from the mountains, the sun shone and the air was mild. To go to his brother's grave was an excuse that would have to be accepted, if Valeri was asked for an explanation of his absence from the library.

In fact his departure was unnoticed, and when he had turned the corner of the monastery wall, no one saw him as he descended the wooded hill to the cemetery.

It was late afternoon, and, owing to the spring floods, the land was empty. In another week the surrounding fields would have been filled with men and beasts tilling the soil, ploughing, harrowing and sowing; and women hoeing in the gardens and the strips where they grew their flax and hemp. But the soil was still too wet to dig the ground, or to sow seed.

Valeri walked quietly through the forest that separated the monastery from the cemetery: he listened to the cawing of the rooks and the cat-like cries of the little red-footed falcons perching among the rooks' nests. Often, as a boy he had climbed up to the nest of some fierce wild bird and surrounded it with a circle of horse-hair nooses in which the hen bird would catch her feet and then fall entangled. Yet in his heart Valeri identified himself with these predatory birds, and he exulted whenever he watched them soar aloft on their pinions: for was he not a Son of the Falcon himself? He held up both sides of his brown cassock as he picked his way from the wood to the small rear gate of the cemetery, and walked thoughtlessly to his brother's grave.

He was close to it before he looked down and was amazed to see a man with his back to him standing beside it and digging. Valeri stood stock still, and, while he watched, the man threw the spade aside and went down upon his knees. From his dress Valeri saw that he was one of the Sultzi. He must be one of the younger sons of Ziklauri, their chief. And there was his brother's murderer starting to dig up his victim, desecrating his grave! Rage, horror, fury blinded him.

Valeri darted forward: he had no weapon, but he saw the hilt of the kneeling man's dagger and snatched it with his left hand from its sheath just as the youth became aware that the monk was towering over him.

'I, I, I, I ca-came to...' the young man stuttered and was springing up and away, with a half-turned head. But he spoke no more and got no further, for, before he was on his feet, Valeri had plunged the dagger into his neck, just above the collar bone. Struck from the left side, the blade went straight down into the heart. The youth pitched forward, and blood spurted into the little hole he had dug at the side of the grave.

To desecrate a grave! To try and dig up the body of the man he had assassinated! To snatch his corpse out of the sanctified earth in which it had been laid! For a few moments Valeri was still blinded by his horror of such an act – beyond anything that he had imagined that the vilest of the Sultzi would be capable. He had caught him in the act, and he gazed at the blood first spurting, and then dribbling, from the man's neck with a fierce and satisfying disgust and rage.

And then, quite suddenly, just as in the pantomime which he had once seen in Tiflis as a boy, there was a transformation scene: what he was looking at changed under his eyes. For, just beside the hole, now brimming with blood, that the man had dug, was a plant, a green tuft of leaves with an early violet in bloom and the whitish buds of flowers that were to follow. And just beyond, on the mound of the grave itself, there was a basket.

Valeri peered. In it were the white shining roots of lily of the valley, the rough leaves of a foxglove, one or two lily bulbs, yellowish ivory and scaly. Everything had changed, was changing, most horribly. The man he had killed, who, he did not doubt, had killed his brother, had come that spring evening to the grave of his victim, not to snatch a corpse, but to plant flowers on his grave. Everything had changed. But the young gardener lay there motionless, his face in a pool of mud and blood, killed at the moment of an act of kindness, maybe of remorse and brotherhood.

Valeri turned and walked away; walked out of the cemetery through the wood, and entered the monastery unperceived. The bell was ringing for the evening service. He would be late: but actually he was not too late, and he mechanically took his place and mechanically knelt and stood and his lips moved mechanically, and, when the service was over, he went to the refectory and drank a glass of kefir and ate a plate of lentils. And then mechanically he went to his cell.

'I cannot understand it. I dare not believe it. Perhaps I did not do it,' he said over and over to himself. It might perhaps have been a vision – except for the rooks beginning to nest and the cat-cries of the little black male, and dappled female, red-footed falcons perched high among the rooks' nests. Valeri did not sleep that night. He lay in the darkness with his eyes open, waiting and making a decision. He would use his pistol, which was hidden in the muniment room, behind the case of bookbinding tools.

In the morning a Cossack galloped up to the monastery. The Archimandrite saw him and the man galloped away. And then more people came. And suddenly the news spread throughout the whole monastery and, without visibly speaking to each other, all the monks knew that the body of Lazar, the young son of Ziklauri, chief of the Sultzi, had been found stabbed to the heart on the grave of the man he had killed, and they all looked curiously at Valeri when he went into the refectory for the midday meal.

Directly it was over Valeri went up to the muniment room and took his seat where he was accustomed to work. Brother Foma did not come in for over an hour. When he did he walked over to Valeri and said: 'Look at me, my Lord.'

Valeri raised his eyes and looked into those of his friend. They were still staring into each other's faces and had not exchanged a word, when one of the novices came into the room and said: 'Our Lord the Archimandrite wishes to see you, Brother Foma.' The little man put down the agate burnisher that he was holding and followed the novice out of the room.

While he was away Valeri looked for his pistol where he had hidden it, but it was gone.

That evening, after Vespers, Valeri was eating a bowl of yoghourt when the Archimandrite came to him and laid his hand gently upon Valeri's shoulder and said: 'Come to my cell, my son.' And he smiled and Valeri left his meal unfinished and followed him.

When Valeri had taken his place on the stool and the door had been shut, Hagystiarchos said: 'Brother Foma has saved you, my son,' and grinned at him through his tangled mane of filthy hair.

'Saved me? No one can save me. I am one of the damned,' replied Valeri.

'A Cossack came with a letter from the Russian General who arrived in the town last month. He demanded that I hand you over for the murder of Lazar, the youngest son of Ziklauri, chief of the Sultzi, who had been found foully murdered on consecrated ground. I called Brother Foma and he swore that you had been in the room with him all yesterday until Vespers. And everyone in the monastery knows that you were at Vespers and in the refectory afterwards until after sundown. Provided that Brother Foma sticks to his story, and provided that I accept it, you are saved.'

Valeri remained silent.

'In gratitude I ask you to give the monastery the wonder-working icon of Saint Anne.'

Valeri said nothing.

The Archimandrite went on: 'I also had a visit from that plaguy fellow the Archpriest, who still has that daughter of his on his hands. It seems that now that you have avenged Djamlet, she is inclined to look on you with favour. What do you say to that?'

'I told you at our first meeting that nothing would induce me to marry,' said Valeri.

'You took a vow also that you would not avenge your brother in the habit of a monk and seek sanctuary here afterwards,' said the Archimandrite.

'I saw him ... I thought I saw him desecrating my brother's grave. He was digging ... he had a spade ...'

'You are telling me this under the seal of the confessional,' said Hagystiarchos. Then he continued: 'I don't insist upon your marrying the girl. It has nothing to do with me. You can stay on until it is time for you to take the vows. But then you must leave. And in gratitude for what I have done, you will give the monastery the icon of Saint Anne.'

'That is for Prince Gurgen, my father. The icon is not mine to give,' Valeri said abruptly, and, bowing to Hagystiarchos, he left the cell, closing the door behind him.

He walked back to the muniment room, where brother Foma was sitting at his work table, peering through his curious spectacles at the manuscript which he was illuminating. He did not look up as Valeri entered the room, nor as he went and stood beside him.

'You perjured yourself to save me this morning. No friend could do more. You meant well and I thank you for your love. But I am sorry that you did. It was wasted effort.'

'Are you going to give yourself up?' asked Foma taking off his spectacles and turning to look at his friend. It had never for an instant occurred to Valeri to give himself up. To begin with, he was a Son of the Falcon and a Prince. He was his own judge in his own cause and no man had the right to judge him. And then to give oneself up implies a belief in human justice, and in the expiation of a crime while here on earth. Both these notions were foreign to Valeri. A Son of the Falcon could punish himself: he could not accept punishment meted out by his inferiors, or his enemies.

'No, I should never do that,' he said surprised and slightly offended. 'Have you taken my pistol?' he asked abruptly.

'Yes, I found it a few weeks ago. I thought it must be yours and that I had better put it away out of your reach,' said Foma.

'Please give it me.'

'Are you planning another murder?' asked Foma looking intently at him.

'I am planning to go away.'

'Where?' asked Foma.

Valeri shrugged his shoulders. 'Where no one can follow me,' he said angrily.

'In that case I shan't give you the pistol,' said Foma.

'Interfering fool,' exclaimed Valeri in sudden rage and walked out of the room.

Back in his cell he looked at his sabre hanging below the crucifix and lifted it down from its hook and then drew it from the scabbard. Then he looked up and down the blade with love: it was so beautiful, with the ripple of the Islamic characters, unwinding their hidden meaning, from the hilt for a full span down the blade. Valeri loved that Damascus blade more than anything, except the shirt that Anastasia had made and embroidered for him. In some ways he loved it more, for the steel would never wear out: it was not personal, but a work of consummate art which could last for ever.

No. He would not sully that blade and leave it for some-one else to clean after cutting his throat with it. It was a service that he could not ask of a weapon which he worshipped. Nor would he destroy himself in the guise of a monk. He was Prince Valeri, eldest Son of the Son of the Falcon, and if he died by his own hand it would be as himself. These details were important. They were what he had to cling to while his soul was in numb agony: a state in which he was in a trance of bottomless despair. He was lying in a ravine, the sides of which were cliff walls of horror and remorse. Never out of his vision was the figure of Lazar – pitched forward on his face, with the blood jerking and then dribbling into the hole in which he had wished to plant a flower to show his sorrow for the man he had so treacherously murdered on his wedding day.

In this strange numbed trance, Valeri took off his cassock and his rough cotton drawers and dressed himself in the clothes he had worn when he came to the monastery. He was slow; his fingers fumbled over the buttons. But at last he was dressed as himself. He took down the crucifix and threw it on the floor and made a slipnoose in his rope girdle, put his head through it and, standing on the stool, fastened it slowly and carefully to the big iron nail from which the crucifix had hung.

'I am coming, Lazar,' he cried and kicked away the stool. He fell such a short distance, less than half the height of the stool, that he did not break his neck, nor was he rendered unconscious. He was suffocating and still aware of his position. Then, as he was blacking out, he heard a cry and was half aware that Foma had rushed into his cell. He seized the sabre and jumping on the stool, cut Valeri down. The body fell, doubled up, almost dislocating the left arm and shoulder. Valeri was unconscious, but not dead, and, directly Foma had loosened the noose, began breathing spasmodically, and he was sick. Foma struggled for some while to straighten his friend's body and lift it on to the bed. Later he cleaned up the cell and, after Valeri had recovered consciousness, he stripped him of his fine clothes and got him once more into his cotton drawers.

CHAPTER TWO

On the night that Valeri first entered the monastery, Irakli slept in the monks' stable on a bundle of hay, taking the precaution of putting his pistols ready cocked beside him. Next morning he woke early and, after feeding and watering his master's mare and his own pony and being given a bite and a sup at the monastery back door, got ready to leave. First he slung his master's precious Martini rifle on his back, then unstrapped the holsters of his pistols from his pony's saddle and transferred them to that of his master's grey mare which he mounted, and, keeping a sharp watch on everyone he saw in the town, rode off leading the pony, to the house of the Armenian Gulerian.

He received a cool welcome.

The servant who opened the door and took a message, did not invite him into the house, and the two boys in the yard laughed and walked away when he asked them to hold his horses. However, without invitation, he led them into the stable, where he saw Djamlet's grey Arab stallion in a loose box.

After keeping him waiting for two hours, Avetis came out and looked at him curiously. 'Haven't I seen you before?' he asked.

Irakli bowed low to the handsome, arrogant figure before him. 'I am the servant of your lamented friend the Lord Djamlet,' he said.

Avetis frowned, shook his head and shrugged his shoulders. 'That was a bad business. It came from having that feud in the family. Living in the past. That's what's wrong with these mountainy people. A bad business.' There was a silence. 'And why have you come here, young man?' he asked sharply.

'I have come to fetch my master's stallion, my Lord.' Irakli gave Avetis this title, though he despised him because he was a merchant and not a robber.

'Why, it is nine months after he was killed! And, in any case, you are making a mistake. Your late master gave me that cursed animal the night before he was shot. It was his last night as a bachelor and we sat up playing cards and drinking. Poor Djamlet had rotten luck. He lost and lost. By the end he had lost much more than he could pay, and he offered me his stallion, and I accepted it, though it wasn't worth what he owed me. I remember I tried to cheer the poor fellow up by reminding him of the proverb: "Unlucky at cards, lucky in love." But he didn't live long enough to prove the truth of it. Smashing young woman, the girl is. Hard lines on her. Someone ought to marry her. But I dare say she was well quit of that mountainy family with the feud behind it.'

Irakli was outraged by every word that the Armenian had said, but he made no reply.

Presently Avetis went on: 'I've been trying to sell that cursed animal for a long time. He bit my groom and savaged my sister's little mare. Now I have found a Russian officer who is fool enough to buy him. So you see my lad – I'm sorry you should have had the trouble of coming. All's well at the Castle, I suppose?' And nodding contemptuously at Irakli he walked into his house and slammed the door.

It was midday; the porter and the lads who had laughed at him had disappeared – no doubt into the kitchen where Irakli had hoped to be given a meal. No one was stirring.

'And to think that my master should have picked a swine like that to be his best man! A dirty tradesman!' Irakli said aloud. He walked over to the stables and looked into the loose-box. There was the stallion. The animal rolled the whites of his eyes and laid back an ear. But he recognised him. Irakli found a halter hanging on a nail, slipped into the box and then he put the halter on the stallion, who afterwards allowed himself to be led out. Irakli took the leading rein from his pony, allowing him to run free, and transferred it to the stallion. Then he mounted the mare and, leading the stallion, rode out of Gulerian's yard, and, with the pony following him, trotted quietly out of the town.

There was no pursuit, and it was not until they had gone several versts and were on the narrow mule-track that trouble started. The track was too narrow to lead the stallion, so he had to roll up the leading rein and drive pony and stallion ahead of him. However, when he reached the first ford, pony and stallion would not enter the water, but scrambled past him, because at that point the track was wider. Irakli left them and rode the mare through the river. He was followed, first by the pony and after a little while by the stallion. It was then that the trouble began. Suddenly the pony dashed past, nearly knocking Irakli and the mare over the precipice, then the stallion came close up behind and began to worry the mare. Irakli unluckily had not got his knout with him and had nothing but a short quirt with which to strike at the animal behind him. The mare grew more and more restive, the stallion more and more enterprising, and Irakli found himself having a rough ride. Then, when the mare for the third or fourth time had let out with her heels, she caught the stallion on the knee. After that Irakli and the mare were left in peace. She had lamed the horse and the last Irakli saw of him, he was staggering along on three legs. When at last the exhausted and famished boy entered the Castle and had been brought before Prince Gurgen, he had a long and confused tale to tell.

At first the Prince could make nothing of it. His son had not visited the Archpriest, but after parading round the town in an incredibly foolhardy manner, had gone to the monastery. Then he had paraded the town a second time, after which he had gone again to the monastery and had dismissed Irakli, telling him he was remaining to become a monk! It sounded complete nonsense. And then the wretched boy, Irakli, had allowed Djamlet's magnificent Arab stallion to be lamed on the way back, and had probably made an enemy of the most important trader in the town, a man who had been Djamlet's friend.

'Get out of my sight or I'll have the skin off you,' he shouted, and the wretched Irakli was glad to creep away into the stable. The stallion had hobbled in, and Irakli was washing and preparing to bandage the broken knee, when Anastasia sought him out with a bowl of hot spiced wine and a plate of smoking sausages which she made him eat, while she sat patiently on a sack of oats. Not until he had finished did she ask him questions and make him tell her the whole story from the beginning until the end. Valeri had clearly gone into the monastery and abjured life, with the intention of carrying out her wishes and ending the feud. She longed to be able to see him and throw herself at his feet in grati- tude. He had given up marriage, rank and property and a free life for her sake – because he loved her and it seemed likely that now they would never see each other again. Only a day's ride away he was living, dressed in a rough cassock, with a cord round his waist, a man forever celibate, while she was bound to the Castle and would never have a chance to leave it and was married to an ancient tyrant whose bed she had to share.

When Nina spoke of Valeri that evening in Prince Gurgen's hearing, he forbade everyone in the Castle to utter his son's name. And he added that no one was to pray for him either.

After he had been to the stable and had examined the stallion's knee, he became so angry that he would have had Irakli flogged if Nina had not reminded him that the boy had run out of the Cathedral, at the risk of his life, to drag Djamlet into safety. But when she said that if the boy had not carried off the stallion, the wretched Armenian would have sold him to a Russian officer, the Prince flared out.

'That damned boy has made Avetis my enemy. The Gulerians are the only rich friends that we had in town. And, for all I can prove, he may have been speaking the truth – though it was unlike Djamlet to play at cards for money. God knows what the truth is.'

'It was Irakli who took the stallion, not you, Prince,' old Nina pointed out. 'You could return him.'

'Avetis would not be too pleased to get a broken-kneed horse back. And it would seem cowardly: I don't like not backing up my men,' grumbled the Prince.

For days on end, he went on talking about the stallion and Avetis and 'that half-wit of a young groom'.

Anastasia often felt like giving him a piece of her mind, but she remained quiet: she felt that she must show as much resignation and self-sacrifice as Valeri. How hard it must be for that splendid young man with his magnificent body and his fiery spirit, to keep his eyes bent on the ground and live with a set of dirty and sexless monks! To spend his life mortifying the flesh and singing fourteenth-century chants.

But when Anastasia spoke to her young sister Tamar, she said: 'It is like Valeri to have done such a beautiful act. I think that the life of a monk must be the happiest that any man can choose. To renounce all evil and embrace the way of God.' She was surprised when the girl replied: 'I think that it is horrible and I cannot understand it.'

'Surely you must see that the alternative was to avenge Djamlet and to keep the feud alive?'

'Valeri is a man – the finest man I know. I would like him to live like a man. If men have to fight and kill each other, that's what he should do, and then...'

Anastasia interrupted her before she could say that Valeri ought to love women and have children like other men.

'He has chosen peace and the Holy Church instead of

cruelty and murder. "Thou shalt not kill," is written in the Gospel. I always hoped that he would not avenge Djamlet, and I rejoice that he has chosen not to do so.'

'I don't care about Djamlet. He was always stuck-up and beastly. But if Valeri was bound in honour to avenge him, why should he become a monk?'

'Honour! What nonsense that is! I hate the idea of revenge. To kill someone because he has killed someone else. That is to live like savages and not according to the word of Christ, who told us to forgive our enemies.'

'If one of the Sultzi were to kill Vasso, would you not want revenge and to have him suffer?' asked Tamar.

'No, I would leave that to God,' said Anastasia and broke off the conversation by walking away.

Tamar would have liked to ask her sister other questions. For one thing, if the finest men like Valeri all became monks, it followed that one would have to choose an inferior kind of man to be the father of one's children. Perhaps it was her duty to rejoice, like Anastasia, that Valeri had chosen to become a monk. But she could not. It seemed to her ugly. Just as so much of the Church was ugly. It was unsuitable that such a magnificent body should be sterile. She hated it, just as she hated that the men in the stable said that her young colt ought to be castrated. And however much Tamar tried to, she was unable to think about Valeri's choice without anger. It was all very well for Anastasia to talk about loving God. But it was Valeri's beautiful body, now hidden under a coarse cassock, that she could not forget. He had given it to God who could make no use of it. She wished that God did not exist, to make Valeri do such a thing.

The weekly round of life at the Castle went on as usual after Valeri's departure. That is to say corn was ground during the week in the very primitive little watermill which would only do a few bushels of grain a day. Then, on Fridays, men brought faggots to the bakehouse and lit the three brick ovens; one very large, one on the right, smaller for white bread, and a third small one for the cakes and pies and roast meats from the kitchen. Faggot after faggot was piled in, and the flames came curling out, and the smoke was blinding at first, but soon cleared away up the chimney above, which served all three of the ovens. While the boy Ramin tended the fires, Souliko, the baker, made dough and kneaded it and set it to rise in the long wooden trough on the hearth below the blazing ovens. The dough was covered over with a sheet of coarse linen to prevent the ashes falling on it. For the most part the bread was rye and rose little, but at one end of the trough were some white loaves baked for the Prince's table, and these rose so that they sometimes pushed up the linen into little mounds like a woman's breasts. The bakehouse was filled with the smell of the burning faggots, mixed with the sour smell of rye dough. When Nina, or any of the women, opened the bakehouse door while the bread was rising, bringing a batch of honeycakes, or a pie to go into the little oven, they would be greeted with a furious shout from Souliko: 'Get out! Get out! Or the dough won't rise!'

And then when the woman had run out and shut the door, he would shout after her: 'Chicken-headed bitches! That's what all you women are!'

It was terrifically hot in the bakehouse, and Souliko worked stripped to his drawers and the sweat ran down his face and dripped on to the dough when he was kneading. It ran down his arms and the sides of his body, and trickled through the hair on his chest. He was a lean, pale man. When once the last batch of loaves had gone into the ovens, he would open the door of the bakehouse and stand there, almost naked, cooling off, even on the coldest days in winter.

Soon afterwards Souliko was transformed into a most charming fellow, wreathed in smiles, and he would welcome the women into the bakehouse to carry off their cakes and pies. When the bread had come out of the oven, the sour smell of rye dough had disappeared and was replaced by the rich smell of new bread, and the shelves were soon filling up with the great round loaves that would last the whole community all the week.

At every baking there was a special little loaf of white wheaten flour, made with sour milk and honey, which Souliko took to the Prince after he had put on his shirt and trousers. And the old man would smile graciously and cross himself three times, before he broke the little loaf and ate a piece of it. After that he would break it into pieces and give one to each of his daughters, who took care to be on hand to enjoy the favour. It was a favour, for even Tamar, who disliked this ceremony, admitted that no bread on earth ever tasted so good.

There was no fixed day for butchering. The number of animals killed, and when, depended on the time of year and how long the meat should hang. In summer it was for only a few days, in winter as much as three weeks. During Lent no animals at all were killed, and they ate smoked hams, sausages and salted and smoked fish.

The sheep or pig to be killed was dragged into the court-yard to a corner where there was a low stone table with a groove in the middle. It was thrown on this and held down by boys, while one of the older men would cut its throat, and the blood would run down the groove and drain into a bucket underneath. Next day there would be blood puddings, liver and offal of all sorts.

After the beast had been flayed the carcase would be hung on hooks under the gatehouse entrance. There were almost always one or two sheep hanging there, and a new arrival at the Castle, seeing them, would be assured that he would not go short of meat during his stay. This was a piece of old-fashioned ostentation upon which the Prince prided himself.

The skins would be rolled up and put with others in a sack. A week or so later, the hides would be brought out, and scraped and painted with soap and saltpetre and oiled with neat's foot oil. Later, the woolly side would be washed and combed, and the skins, which had smelt so rank, would become supple and smooth and smell only of clean wool and leather. Coats and hats would be made of them.

Once a month Nina collected the baskets of dirty linen and there was a big wash. All the morning the wash house would be filled with clouds of steam and the shrill voices of women, sometimes laughing, sometimes quarrelling, or giving each other unwanted advice. The men all learned to keep out of the way on washing day. The most sensible thing was to go off with a lump of black bread, a sausage and a couple of apples and round up the sheep on the mountain. When they came back they would see long lines of linen hanging outside the Castle walls. The tired women would welcome them with weak smiles, and there was a makeshift supper.

Sometimes people would come to the Castle – it was seldom complete strangers like the Persian Mustapha Sasun and his wife. There were four or five regular pedlars – usually a man and his wife with an ass, its panniers loaded with what they had to sell. There was an Armenian who offered nails, copper wire, small tools like gimlets, bradawls, hammers and screwdrivers. His woman had a basket with scissors, needles, cotton reels, buttons and gold and silver thread for embroidery. There was a Persian cobbler who came with women's shoes and slippers. In spring and autumn there was a bee-man who led a mule loaded with straw hives and who would buy honey and wax, and give advice. He often stayed a week or two. Once there was a solitary Russian gipsy with a dancing bear, but he went on and over the pass, and never came back. And then there were the Tatar caravans – usually half a dozen men and boys with a long string of camels taking Russian goods to Turkey, or Persia, and coming back with carpets, silks, bags of dates, spices and metalwork. These caravans seldom paused at the Castle, or greeted any of the men they met beside the track. But there was one old Tatar who knew the Prince, and would stop to sell bricks of tea on his way south and bring a bag of green coffee beans on the way north. For Malik and the Prince coffee was a rare luxury, and on special occasions they would drink a few cups of thick Turkish coffee together. It was not a Christian habit, and the Old Prince was rather shy about admitting to it among men of his own rank, or to ecclesiastics like the Archpriest.

The two sisters, Elisso and Salomé, had accepted the life of the Castle while they were children and believed that just as spring followed winter, and summer spring, so their own lives would blossom and bear fruit. But this happy state changed after the death of Djamlet and the disappearance of Valeri. They were sixteen and fourteen: their half-sister Iriné was nineteen, and they became aware that there was nothing for them to look forward to. The Old Prince would never take them, or Iriné, to the town. Anastasia treated them as children and kept aloof. Tamar they hated, because her beauty was of a different type and she kept herself apart from them. Between them and Iriné there was jealousy and contempt. Salomé, the younger, was the more intelligent and passionate.

'Don't you understand,' she exclaimed one night, 'our father would think any money given in dowry with us as wasted. He only wants men – fighting men who would marry us and come to live here and serve under him. And who wants to do that and pit himself against the Sultzi? We shall go on living here, like Iriné, until we are both old maids, kept busy knitting socks for Vasso, or embroidering shirts.'

'We must pray for husbands,' said Elisso. 'Although I am a Princess, I would marry an Armenian shopkeeper who lived in the town.'

'No such luck will come to either of us,' replied Salomé. 'I would go gladly with any fighting man who rode his own horse and had his own sword by his side.'

'You must remember that you are a Princess,' said Elisso. 'Leave the stable boys to Tamar. If you get into trouble with any of them, Father will put you into a nunnery.'

'I would rather run away with a Kurd. There are decent men among them, like Malik. Better be one of four wives, than an old maid.'

Her sister was shocked. 'Be careful what you say Salomé. Remember that Saint Anne can overhear us talking.'

During winter, and in early spring, Prince Gurgen was always quarrelsome and unhappy. For the months from January till April were the months of safety. No raids from over the mountain passes to the south were possible owing to the deep snow, and, down the river, sudden freshets were liable to make the fords too deep for passage by a man on horseback; then the mule-track was cut in two. For this reason it was dangerous for a raiding party of the Sultzi to venture upstream. If the river rose suddenly, their retreat might be cut off, or made perilous. Then, after the thaw in the high mountains, came the torrents of spring when all communication with the town was cut off for two weeks. These months, when Prince Gurgen knew that no enemy could come near his stronghold, were for him times of intolerable boredom. What made it worse in spring was that most out-of-door activities were impossible. In January and February hunting took up much of his energy, for there was abundance of game. But once the snow higher up had melted, it became difficult to get about in the mud, and every streamlet was a problem. Nothing could be done in the four great fields. The earth was too sodden. There was no need to send out sentinels, or for the men to carry arms. There was no telling what the Sultzi might be doing, or what plans the Russians might not be making for pushing right up to the Persian and Turkish borders. The Prince's disgust with this state of affairs found expression in violent explosions of anger.

One such resulted from Anastasia speaking to him of the

desirability of having their son Vasso taught to read and even to write a little, and she was injudicious enough to suggest that: 'We might get in some man from one of the religious orders.'

Prince Gurgen shrieked: 'A monk! Good God! You should like to turn the only son I have left into a snivelling monk! God damn all women! Do you understand? I will never have another of those miserable hypocrites in the house. By God, if there's one thing I hate and despise it is monkery. That old Turkish bastard Hagystiarchos, with the lice falling out of his beard! He ought to be put on a bonfire with the rest of the rubbish, the old billygoat! Oh, I know, you women are so damned inquisitive. You want to pull up the cassock and see if it's a proper man underneath...'

Prince Gurgen was shouting, but in spite of seeing that his master was beside himself with rage, Malik came into the room, and said in a loud voice 'My Lord...'

The Prince looked at him, flabbergasted. The leader of his men appearing so tactlessly was so surprising that he actually forgot what he had been shouting at Anastasia about.

'Well, what do you want?' he asked at last.

'A pigeon from Nina's cousin has come into the loft with a message.'

In the town there lived an old man, a cousin of Nina's, who was a pigeon fancier. At Malik's suggestion, hidden away behind his tumblers and fantails, was a coop of homing pigeons which had been reared by Malik at the Castle. News of paramount importance could thus be sent by pigeon post to the Castle in an emergency. The idea had only been accepted by the old man the year before, and this was one of the first birds to bring a serious message. Its arrival at a time when the mule-track was impassable, and the news it brought, was such as to lead Malik to interrupt the Prince while he was shouting abuse at his wife. Although the Prince could sign his name, neither he nor Malik was capable of reading the message carried by the pigeon, and they were dependent upon a boy of fourteen, whose leg had been mal-formed at birth and had been sent to the hospital in the town, where he had lived his first ten years. He had learned his letters in the town and to read and speak Russian, and had returned a cripple, who spent his time reading and catching trout in the river. He was an expert fisherman.

So, when the Prince asked shortly: 'Well, what has your pigeon got to tell us?' Malik beckoned to the crippled boy standing behind him and said: 'Read it to my Lord, Vakhtang.'

Vakhtang bowed awkwardly and, holding a little band of paper in his hands, read out: 'Lazar, the murderer, found dead, stabbed with own dagger on Djamlet's grave.'

Prince Gurgen gave a shout of exultation and ran straight out of the room to the icon of Saint Anne. There he flung himself on his knees and began a long prayer of thanksgiving, prostrating himself, and humbling himself for having doubted her goodness and for having assumed that his beloved son Valeri had rebelled against his authority, when he had re-venged his brother with consummate brilliance.

For although, wisely enough, nothing was said about who had killed Lazar in the message, Prince Gurgen instantly guessed that it was Valeri who had avenged his brother. The cemetery was close to the monastery – who else could it be? And what skill: to kill the murderer with his own weapon and on the grave of his victim!

After the crippled boy had read out the message and the Prince had run out of the room, Anastasia, who had turned very pale, went up to him.

'Read it again, slowly and carefully,' she ordered; and, when Vakhtang had read it, she took the little scroll of paper out of his hand and looked at it for a long time. She had taught herself to read a few words. At last she gave it to Malik and went quickly into the next room, where she threw herself down and burst into a storm of tears.

She was still lying on the divan, but the tears had dried

on her face, when her husband, after his burst of prayer, came back into their room and found her.

'I feel so ashamed! I have been so unfair! For months now I have believed that Valeri could have betrayed our honour, that he could have been such a coward as to seek safety in a monastery. I have ordered everyone to leave him out of their prayers! I have tried to cut him out of my thoughts and all the time was hating him. It never occurred to me he would have imagined such a clever trap. I wonder how he managed to lure that young villain Lazar to the grave of Djamlet?'

'I do not believe that Valeri killed Lazar,' said Anastasia icily.

'Don't believe it was Valeri! But it's obvious. Who else could it possibly be? We have no one, on our side, in the town, who would take such a risk ... And may I ask you, madam, why you don't think it was Valeri?'

'It is sacrilege to kill someone in a churchyard. It's consecrated ground. And Valeri would never disguise himself as a monk to murder anyone. He would do it openly. He would never stoop to such vile treachery. You judge him by yourself...'

Prince Gurgen sprang at his wife and slapped her in the face, screaming: 'Get out, you foul woman, before I strangle you. Get out, you crazy bitch. Get out!' He rushed at her and hit her again and again in the face. Finally he pushed her out of the room and shouted for Nina. When she appeared he said: 'Take your mistress to the top room in the tower and lock her up. She has gone mad ... says terrible things. And don't let her have Vasso up there. She might corrupt him.'

The Prince was trembling and, to his annoyance, found he could not control his shaking hands.

Anastasia's nose was bleeding. But Nina did not seem agitated by the scene. 'Come my dear, I'll get you a cold compress for the back of your neck. That will stop the bleeding.' The two women went away and, when they were out of hearing of the Prince, Nina said: 'You have put him in a passion, my dear. It's bad for his heart. It will take a long time for him to calm down now. Much better keep away, as he says. I'll have the room ready in no time. I'm sure you could do with a good rest yourself.'

Anastasia did not mind where she went, so long as she could be alone. What was so terrible was that in her secret heart she believed that her husband was right and that Valeri had killed Lazar. 'Could it have been an accident?' she wondered. 'Valeri is not treacherous...'

But if the Prince had convinced his wife, her words had raised terrible doubts in his mind.

'After all, it's pure assumption ... but of course it couldn't have been anyone else. It would have been too dangerous to put his name in the message on the pigeon's leg. It could not have been anyone but Valeri, particularly as the body was found on the grave of Djamlet and the cemetery is so close to the monastery, with only that little wood in between.'

Directly Prince Gurgen had had time to think about the consequences of Djamlet having been avenged, he determined to carry out his vow to take the wonder-working icon of Saint Anne to his son's grave at the earliest possible moment.

He ordered Malik to go upstream to the lake and put in marked sticks so he could measure its rise and fall every day, and he himself went down every morning to look at the gauge and see if it had risen or fallen at the ford during the night. Meanwhile every preparation had to be made. The expedition was dangerous, but the sooner it was completed the better. If they could make it while the water was still high, they would be unexpected and might steal a march on the Sultzi, while those ruffians were making preparations for a large-scale raid to revenge the death of Lazar – a raid he felt certain that they would make before long. The prince decided that he would, of course, leave Anastasia behind, and that he would take Vasso with him with old Nina to look after him. He would leave Malik in command at the Castle.

The party would therefore consist of himself, Vasso, and Nina with five armed men and Irakli and another lad to act as scouts. This was a very small party if they ran into trouble, but it was essential to leave Malik with enough men to defend the Castle, with the flock of sheep and goats and the girls.

For days the preparations went on. The Prince, Vasso and Nina had to be in full mourning for the service. The armed guard would wear black bands round their left arms and round their tall white sheepskin papakhas. Even the horses and pack camel would have black favours. Prince Gurgen himself took the icon of Saint Anne out of the surround and frames, and wrapped her in white linen. He stowed her away in the long wooden box in which five four-foot-long brass taper holders, which the attendants would carry during the service over the grave, were packed, together with the white surplices the two boy acolytes would wear, and the bag of incense which would be burned. The level of the river had dropped, and there would be no great difficulty in crossing the fords on horseback. The camel and ponies carrying packs could be pulled over if they hesitated. They had long ropes in case of trouble downstream.

At dawn, the two scouts were sent off on their ponies, still swallowing down their breakfasts of bread and onions, and, an hour later, the main body started. The river was rising, but none of the animals missed their footing, or went down. Two hours later they reached the place where the mule-track fell down to the side of the river and there was a crossing over what was normally a wide and shallow stretch of pebbles. Now it was a fast-running, wide flood, and the difficulties were obvious. Moreover, as the river was rising fast, the crossing had to be made at once, or not at all. Faced with this problem, Prince Gurgen showed himself an experienced and accomplished leader. He rode over himself, leading the pack-camel with the box containing the icon of Saint Anne, and unwinding a rope which he fastened around a rock where he also tethered the camel. He then rode back and personally brought Vasso and Nina over, supported by the rope, while all the men but one old fellow got across as best they could. When they were all over, the man who had been left on the far bank unfastened the rope and tied the loose end to his horse's girths and, though the animal lost his footing twice, they pulled him over. Two of the pack-ponies went down and were swept downstream into the deep pool below, but each managed to swim to the shore. By the time that the whole party were across, it was obvious that there would be no return.

The crossing had been so difficult and exhausting that Prince Gurgen decided to call a halt, so that a fire could be lighted of driftwood and that they could warm and dry themselves. Everyone was given a tot of vodka, and tea was brewed.

While they were almost ready to start again, Irakli came tearing back at a gallop, his pony sending stones flying into the ravine beneath him. When he reached them, he threw himself off his shaggy pony and rushed to the Prince. 'My Lord, the men of our blood are out in force. They will now be about five miles down. There are about twenty of them. I counted fourteen myself, scrambling up the hillside and taking up positions behind rocks. They are waiting for us and somehow must have got word that we are coming.'

Prince Gurgen actually smiled at the young man and replied: 'You have done well – very well. Go back and rejoin your comrade, but on no account allow yourself to be seen. Be sure to leave your pony well out of sight and remember that they may have a sentinel high up, with a long view of the mule track. If they make a move, return and report here immediately.'

The Prince went back to the river and drove a notched

stake into the river so that he would know whether it was still rising, or had fallen, if they were trapped. When he rejoined the party, he told Nina to brew some more tea. When it was ready, he drank a cup and walked down to the river to look at his stick. The water was rising fast, and retreat would be impossible until it fell. The alternatives that presented themselves to his mind were first to stay where they were, until attacked. In that case the Sultzi would have every advantage. They would be on higher ground, would outnumber them four or five to one. On the other hand they might advance, and, by some ruse, avoid the fight which the Sultzi would inevitably win – winning with it the wonderworking icon of Saint Anne. Prince Gurgen sat down on a stone, drank another cup of tea. There was only one possible way of saving Saint Anne, which was by a sacrifice which appalled him, but which had a quality which was as magnificent and terrible as anything in the Old Testament.

Vasso and Nina were sitting in the shelter of the rock round which he had tied the rope to help get the animals across. He took off his long black cloak and handed it to Nina. 'Turn your back on me and hold up this cloak so no one can see behind the rock,' he commanded. Then, taking Vasso by the hand he led him into shelter behind the rock and sat down on a large smooth boulder and took the boy on his knee.

'There is a world made of crystal where everyone is happy. It is full of laughing little boys like you and of beautiful girls with long golden hair, who shed tears of pity when they look down, and sing songs of joy like the mountain thrush in spring, when they look up and meet the eyes of those around them. You will go there, Vasso, and play with those laughing children and they will kiss you and caress you. Would you like to go there?'

'I don't know,' he replied, looking at his father distrustfully, for he was puzzled and embarrassed by what he had been told.

71

'I am sure you would like to do something very brave and wonderful, so that men talked of you forever,' said the Prince.

'I don't know,' repeated Vasso.

'Will you do what I ask you?'

'I would do anything that Mummy asked me,' said the little boy.

'Your mother would ask you if she were here. Because if you don't do what Papa asks, the bad men of our blood will go and set fire to the Castle and burn your mother. She is in a room at the top of the tower, locked up so she cannot escape and the flames will come crackling up the stairs and they will burn down the great wooden door and they will reach in and burn your mother alive,' said the Prince. Then, as the child shrank away from him, he added quickly: 'But if you do what Papa tells you you can save her and she won't be burned, or hurt at all. Will you save her?'

Vasso nodded his head gravely and murmured so low that the Prince could not hear his words.

'Speak a little louder.'

'I will not let Mummy burn,' said the child.

'You must say: "I give myself willingly to save Saint Anne, and I forgive you, Papa," ' said the Prince coaxingly.

Vasso found the courage to say clearly: 'I give myself to save Mummy and Saint Anne and everyone, and I forgive you Papa.' Then he laughed, for it sounded funny to be forgiving his Papa, instead of the other way round. The Prince stooped and kissed his son and stood up.

'Now shut your eyes and turn round,' he whispered.

The boy did as he was asked, and the Prince took his son by the throat and pressed with his thumbs on the windpipe. The child struggled madly, so that it was all he could do to hold him. It seemed an immensely long time to the Prince before the struggles slowed down, then, stepping on the boy's insteps so as to hold him down, he jerked the little head up and with the edge of his right hand hit him a

72

tremendous blow just below the base of the skull, a blow which dislocated the boy's neck. Then the old man let go of the boy's body and fell on his knees beside him. After a moment, gasping and with the sweat pouring off his face, he got up and fetched the box with the icon in it and the long brass taper holders. He knelt down and undressed his son. The body was very soft. Some of the clothes clung, and he tore them as he pushed them off, and found it difficult. When he had the naked body lying before him, he drew his dagger and made a quick cut in the child's belly below the navel. For the first moment, there were revealed two gleaming edges of white fat; then the blood began to trickle from the tissue in little threads of red over the white, and then flowed over and completely covered it. The Prince took the icon of Saint Anne, unwrapped it, gazing fervently into her strange blue eyes. He pushed his hand through the cut he had made and after withdrawing it, he pushed in the icon, burying it under the warm and steaming intestines of his son. He called then to Nina and, getting up, went and took his cloak from her. No one was looking. The men were all squatting round the fire in a group smoking and waiting until their leader had made up his mind what orders to give them.

'Wash our angel. Wrap him in a clean linen. Leave his face and breast bare. Then put him in the box.' While Nina was carrying out his instructions, he stood by the rock, holding his cloak so that if any of the men chanced to look his way they would not see what she was doing. When she had finished, he carried the brass rods to his men and told them to sling their muskets reversed, with the muzzles pointing downwards. Then he gave each of them a brass rod with an unlighted taper – with Nina's help he lifted the box back on to the camel.

'Tear your clothes and put ashes on your head,' he ordered her. Soon the funeral procession set out: the Prince rode first, holding up a crucifix in his right hand. Then came the

73

camel, led by a boy on his pony. Then Nina riding, and, after her, the escort of five men riding in single file each carrying a brass rod in his right hand.

All these preparations had taken two or three hours, and it was afternoon, with the gorge in deep shadow, before they reached a place where the track opened out in a flat space. A challenge rang out and shots were fired.

Prince Gurgen, with his head bare, and the crucifix held high, rode slowly on at a foot pace; then halted, as a dozen of the Sultzi rose from behind near-by rocks and surrounded him. The camel halted, and the whole procession came to a stop.

'Do you surrender, old man?' cried Ziklauri, riding up.

'I go to bury my son,' said Prince Gurgen.

Ziklauri gazed incredulously at the little party. One of the Solutz poked the muzzle of his musket into the Prince's ribs.

'None of your treacherous tricks,' he hissed. But Ziklauri waved the fellow away.

'Show me the corpse and I'll let you pass,' he said.

The Prince wheeled his horse round and pointed to the box on the camel. Then he called out: 'Nina, show Vasso to this man of our blood.'

Nina untied the leather thongs and then lifted the linen shroud covering the child's face and chest. Ziklauri rode up and looked over into the box. The camel backed away. But the leader of the Sultzi had seen enough. He took off his papakha and crossed himself.

'How did the boy die?' he asked gently.

'The Lord giveth and the Lord taketh away. He slipped when he was climbing Rusudan's rock, birds' nesting,' said the Prince.

'Yes, I saw that his neck was broken,' said Ziklauri. The sight of the dead child had upset him. There was a silence.

'Well, you can go on your way, old man. But I give you warning that I am coming soon to your Castle to collect the icon of Saint Anne. Give it to me freely and you shall live the rest of your life in peace. I have no wish to harry men of my blood.'

Prince Gurgen did not seem to hear what Ziklauri was saying. He mumbled stupidly. Nina covered Vasso's face and did up the thongs of the box. Then wheeling his horse, and, still holding the crucifix aloft, the Prince gave the signal to go on. The Sultzi remained in a group. After a while they turned their horses' heads upstream and trotted off in single file. It had occurred to Ziklauri that it was a golden opportunity to burn the Castle and capture the wonder-working icon. However, when they reached the river crossing, they found the ford impassable. It was a raging torrent in which no animal could keep its footing. They were forced to turn back and follow the funeral procession. But Prince Gurgen had increased its pace to a sharp trot directly he was out of sight of the enemy, and his party was not overtaken.

He led the cavalcade straight to the cemetery and, after giving his men orders to dig a grave next to that of Djamlet, he led the camel into a far corner. There, while Nina kept guard, he unwrapped Vasso's body and opened the wound to extract the icon. Rigor mortis had set in, and Saint Anne seemed to have glued herself into the child's belly. At last, after a long struggle, he got the panel out. He wrapped it up in a piece of linen from the shroud, put it inside his shirt and then, leaving Nina to prepare the child's body for burial, he rode off to the house of the Archpriest. He was received with the utmost cordiality.

'Come in, come in, most honoured Prince.... Fetch vodka for the Prince.... A plate of caviare for the Prince,' cried the fat little ecclesiastic. But he saw at once that his honoured guest had something wrong with him. For one thing saliva was running out of the corners of his mouth and dribbling from his beard. 'Here, drink this, Prince,' he said handing him a glass of vodka. The Prince drank it, but the saliva still dribbled.

'Allow me, Prince,' said the Archpriest and producing an enormous handkerchief from the pocket of his kaftan, he began wiping the Prince's mouth and beard.

There was a spot of blood on his shirt too. The old fellow was in a bad way.

'Please arrange for three services,' said the Prince at last.

'Three services!' exclaimed the Archpriest.

'Yes, three. If Saint Anne so wills it, my son Vasso must be buried. Then there must be a service with her wonderworking icon over the grave of Djamlet and another service over the grave of Vasso.'

It was a long time before the old priest could get the story clear. The boy had broken his neck birds' nesting – the Prince seemed to believe that Saint Anne might bring him to life again. And he had brought the icon with him, to have the service over Djamlet's grave, as he had vowed.

Finally he got the Prince to sit down, to drink more vodka, and he called his daughter in to look after him, while he sent his servants flying in all directions to arrange for the funeral that evening – the Prince would hear of no delay – and for the service with the icon of Saint Anne over the graves in the cemetery, next morning. He was sure that one service would do for both graves. Then the Prince would, of course, stay in the Archpriest's palace. A room indoors would be found for Nina. The men and boys could sleep in the stables.

There was an immense amount to be done. Katerina, the Archpriest's daughter, was a solid young woman who was used to getting her own way. Djamlet had seemed to her just the right sort of husband and she regretted him, but she found his father disconcerting, to say the least. He sat there with his eyes staring, and with saliva running down his beard and the only remark he made was to say, 'I forgive you, Papa,' – which she misheard and asked herself: 'What on earth has he got to forgive Papa for? We weren't responsible for his son being shot, and anyway it was some time ago.' Then she noticed that the Prince's wrist and right hand were bloodstained.

'You must come and have a wash before the funeral, and I must get into my black dress.'

She actually succeeded in making the Prince stand up and follow her to his room, where she brought him soap and water and a towel.

'Give yourself a good wash, Prince. You've got blood on your wrist. Did you cut yourself?'

The Prince washed himself after she had gone away, then he took Saint Anne out from under his shirt and washed her face and the blood off his own chest, and at once felt better. He stopped dribbling and looked about him. Then when the girl came back in her black frock he looked at her and said to her surprise:

'You look very healthy, my dear.' He drank two more glasses of vodka and then they got into the tarantass with the Archpriest wearing his surplice and dalmatic, and drove off to the cemetery. It was nearly dark by the time the funeral was over and they then drove back to the Palace. The Prince was very tired and though he didn't dribble, he started shivering and could not keep his hands still. Katerina insisted on his drinking a bowl of soup. Then she packed him off to bed. That night Prince Gurgen looked for a long time at the icon of Saint Anne. Her varnished face was unchanged, but the worm-holes at the back of the panel were full of clotted blood.

'He gave himself to save you,' said the Prince reproachfully, 'and now his body is lying in the clay.' She had performed no miracle. 'Perhaps,' thought the Prince, 'I ought to have left her in the body. Then she would have *had* to do something. But it might have made her angry with me if I had buried her. It's difficult to know about women.'

The service next morning with the icon blessing Djamlet and Vasso in their graves, was a strange affair because Prince

Gurgen and Saint Anne were scarcely on speaking terms. He felt that the mother of the Virgin had let him down badly. He had counted on a miracle – but she had not performed one, and, by the time the service was over, it was clear that she was not going to do what she was in honour bound.

But, oddly enough, this brought Prince Gurgen and Saint Anne close together. They were in the middle of a quarrel and, like a married couple, they did not wish for any outside interference. The Prince was therefore in no responsive mood when the Archimandrite Hagystiarchos caught him by the sleeve and began to lead him aside, just after the service was over.

'Just a word with you my Lord. You no doubt know that your son Valeri, under pretence of being a monk, killed Lazar in the cemetery. The Russian Governor of the town demanded that I should hand him over. I refused and I saved your son's life. He had confessed his crime to me. I cannot keep a murderer in the monastery, and at present I have him locked up in his cell, which is why he was not at the service this morning, or at the burial service last night. But I will set him free to go home with you, if you will present the icon of Saint Anne to the monastery in gratitude for our saving, and sheltering, your son.'

Prince Gurgen stared at the Archimandrite as though he had not understood what he had said. However, after a pause, he said 'No!'

'Surely you will give the icon to the monastery in order to save your son's life?'

Prince Gurgen giggled.

The Archimandrite went on: 'You understand I cannot allow a murderer to take the vows as a monk. If you refuse to give us the icon – and really there could be no better place for it than in our monastery, I suppose I shall have to hand over Prince Valeri – though very reluctantly – to Ziklauri, the father of Lazar.'

Prince Gurgen suddenly began laughing hysterically. He went on laughing, laughing and laughing. The sound of his laughter rang through the cemetery, and all the people who had been leaving after the ceremony turned to see who was behaving in such an indecent way. But the laughter went on.

After the double ceremony of exposing the icon of Saint Anne over the graves of Djamlet and Vasso, and his burst of scandalous hilarity, Prince Gurgen ordered his men to return in the same order as they had come: with reversed slung muskets and carrying the brass taper rods. He thought that by continuing to exhibit the trappings of a funeral, the party might escape attack. In this he was right. There was no ambush; no sign of an enemy along the track. However, the river was still high and, in crossing the ford, the pack camel lost her footing and she and the boy leading her were swept away and drowned. Their bodies caught on a rock low down in the rapids, but could not be recovered. The boy's pony managed to swim ashore.

Prince Gurgen, who had had a narrow escape himself, was very much shaken by this. He had very nearly put the icon of Saint Anne back into the box on the pack camel, but at the last moment had decided to carry her himself. He thought that she had saved him and let the camel and its leader drown. But the death of the lad shook him also. Vasso had given himself freely; this poor boy had been swept away without warning. There were too many deaths. And the saliva began to flow out of the corners of his mouth.

Late in the afternoon, the wet and exhausted little party rode into the Castle, and to his astonishment, Anastasia was standing in the doorway to meet them. The Prince, on his departure, had ordered Malik to keep her locked up in the tower, but she had forced her way out that morning, past the girl who had brought her breakfast, and had then defied Malik to carry her back to the top of the tower by force. He had not accepted the challenge.

79

'Vasso,' she called out, as the party came to a halt and dismounted in the yard. Then looking closely, she saw that her son was not there.

'Where is he?' she demanded. The Prince did not reply, but pushed past her into the hall. There he drew the icon of Sainte Anne out from under his shirt, unwrapped her from a band of linen, and silently carried her to where the lamp was burning before the empty frame.

'Where is Vasso? Where is Vasso?' screamed Anastasia.

None of the men looked at her, or seemed to hear her.

At last Nina pointed to the icon which the Prince had slipped back into the great silver-gilt surround and said:

'Saint Anne is his granny now. He is sitting on her knee and I'm sure she spoils him, the darling. For her it's just like what it was when Jesus was Vasso's age.'

'He's not dead!' exclaimed Anastasia.

'Dead and buried,' said Irakli.

After restoring the icon to her position, Prince Gurgen had gone to the inner room. Anastasia rushed to it, but he had bolted the door from the inside. Baffled there, Anastasia turned to Nina and seized the older woman by the arms.

'Tell me everything!'

Nina struggled and freed her right arm from Anastasia's grasp. She crossed herself.

'Vasso, who is now one of the Saints in Heaven, gave himself freely to save Saint Anne,' she said.

'All of us, including the Prince, owe him our lives. The Solutz were waiting for us, five to one, but when they saw we were a funeral procession, carrying Vasso's body, Ziklauri let us pass,' said Irakli who had come up to the two women.

Anastasia sat down and began wringing her hands. Sometimes she gave a low moan.

'Help me with her, Irakli,' said Nina. 'We will take her up into the tower, where she will be away from the Prince.'

Together they lifted her and, putting their arms under

80

hers, led her up the stone staircase. Anastasia moved like an automaton, dragging her feet.

'I can manage by myself,' she said but made no effort to do so. Half-way up the staircase, she stopped and said in a dreamy far-away voice: 'So his father killed him.'

She seemed disinclined to make the effort to climb further, and Nina and Irakli began to pull her up the steps.

Suddenly she shook herself free, standing up to her full height: 'His father killed him, and you let him do it.'

'Vasso saved all our lives by giving his own,' said Irakli. 'He gave it freely and he forgave his father. I heard him say: "I forgive you Papa",' said Nina.

Anastasia looked at them with eyes blazing with hatred. 'Cowards. To let that unnatural beast...'

For a moment she looked as though she intended to fight her way past them down the staircase. She had regained her strength. Then she turned and ran lightly and fast to the last storey, and then up the wooden ladder to the roof of the tower...

Nina followed slowly, for she had had a full day and was very tired. She heaved herself up the ladder and then put her head out at the top and looked round: there was no one on the roof. She climbed out on to it, nevertheless. When she looked over the castellated parapet, there was a little group of heads looking at something on the ground. Nina held very tightly to the rungs of the ladder as she climbed laboriously down.

Next day the Prince gave orders that a grave should be dug where the camel-track forked, about a mile upstream, just below the lake. Anastasia's body was dropped into it, a stake driven through her above the navel and the grave filled up. Prince Gurgen did not attend the ceremony.

For a few days he busied himself in constructing a shrine to the memory of his son Vasso, in front of the chapel which held the icon of Saint Anne. In it there were many relics which would acquire value after the boy was formally

81

beatified; for the Prince felt sure that he would be made a saint. Thus there were the clothes he had been wearing, a length of blood-stained linen in which his body had been wrapped and some of the child's toys. Every few days his father had a new idea and would discuss whether to add the child's shoes, or a whipping top, with Nina. When the Prince was satisfied with the shrine, he held a service at it during which it was sprinkled with Holy Water and he addressed his family as follows:

'There are few families in Georgia which are as old as the Sons of the Falcon. Thus there is no need for us to bow our heads before anyone. But we are not unduly proud of our antiquity. None of us, I think, would wish to boast of his pedigree. We are men, sons of Adam, conceived in sin and prone to sin. We are as God made us. But we can all be proud that one among us – a pure and innocent child, is now one of the Saints sitting in Heaven. We knew and loved him; we, all of us here, humble ourselves before him. Saint Anne has taken him to herself.'

Here the old Prince could say no more because of the tears that blinded him and the sobs that choked him. At last he managed to say: 'So I have assembled these few relics ... the toys he loved ...' And, at that, he completely broke down and Nina took his arm and began leading him to his room.

He was able, however, to hear Iriné saying:

'I wonder who is the next of the family going to be made into a Saint by Papa? I think that Salomé would look very pretty in a halo, or has Elisso more of the Saintly character?'

None of the men who had been in the party which carried Vasso's body to be buried were willing to talk about the child's death. It was only Irakli who had spoken freely. But it was whispered everywhere, and after Anastasia's suicide the women of the Castle looked at the icon of Saint Anne with fear and prayed to her more often and more fervently. She could kill. Behind the set smile of her face

82

and her living blue eyes, she was soaked in blood. And who could tell? She might exact another human sacrifice.

Tamar alone did not fear her, or pray to her. After Anastasia's burial at the crossroads she felt that her life was over. She would not worship the icon or remain a Christian but become a Muslim or a pagan worshipping fire and thunder, and the winds and waters, like her mother's people. She was alone, and she decided that the best ending to her life would be to kill Prince Gurgen. But she had no sooner made this decision than the Prince sent for her and, looking at her distraught face, said to her: 'It is terrible for you, my poor child. Understand that you shall always have a home here with me, as long as I live and that I regard you, and that I love you, as one of my own daughters. Judge not, that ye be not judged. We are all sinners and need forgiveness.'

Tamar looked up at the old man and was horrified to see that he was sobbing and that there were tears running down his cheeks. She could not think of any words and looked at him in silence.

Presently he recovered himself enough to say: 'Of course all her jewels and dresses belong to you. They are all yours ... That is only right ... But I implore you, Tamar, not to wear the dresses she used to wear every day when I am there ... I could not bear it...' And bursting into loud sobs, the Prince waved his hands in despair and ran back to take refuge in his bedroom.

Tamar's first thought was to refuse to accept the jewels and dresses. She had no intention of being indebted to the Prince. But then she reflected that they were hers by natural right and that Anastasia would have preferred her to have them than to see them distributed between Iriné, Elisso and Salomé.

The jewels and wardrobe amounted to a large chest full of splendid clothes and a locked jewel box containing many rings, bracelets, necklaces and jewelled belts. Tamar accepted them, but made no changes in her dress. But she took a silver belt and a ring, set with pearls and rubies, for ordinary wear. More important in her eyes was a Circassian dagger that had belonged to her father. It had a straight steel, double-edged blade bevelled from the central rib, an engraved cross piece at the hilt and a grip bound with gold wire. It was a beautiful weapon, except that the scabbard was old and shabby, and the leather torn.

It would be easy to drive it into the old man's chest, and then she imagined herself folding her arms and saying: 'My sister is avenged for the unutterable wrongs that you did to her.' Tamar brooded on this plan, but it gave her little satisfaction. She remembered what Anastasia had said herself: that she would not seek revenge if Vasso were murdered, and that Valeri had not sought to revenge the death of Djamlet. It had happened. So perhaps the punishment of Prince Gurgen should be left to God. She could imagine herself standing with folded arms over the Prince's body saying: 'Anastasia is avenged!' But she could not see herself saying to Valeri with an equal satisfaction: 'I have killed your father!' – and baring her bosom to the knife, so that he could stab her.

With all these contradictory ideas whirling in her head she clutched the hilt of the dagger under her cloak and put off the execution of her project from day to day.

Meanwhile changes at the Castle were about to occur.

A week after Anastasia had been impaled at the crossroads, Prince Gurgen summoned the cripple boy, Vakhtang, to his room and dictated a letter to the Archpriest. It ran:

'Most reverend Father in God,

'I am in the hands of God, who giveth and taketh away. His will be done. I throw myself on His infinite mercy. Since I last saw you, I have lost my wife and I have the honour to ask you for the hand of your daughter Katerina in marriage. She is a fine healthy girl who will bear me sons. I will take her with half the dowry that was offered before, in consideration of the fact that I am an older and wealthier man.

84

If you look upon this proposal favourably, she will become the mistress of this Castle, a higher position than she would have had before.

'Owing to the disturbed conditions that prevail, I cannot venture to the town, but it would be quite safe for you and my bride-to-be to come to the Castle, and you can bring a priest with you. The ceremony can take place in our old chapel in front of Saint Anne. Please send an answer back by my messenger and, if God so wills, on what day I may expect you. I crave your blessing, Holy Father in God.

Gurgen
Son of the Falcon and Prince.'

Katerina Paphnuty had received the best education of any young woman in the town. She had not only been taught embroidery, cross-stitch and needlework of every kind, the making of jams, pickles and preserves, the supervision of the kitchen and management of servants, but she had been taught to read Georgian in the two alphabets, a good knowledge of Russian and a slight knowledge of Turkish and Armenian. Besides this, she could play the balalaika and dance the leezginka as well as any girl of her class and generation. She was well aware of her superior accomplishments.

When Prince Gurgen's messenger came to the door and produced his master's letter from under the sole of his boot, it was taken to her. She ordered the messenger to be given a good meal in the kitchen and carried off the letter.

'Papa, that old monster, the Prince Gurgen, has had the grace to send a letter, thanking you for your kindness to him during that ghastly visit. It's rather late in the day, but no matter for that. Shall I read it? It will save hunting for your spectacles.'

'I'm sure it concerns you more than it does me. It was you who made him wash his face and packed him off to bed,' said the Archpriest.

Katerina opened the letter and, after glancing through it,

left the room to think over its contents. The offer was well worth serious consideration. Prince Gurgen was almost eighty and was unlikely to live more than another five years and, even if he did survive for ten, would certainly become senile. She would be mistress of the Castle – virtually its ruler – and after Gurgen's death its actual ruler, provided that Valeri took the monastic vows. That would have to be arranged. If she were the ruler, she could make peace with the Sultzi: Ziklauri was a reasonable man – and live in perfect security. The feud and vendettas were out of date now the Russians were come to stay. She might even reunite the clan under her rule. Thus the distant future was rosy. Against that must be set the immediate present. She would be marrying a tyrannical and physically repellent old man, who dribbled when excited, and who was reputed to have murdered many people and who had just driven his third wife to suicide. And, while he held the reins, the feud would go on. She had to decide whether she could put up with the immediate prospects for the sake of power later on. But what was the alternative? Her father, she knew, wanted her married as soon as possible, no doubt because of his relationship with widow Tara.

Until the Prince's surprising offer, the alternatives had been unpromising. A divinity student, Alexander Babishvili, who had finished his studies and only needed to get married in order to be ordained, had been actively pursuing her. He had sent a matchmaker to the house, had asked the Archpriest's permission, and had proposed to Katerina personally on three occasions. As a result Mr Babishvili had become an habitué of the Archpriest's house. It was, however, essential for him to marry someone quickly. Katerina was a wonderful match for him, as her father would be able to push him in his profession. But it was not a very wonderful match for her. It would mean being a hard-working priest's wife for years, and the utmost her husband could look forward to, with the greatest good luck, and family influence, was to become an Archpriest like her father – the highest rank open to the married priesthood.

The alternative to Alexander Babishvili was a Russian officer. That is to say a foreigner who would only marry her for her dowry and might easily lose it at cards when the honeymoon was over. Even if he were an honest and affectionate man, he might at any time be recalled from the Caucasus and posted to some distant part of the Russian Empire, where she would be a foreigner in exile, despised by the Russian women, wives of her husband's fellow officers. There had been one offer of this kind, but she had managed to persuade her father that the man was of bad character and to shelve it. The Prince, however displeasing to her personally, was a noble and offered something for the not too distant future. If she could get her father to promise her the other half of the dowry, she would be safeguarded if the marriage proved unendurable. But it would be a good plan to look at the Castle first, before committing herself irrevocably.

When she went to preside over the samovar, and give her father the Persian rose-petal jam that he adored, he remarked: 'Oh, you never read me the Prince's letter. Apparently he expects an answer. His messenger sent word up from the kitchen asking when it would be ready.'

Katerina gave her father his cup of tea and stooped to kiss the top of his head.

'The letter was not only one of thanks for your hospitality; it was to tell you that his wife is now dead.'

'So the messenger told Vatya in the kitchen. The wretched woman, driven mad I suppose by that old villain, flung herself off the roof of the Castle into the courtyard. The Prince had her buried as a criminal, at the crossroads, with a stake driven through her body. Of course, as it was suicide, he was legally justified. But it shows how barbarism prevails.'

'Terrible. But one must sympathise with the old man in

his loneliness. In a few months he has lost three sons – for Valeri as a monk must seem as good as dead to him – and now his wife. Yes, even if it is partly his fault, I feel deeply sorry for him. He is such a splendid figure of a man too.'

Katerina's words surprised her father, but they also warned him that he might have been adopting the wrong tone.

'Well, perhaps my first judgement was too harsh. Of course I'll send my sincere condolences. But it seems scarcely matter for an urgent reply.'

'Well, there was more in the letter. It's such a nuisance that you have mislaid your spectacles.' (Katerina had hidden them until the Prince's letter should have been answered.) 'He says that he was much impressed by me – just imagine – and he invites us both to visit him at the Castle.'

'Good Heavens! Whatever for? It's an impossible journey. Riding all day along a path by dizzy precipices, with bandits behind every rock – and all to be given a glass or two of home-made sour wine and a roast lamb and goat cheese at the end of it. What a mad idea!'

'Darling Papa, I am longing to go. It will be wildly romantic. I have always wanted to see the Castle. Djamlet gave such a wonderful description of it. And I think the Prince is a tiny bit in love with me. I know the journey's tedious and difficult. But do let's go. There will never be another opportunity.'

'I suppose the old fellow wants to return my hospitality. Well, if you really insist on going, I shall have to give in, Katya – but I do so with a bad grace. I warn you – we shall both be bored to tears. Write a letter accepting, and give it to the messenger with five roubles.'

Katerina danced away like a little girl and wrote: 'Most Honoured Prince, Son of the Falcon,

'Your letter has greatly surprised me and my daughter. Katerina is much flattered by your honourable proposal. There are, however, many matters to be discussed and considered and a marriage settlement to be drawn up, and my daughter and I would like to visit your Castle and enjoy your hospitality. I feel most deeply for you in your recent loss which must have been a terrible shock to a man of your sensitive nature and upright feelings. You may expect us next Thursday.

'Your friend in God and sincere well-wisher,

'Paphnuty
'Archpriest'

The letter was sealed and the messenger dispatched. Katerina thought a tip of five roubles excessive for a mountainy lad and gave him three, keeping the other two for herself. That evening, before sitting down to their regular game of chess – which Katerina had difficulty in not invariably winning – she stood behind her father and put her hands over his eyes before saying: 'I did not tell you all the contents of Prince Gurgen's letter. So now, Papa, I'll confess. It contained a proposal of marriage.'

'What? Who does he want to marry you off to?'

'Don't be so stupid. Of course he wants to marry me himself.'

'That is proof that he is mad.'

'Papa, that is not polite to me! Anyway I want to see his Castle. He is rather an old dear. He offers to take only half the dowry you agreed to for Djamlet.'

The Archpriest was so upset that the game of chess never got started.

Twice a week the Archpriest would put on his cloak, take his pastoral staff and, going down to the bottom of his garden, open a wicket gate which led to the lodge occupied by his neighbour, the widow Tara. Directly he arrived, he signed her with the cross, she curtsied and pulled down the blinds in her living-room and then brought in the samovar, teapot, two glasses in wicker holders and a tray of Persian sweetmeats.

Every visit was the same. Each asked about the other's

health and thanked God that it was no worse. Each asked what the other had been doing and related the tiny incidents of the day. Then each of them drank three cups of tea with sugar and lemon and ate sweetmeats. Then they got up and went into the bedroom.

'Since you have been a naughty boy, Nursie has got to punish you,' said the widow Tara in a soft voice. The Archpriest pulled up his shirt and pulled down his breeches and lay on his face on the bed. The widow took a bundle of thin birch twigs out of the wardrobe and gently swished his buttocks, with each stroke getting a little harder. After the fourth she stopped to slip her fat little hand under his groin and feel his member. Then she would give a sharp stroke and feel again and usually by then the naughty boy was gasping and crying out. A little later he would roll over and the widow would bring a clean napkin and wipe his belly and penis.

'Be a good boy and say you love Nursie,' and the Archpriest would whisper feebly: 'I love my Nursie, I love my Nursie. Don't beat me any more.' The widow Tara would laugh a self-satisfied little laugh and, after handling his shrinking genitals, would say: 'All over now,' and go out of the room, while the Archpriest dressed himself, then went back into the living-room, where the widow Tara had two little glasses of vodka poured out on a tray.

Strangely enough this couple loved each other, and their perverted and disgusting relationship made them happy and contented.

The day after Prince Gurgen had sent his letter, the Archpriest paid widow Tara one of his visits and, after his flagellation, told her about the Prince's invitation and offer and that he had mislaid his spectacles and Katerina had let out the contents of the letter bit by bit, and that he had been cajoled into agreeing to make the hazardous journey.

Tara nodded her head and put out the tip of her pointed little tongue. Then she pressed the tips of her fat little fingers together and said, smiling: 'I have to tell you what I feel, because we are such old friends. I think it is rather heartless of Katerina to want to marry anyone. You are very dependent on her and will be lonely when she has gone. I shall do what I can, but it won't be the same. Who will play chess with you? I admire Katerina very much, but it is heartless of her to want to marry.'

'What absolute nonsense. I have always wanted her to marry and I would never stand in her way,' said the Archpriest.

'I know, I know what a good father you are,' said the widow.

'I want her to marry. Only I feel it cannot be right to hand over an innocent girl to that bloodstained old man, who has just driven his third wife to suicide. Besides that, he is four times her age.'

'Yes, there is all that to consider,' replied the widow Tara, putting the points of her fingers together and putting out the tip of her pretty little tongue again. 'All the same, I think that you should visit the Castle and then your daughter can see the drawbacks for herself. It is always better to let children make up their own minds than to use authority – particularly because Katerina is a very sensible person and is bound to agree with you and to do what is best. The final decision will rest with you.'

The widow hated Katerina who returned the hatred threefold. In spite of her youth and innocence, she knew all about what went on behind the closed blinds during her father's visits. Yet both women were allies. That is to say both wanted Katerina's marriage and when the Archpriest got worked up over trifles, would do their best to help each other soothe him down and manage him. Katerina also was aware that her father's relationship with the widow might have been much worse. If Tara had not existed, there might have been scandals.

The party that set out the following Thursday consisted

of Katerina, the Archpriest, the divinity student Alexander Babishvili and Vatya, the manservant. The Archpriest and Alexander rode mules, Katerina her piebald mare and Vatya a pony. In addition there was a camel loaded with trunks, bags and boxes, with a very small boy perched on top. The party was unarmed, though at one time the Archpriest had played with the idea of hiring two Tcherkesses to act as guards. Katerina had felt sure that they would cause trouble at the Castle and that her father's position would protect him.

The journey was uneventful, and, as the river had fallen to its summer level, the crossings were easy and the Archpriest rode into the Castle yard immensely pleased with himself for having accomplished it.

At the Castle they had been sweeping, polishing, dusting and throwing away rubbish for nearly a week. The great hall had never looked so magnificent: the carpets that hung on the walls had all been beaten and glowed with a rich beauty, a great fire blazed, even Saint Anne's silver gilt surround had been polished and shone more than ever.

Prince Gurgen washed, curled and perfumed and wearing his most gorgeous clothes, came out to meet the party. He kissed Katerina's hand before helping her to alight, and threw his arms around her father, kissing him on both cheeks. He then ushered them into the hall and showed them to two rooms in the tower strewn with rushes, the walls covered with rugs and tapestries, and bunches of wild flowers everywhere. The fact of having carried through such an adventurous, and perhaps hazardous, journey so successfully put the Archpriest into the best of tempers and made him think well of himself and in consequence of everyone else.

Several glasses of vodka, followed by crayfish soup served with little pies stuffed with caviare and smoked eel, a roast sucking pig stuffed with buckwheat and cherry tarts smothered in whipped cream, all washed down with an excellent wine from Kakhitia, completed a memorable evening

– and when the Prince asked for an immediate marriage, the Archpriest replied: 'Tomorrow,' meaning that they would discuss it then. Katerina however said at once that the settlements must be drawn up. Once they were out of the way, she was quite ready for an early marriage.

The marriage was in fact celebrated three days later, but before it could be consummated, matters of moment had occurred.

CHAPTER THREE

The Archimandrite Hagystiarchos was superstitious and the Prince's laughter in the cemetery had terrified him. He could not see a reason for it. How could the Prince laugh in such a place; at such a time? He could not guess that his offer to exchange Valeri for the icon had been made to a man who had just murdered his son Vasso in order to preserve it; and that to the Prince there was a quality of nightmarish fantasy, after that horror, of being asked to exchange it for the life of another son. The Archimandrite thought quite simply that Prince Gurgen was in league with the Devil. The icon itself might be a false image of diabolic origin – none the less valuable for that. Or it might be that the Prince wanted Valeri to be handed over to the Sultzi. Anyhow the Archimandrite saw that he had said the wrong thing.

Immediately after the news of Lazar's murder had spread through the monastery, and before he had seen Valeri, Brother Foma had discussed it with the farm Bailiff. He had said that it was quite incredible that Valeri – who had obviously committed the murder – should have come upon Lazar at the grave by pure chance. He must have been told that Lazar would be there and that his informant could only have been the Archimandrite.

'The whole business has been most cleverly cooked up. That old Turkish bastard agreed to take Valeri in here disguised as a novice and to act as his spy. In some way he decoyed Lazar to the cemetery, or anyhow got wind of the fact that he was going there at that particular time, so that Valeri could murder him, disguised as a monk. But you ask:

"What did our Archimandrite stand to gain out of this?" I can tell you. I am willing to bet that the wonder-working icon of Saint Anne will shortly be presented to us. That's the way the world works.'

The Farm Bailiff was an old friend of Brother Foma's; these ideas greatly impressed him, and he repeated the story, under pledge of secrecy, to the Bursar. It was not long before it reached the ears of the Archimandrite himself.

Half an hour after he had told the Bailiff this version of Lazar's death, Foma had seen Valeri and had looked into his eyes and would have hotly denied the story he had put about. He knew that Valeri had not planned to kill Lazar, and that he was in torture because he had. But the mischief was done. The day after he had cut down Valeri in his cell, Brother Foma disappeared. The last thing that he said to Valeri was: 'After Lazar's death, I told the Bailiff that I thought that your coming here was a put-up job and that the Archimandrite had decoyed Lazar to the cemetery and that the monastery would get the icon of Saint Anne in exchange.... Directly I had looked into your eyes, dear friend, I knew that what I had said wasn't true and that your soul was in torture. But the story had got round and that Turkish bastard has decided to have me out of the way so that if there is an investigation I cannot be questioned. By the way, you had better take your pistol from where I hid it behind the Armenian books, and hide it and your sabre somewhere safe. I think that you are in danger, though not immediate danger.'

'You are my *kounak*,' said Valeri.

'Willingly, but what does it let me in for? Am I saddled with my *kounak's* blood feuds?' asked Foma.

Valeri laughed. 'You are a cautious fellow. No you are just my blood brother. And I have no *gaujas* for you to inherit if I am killed.'

The two friends embraced, and an hour later Brother

95

Foma had vanished. Valeri took his advice and hid his pistol and his sabre behind a stone coffin in a dark corner of the crypt.

The day after Brother Foma's disappearance, Valeri woke to find himself locked into his cell. Thereafter he was served by two monks, one to spy on the other, who maintained absolute silence. He asked for books, but received no answer. He was a prisoner in his cell. Although this was confirmation of Foma's warning, it was totally unexpected.

In normal existence thoughts and images flit across the mind like the shadows of clouds chasing each other across the landscape. The thoughts, the images, the ideas, follow one another, leaving little behind them. But when normal life is interrupted by the will of another, forcibly imposed for day after day, the gay sequence is broken, and one thought, or train of thoughts, sinks deep. It is not that the prisoner has *time* to think – for thought is instantaneous – it is that his thoughts repeat themselves over and over again, because there is nothing outside to interrupt them, or to change and force them to develop. And this constant repetition changes the prisoner's character.

So it was with Valeri. At first he felt rage, suffocating rage, at the arbitrary act which led to the disappearance of Brother Foma, who might be dead, poisoned perhaps, or lying miserably in some dungeon. Then he himself was being held a prisoner, kept in complete ignorance of what was going on in the world – held a prisoner, not in punishment for the crime of murdering Lazar, but as a hostage to be exchanged – perhaps for the icon, or sold to Ziklauri.

He had come like a child the year before to the Archimandrite, a child who believed that if one could not be both warrior and saint, like Saint George, one could humble oneself and be a Christian. Hagystiarchos had naturally believed that he was a cunning conspirator, planning to commit a murder under the protecting cloak of religion. It was natural for him to think so, because it was what he was himself.

That was, in fact, what the vast organisation of the Church was for – to commit crimes, to perpetuate frauds and to filch money from the innocent with impunity. And the men who directed the Church were simply a band of lazy criminals who lived without working on the credulity of the common people and at their expense. The monks in the monastery were organised in a network of spying. And this state of affairs, this exploitation of mankind by criminals in the name of Christ, had existed for centuries: here in Georgia for fifteen hundred years!

Such was the conception over which Valeri brooded day after day, finding continual new evidence for it in his memories. It was the priesthood which had created this monstrosity that battened on the poor it was founded to help – and on the fears of the rich whom it was supposed to guide into the paths of virtue. Then he recollected that he had been told that, almost alone among religions, the Mohammedans had no professional priesthood. Perhaps they were able to worship God without the intervention of crime and lying and fraud and the exploitation of the simple and innocent.

He would go and study at Alexandria – but he was forgetting. He had no future. But at least, thanks to Brother Foma, he had discovered the truth about the Christian Church, and, even if the Archimandrite had him put to death, he would die with his eyes open. That was something at which to rejoice, even though he was a mere counter in a bargain – to be sold to the highest bidder, or to be quietly knocked on the head. He knew that his father would never surrender Saint Anne for him, or pay much of a ransom. Anastasia would do what she could, he thought. What would Ziklauri pay to have him killed? Everyone who had met the man spoke well of him.

It took the Archimandrite a week to get over Prince Gurgen's satanic laughter in the cemetery. Then he sent a message to Ziklauri to come to discuss a matter of the utmost importance. The leader of the Sultzi obeyed the summons reluctantly. He did not care for Hagystiarchos, and, when he entered his cell and was waved to a stool, he first dusted it and then moved it as far as possible from the hairy, unwashed monk.

The Archimandrite was puzzled by this, because during the last interview he had had with the Russian Governor, that exquisitely washed and scented gentleman, in his new uniform, had behaved in precisely the same way. Possibly it was a new fashion: to sit apart.

After a few compliments which Ziklauri seemed not to notice, the Archimandrite began: 'I wanted to discuss the ownership of the famous icon of Saint Anne, now in the hands of a kinsman of yours, Prince Gurgen of the elder branch of the Sons of the Falcon. You may not be aware that he brought it with him for the funeral of his little son Vasso, just over a week ago.'

'So I have heard,' said Ziklauri. Then he went on: 'I did not attack or search those in the funeral procession, or interfere with their free return, though I was criticised by my council for not doing so. Respect has to be shown to the dead and to the bereaved.'

The fact that Prince Gurgen had been able to bring the icon into the town and take it away with him had been galling, and it had needed Ziklauri's utmost authority to prevent the Prince's party from being attacked on their way back to the Castle. It was, Ziklauri thought, very tactless of the Archimandrite to refer to it.

'Prince Gurgen is now an old man and he is unlikely to beget any more children,' said Hagystiarchos. 'He has only one remaining son, and, in the event of anything happening to him, the elder branch of the Sons of the Falcon would become extinct.'

'Well, the son you refer to is a monk in your monastery, which is not supposed to be a very good breeding ground for legitimate heirs,' said Ziklauri, stressing the word legitimate and laughing. It was the turn of Hagystiarchos to feel annoyed.

'The man was admitted as a novice. He has not taken the vows and he will not take them,' said the Archimandrite.

'So he has changed his mind, has he?' asked Ziklauri.

'A novice cannot take the vows unless he keeps to the rules of the Order. My Lord Valeri has broken the rules.'

'Whatever can he have done?' asked Ziklauri with studied carelessness. 'I thought he was Brother Foma's best pupil, learning to read and write three languages at once.'

The Archimandrite was obviously nettled by this tone.

'As you know well, after the murder of your son, there was an inquiry, and suspicion fell upon the Lord Valeri.'

'Yes, but I believe you swore that, to your own personal knowledge, he was in the library working with Brother Foma for the whole of that evening,' said Ziklauri.

'Nothing of the sort. I swore that the librarian of the monastery, Brother Foma Ilyitch, swore that my Lord had been with him all the afternoon and evening working in the muniment room. Brother Foma is no longer with us.' Here the Archimandrite crossed himself, 'and I have heard that he made a partial confession on his departure, that he was lying. I am now investigating the matter. But, in any case, suspicion rests upon Lord Valeri, and I could not, as a matter of conscience, permit him to take the vows. So the question is: how am I to get rid of him?'

'I imagine, perhaps wrongly, that you still have enough authority to throw him out whenever you please,' said Ziklauri contemptuously.

The Archimandrite appeared not to have heard this insult, but went on: 'If the elder branch should die out it would be greatly to your advantage. You would inherit the historic Castle, the ancient stronghold of your family, and its lands and, incidentally, the icon of Saint Anne. If you will agree to give the icon to the monastery, I am in a position to help you to your inheritance.'

There was a silence.

'The old fellow was laughing at you after the ceremony in the cemetery of blessing the dead. I suppose he was refusing to give you the icon in exchange for Valeri. So now you are offering him to me,' said Ziklauri.

'I don't know what makes you say such things. You know that the old Prince is not quite right in the head,' said the Archimandrite.

'What you are proposing to me, is that, if I can get hold of the icon, I should sell it you for the life of Lord Valeri,' said Ziklauri. Hagystiarchos smiled and twisted the ring on his finger.

'I think that proposal is premature. I haven't got the icon and Prince Gurgen may live to beget several more sons. Moreover, it strikes me that such a proposal comes strangely from a Prince of the Church that preaches: "Forgive your enemies." Frankly I am not attracted by the idea of buying a man in order to put him to death. I would prefer Lord Valeri to take the vows. I have said, over and over again, that if Prince Gurgen would surrender the icon, I would never harry him again. I was very much distressed by Lazar's murdering Djamlet outside the Cathedral. He did it just on the spur of the moment, as a boy might shoot a peacock in his neighbour's garden. The temptation, if you are holding a gun at that age, is very great. He was ashamed of having done it and it was because of that shame that he went to plant flowers on Djamlet's grave and came by his death. I loved him, and I shall always remember his digging up those roots of flowers to take to the grave, which was an act most beautiful and worthy of him.' Ziklauri paused, aware that he had said more than he had intended. Then he continued recklessly: 'I don't want revenge. I only want the icon that rightfully belongs to all the Sons of the Falcon, and we, whom you call the Sultzi or the Solutz, are the majority.' Having spoken the truth, Ziklauri got up from the stool to leave. But he suddenly sat down again. It had flashed into his mind that if Hagystiarchos could not sell Lord Valeri either to his father, or to himself, it was possible that he might poison him. Ziklauri could not think of any reason why the Archimandrite should want to poison Valeri – there was no obvious advantage to be gained by his doing so – but Ziklauri knew that one murder begets another and that once a poisoner, always a poisoner. There had been rumours at the time of the Archimandrite's succession – his predecessor's death had been sudden. Then Brother Foma had disappeared suddenly, and although the Archimandrite said that he had sent him on a journey because of his learning, there was no reason to believe him. The journey might be a euphemism for beyond the grave and his learning that he knew too much. Besides that, Hagystiarchos had crossed himself in a suspicious manner when he had spoken of Brother Foma's having left the monastery.

So, while the Archimandrite stared, Ziklauri said: 'My Lord, I think that I may be being too hasty. Though I do not like your proposal, it needs thinking over. I may feel differently when I have the icon in my hands, which may be sooner than either of us thinks. We might possibly come to some arrangement. I make no promises. Let us leave it open.' Then, giving the very slightest of bows, Ziklauri left the Archimandrite's cell.

As soon as the door had closed Hagystiarchos actually laughed. 'That man, Ziklauri, is a shrewd fellow. He almost took me in with that ethical tone. "Not attracted by buying a man in order to murder him." And then, "We may come to some arrangement." I bet my life that he comes back with an offer to lend the icon for church festivals, but that it should remain his property. A shrewd fellow.'

The prospect of haggling over the icon with Ziklauri appealed to him. He could be as tough as any mountain tribesman. And as long as he had Valeri under lock and key, he had the advantage.

'Really for a fellow like that to think that he could get

the better of an old Greek by putting on that act: "I don't want revenge." ' So the Archimandrite mused and chuckled during the hours when he should have been reading the Divine Office or telling his beads.

The Sultzi, or Solutz, as they preferred to call themselves, had made their stronghold in an ancient earthworks, popularly supposed to be a Scythian camp, which was only about fifteen versts from the town, on higher ground. Within its wide perimeter and stockade, they had built an oval group of cabins and log houses round the central well, with its long cantilever balanced pole which dipped and raised buckets of water. Whereas at the Castle there was only one ruling family, that of the Prince, power among the Solutz had split up among the families headed by Ziklauri's uncle, younger brothers and cousins. The leadership was therefore quite unlike the autocratic rule of the Old Prince. Ziklauri, though the undisputed leader, governed through a council which included one member of each important family and which was in essence, that of the Russian village *mir*.

Recently there had been complaints that since the coming of the Russians, Ziklauri had been too pacific. It is always easy to criticise those in power for being too cautious. The party to ambush Prince Gurgen had been organised by Ziklauri to allay this dissatisfaction. But in the event, it had been a failure; the Sultzi had been outwitted, and Ziklauri's refusal to allow the funeral party to be attacked, even on its way home, had added to his unpopularity as a leader.

At the last meeting of the council, there had been a demand for an all-out attack against the Castle. It was urged that, with their great preponderance of numbers, it must be possible to capture it, killing the male defenders. The booty would be great – flocks of sheep and goats, fertile fields, the younger women, the treasure that Prince Gurgen was said to possess and, above all, the wonder-working icon of Saint

Anne. Moreover it would settle the succession and Ziklauri would become the head of the clan. Surely that must mean something to him?

His critics, moreover, pointed out that, since the coming of the Russians and the establishment of their Governor in the town, it was becoming more and more dangerous to live by robbing passing merchants or extorting 'protection money' from its traders. But the Russians would not mix themselves up in what was simply a family quarrel, if they attacked and captured the Castle. Ziklauri listened to all these arguments, and, when he rose, it was to reply that he agreed with most of what had been said. He had not allowed the funeral party to be attacked because he believed that decencies had to be observed, but he had, for some time, been planning the investment and capture of the Castle. It had not been possible – or would have been very rash – during the winter and during the spring floods. Now that they had subsided, the sooner the attack was made the better. He planned, if they were successful, to take over the Castle and to establish a large part of the clan in its historic home and to improve greatly the cultivation of the fields and orchards. There was also, he thought, the possibility of starting a fishery in the lake, higher up the river. They could exact tolls from the Tatar caravans which used that route.

The plans that he put forward not only silenced his critics but converted them, and one after another gave his vote for Ziklauri's proposals and promised his full support. Preparations for the expedition were made rapidly: arms examined, powder flasks filled, bullets moulded, wads stamped out of sheets of greasy felt, boxes of percussion caps bought, swords and kinjals sharpened. The chief armament, however, was an ancient Russian mountain gun which Ziklauri had obtained illegally from the superintendent of the arsenal at Vladikavkaz by a cash payment of two hundred roubles and the promise of three hundred more, after the Castle had been taken. This piece of ordnance was to be carried by two camels, while two others were loaded with cannon balls and bags of powder. Eight scaling ladders and four casks of naphtha oil were also part of the equipment. The party consisted of thirty-eight men, four boys and four women. Rations for a week were taken, in case the initial assault failed and a siege were necessary. The Solutz camp was left practically undefended, with only the older men, boys, women and children to occupy it. The camp was also denuded of horses, mules and camels: only the brood mares and two stallions and some donkeys were left. Two days after the Archpriest and his daughter had arrived at the Castle, Ziklauri and his men set out at midnight and before dawn had reached the point where the track was completely hidden from the open country by the turnings in the mountains. Ziklauri thought that during the visit of Katerina and her father – and during the wedding likely to result – the Old Prince might be caught off his guard. In this he was more successful than he had expected. Soon after midday the expedition had reached the second crossing of the river, without seeing any trace of a sentry. After they had forded the river, Ziklauri called a halt for several hours, during which beasts were fed and watered and all ate a good meal and rested. Ziklauri posted lookouts up the side of the defile, but did not send men forward lest they should give away the presence of the Solutz.

He planned to pitch camp by the river below the aoul and to invest it from both sides. His attack would open with a bombardment with the mountain gun directed against the entrance of the great courtyard. When defenders appeared, his men, concealed behind rocks, would open musket fire. As soon as it was dark, men with scaling ladders would creep up to the Castle walls, while others would create a diversion by carrying the casks of naphtha up to the walls and setting them on fire in an endeavour to burn the great gateway previously battered by the cannon. During the blaze his men would scale the walls from the opposite side. Ziklauri himself would direct the attack by signals from a rock on the mountainside overlooking the Castle. Once the attack had been co-ordinated, he would descend and join those scaling the walls. The Solutz were able to make all their dispositions for attack without being detected, for a simple reason.

The boy Ramin had been commandeered by Nina to heat the small brick oven and to bake some hundreds of cheese-cakes. While he was employed in raking out the ashes preparatory to putting in the first batch of lemon curd tartlets, Malik had come up to him and said: 'Off you go my lad. You are on sentry duty tonight.'

But Ramin had a passion for lemon curd cheesecakes. It seemed to him only reasonable that he should put in the first batch. They would only take five minutes in the hot oven – and he would be able to see if they were well done before he went off on his solitary vigil. Unfortunately the oven was too hot, and the first batch were a failure. He had to wait and let the oven cool down before risking the second batch. Ramin was a real connoisseur of cheesecakes, and he was not satisfied with the second batch. He thought that the third would be perfect. They were. But by that time he had been joined in the bakehouse by Elisso and Salomé, who began devouring them.

'Hold hard,' he said. 'I'll fetch Nina if you eat any more.'

'You wouldn't give me away to that beastly old nanny goat would you?' said Elisso and put her arm round his shoulder. Ramin stayed and cooked all the cheesecakes. Elisso promised to come to the woodshed, and by that time he had forgotten that he ought to be out alone, hiding behind a rock. Malik would have to send someone else. He could not do two jobs at once.

It was the day of the marriage. The ceremony had, however, been delayed for some hours by the fact that the bride's father was too drunk to give his daughter away. Katerina, who knew that her father would agree to anything that was said to him when he was drunk, had made too sure of his acquiescence in her marriage the night before, and the Archpriest lay like a log the next morning, defying her efforts to arouse him. A cold compress dipped in river water and wrung out and applied to his forehead and the back of his neck did not even make him shiver. He had passed out, it seemed for a long time. Katerina even tried torture—she stuck a needle into his thumb—but the old man appeared insensible to pain. Finally she went to Nina and asked her to wake him up.

'Leave him to me,' said the old woman and, sure enough, she was able to produce him two hours later, fully caparisoned in his ecclesiastical robes, in a condition fit to take his part in the marriage ceremony, which was conducted partly by the Archpriest, assisted by Alexander. Her secret – in case any one is faced with a similar problem – was to open his mouth and pour in a mixture of hot brine and vinegar.

The wedding was held in the chapel of the Castle – a chapel which was no more than a large alcove out of the great hall – an alcove in which there was a minute altar, the icon of Saint Anne, with the lamp lighting up her face and living eyes, and, in front of the altar, the curious heap of miscellaneous objects which composed the Shrine of Vasso – martyr or Saint had yet to be decided. This heap of relics was in everybody's way, and Katerina had gone so far, earlier in the morning, as to suggest to Nina that they should be moved.

The old woman's face set like a trap, and she said: 'I warn you not to speak of such a thing. Prince Gurgen would think it an ill omen for his marriage.'

Privately Katerina determined that she would get rid of the shrine – but she supposed it would be more tactful to wait and to remove the objects which composed it one at a time, until there were no relics left. She had been shocked also to find out that the young girl with rosy cheeks and light brown hair who had been chosen as one of her brides-

maids was the sister of her predecessor. She had hoped that
the Prince would have removed all the traces of his former
marriage. Instead of which there was the heap in front of
the altar to the memory of her son, and her sister, to whom
the old man had given his wife's jewels which ought rightfully to have been hers. Well, the girl was obviously of
marriageable age, and the sooner a husband was found for
her the better. Alexander had to marry in order to be ordained – and would be perfectly suitable. She would drop a
hint that his promotion later on might depend on it.

The ceremony lasted a long time, and Tamar, forced to
witness it at close quarters, found it disgusting. The Archpriest was obviously so drunk that he did not know where
he was, or what he was doing, and Prince Gurgen was un-
steady on his feet – though whether from vodka or old age
seemed to her uncertain. Alexander's reference to the text:
'It is better to marry than to burn,' was unsuitable, and
became comic when he urged the pair to have a multitude
of children. Applied to the Old Prince such advice was simply
disgusting. He ought to have been in his grave long ago. The
chapel was dark and crowded; it smelt of incense, jasmine,
spirits and human bodies.

When at last the marriage ceremony was over, the Prince
and his bride sat side by side on two chairs raised above the
level of the floor, and all the people of the Castle came
forward and bowed, or curtseyed, to their new mistress and
were allowed to kiss her hand.

When it came to Tamar's turn, Katerina half-rose from
her throne and pulled the young girl to her, kissed her on
each cheek and exclaimed:

'Just think, I had never been told of your existence! You
must think of me as your sister! What a lovely creature!
Never fear. I shall find a husband worthy of such a pearl!
You can rely on me.'

Tamar retreated scarlet with rage, saying to herself: 'I
must run away.' So full was she of this thought, that she

scarcely noticed that the kisses that Katerina bestowed on Elisso and Salomé were more perfunctory and that Iriné had been merely allowed to kiss Katerina's hand.

When the presentation was over, Katerina and the Prince retired. As they were leaving, they heard Iriné saying: 'I am sure Papa will arrange half a dozen more marriages for himself before he thinks about marrying his daughters.' A remark which produced a guffaw from Salomé and a loud: 'Hush Iriné,' from Elisso.

Shortly afterwards, dancing began with the bride and bridegroom dancing the leezginka. Prince Gurgen cut a fine figure. He was dressed in the full panoply of a Georgian warrior: baggy velvet breeches tucked into top boots, a white embroidered shirt, a dark red silk Persian scarf wound round his waist with his kinjal thrust through it. He had sobered up a bit, but he did little except stamp his feet and bend his arm in front of his face at the right moments. Katerina, who was wearing a white smock over full but transparent Tatar trousers, with a sash and kerchief of dark red silk and golden shoes with upturned points, held a fluttering veil of scarlet in her right hand, and with tiny, almost imperceptible steps, turned and twisted, ducked and wheeled about her partner, waving her fluttering veil and gazing at him over her shoulder, as she glided past him, all with the utmost provocation, while he stamped his haughty indifference.

Then, when she remained immobile, he bent his head, took three steps to the right, then three steps to the left, reversing his bent arms. At the climax, he drew his dagger and threw it down, so that it stuck quivering in the floor, as his partner flung herself into his arms. The dance was wildly applauded, and the Prince, preserving his dignity, but out of breath and giddy, took his place on the divan.

Next came Nina and the Archpriest. But Katerina's father had not taken four steps before he lost his balance and, his legs sliding in front of him, fell heavily to the floor. He was helped up and led to the divan where he subsided beside his son-in-law and two minutes later was asleep.

This fiasco was followed by a dance in which all the younger ones took part, Malik partnering Katerina, and Irakli, Tamar. The dancing went on and on, one following another. Then the floor was cleared for Tengiz and Ramin who squatted, and threw out their legs alternately, but managed to preserve their balance. Their exhibition ended with their jumping up and walking out of the hall on their hands.

Drinking followed the dances, and then two long tables were set up on trestles, with chairs for the Prince and Princess, her father, his daughters, and for Malik and Nina, but with benches for the young and humble. Tamar took a seat on a bench with her friends the stable boys, but was noticed and summoned to take the chair provided for her between Alexander and Malik.

'You would have had more fun down there than stuck between an unfledged priest and an old badger like me,' said Malik sardonically.

'If one can't get thrushes, one has to eat blackbirds. I like you well enough, badger though you are,' replied Tamar. Katerina had not had time to drop her hint to Alexander, who did not address a single remark to the neighbour on his left.

The banquet began with an egg and lemon soup with little pies stuffed with caviare. Meat followed. There was a whole roast lamb, three roast sucking pigs, a haunch of venison, a roast goose, three pheasants and a covey of partridges. Alexander delivered a grace that no one listened to, and then they fell upon the food. With the meats were jellies and sauces, pickled mushrooms, red cabbage and salted cucumbers. The meats were followed by flaming pancakes, by cherries and greengages preserved in brandy, by quince, apricot and peach loaf, by halva and by a huge wedding cake, surmounted by a falcon with its wings spread, made of marzipan, with its breast spotted with currants and its wings and tail striped with powdered cinnamon.

While the company feasted, it was entertained by a harper, a bagpiper from the mountain, and by three men playing the balalaika.

There was plenty to drink, and the mixture of vodka and sweet Georgian wines may be one reason why several diners either disappeared under the table, or reeled into the yard to empty stomachs overburdened with such rich fare. At the end of the meal, Malik rose and proposed a toast to the bride and bridegroom which even Tamar found herself drinking. She was flushed and felt that at the moment she could not have cared less.

When they rose from the feast and the dishes and tables had been cleared away, an attempt to continue dancing was made by the young women, but only two or three of the men were able to stand upright, and even these clutched at their partners from motives either of remaining perpendicular, or of lust, or both.

It was during the last attempt to prolong the orgy that the door was suddenly flung open, and the cripple Vakhtang, who had chosen to remain sober, appeared and shouted: 'The Sultzi are upon us!'

At that moment a heavy explosion and the sound of splintering wood confirmed his words. Nina and Vakhtang secured the door. The men gazed about them stupidly. Even Malik, who had seemed sober half an hour earlier, waved his hand and said with a broad smile: 'Tell the bastards to come back in the morning,' and then lay down in a corner.

Prince Gurgen staggered out from his bedroom and tried vainly to draw the sabre he was carrying from its sheath. After the third pull he succeeded. The Archpriest was asleep and nothing would wake him. The ascetic neophyte Alexander fell on his knees and vomited over the shrine of Vasso, Saint or martyr. There were two more explosions and crashes as the Solutz tried to blast their way into the yard. Then, as there was no reply, the men carrying scaling ladders ran up and set them against the walls on the opposite side.

But suddenly Tamar seized a rifle and, calling out: 'Follow me girls,' ran up the stairs of the tower. Salomé at once seized a musket and, having fired one before, took with her a powder horn, a bag of bullets, a box of percussion caps and ran after her. From the top of the tower, Tamar looked down and saw a man already astride the wall of the yard and preparing to drop down into it, while another man pushed up the ladder behind. She aimed and fired, and the man, flailing his arms, fell into the courtyard where he lay motionless. There was another shot and another man fell, and Tamar saw Salomé beside her.

'Good work,' she cried. The whole of the yard was lit up by flames. The cask of naphtha had been lit beside the main gate, already splintered by the cannon balls, but holding firm.

And then, suddenly, before Salomé had rammed down the bullet on her second charge, a tremendous shiver ran through the earth. It was repeated more violently, and Tamar saw the men on the ladders leap down and run back aghast, as the walls of the Castle shook, the earth rocked and, with an immense roar, rocks on the sides of the mountains came crashing down. The cask of burning naphtha which had been blazing against the door of the yard began to roll down the declivity to the river, pursuing, with a pathway of fire, the men running before it to safety. The Castle rocked like a ship coming afloat in a rising tide, but its foundations were solid and it stood firm. And, in the light of the blazing naphtha, Tamar saw the besiegers of the Castle flying down to the river. There were deep sounds from within the earth and then a sound of rushing water. A few minutes later the cask of naphtha was quenched and all was darkness.

What Tamar had watched from the tower, Ziklauri had seen from the mountainside as he was scrambling down to join his men, after giving the signal for the attack. But just as he realised what was happening, he was hit by a flying stone and knocked insensible. When Tamar and Salomé had felt their way down the stairs of the tower in pitch darkness, uncertain whether the stair had collapsed below them, they found the Great Hall empty, but all the inmates on their knees in the chapel, in front of the icon of Saint Anne, whose pale eyes looked out unmoved at her incapacitated worshippers, too terrified and too drunk to utter intelligible words of prayer. Tamar looked at them with loathing. Then she picked up a torch, lit it at the log fire and went out into the yard to see if the man she had shot was alive and in need of help. He was dead, and the blood and brains spattered on the stone floor showed that he had fallen head first from the wall above. The man that Salomé had shot was dead too.

'Well, that's that,' said Tamar. She thought that she was indifferent to the fact that she had killed a man – but as she walked back to the Great Hall she had to run into a corner of the yard, where she vomited. Then as she went through the Great Hall and up to her room still feeling sick, she reflected that Anastasia was perhaps right and that it was always a mistake to kill people. But how could *she* tell if she had never killed anyone? she asked herself.

She lay down on her bed but she did not sleep. Occasionally there were little shivers; it was as though the earth were frightened by the recollection of its own strength.

CHAPTER FOUR

What is called the epicentre of the earthquake was, however, nearer to the town than to the Castle. Indeed if it had not dislodged the wall of rock that dammed the lake, its effects in the defile would not have been exceptionally severe. But in the town it had demolished two whole streets, fire had broken out and many citizens, like the widow Tara, had spent an hour or two screeching with fear, and chilled to the bone, in their nightgowns in their gardens. That lady had been guided well by her instinct, for in the lodge the ceilings had fallen, and it is possible that if a half-brick had hit her she would have shared the fate of the two hundred persons who were killed.

Most spectacular were the effects of the earthquake on the monastery – one of the outside walls being split in two leaving a gap in the masonry.

Valeri, who was asleep, was woken by the first tremors and the deep subterranean rumblings. He scrambled out of bed in the darkness, lit a candle and suddenly saw that the door-posts of his cell had separated and were further apart at the top than at the bottom. He put his shoulder to the door and the tongue of the lock drew and the door burst open. He pulled his cassock on over the precious shirt in which he slept, put on his sandals and walked out. The violent rumblings underground and the crash of falling masonry were a bass accompaniment to the high-pitched cries of the monks gathered before the altar on their knees. Valeri, carrying his candle, paid no attention to them, but rapidly descended into the crypt of the church, although the steps of the stone staircase were sliding gently to and fro beneath his feet. There he found and girded on his hidden sabre and his pistol and went up. He would have found it difficult to find a way out of the monastery, for its doors were locked and chained every night, and the windows criss-crossed with iron bars, had he not suddenly seen the breach made in the outer wall, which was just wide enough for him to push through sideways. He made his way to an open space at some little distance and there lay down and waited for the dawn.

At first light, Valeri took the road or mule-track up the river to the Castle. In many places it had disappeared in a slide of rock into the gorge below. At some of these it was necessary to climb high up and pass with difficulty from rock to rock and then slide down again to where the track remained. Progress was slow, and he had not reached the first river crossing when he caught sight of an armed man moving towards him.

In the next moment the man had seen him, and had thrown himself under cover of a rock. To Valeri it seemed absurd that, in the midst of so much devastation, men should be enemies, so he held up his arms in the air and walked on. No shot was fired and, when he reached the rock, Ziklauri rose from behind it. As he still held his rifle at the ready, Valeri turned his right side towards him, and said: 'You can take my pistol out of my belt, if that would make you feel more comfortable.'

At the same time he noticed that Ziklauri's neck was covered in dried blood and that his ear was still bleeding. At Valeri's action, Ziklauri spoke, and his voice sounded as though from far away, like that of a dead man.

'Are you part of the Church militant? A monk with the cross on his chest and a sabre and pistol at his side? No, I don't want your pistol, Valeri. Sit down and tell me how you come to be here. You see before you a ruined man.'

'The monastery was shattered. I escaped through a breach

in the wall. But how do you come to be here and how wounded?'

Ziklauri looked dazed and did not reply, so Valeri repeated his question. At last he answered: 'The icon! It can only have been that damned icon. I think she is not Saint Anne, the mother of the Holy Virgin, but the wife of Lucifer – some un-Christian creature.'

Valeri laughed. 'Are you blaming her for the earthquake?' he asked.

'Who else?' replied Ziklauri. 'I brought all my fighting men, and four women to cook for them, to storm the Castle. We had a cannon, scaling ladders and barrels of naphtha. There was no defence after our attack, except two shots from somebody on the top of the tower. I had given the signal and was climbing down to join in, the naphtha barrels had been lit, the men were on the ladders – and, at that moment, the earth trembled, rocks began tumbling down. My men jumped off the ladders and ran down to their horses, and a barrel of naphtha rolled after them, spreading a path of flame. And then five minutes later they were all swept away by a flood of water, and then, as the naphtha flickered out, something hit me. When I recovered, I was alone and all was over.'

'Why were you on the mountainside and not with your men?' asked Valeri.

'To give the signal for attack with scaling ladders when both sides were in position. After giving the signal, I could be with them in two minutes. The earthquake began just after I gave the signal, and I waited to see what was happening. There was nothing I could do to stop my men running back to the river, to their horses, once the earthquake had begun. If the water had not swept them away, I could perhaps have rallied them for a second attack, or for a siege. But as the icon was responsible for the earthquake, it would have been useless to defy her again. She had made a clean sweep.'

Valeri remained silent, and presently Ziklauri asked: 'Why do you doubt the powers of that icon?'

Valeri shrugged his shoulders. 'I don't think that the earthquake had anything to do with your attack. As I came away from the monastery, I could see that streets of houses in the town were burning. It was just bad luck that your men ran downhill and met the flood. The wall of rock holding the lake must have been broken and then the lake emptied itself. Do you think there were any survivors besides yourself?'

'I've seen no traces. But before I decided to come away, I saw Malik leading out a well-armed search party, on the other side of the river. Luckily for me, I wasn't noticed.'

'If any of them were washed on to the fields, they might have escaped,' said Valeri.

'Are you planning to stay at the Castle?' asked Ziklauri.

'I don't know; I must talk to Anastasia about it. I shall stay if she wants me to.'

Ziklauri gave Valeri an odd look. 'What Anastasia is that?' he asked.

'Princess Anastasia, my father's wife,' replied Valeri haughtily. He was surprised by the question. Then he added: 'What I do, what my plans are, depend a good deal on her. If I can be a help to her, I'll stay. If I'm an embarrassment, I shall ride off.' He looked up at Ziklauri wondering why he should have made him such an intimate confidence and saw such a strange look on his face that he asked at once: 'What's wrong?'

'So locked up in the monastery, you never heard.... It's too awful. It's too terrible,' said Ziklauri, speaking very softly as though he were talking to himself.

'What haven't I heard?' asked Valeri.

'The Anastasia that was your father's wife ... she threw herself off the top of the tower ... it was when she heard of the death of her little son, Vasso.'

Valerie put his hands in front of his face and bent his head. Then Ziklauri could see his body rocking to and fro on the boulder he was sitting on. A few tears ran between his fingers, but he said nothing. There was a long silence and then, collecting himself, he said: 'Tell me all.'

'Well, I don't know everything. I don't know the whole truth. I only know the gossip that came to the town brought by the Armenian pedlar, who turned up as they were burying her. According to him, when Prince Gurgen came back to the Castle, after the burial of the little boy and the service over Djamlet's grave, his wife, the Lady Anastasia, ran up to the top of the tower and threw herself into the courtyard below. And the pedlar saw her buried at the crossroads above the lake and a stake was driven through her body. The men digging the hole in which she was thrown told him they were doing it by the Prince's orders, because she had killed herself.'

Then as Valeri said nothing and made no movement, Ziklauri continued: 'It would seem from that, that the death of her only child came as a shock to her, in which case Gurgen was lying to me when he told me that the boy had broken his neck from falling off Rusudan's rock when he was birds' nesting.... But the child's neck was broken. I saw that for myself.'

'How did you come to see it?' asked Valeri.

'It was common knowledge that after Djamlet's death the old man had sworn an oath to bring the icon of Saint Anne to the cemetery and hold a service over Djamlet's grave, and, soon after you killed my poor boy Lazar, I got wind that he had planned to come on a certain day. So we ambushed him. But it turned out that they were a funeral procession to bury the body of the child. I asked to see the body of the child and was shown it – there was no possibility of mistake. So, out of respect, we let them pass. But they had the icon with them, hidden somewhere. Only of course we didn't search. But what worries me is that, if what Gurgen told me was true, Anastasia must have known of the child's death before they set out. And surely she would have gone with them to the funeral, unless she was mad? And if she didn't know, Vasso must have met his death on the road – before the ambush. Not birds' nesting. But his neck was broken – he might have been strangled ... who strangled him?'

Valeri remained silent.

After a time Ziklauri said: 'Of course if you never heard of Lady Anastasia's death, you cannot have heard of Gurgen's remarriage.'

At that Valeri lifted his head, and stared.

'Remarriage? Who on earth to?' he asked.

'To Katerina, daughter of the Archpriest. She and her father came to the Castle with a young fellow who is waiting to be ordained a few days ago, and the widow Tara told everyone in the town that the girl was going to marry the Old Prince. I don't know whether the marriage has taken place. The earthquake may have interrupted it. Anyway I thought it was a good time to attack the Castle, only I didn't know Saint Anne had such power.' Valeri still did not speak and after looking at him, Ziklauri rose from the rock on which he was sitting and walked up to him, patted him on the shoulder and then bent down and kissed his forehead. 'I am sorry, but I had to tell you,' he said.

Valeri suddenly went down on his knees before him, caught the edge of his chokha and said:

'Can you ever forgive me for my crime? I swear I did not know what Lazar was doing. I saw him digging at the grave.... But that does not make it any less.'

'I guessed that long ago, my friend. Evil deeds breed evil deeds, and we must put an end to them, so I bear you no evil,' said Ziklauri.

Valeri suddenly burst into tears. And, still on his knees and sobbing, he said: 'Thank you, Ziklauri. You are a good man. I cannot forgive myself ... never ... never. My crime has marked me ...'

'Come, my friend,' said Ziklauri. 'There has been too much

blood between us. Let us be friends from now onwards.'

Valeri stood up, brushed away his tears and said: 'May I call you my friend? You are the best man I know after Brother Foma. I will see that any survivors of your men at the Castle are well treated and sent back to you.'

He stood, suddenly looking taller and stern.

'I must go on my way now, for I have much to do. But first let me wash away the blood and bandage your wound.'

'That is nothing,' said Ziklauri, but he went with Valeri back along the track to where a rill of water dripped out of a rock, green with liverworts. Valeri took his handkerchief and washed away the blood and then gently inspected the gash in Ziklauri's scalp and torn ear. Then he rinsed out the handkerchief in the spring water, and made it into a pad to cover the wound and bound it in place with the silk scarf which he was wearing round his waist, under his cassock. Before parting, the two men embraced, and then each of them went picking his way among the rocks, without looking back.

As Valeri came in sight of the Castle, he saw men with long rods raking about in the river, and other men picking up large pebbles that had been washed on to the fields and throwing them in heaps to cart away. They looked up at him as he passed by, but none of them recognised the tall monk striding along. Only when he had reached the gateway did he come face to face with Tinatin. the wife of a shepherd, who cried out in astonishment and ran back into the yard. A moment later Valeri found himself surrounded by women and one or two young boys. All were exclaiming with delight and began asking his blessing – for, in his cassock, he was not just the Valeri that they had known, but a Holy Man of God. The men were all at work, as he had seen, either searching for what they could find in the river, or trying to undo the damage that the flood waters had done in the fields.

'Blessings be on us, the young Master has come back.'

cried Nina, running to him and trying to kiss his hand. But Valeri put his arms round her and kissed her on each cheek while she struggled with him, trying to drop a curtsey in respect. When he released her she ran back to carry the news of his return to the old Prince.

'Where are the prisoners?' he asked the crowd of women standing round him.

'They are locked up in the round house, my Lord,' one of them answered.

'Get the key and unlock the door!'

Old Herakli, who had been made gaoler because he had a bad leg and could not join in a search party with the other men, came hobbling up. When he had unlocked the door. Valeri looked in and saw five men and a girl, tied up, wet and shivering, standing against the wall.

'Let them loose at once,' ordered Valeri. Then, addressing the wretched prisoners, he said: 'The feud between us is over. I have made peace with Ziklauri, and you are our guests. You will be given food and dry clothes and when you are well rested, you will be sent home.' Then he turned to the waiting crowd of frightened and astonished women. 'Light a fire, prepare a meal. Give all these men warm dry clothes.' Then catching sight of Tamar standing apart, he said to her: 'Dearest sister, take this poor girl under your care and give her everything she needs.' The whole of this scene had taken only two minutes, and then Valeri turned and saw his father standing in the doorway. He thought that he looked much older than when he had last seen him.

Valeri walked up to him, but did not kneel or ask his blessing or kiss his hand, or cheek, but only said: 'I have come back, Prince Gurgen.'

'What is going on here?' asked his father.

'The feud with the Solutz is over. I have made a binding peace with Ziklauri – and so I have given orders that these poor fellows should be cared for until they are well enough to return home,' said Valeri.

'Yes, yes, yes, there is much to talk about.' Then drawing himself up with dignity the Prince said: 'You are welcome home, my son. I was unjust to you, and it is for me to ask forgiveness. I thought you were a coward, but you avenged your brother, and I honour you for the deed. If Ziklauri has sued for peace to you, you were right to grant it.'

' "If the light that is in you is darkness, how great is the darkness thereof". Do you know that text, Prince? I like it better than the cowardly one of "Judge not that ye be not judged".'

The old Prince was puzzled, but replied: 'Of course you have learned a lot of the Scriptures ... I say you are welcome.' Then he turned and shouted: 'Bring vodka and caviare and pickled cucumbers.' As Valeri followed his father into the Great Hall, the old Prince said confidentially: 'There have been many changes.' Then, taking Valeri by the sleeve, he led him to the little chapel with the icon and pointed to the heap of relics that made up Vasso's shrine.

'Say a prayer and make an offering to that young Saint; it was he who saved Saint Anne, and it is to Saint Anne that we owe the destruction of the Sultzi and the safety of the Castle, last night.'

Valeri pulled the big crucifix he was wearing over his head and threw it down among the other relics, saying: 'You can add that to the junk heap of expiation,' and gave a strange laugh.

'Kneel to Saint Anne, my son.'

'Did you kill your own son?' Valeri asked abruptly.

'I was the instrument of the Holy Martyr and obeyed his wishes in order to save Saint Anne from the Sultzi.'

'You murdered your own child in order to save your own life and a piece of painted wood,' said Valeri.

The Prince crossed himself and fell on his knees, so that Valeri could no longer see his face.

'God and Saint Anne forgive him, for he knows not what he says,' the Prince prayed aloud.

'And by that murder of her child, you drove your wife to kill herself,' said Valeri over his kneeling father's shoulder.

'May Saint Anne forgive her for sin,' murmured the Prince.

'You buried your own wife at the crossroads and drove a stake through her body,' said Valeri with mounting fury.

'I did my duty. She was unfit for consecrated ground,' said the Prince Gurgen in terrified tones.

'And immediately afterwards you are marrying a girl who knows nothing of your crimes,' thundered Valeri. He turned away and saw Katerina standing close behind him. How long she had been there, and how much she had heard, he could not tell. He nodded to her and walked into the yard.

There he saw a knot of women waiting for him, and suddenly his self-command deserted him, and he turned back and ran up the stairs of the tower to the little room that had been his.

He pushed open the door and, without noticing that the room had been occupied since it was his, flung himself down on the couch. But he had no sooner lain down than he jumped up again. There was no comfort anywhere. He could not just hide and cry like a child. Anastasia and Vasso were dead: his father mad, or next door to it. There was nothing he could do, and there could be no question of his living in the Castle again. He walked up and down the room restlessly, unable to keep still, and, on one of his turns round the room, noticed the things lying on the table: a girl's white blouse, a pair of women's stockings, an amber necklace which he remembered Anastasia wearing, a brush and comb. And then a Martini rifle propped in a corner. Some woman must be living in the room – yet there was still the skin of the snow leopard he had shot on the couch, and the horns of his first big horned sheep over the doorway. He stared for a moment and then began to look into a box full of bracelets and brooches, all of which must have belonged, he thought, to Anastasia.

When a knock came at the door, he jumped guiltily before he went to it and opened it.

Tamar was standing outside with the girl of the Sultzi, newly dressed in dry clothes, behind her. Valeri stepped back.

'This is your room now, isn't it,' he asked.

'Forgive me for living in it while you were away. I've looked after all your gear and have come now to take my things away.'

'Isn't this the necklace Anastasia used to wear?' he asked picking up the rope of big amber beads.

'Everything beautiful that I have got used to be hers,' replied Tamar. Then she went on: 'I wanted to kill your father after her death. I sharpened my little dagger and planned to plunge it into his heart...' Valeri shuddered violently at her words. The memory of Lazar's body, spurting blood into the little hole that he had dug in Djamlet's grave, was there before him. Tamar broke off what she was saying and watched him, as he put his hands over his face to try and shut out a vision that was unbearable. Valeri gave a last shudder, then dropped his hands and looked at Tamar with an expression of complete exhaustion.

'Tell me everything.' He was sitting on the couch on the snow leopard skin. Tamar sat down opposite him, and, looking over her shoulder, Valeri became aware of the girl of the Sultzi standing in the doorway behind Tamar. She had drawn a central parting through her mane of black hair and was plaiting one half of it into a pigtail. It was clear that Tamar had forgotten her existence and that the girl was listening. But Valeri did not wish to interrupt Tamar or she might not speak again.

'It's difficult to explain. After Anastasia's death, when he had treated her so shamefully, your father called me to him and gave me all her jewels and all her dresses and said that he loved me like one of his own daughters and that I should always have a home in the Castle. I had my hand on the hilt of my dagger and was ready to spring on him, when he asked me not to wear any of the dresses that Anastasia usually wore, because he could not bear it – and then he burst into tears. So I could not kill him then, and later I remembered that Anastasia hated the feud, and would not want me to avenge her. Since then I have done nothing, because I really do not know what I *should* do. Please tell me what you think....' And Tamar looked up at him angrily, screwing up her blue eyes.

'Dearest Tamar, dearest Tamar, I understand what you have suffered, and, all alone as I was, locked in my cell,' said Valeri. He stood up from the couch, and, as Tamar stood up, he put his arms round her and kissed her, first on the cheek and then on the lips.

'I suppose you know, without my telling you, that Anastasia was the only woman I have ever loved...' As he said this Valeri looked over Tamar's shoulder. The Sultzi girl was still standing in the doorway. She had finished the plait on the right hand side and had begun the one on the left.

Valeri looked at Tamar: her lovely face – and at that minute he realised for the first time how lovely she was – was set in an obstinate expression.

'Anastasia was all I had, but I did not love her as I should have done and as I know that you did, because she held herself back from me and treated me as a child. And then, a year or two ago, I realised that she had sacrificed herself for me. That if I had not existed, she would not have married your father. And that made me ashamed. She ought not to have done that. Instead of making me feel gratitude, it made me feel despair and also, now that I am in the same situation, contempt for her weakness.'

'What do you mean – the same situation?' asked Valeri.

'That woman, whom your father has just married, is set on marrying me to that scared divinity student Alexander. It's funny really. He doesn't want to marry me – I frightened him out of his wits. I told him I had shot one man and might shoot another.... But Katerina wants to get rid of me, so it's marriage for me or, perhaps, poison. The other girls – Salomé and Elisso – are desperate. She plans to put them in a nunnery. Salomé told me that she meant to get herself with child so as to stop that.'

Valeri looked up. The Sultzi girl, who had left half her plait unfinished, suddenly began moving her fingers again when she met his eye.

Valeri was puzzled. There was too much for him to take it in all at once. He wanted more facts and time to think them over. But since listening to Tamar the violent personal emotion he had felt, when he first entered the room, was gone. For he was facing the problems of these women. He had forgotten his own despair in thinking how he could help Tamar and his sisters. Suddenly he felt very close to her: she and he were one – or rather talking to Tamar was like talking to his younger self, to the boy he had been before he entered the monastery. Thanks to her, he was no longer alone.

He took Tamar by the hand and, to her astonishment, tickled her palm and laughed at her look of surprise.

'We trust each other don't we? And we can help each other. You know I shan't stay in this hell hole. I am actually on my way to ... well ... probably to Alexandria. Perhaps I ought to explain that while I was a prisoner in the monastery ...'

'A prisoner? Were you a prisoner?' interrupted Tamar.

'Yes – but that's a long story – while I was a prisoner, I discovered the truth about religion – no, I don't mean religion – we all have our religions – I discovered the truth about the Church. It is an organisation exploiting simple people, and we are all simple people, by scaring them with the fear of Hell and promising them Heaven – in return for cash usually – and all so that a class of people, liars and criminals – should be able to live at their ease. That is the Christian Church. Of course Christians are good and bad like everyone else. It's only some priests and the Bishops and the

Archimandrites, I am saying are criminals. So I am going to Alexandria. I mean to study the Mohammedan religion and see if it's better. You see, I want man to live again as he used to do in the Golden Age, when there were no priests, no icons and none of this fear that makes men cruel.'

Valeri paused and wiped his eyes. He felt angry and ashamed, because by speaking his thoughts he had made himself cry, like a child. He swallowed and went on : 'There was a monk who was my teacher, Brother Foma, and it is thanks to him that I started to think for myself. He has disappeared. The Archimandrite may have poisoned him. If he is alive, I want to find him. You understand : it is only by thinking and thinking and finding out the truth that all these horrors and abominations and evils can be overcome. My father would never have murdered the child he loved...' At this point Valeri burst into tears, and then making an effort went on : 'if he had not been brought up to believe in miracles and holy images and been told lies all his life by priests. Lies, lies, lies! It's all lies. Really I pity my father. I condemn him and probably he condemns himself. But the only way, the only way to overcome these cruelties is by finding out and teaching the truth. But before one can teach it, one must find it out.' Valeri had recovered himself and said calmly and almost drily : 'So you see what I am planning to do is very important.'

The Sultzi girl was still staring at him. Tamar had moved a little, and he could see that the girl had a beautiful body and the most wonderful eyes. At first glance he had thought that they were very dark, or black. But now he saw that he had thought that because she had black lashes and black eyebrows. Her eyes were really very dark blue. But her lips were coarse.

Valeri wondered why she stared at him like that. Probably she had not understood a word that he had been saying. But what did it matter? The girl meant nothing to him.

Only those eyes ... Tamar was looking at him rapturously and saying: 'I know, I know, I understand.'

Perhaps Tamar did understand – but was it right for him to have said so much? Or to have said anything at all? The truth is so important: only one ought not to speak unless one is *absolutely* sure. And perhaps he had exaggerated.

'All that I meant to say was that I am not staying here very long. But while I am here, I will do what I can to help you and my two sisters. Now, can you find that wretched young divinity student they brought with them, the one Katerina wants to marry you to? I will try and put the fear of God – no, just fear – into him. Ask him to come here. And take this girl of the Solutz away. She has been listening to every word we have been saying to each other. She distracts me.' Tamar started, turned round and saw the girl of the Sultzi. 'Come along, long ears,' she said, and catching her by the wrist, dragged her away from the door, down the stairs. The girl went unwillingly, turning her head to give Valeri a last look.

Left alone, Valeri shut the door, pulled off his cassock, combed his hair and taking a big gold ring set with rubies and emeralds out of his pocket, he pulled it on to his third finger and waited for Alexander. The only thing to do with priests was to lie to them, and so beat them at their own game.

There was a tap. Valeri opened the door, and Alexander raised his hand in benediction. Valeri at once turned his back on him and walked across the room. Then he turned to the discomfited young man, who had been surprised to see Valeri in his fine clothes, but recovered himself sufficiently to say: 'If I can be of any help to you, my son...'

'It is you who are in need of help, not me,' said Valeri firmly. 'I have sent for you because I want to help you. My father's new wife, Katerina, is a warm-hearted and generous woman, and through her father, has great influence in the Church. She has a brave character also and will make a

127

splendid head of this household. Now she is making a match for you with that girl, Tamar...'

'I had no idea that you were interested in my affairs, Prince Valeri, and really perhaps I am the best judge of them,' began Master Alexander, but Valeri interrupted him.

'Unfortunately Katerina has no idea of Tamar's character. It, I am sorry to say, is a bad one. She is proud, head-strong, unruly and violent-tempered. She has never loved anyone, even her sister. If you marry her, your life will be filled with scandals. She will scratch your face, pull out your beard, scream so that the neighbours will hear – and you will never know whether your children are your own or the postboy's. She is a savage and might, any night, if the fit took her, wake up, stick a dagger in your heart and run away to her Mohammedan tribesmen over in Turkey. You must at all costs avoid marrying Tamar.'

Poor Master Alexander looked at Valeri pitiably. What he had just heard agreed all too well with his own experience of Tamar. He sat facing Valeri with his mouth open, unable to say a word. 'Now my sister Elisso – if only she were to be your bride, your life would be peaceful and happy. But she wishes to be a nun. And, as you know better than any-one, once a girl feels that she has a vocation, it is difficult to make her change her mind.' Valeri looked with amusement at the shattered figure before him. His words seemed to have had an effect.

'Well, I just wanted to warn you. In your own interests, of course.' And Valeri rose and bowed to his visitor in token of dismissal.

Master Alexander retired greatly perturbed and puzzled by the conversation. How was it that Valeri, who had only reached the Castle an hour or two before, knew everything that was planned and going on in it? What Valeri had said about Tamar was true. She was a little firebrand, who had the makings of a virago in her. She had slapped his face when he had spoken to her of marriage, and she had boasted that she had shot one man and would like to shoot another. Valeri's sudden appearance at the Castle, his commanding manner, his fine clothes, and his refusal to ask his blessing, or to treat him as a priest, had impressed Alexander. Then, with a few words, he had reduced Prince Gurgen to a slobbering dotard and Katerina to a condition of wild-eyed hysteria. Though she would of course recover, Alexander felt that it was essential for him to keep in with Valeri. His own influence would be as great if he were able to exchange that termagant Tamar for Elisso, a sweet girl and the Prince's own daughter. He must marry immediately, as his ordination depended on it.

The five survivors of the Sultzi had been fed, taken to the bath-house and given dry clothes. They presented themselves, one by one, in the great hall, where they looked about them timidly. They were men of a kind that Salomé and Elisso had never seen before. They were not nobles but, on the other hand, they were not serfs, or servingmen, or artisans, or pedlars. Though he was shy, when one of them asked Elisso to show him the icon of Saint Anne, he spoke to her as an equal – and when she asked if he were a son of Ziklauri, and he replied that the only son that Ziklauri had left alive was talking to her sister in the alcove at the other side of the hall, he spoke of Ziklauri and his son as equals, and she felt sure that he was right in that assumption.

While she was talking to him, the search party under Malik came back into the yard, bringing with them four bodies that they had recovered from the river and had tied on to two hurdles drawn by mules.

Nina had been keeping a lookout and went to meet them to tell them of Valeri's return and the new state of affairs.

'Well, what are we to do with these fellows?' asked Malik pointing to the corpses. 'My chaps have divided up all their belongings – even to the crosses round their necks – and they won't want to give them back.'

'Prince Valeri said the prisoners would be sent home to-

morrow. Can't you hide the bodies until they are gone?'
suggested Nina. So the two hurdles were dragged into the
granary and locked up there and Malik warned his men not
to speak a word about having found them.

The precaution was, however, unnecessary as after Malik
had greeted Valeri, who took him in his arms and kissed
him on each cheek, and they had got to talking of what
was to be done next day, Valeri said that the Sultzi would
wait until after the funeral of the two men who had been
shot down from the ladders, so Malik spoke of the four men
picked out of the river, and Valeri gave orders that four
more coffins should be knocked up by next morning, and
that their possessions should be returned and their appearances tidied up, as the Sultzi would certainly wish to identify
them before they were buried. Next morning there would be
a grand funeral conducted by the Archpriest and Alexander,
which everyone would have to attend.

By the time Valeri had seen to all these details, Katerina
had recovered herself and had ordered a grand dinner to be
prepared in honour of Prince Valeri's return. There were
plenty of delicious left-overs from the wedding feast, which
could be used up.

Meanwhile Alexander had sought out Elisso and got her
into a corner where he could talk to her without being overheard.

'My child, I am told that you think that you have a
vocation to enter the ranks of the Penitent Sisters. Is that
the truth?' Elisso hesitated, then she looked Alexander
straight in the eye. What she saw there was repellent. The
horrible young man was attracted by her. Perhaps having
his face slapped by Tamar was making him switch to her.
The truth, that she was terrified of being shut up in a nunnery, would never do. She would have to lie.

'Yes, Father. I can only love our Saviour. I dream of washing His feet ... Saint Anne appeared to me in a vision ...'

'The love we bear Our Lord may take many shapes....

The duties of a wife are the highest to which woman can aspire, just as the duties of a Consecrated Priest are that of Man. If I were to ask your Father for your hand in marriage...' But Father Alexander got no further. The Princess Katerina was walking up to them.

'Oh, here you are Alexei. Run along Elisso....'

Elisso ran, and Katerina continued: 'I want you, before the usual grace at dinner, to say that this is a very special occasion, because we have here the Lord Valeri as our guest, as welcome as he was unexpected. And that, thanks to Saint Anne, the ancient quarrel with the Men of our Blood is healed and that we have here in the Castle, the son of Ziklauri and four men of the Solutz, gathered in the home of all our ancestors, partaking of the hospitality of the head of the family, Prince Gurgen.'

This speech was never made, nor was the feast that Katerina had planned, to use up the left-overs, ever eaten.

Nina had taken it upon herself to inform Valeri of the Princess's project before beginning to execute her new mistress's instructions.

Valeri found her still talking to Alexander.

'I am deeply grateful to you for planning to give a little dinner in my honour, but I must ask you to postpone it,' he said.

'Why so?' asked Katerina.

'Because I, whom you seek to honour, ask you – and because the men of the Solutz here are mourning their dead.'

'What on earth has that got to do with us?' she asked haughtily.

'It has this. We must show as much respect to their dead as they showed to the corpse of poor murdered Vasso.' Then, as Katerina started back at the ferocity which he put into his last words, he added more mildly: 'And, if you want the children you bear to my father to escape the fate that has already attended five of his sons, leaving only me alive, you must, at your peril, keep the peace which I made this morning with Ziklauri.'

Katerina listened and said: 'I see that perhaps I was injudicious. But your father will be terribly disappointed. Well, we'll have a little, quite private, celebration in our room, with only you and me and our two parents.'

'Tell my father that I am tired after a long day and that I have much to think over before my departure, so I shall eat alone in my own room.'

At the word 'departure' Katerina looked at Valeri wildly. Then she made an effort and said: 'What can I get you for supper?'

'I will ask Nina to bring me a glass of wine and a piece of your wedding cake to my room,' said Valeri. But when he had said good-night to Tamar and his sisters, he went into the cellar and helped himself to a bottle of vodka and a pitcher of water. Soon afterwards, Katerina herself brought him wine, bread, caviare and a piece of the wedding cake. He took them from her at the door, thanked her and closed it in her face, before she could make an excuse to enter. Then he poured the wine out of the archer's squint and threw the wedding cake after it. He ate bread and caviare and drank glass after glass of vodka, putting a very little water with it. It was a long time since he had drunk spirits and a delicious deadening of pain, acceptance of life and indifference to what the future might bring, stole over him with every glass.

It was past midnight, and he was lying naked on the skin of the snow leopard, when he was woken by hearing something scratching at the door.... Valeri wrapped a cloak round him, picked up his pistol, cocked it, and opened the door. The girl of the Sultzi was standing there in nothing but a thin silk shift. She slipped under his arm like an eel and taking hold of the door pushed it shut behind her.

'I have come Prince, to tell you that your secrets are

safe with me,' she said and then slipped her arms under his cloak and pressed her body to his naked one.

'Secrets? But what are you doing here?' muttered Valeri, dazed.

'You killed my lover Lazar, the son of Ziklauri. He was only a boy – an unstable boy, and I know he had done wrong. I meant to kill you and avenge him, until I heard you talking. You are a man. But you owe it me to make up my loss. I would have killed you in revenge. But instead I ask: may I take you in his place.'

Valeri's eyes swam. The floor moved up at him.

'Funny girl ... funny things happen to me. That's what I mean.... Funny,' said Valeri indistinctly.

'You are drunk, my darling. Lie down now and don't worry. You will be all right in a minute. It will soon pass.'

Valeri staggered, the girl took the pistol away and half pushed, half led him to the couch. He fell back on it and felt her cradling his head and whispering tenderly. After a time he opened his eyes and he was looking at her naked body in the light of the guttering tapers. Then she was moving him, touching him and guiding him. His body took control and he was whirled aloft in the high spaces above the abyss below, and the girl was crying out and digging her nails into his shoulders, then he was kissing her tenderly and she was murmuring something.

When he woke, hours later, he was alone, lying under his cloak which had been tucked carefully round and under him, with a cushion put under his head, and a shaft of the risen sun was pouring in at the archer's squint.

There was just time for him to get dressed, swallow a cup of cold tea and attend the funeral.

First came the Archpriest in his magnificent green and gold chasuble, carrying his pastoral staff, Master Alexander in his alb and with an epigonation hanging between his fingers – then the six coffins each carried by four bearers, with the five men of the Sultzi, three on one side and two on the other, walking beside the coffins, each carrying a brass rod with an unlit taper. Then Valeri's visitor of the previous night, draped from head to foot in black and with her face half veiled, followed. After her came Prince Gurgen in full dress, leaning on the arm of his young wife. Then Prince Valeri and Tamar and Iriné, then Nina and Malik. After them came the less important members of the Castle establishment, with the maids and stable boys bringing up the rear.

Elisso and Salomé were unaccountably absent, but the only person who commented on this was Valeri, in a whisper to Tamar, walking beside him.

'I expect that they overslept,' she said and blushed.

'I nearly did myself. In fact I don't know how it was I woke up,' said Valeri.

'But I know,' said Tamar. 'I woke you. Do you know that you left your door unlocked and your pistol loaded and cocked upon the table, and a bottle of vodka with three quarters of it gone? You had drunk all the rest. I could have blown your brains out and everyone would have thought that it was suicide.'

'Were you tempted to?' asked Valeri.

'No, but that girl in black ahead of us, might have been, if she had happened to come into the room. She told me that she was going to be married to Lazar.'

Valeri did not reply.

'Aren't you ashamed of drinking so much?' Tamar asked.

'Hush. We are nearly there,' answered Valeri.

The graveyard was the feature of the ceremony which left much to be desired. It was situated under the cliff at the corner between the river and the wild pasture that sloped to the first of the four fields. It had at one time been surrounded with a wall of dry earth and stones which had been lime-washed over a century before. Some of the walls had long since fallen, and the flood had swept away a length of what remained, on the river side. The decline in numbers of the Castle establishment in recent years had led to fewer burials, all of the humbler sort, and the practice of burying members of the Prince's family in the town cemetery had also reduced the usefulness of this homely graveyard. Thickets of brambles and suckers of wild plum had sprung up everywhere. Then the digging of six fine new graves, in two rows of three, had excited the curiosity of a flock of goats, and as the procession approached, these inquisitive animals leapt up from the graves they had been inspecting and bounded away to vantage points from which they could watch the subsequent proceedings. The heaps of earth beside each grave were sprinkled with their droppings. All this might have been ignored. But as the Archpriest toddled to the first grave in soporific dignity, he was suddenly confronted by a pair of horns, a black and bearded face, and a pair of impious eyes, which suddenly disappeared again from the edge of the grave over which they had been looking.

The Archpriest came to a sudden halt and the procession behind him likewise.

'Get thee behind me, Satan,' exclaimed the old man in quavering tones.

'What, has the Devil got in there first?' exclaimed one of the bearers of the first coffin, who had been keeping his eyes on the ground and had not noticed the flock of goats.

'Old Nick is waiting in the grave to carry one of these fellows off to Hell,' jested another bearer, somewhat tactlessly.

The nearest of the Sultzi was fortunately made of sterner stuff. ''Tis naught but a billy goat. They have been fighting and t'other must have butted him in and he can't scramble out,' and handing his brass rod to a companion, he leapt down into the grave and soon ejected the animal.

'By God, it is wet and muddy down here. No wonder he couldn't jump out.' The man who had so readily jumped in, needed helping hands to get out. His boots were full of water and his clothes covered with wet mud. He was, however, in a good humour, and said: 'We had better bury Sasha in there,' and, turning to the Archpriest, he explained: 'Sasha was our shepherd. He lived all his life among goats and would like to know that one had been keeping his grave warm for him.'

A titter of laughter ran round the ring of graves. Sasha's coffin was brought to that grave. Then the coffins were lowered on wide bands of webbing and the funeral services began. The Archpriest and Alexander each performed three services – but they performed them at the same time – with the result that the mourners were treated to syncopated burial services which at moments partook of the character of a glee, such as Three Blind Mice.

The graves were filled in. The men of the Solutz handed in the brass rods (of unhappy memory to some of them). The sun shone and, mounted on a very scratch collection of ponies, they were sent off with enough food for a midday meal and Irakli and Ramin to bring the ponies back.

At the last moment, before their departure, there was an unexpected scene. The girl of the Sultzi suddenly flung herself full-length at the feet of Prince Gurgen and craved a boon. The procedure of 'craving a boon', though well-known in legend, had not been witnessed by anyone present, or heard of during the lifetime of the eldest of them.

'Take me under your protection, Most Noble Prince Gurgen, Son of the Falcon. Allow me to stay for a space in your Castle.'

Valeri who was standing between Tamar and the suppliant, preserved an icy demeanour, which he was far from feeling.

'Granted, to be sure, dear child,' said Prince Gurgen and bent stiffly to help her rise. But she bounded up like a leopard, kissed the hand of the Prince and was kissed by him on both cheeks, after which, with no explanation on her part, the men of the Sultzi set out for home. The Prince did, however, extract one piece of information from the new inmate of the Castle, which she had refused to tell either Tamar or Valeri.

'What is your name, my dear?'

'Shorena. I am named after the girl who preferred the master builder of the Cathedral to King Georgi as her lover.'

Iriné, who was standing near, went into a hoot of maniacal laughter. Everyone looked at her, but she did not explain that she thought it comic that the Old Prince had succeeded in recruiting another unwanted girl. Competition between them would be stronger than ever. When everyone thought she was quiet she said in a penetrating voice: 'Why didn't she ask him to divorce Katerina and marry her instead?'

Valeri went to the stables, for during the previous evening he had had no opportunity to look at his mare. The stableman Herakli, who had one leg shorter than the other as a result of a bad fall when he was a boy, and who looked after her, came out.

'She is in perfect condition, sir. She foaled six months ago – a lovely young filly – a grey like her. The little thing is out with the others. They were in the high meadow when the flood came and got no harm.'

Mention of this young filly reminded Valeri of the colt he had given to Tamar and he asked about him.

'He is a beauty, be two years old in October. She has him tame as a dog. She'll have no trouble breaking him. Only she won't have him cut, and he'll be an infernal nuisance later on.'

'Well, give my mare a good grooming and a good feed. I shall want her in a little while.'

When he got back to his room, Valeri found Tamar waiting for him.

'Elisso and Salomé have disappeared,' she said.

'Disappeared? Where have they gone?' he asked.

'Promise on your sacred honour not to tell anyone, if I tell you?'

'I don't seem to keep those sacred promises very well. However I won't give them away.'

'They have eloped with the Sultzi. Salomé with Ziklauri's son, the fair one with blue eyes, Elisso with that dark, older man whose eyebrows meet over his nose. They set off on their ponies while everyone was at the funeral, so as to get away without being noticed.

'Salomé! What a girl. She actually shot and killed one of the Sultzi two nights ago and now she has eloped with one of the survivors! But Elisso! That surprises me. I didn't know she had so much spirit.'

'Well she got the idea that your father might put her in a convent and then Alexander started to propose to her last night and the dark Sultzi fellow was very taken with her . . .'

Valeri laughed. 'Alexander is a quick worker. I gave you such a bad character when he came to see me. I said you were a savage and might kill him and run away to your tribe at any time.'

'So I may. But the occasion won't arise with him.'

'I've told Herakli to saddle my mare, and I'm leaving in a few hours' time,' said Valeri.

'Then, like the Sultzi girl, I crave a boon.'

'What is it?'

'Oh, you have to grant it in princely fashion like your father before I tell you what it is. Not that I shall pay any attention if you refuse it.'

'In that case I may as well grant it.'

'Well, I am coming with you. I shall wear boy's clothes.'

On the previous day Valeri would have told her that this was utterly impossible. That he was setting off on an adventure into the unknown – that he might go as a student to the University in Cairo. But Shorena's visit the previous night had made him look at women with new eyes. He would prefer Tamar to the Sultzi woman as a companion – but in his secret heart he had wondered if that woman

138

might not want to come with him and whether he would have the strength to refuse if she did. So he asked: 'But where do you suppose that I am going?'

'You are coming with me, to my mother's people. To the Circassians who have taken refuge from the Russians in Turkey.'

'I see you have got it all planned out,' said Valeri. Then, as she said nothing, he added, 'It's a good idea. We can have a shot at it, anyway. If you want to stay with them, you can while I go on to Constantinople or Alexandria.'

Tamar gazed at him speechless and wild-eyed with happiness, so he took her in his arms and kissed her and said: 'Well, comrade, when will you be ready to start?'

'Whenever you like. Do we take a pack-pony or carry everything in saddle bags?'

'I hadn't meant to take a pony, but now that we are two I think it would be just as well. It would carry a tent and enough food to last us a week or so.'

These changes of plan were followed by another. Tamar begged they should take her young colt, which would be ready for breaking in by the winter. He would run alongside them and be no trouble. So she had to go out to the high meadow and catch him and bring him in. Then there was a tent to be found, and a pack-pony to be chosen. So that their departure was postponed until the morning after the next day.

Fortunately everyone in the Castle was so much shaken up by the earthquake and thrown into such turmoil by the disappearance of Elisso and Salomé that nobody paid any attention to what Valeri and Tamar were doing.

The Prince ordered two search parties to be sent out – one up the river and the other down, and Alexander held a service of intercession for their safety in front of the icon of Saint Anne.

Nobody suspected that they had eloped with the Sultzi – though it was hoped that if they had been carried off down river, the Sultzi might overtake their kidnappers and rescue them. The search party that had been sent off up the river under Malik returned shortly afterwards. He reported that there was not a footprint to be found upon the level sands between the river and the cliff wall and that no man or horse had passed that way since the flood that followed the earthquake. Suddenly someone noticed that the girls' ponies were missing from the stables. This indicated that they had gone willingly. Alexander suggested that perhaps Elisso had persuaded Salomé to go with her to the Convent of the Penitent Sisters.

All these speculations were set at rest the following after-noon when Irakli and Ramin returned with the second search party which they had met on their way back with the ponies. They related how the party of the Sultzi had caught up with the two girls, who were waiting for them about ten miles down the track, and how they said they were going to be married as soon as they reached the town. Salomé had even sent a message back to her father asking that her dowry be sent to the encampment of the Sultzi by return. Elisso had sent a more humble message, asking for-giveness for not having consulted him.

When Prince Gurgen understood what his daughters had done, rage overcame him. He bounced out of his room in his shirt and breeches, with his hair unbrushed and his beard sticking out at different angles, shouting for Malik. When he appeared the Prince demanded: 'How many men can we put in the field this afternoon?'

'Which field?' asked Malik, puzzled.

'Armed and mounted, ready to raid the encampment of the Solutz by nightfall? I can't let my daughters sleep an-other night with that scum. We might be in time to stop the weddings.' Then, as Malik did not reply, he went on: 'I tell you what ... we'll take that cannon of Ziklauri's and knock down their stockade with it. Then set fire to the place. Smoke them out like wasps. Turn the tables on them. They dared attack here during my wedding. We'll do the same, during theirs. Saint Anne will come with us and will finish the job.'

Malik considered. 'The cannon, to be sure, is buried in sand. It will want digging out and cleaning. And there will have to be cannon-balls cast.'

'Well, don't hang about arguing. Get it dug out and washed clean immediately. Tell the smith to start melting lead and casting cannon-balls.'

Malik bowed and retired.

'Two of you chaps dig that cannon out of the sand and get a mule to drag it into the yard,' he ordered. But he did not bother to give the smith instructions. The fit would pass, and the Prince would see reason. Meanwhile the old Prince was saying that Valeri had been swindled by Ziklauri, who ought to have been made to pay tribute and swear fealty.

Katerina was glad to see the girls go, but she had no intention of allowing the Prince to reopen the feud, or to risk defeat at the hands of the remaining Sultzi. Irakli reported that nine of them had somehow escaped from the flood and had made their way home.

When the Prince had cooled down a little, she pointed out, supported by Malik, that the stronghold of the Sultzi was within the Russian zone of influence. The Russians would not allow a pitched battle to take place so near the town without interfering, and, if they were stirred up, they were quite likely to send a punitive expedition against the Castle. This argument was a trump card, and Prince Gurgen was forced to defer operations against the insolent enemy until the Russians should leave Georgia – an event which the Prince had been confidently expecting all his life.

Having secured a victory over her old husband on one point, Katerina went on to the subject of Iriné.

'I know that you say she is not quite responsible – but really you must put your foot down and get rid of her.

She makes a point of bringing out an insulting remark, loud enough for one to hear, just when one is leaving the room. You are much too sweet a character, darling. But I am not, and next time Iriné opens her mouth, I shall give her a slapping.'

Prince Gurgen shook his head sadly. 'You don't understand. Iriné, and the things she says, are a punishment for my wrong-doing. Those words are not the poor girl's own words – they are put into her mouth at those awkward moments by God, to chastise me for having seduced her innocent mother when she was only a child.'

'Nonsense. You are much too sensitive about what other men are always doing. God's words indeed – the girl is a spiteful little bitch.'

'Do not blaspheme. I know what I say is true. Iriné is a cross that we both have to bear, and I forbid you to take any notice of her words. I forbid it!' And Prince Gurgen banged his fist on the table and looked so fierce that Katerina thought it best to change the subject – though what the old man had said was really crazy. Katerina had lived all her life in God's house and knew that one can arrange things to suit one's convenience without referring to Him.

'Surely now the Sultzi have carried off your own daughters you are not going to keep that awful Sultzi woman, Shorena, here? I can't think why you saddled us with her in the first place. I think that she is just a spy.'

The Prince drew himself up to his full height.

'It is due to me to keep her.'

'What on earth do you mean? You have no right to introduce a strange woman – and a woman of that class – into the Castle directly after my marriage. I demand that you turn her away.'

'It is the first time that one of the Solutz has ever craved a boon from the Son of the Falcon. As a matter of fact it is the first time *anyone* has ever craved a boon from me.'

Katerina laughed. 'That's all stuff and nonsense. We are

not living in one of Sir Walter Scott's novels – but I forget you can't read Russian. You are a romantic old darling, but you are going to turn that woman out of the Castle at once.'

'Katerina. My wife cannot dictate to me on any subject. Least of all where my honour is involved. I granted her boon and I, the Son of the Falcon, shall, as always, keep my word.'

Katerina had been defeated twice in succession. Prince Gurgen gave Katerina another surprise that night. He deflowered her.

When all was over and she had somewhat recovered, she thought it might be a good moment to renew the attack on the Sultzi woman. 'Darling, I am going to crave a boon of you, you wonderful man.' A snore was her answer.

The first three brides for Alexander were not available, but, as a last hope, Katerina asked herself why shouldn't he marry Iriné? There was nothing wrong with the girl physically – in fact she was undeniably handsome: her only fault was that she would say things that no decent, well-brought-up young woman would dare to utter – and say them at the wrong time and in the wrong place. That was what her craziness amounted to – and perhaps if she were the wife of a priest she would learn better. Katerina dropped a hint to Master Alexander who was unexpectedly receptive. Actually he liked Iriné's looks better than those of either of her half-sisters. There was, however, the fact of her illegitimacy. Katerina was realistic on the subject. 'If you marry her, I will force the Prince to give her a dowry of thirty thousand roubles. After all, just look at what he has saved by Salomé and Elisso's elopements.' The sum was more than Alexander had hoped for in his wildest dreams.

That evening he took Iriné by the hand and led her into an empty room. She went with him meekly.

'Will you marry me, Iriné?' he asked bluntly. No good beating about the bush.

'Tell me, is marriage decreed for the procreation of children?' asked Iriné rather surprisingly.

'Yes, dear Iriné. It is so ordained in the marriage service.'

'But,' and here Iriné affected great coyness, 'if we married, would it be possible for us to be blessed with children?'

'Without a doubt. Most certainly. If God so wills,' said Alexander, who was becoming embarrassed.

'But have you got any balls? Because, unless you have...'

Alexander Babishvili let go of her hand and jumped to his feet.

'I won't marry you unless you show them to me, because I don't believe you have any.'

Alexander turned his back to run.

'Don't be so shy. If we got married I should have to see them one day, if they exist...' Iriné called after him and then went into fits of laughter.

'That girl is possessed of demons. She must be exorcised,' Alexander reported to Katerina.

'Well, arrange for an exorcism, and perhaps if it is successful...' said Katerina.

'Not by me. Not by me,' said Alexander shuddering. After that he was careful to avoid both the person and the subject of Iriné. All that money lost and influential connections! And he must marry at once in order to be ordained! It was enough to drive him mad.

Although Valeri had been fully occupied all the afternoon and evening in the preparations for taking Tamar with him on his adventure, when he went to his room that night it was with eager anticipation, and the question: would Shorena come to his room? He was a very different man from the night before. Then he had been physically exhausted and had got drunk to deaden his sorrow and horror. But in twenty-four hours he had recovered. He was looking forward eagerly to the future. The idea of taking Tamar to her mother's people had captured his imagination; his sisters had escaped from the double tyranny of Katerina and of his father, so that he no longer need feel responsible for protecting them. Moreover he had only drunk one small glass of vodka and two of wine. He took off all his clothes and lay down on the leopard skin, waiting. It was too much to expect her to come. It was crazy of him even to want her to come. It would probably be better if she did not come. She certainly was not coming. But he waited as intently as a cat at a mousehole – and for the same sound – a light scratching.

There it was – a fingernail drawn lightly down the heavy wood. He tingled with excitement and relief and instantly was at the door. He took her hands, drew her in, flung his arms round her, and found her mouth – then drew back to look at her. He was in ecstasy, in triumph and at the same time he was able to see how coarse Shorena was compared with Tamar. Her mouth was heavy with thick lips, her face framed in two plaits of coarse black hair. Under her transparent silk covering, he could see that she had beautiful firm breasts with large nipples, a beautiful belly and slim waist, but that her thighs and calves were heavy. But when he met her eyes, he knew that she was the woman he wanted. Her coarseness was, in an odd way, a liberation. She was a woman who knew exactly how to give him the greatest pleasure and could use his body to extract the uttermost pleasure for herself. She had come for that and that alone. There was no pretence that she wanted anything but his body, or that she offered him anything more than the opportunity to enjoy hers. Yet her lovemaking was not animal: humans are infinitely more sensitive, imaginative, ingenious and beautifully various in the act of love than any of the beasts. The delicacy of human love can be matched by the butterflies perhaps; though, living in a more permissive society, they can never know the fierce pride of exclusive possession.

Valeri knew that he had to speak. He could not leave her tomorrow without a word.

'I am going away tomorrow, perhaps for a long time. I cannot live here in the Castle, while my father is married to Katerina,' he told her.

'I shall wait for you,' said Shorena.

'I shall be away for a long time.'

'Yes, I heard what you said to Tamar.' He thought that she was not really interested in where he went, or what he did, only in him when he was there. All she had understood was what she knew before: that he could not live in the Castle while Katerina was its mistress. When Katerina went, he would return.

'I am taking Tamar to her mother's people. They are Circassians who fled from the Russians into Turkey. And I might go and study in Alexandria.'

What he said meant little. Circassians who flee from Russians, that she understood. But of Alexandria and studying there, nothing at all.

'I am your woman now. I shall wait until you come back. I will wait all my life for a man like you,' she said, and Valeri knew that she meant it.

At that moment Valeri knew that he would come back to those big firm breasts, that slender twisting waist, the strong hips and the heavy lips that clung to his. It was useless to try and explain more.

'Yes, I'll come back,' he said and while he was saying it, knew that it was true.

When in the early hours, Shorena roused herself from sleep and slipped quietly off the couch and out of the room, Valeri, only half awake, was lazily aware that he had been strengthened and completed and that he was more sure of himself than ever before and he fell into a profound sleep. A few hours earlier, his eighty-year-old father had had similar cause for satisfaction.

CHAPTER FIVE

Tamar came to Valeri's room to wake him at dawn, and, as soon as she had done so, she noticed a pair of slippers by the bed – a pair of Anastasia's old slippers which she had given to the Sultzi woman, Shorena. She said nothing about them, perhaps because Valeri was speaking.

'I'll be ready in five minutes. We must get away before my father or Katerina is stirring.'

Nina, who had finished milking, was the only person awake and moving in the great hall. She exclaimed: 'The Lord bless us,' and crossed herself on seeing Tamar dressed in boy's clothes, but Valeri explained: 'I am taking Tamar back to her mother's people – perhaps only to visit – perhaps to stay.'

'Ah, you are taking her to the Tcherkesses! That's an idea.' And Nina nodded her approval and understanding. Then she said: 'Come with me, my Lord, and you too, my girl, and say a prayer to Saint Anne, our Saviour.'

Valeri hesitated, but he would not wound the old woman at that moment, so he went with her, Tamar following behind, and the three stood looking at the strangely living, light blue eyes in the little painting, lit by the flame of the eternally burning lamp. Nina fell on her knees and began murmuring her prayer, but Valeri and Tamar stood, as neither would kneel to that blood-soaked image. So they stood silently watching, looking first at the icon itself, then at the heap of Vasso's toys and old clothes, and then at the grey elf-locks and dirty neck of the old woman bowed down in her old brown dress, with the strings of her apron tied at the back. At last Nina finished her prayer and pushed herself back on to her legs. Then she went with them into the yard, where Malik and Herakli were waiting with the saddled horses and the pack-pony.

Nina kissed them each three times and signed the cross over them, and then Valeri wrung Malik and Herakli by the hand and they mounted. Malik watched them go in silence, but Herakli called out, 'Good cheer, Master,' as Valeri let his impatient mare have her head and rode out of the yard, leading the pack-pony. Tamar followed, and then Herakli let Tamar's colt out of the loose box, and it galloped out of the yard after her.

They did not speak until they had ridden all the way up to the lake, which was reduced to a mudflat with a broad central ribbon of water. Valeri had let the pack-pony go free as he rode up the last treacherous part, where one had to hug the cliff wall, and the pony, following its instinct, kept on safe ground, sometimes rubbing its pack against the rock. The colt straggling behind Tamar's mare did the same. Perhaps he remembered the time when he had come down that descent when he was only two or three days old.

When they were at the top, Valeri reined up and waited for Tamar to draw level with him.

'Farewell to Christ and good riddance to the Christians,' said Valeri.

'So we are turning Turk, are we? Luckily I'm in boy's clothes, or I should have to wear a yashmak!' When she had said that, the thought came: he has been getting in practice to have two wives already, but she could not speak of the slippers she had given to Shorena, by the bed.

Valeri laughed. 'I don't suppose we shall meet many yash-maks, or veiled houris, up here.'

'But don't you wish you could?' Tamar commented silently to herself.

The sun was hot. They followed the river up through the

148

forest. It no longer ran in a gorge but in an open wooded valley, for the limestone had given way to intrusive volcanic rock. The vegetation had changed also, conifers replacing birch and deciduous trees, and heather, box and butcher's broom. As they climbed higher they found more and more flowers in bloom: yellow foxgloves rising above the wet tumbled stones where a rivulet came under the trees, blue campanulas of many kinds flowering where they could get the sun, late-flowering orchids and gentians and eyebright everywhere. Then, suddenly, among the pines in more open order, came vast extents of rhododendrons in a blaze of white and yellow and magenta. When the valley opened to a grass plat, they stopped to eat, hobbled their horses and let them graze. Then they lay on their backs, stretched out in the sun. Valeri put his arm out and touched Tamar on the shoulder, but she moved away. Valeri slept for a little while, but she remained awake, looking at the sky, at the massed rhododendrons under the tall scattered pines and wondering, uncertain.

Directly Valeri woke, they caught their horses, unhobbled them and went on, Valeri leading, the pack-pony next, then Tamar and the colt bringing up the rear. Tamar was happy to get away from the Castle. It was the dream she had been longing for – and yet it was not quite her dream. She could not forget that pair of slippers by Valeri's bed, and she looked at his back, jogging along the trail ahead of her on his mare, resentfully. She knew she had no good reason for resentment, but she felt it all the same. After two or three hours, the scenery changed, the open forest and rhododendrons gave place to thicker forest and sharper hills. Then they came to an open pasture with the river, now reduced to a stream, running through it, all shut in by dark pine-woods, above which were snowpeaks which seemed close at hand.

'We had better camp here tonight,' said Valeri. 'We don't want to go above the tree-line. We shall have plenty of grass

149

for the horses and firewood and shelter here. We'll tackle the pass tomorrow.'

They chose a place between the edge of the forest and the stream for their tent which they pitched together. While Tamar unpacked and set out the food and the rugs they would need for the night, Valeri went into the forest with an axe to collect firewood.

'I saw a bear,' he said when he came back. 'He had been eating whortleberries, the ground is thick with them there – and I saw him for a moment running away uphill, among the trees.'

'What a pity you hadn't got your gun,' said Tamar.

Valeri shook his head. 'He didn't give me a chance to shoot, and, anyway, what should we do with a dead bear? But I expect there are all sorts of game up here. Wolves and leopards and deer and horned sheep higher up among the rocks.'

While Tamar was cooking, Valeri drove two pickets of the split pine branches deep into the ground and then stretched a rope between them and tied the horses to the rope, though Tamar had to come out to catch the young colt by his head-stall. Valeri did not want them to wander away, or to hobble them so that they could not put up a good defence with their heels, in a place where there were bears and, no doubt, wolves about.

They ate and had not finished when darkness fell, and Valeri threw more branches on the fire so that they could find the cheese which they had lost. Then he put on bigger logs which would burn nearly all night and they crawled into the tent and wrapped themselves in the rugs for sleep. After Tamar had lain down, Valeri sat upright and leaned over and kissed her. She said nothing, but shivered a little and drew away as far as she could on her side of the tent. After Valeri had lain down again she said: 'I expect you would rather that Shorena woman were here. I'm sorry, but I can't take her place.'

Valeri was silent for a while with surprise. Then he replied: 'So you know about that, do you?'

'I saw her slippers by your bed, when I woke you this morning.'

'Well, I don't regret her coming last night. But I don't want her here now. I would far rather have you with me, Tamar, just as you are.'

Tamar gave what she hoped was a sarcastic grunt and soon afterwards fell asleep. Though Valeri was tired and in want of sleep, he lay awake watching the flames leaping up in the fire outside and listened to the occasional hoot of an owl in the pinewood, or the nearer snort of a horse.

While it was still starlight, with only a faint pallor in the northeast, Valeri woke up and went outside. It was very cold, and the grass soaking wet, with icy cold dew for his bare feet. He stirred up the embers, threw on another couple of logs and went back to crawl under his rug. Tamar was invisible in the darkness of the tent, but he could hear her give a deep breath and then stir slightly, disturbed in her sleep by him.

She woke first. The sun had risen, there were long shadows in the corners of the glen, but the tent itself was in sunshine. It was bitterly cold, and she hastily pulled on the trousers and the jerkin she had discarded the previous night. Then she wrapped her rug around her and went out to blow up the fire. When she had put a pot of water on to boil she went and stroked the muzzle of her colt and blew a breath into his nostrils, which was a magic trick to make him love her.

Soon the pot was boiling, and she brewed tea and crawled into the tent on all fours, carrying a cup of it to Valeri, who woke up and looked so pleased and charming that she kissed him without thinking. Soon, both wrapped in rugs, they were sitting side by side, in the mouth of the tent, drinking tea and munching slices of rye bread and pieces of raw bacon.

'We shan't get any more of that. The Mohammedans don't eat pig,' said Valeri.

'Oughtn't we to save it?' asked Tamar.

'No. We must eat it up. Seeing us eating pig will make them think we are unclean.'

So Tamar cut herself a good rasher and toasted it over the fire. When Valeri said that the smell was so good that he wanted one too, she gave him hers and toasted herself another. After breakfast, they watered the horses and let them graze while they struck the tent and packed up. An hour later they were out of the trees and among dwarf alpine rhododendrons. Then these also fell away, and they were winding about on a mountain upland studded with granite boulders and luxuriant with wild flowers of every sort. Often they saw Bobak marmots, golden brown and short-legged, which galloped with tremendous energy to their burrows and then turned to look at the intruders with disdain. Overhead two eagles wheeled and in front of them rose the mountain they must pass. It was very hot and at that altitude the horses breathed deeply and sweated as though after a race, though they were only walking. They themselves were overheated. They rested for the midday meal in a wide valley where the stream came down tumbling from rock-pool to rock-pool.

Tamar said she would bathe and went to the side of the stream to undress, and when Valeri had hobbled the horses, he wanted to make a fire to brew tea, but they were above the tree-line and there were no sticks, something he had not thought of. By the stream, however, there were some reeds and the dry stalks of some kind of hemlock or angelica. He gathered a bundle which might make a blaze to heat water for tea and then reached the pool where Tamar was swimming. She was lovely and naked and laughed and waved her hand to him. 'It's icy!' she shouted, and next moment he saw to his horror that she had been swept to the far edge

152

and was helpless in the rush of the current which flung itself, in a miniature cataract, on to rocks eight feet below. But she caught a rock in the centre and clung to it hanging on the lip of the waterfall, helpless. Valeri ran as fast as he could and showed her the rope he had brought to bind up his bundle of dry reeds and stalks and threw one end across to her. The water snatched it, took it past her and she caught hold of it with one hand, holding on to the rock with the other. Valeri braced himself. 'Hold on with both hands,' he shouted, and with a steady pull had her in safety at the side of the pool. She came out frightened, and next moment he had her ice-cold body in his arms, pressing her to him and kissing her. She was pink all over, pearled with drops of water, with little rivulets running from her wet hair over her shoulders and down into the small of her back. Her breasts and nipples were tiny. It was the first time Valeri had seen her naked, and he could hardly bear to let her go, for her to dress, while he lit his bundle of reeds and boiled the water to make four cups of tea.

They camped that night early at the foot of the pass, for Valeri did not know how difficult it would prove and thought it better to have the whole day before them in case they had to lead the horses over one by one. Even before the sun set, it was bitterly cold, and, owing to his lack of foresight, they had no fire to keep them warm. They put their rugs together and, wearing all the clothes they had got, lay fully dressed in the tent, holding each other close for warmth. In spite of the intense cold, Valeri would have liked to make love to Tamar, and she was secretly hoping that he would and longed for an opportunity to respond. It seemed to Valeri wrong to take advantage of so young and inexperienced a child who was, besides, almost like his own sister. Eventually they fell into an uneasy coma.

Valeri woke early but waited until the sun had warmed the air. When he decided that they must move, he found that Tamar was warmer than he was. They had a miserable breakfast of bread and cheese and a cup of vodka each. Then they packed up with numb fingers, and set off for the pass. The horses were as dispirited as they were themselves. They had warmed up by the time they came to the steepest part, where they had to dismount and coax their horses up a track which had become almost like a staircase. There were one or two patches of snow in places which the sun reached for only a few minutes in the day.

At last they came out on to a small level patch at the summit, from which they could see the vague hills and broken country of Persia or Turkey below them. But when they turned and looked north, from where they had come, with the sun behind them, they could see in detail the ranges of hills they had traversed, and the plains reaching up to the Caspian Sea beyond: a view extending for a hundred miles and more. The descent facing them was easy, and soon they were able to ride abreast. The soil was more arid, and the forests below them sparser. Although they were both very hungry they pushed on, because they wanted to find a spot where there was both wood and water. Suddenly they came out of a sparse forest of tamarisk and found themselves in a huge circular field of luxuriant grass, ringed by mountain. It was, perhaps, the crater of a huge extinct volcano. Hundreds of horses were grazing near by, some of which pricked up their ears and ran to meet them. They were soon followed by two small boys wearing old fur caps and riding barebacked on ponies. They rode up to them fearlessly, calling out greetings that neither of them could understand. These boys were followed by others, and in a very short time they found themselves the centre of a bunch of half a dozen eagerly talking and gesticulating boys, addressing them in an incomprehensible tongue. Most of them were dressed in ragged shirts, with full woollen breeches which reached half-way down the calf of the leg. Their bare feet were thrust into loops of webbing or rope thrown over their ponies' backs. These served as stirrups. Two of the older boys had saddles and wore shoes. All of them wore sheepskin caps: sometimes they were astrakhan.

The boys pointed to the right and they went with their new friends to where a fire was burning beside a stream, bordered by willows. All of them flung themselves off their ponies, and Valeri and Tamar also dismounted, tied up their horses and sat down in the circle of boys, in the centre of which a large iron pot was set by the two boys who had been cooking by the fire. Tamar had to rummage for two spoons. Then they joined in, urged on by a boy who thought they were not eating enough or fast enough, and kept opening his mouth and waving his fingers in front of it, to urge them on. Another boy brought a wooden box full of reddish crystalline salt and scattered some in. The soup was made of lentils and mutton bones. Eating was serious, and the boys dipped their spoons regularly and did not talk much. When the pot had been finished to the last drop, the other pot was brought from the fire. It was full of rice with pieces of mutton and a few handfuls of raisins and dates. It was delicious and, urged on by gesture, Valeri and Tamar set to with as much diligence as their neighbours. Then the boys began telling them their names: the big boy who boasted a saddle and stirrups and shoes was Ameer. Another boy, next to him, was Ghulzi, a third Ali and a fourth Mohammed. Tamar called herself Timur, hoping it would not sound too strange.

Then, while some of the boys stretched themselves to rest on the ground and others chased each other in and out of the willows, Ameer, the boy in authority, made signs to Tamar and Valeri that they should go with him.

They mounted and rode with him to the far side of the prairie and from there followed a stream which led into a wooded valley. Dogs rushed out barking and snarling at the horses' heels. There were many sakls there – for that is what Valeri called them, as they were just like the sakls of the nomads that he had seen in a settlement near the town. That is, they were big circular huts, built of branches and sods of turf, with their roofs covered with turf – a hole in the middle to let out the smoke from the fire which burned in the centre.

Men and women came out to look at them and shouted questions, but Ameer seldom bothered to reply and led them to a large sakl, near the stream and shouted. A man and a woman came out. The man was short and dark with long twisted moustaches; the woman clearly a Georgian, though dressed in the sack-like dress of the Mohammedan tribeswoman. After Ameer had spoken, she greeted them haltingly in Georgian, and they alighted. The man took Valeri by the hand and the woman said that her husband would like them to be his guests. Valeri explained that they had come over the pass and were on their way to visit the Circassians. The woman said she had not heard of any Circassians and that the people they were among were Turkomans. They unloaded their pony and would have set up their tent, but the woman explained that they must stay with them in their sakl and added that they would be safer there.

They were at once invited to eat again, and although not hungry, Valeri told Tamar that they must accept, as he remembered that among Mohammedans the stranger who breaks bread with his host forges a bond between them. They were given bowls of mare's milk, barley bread and dates and raisins. The name of their host was Mirza, his wife Mzekala. She explained that every summer the Turkoman tribesmen, whose home was in the hills farther south, brought their flocks of sheep and horses to graze in the high mountains. In a few weeks they would start their trek back – a week's journey – to their own country. She herself was the daughter of two Georgians who had been taken as slaves, when they were children, by the Persians after they had captured Tiflis, but she had been born in Persia. When she was ten years old, her parents had run away, taking her with them. Their pursuers had overtaken them and killed them when they were sheltering among the Turkomans, but she had been away, playing with the children, and the tribes-men pretended they had never seen her, and brought her up as one of themselves.

This story was told as they sat in the sakl in front of a glowing fire of charcoal embers. Occasionally the woman would scatter pine cones on it and then a blaze would light up her face and the walls of the sakl, revealing the carpets on which they slept, the heaps of saddles and harness in one corner, cooking pots in another, guns slung on the wall, and the baby's cradle. They had two other children who came and stared at Tamar and then hung their heads and five minutes later were firm friends.

Tamar felt that she could trust this woman and took the opportunity when Valeri and Mirza had gone out to look to the horses, and the children had run out, to go up to Mzekala who was suckling her baby. Mzekala looked at the strange boy in surprise and hid her breast from him. Then Tamar said: 'I'm not what I seem. I'm a girl, and I ask you to help me to keep my secret while we are your guests.'

Mzekala settled to give her baby the breast openly and smiled knowingly. 'Well, I thought your voice was odd for a lad of your size. I thought you were a bit womanish and that your friend was one of those men who like boys better. You know, when you get to the towns lots of the men will be after you. Luckily my husband isn't like that, and there are not many of the tribesmen who are. Most of our men marry when they are young. Among us you'll run into more trouble with the girls coming to flirt with such a handsome boy as you are, and to provoke you into making love to them. You'll find them taking all sorts of liberties.'

Tamar sometimes wondered whether it was because she was dressed as a boy that Valeri avoided her, or whether it was because he was thinking with longing of Shorena. She saw very little of him after they had gone to live in Mirza's sakl. He would go off early in the morning on his mare and join a group of the men, one of whom, Rahman, talked a little Georgian. He would spend hours helping to herd horses, to brand yearlings, to break in two-year-olds, and then in sitting around a fire in the evening after work was done. And then when he came back at night he apparently preferred to talk to Mzekala than to Tamar.

Her first adoration was gone. Why, when she most needed his companionship, did he neglect her. Why did he linger on with these herdsmen? What was the reason for this idleness? What Tamar did not guess, and of which Valeri was himself almost unconscious, was that everything that had happened in the few days after he escaped from the monastery, everything that he had found at the Castle: Vasso's murder, Anastasia's suicide, his father's remarriage, had been a profound emotional shock, after which he needed a long period of rest in which to recover. That he, almost unconsciously, neglected Tamar was because her presence brought back all the horrors of the Castle and his lasting grief at Anastasia's suicide. It was because he was trying not to think of Anastasia, not because of any lecherous longing for Shorena, that he avoided Tamar. Indeed he rarely remembered Shorena and, when he did, it was with a happy smile. A wonderful woman to whom he would always be grateful, for she had come at the right time.

Each day started in the same way. Then each was different. In the morning, early, Tamar would go with Mzekala into the fenced enclosure where their four brood mares were shut up for the night apart from their foals. Together they would catch the reluctant brown mare, put a nosebag with a handful or two of oats in it, or some locust beans, on her, and Tamar would hold her head, while Mzekala would milk her little black velvety udder with her right hand into a jug she held with her left. The mare was always more fidgety than a cow. Mzekala would seldom take more than a pint from each of the mares. Tamar would talk to the creature who tossed her head, throwing up the nosebag so as to get the last bean out of the bottom, and, although not minding being milked, felt she had to put up a show of independence. One of the mares was able to hold back her milk and needed coaxing and petting before she would let it down. One of them would kick forward at the little jug, and Mzekala would swear and hit her as hard as she could with her open hand.

When they had been milked, the mares were let out to graze by themselves, and the foals were not turned out for an hour or two, when their mothers would have milk to give them. The bucket of milk was mixed with some of the previous day's koumiss and put near the fire, covered with a cloth. By evening it was fermenting strongly, and it formed a chief part of their evening meal.

Tamar's colt had grown into a magnificent animal. He was a trifle taller than his sire, but with the same lovely Arab head and splendid proportions. All he had inherited from his dam was her skewbald colouring and her hardiness and strength. It was time to break him in to the saddle, which Tamar proceeded to do with Mirza's help.

First there was the business of bitting him and making him run in circles on the lunging rein. Then saddling him and exercising him with a 'dumb jockey' – in this case a sack of corn strapped to the saddle. In spite of his fire, the colt which Tamar had called Byron, after the English poet who had died in Greece fighting against the Turks, was so fond of her and of her caresses that he let her have her way. The first time that Mirza mounted him, he bucked and reared, but Mirza was a fine horseman with good hands and he did not punish him, and the horse was intelligent enough to understand what he wanted and very soon to enjoy being ridden.

'They keep telling me that he ought to be cut, but I would like to keep him entire,' said Tamar.

'It would be a shame to do that. He's one of the best horses I have ever handled. I would like to breed from him,' said Mirza. Tamar did not forget this remark.

Sometimes one of their neighbours would come round to say that he had killed a sheep, and they would go to his sakl, where the men would sit in a circle round a metal bath tub heaped with rice and roast mutton. The men would cut pieces of meat off the joints with their knives and then scoop up a ball of the rice, yellow with saffron and strongly spiced with garlic, peppers, cardamom and coriander. When they had eaten their fill and the relics of the feast had set with cold mutton fat, the woman of the house and a daughter would carry off the tin and afterwards would bring them coffee, and the men would light a pipe and talk. Though Valeri and Tamar could not understand what they said, they knew that the men were not telling anecdotes, or making jokes, or relating personal experiences, but were uttering pearls of wisdom. For after each pithy sentence the listeners would either nod their heads in agreement, or shake them doubtfully, or shrug their shoulders. One by one, they would look at the sun and start up and go off to the task they had set themselves that morning, without a word of thanks, or a good-bye to their host. All salutations and ceremony were reserved for the time of arrival and the acceptance of the first mouthful.

At the setting of the sun, one of the older men who wore a turban would cry out the name of God in a piercing high-pitched voice, and some of the men would kneel and put their foreheads to the earth, while others and the women paid no attention. In the evening, there was always a big bonfire somewhere and the sound of the accordion, and then, in the light of the flames, boys and men would begin dancing. Valeri and Tamar would wander over to watch. Sometimes the girls danced, sometimes the young men, but they did not dance together like the Georgians, and each sex seemed to watch the other surreptitiously.

Mzekala's warning about the girls proved true. Two or three of them would wander by Mirza's sakl, and, if Tamar showed herself, the boldest of the girls would call out and the other girls would giggle. One day Tamar thought she would try being enterprising and walked up lackadaisically to the girl who was making the remarks and, when she was facing her, suddenly thrust a hand into her bosom and gave a slap on the bottom. This produced a shriek, and the girl jumped away like a wild cat. Tamar gave a complacent laugh and went back into the sakl. After that the girl always glowered at her angrily, if they chanced to meet.

One morning the boy who had led them to Mirza's sakl came along and, with Mzekala translating, invited Tamar to come with him to a shooting match, and to bring his gun. Mzekala assured her that it would be all right, so Tamar saddled her mare, took her Martini rifle and cartridges and went with him. They rode over to the far side of the prairie where the grass was poor and white. There was already a group, or rather two groups, of boys, most of whom were armed with bows and arrows, though a few had old flint-locks. A row of targets had been set up against the side of the hill, and two of the older men were in charge of the proceedings. The boys were being trained to shoot. The targets for the archers were turf, and planks for the boys with guns. One of the groups of boys were the shepherd lads, the other the horse-herders. Each of the archers had nine arrows. He shot three at the target standing, three from the saddle with his horse standing, and three riding past the target at a trot. Several of the horse-herders were successful in shooting arrows from the saddle with their horses trotting. They were far better than the shepherd lads, because they spent much of their day on horseback, rounding up the herds of horses, while the shepherds were lying asleep by their flocks.

When all the archers had shot their arrows came the turn of the boys with guns. They only had three shots each, because of the expense of powder and bullets. Tamar was at an advantage, though she did not realise it, because her Martini was a far more accurate weapon than their old guns. For this reason she came out well, hitting the target both

161

standing and from the saddle with her horse stationary. She missed when firing at a trot. One of the shepherd boys was, however, a brilliant marksman and hit the target with each of his shots. For that reason the team of shepherd gunners was judged to have won. The man marking had a pail of lime and, after each hit, smeared whitewash over the bullet hole. Ameer had bad luck. He hit the target standing, but just as he fired from the saddle his pony stamped because of a horse-fly, and he missed the target when riding at a trot. However he was very proud of his friend's success – Timur had shown that he was a good shot and no milksop.

One evening Mirza took them to a far corner of the prairie where eight young men were playing a game on horseback, something they had never seen before. Each of them had a long stick with a wooden head with which they hit a lump of wood while riding. There were four of them on each side, and their object was to drive it in opposite directions. It was not long before one of them lost his seat and fell while going at a gallop. One of the spectators at once took his place, while another went to catch the pony of the man who had been thrown. Neither Valeri nor Tamar had imagined that such skilful riding was possible, or that ponies could be so well trained, for they seemed to understand just what was required of them and to enjoy the game as much as their riders.

Valeri would have liked to have learned this wild game, but Mirza told him bluntly that he was not a good enough horseman, and that the young tribesmen would find him a nuisance if he asked them to teach him. Valeri was furious when Mzekala translated this in her bad Georgian. He realised it was true and went out alone on his mare that afternoon to try and knock a lump of wood about with a long stick.

Tamar had been full of excitement about her success in shooting and boasted to Valeri about it, suggesting they should practise together.

To her surprise he said: 'We have found the most wonderful people here living in the Golden Age. I hope you will want to settle down, because I should like to live with them forever.'

Tamar gazed at him in astonishment. 'I thought we were only staying for a few days, and then going on to find my mother's people. You talked of studying in Alexandria.'

'I suppose I did at one time. But don't you feel that this primitive life gives you everything that one can possibly want?' Valeri was obviously in earnest.

Tamar thought he must be crazy and replied: 'Well, I'm a woman. I don't propose to live the rest of my life disguised as a boy. And we are living on these people as their guests.'

Valeri looked a little ashamed of himself and said: 'Forgive me, my dearest sister. I have been neglecting you. And of course you are anxious to find your mother's people.'

Tamar wondered if she were always to be Valeri's dearest sister and whether some Turkoman woman had been setting her cap at him as that Sultzi woman had done. She felt deeply critical of him. He had set off in order to denounce the Christian religion to the Turks and to study the wisdom of the Arabs at Alexandria, and here he was, a few weeks later, wanting to settle down for life with a lot of nomads. Perhaps he would not think that they lived in the Golden Age if he could speak their language.

A little later he asked her to saddle her horse and go with him to a secluded spot and try and knock a bit of wood about with a long stick.

She refused, and, after he had gone off alone, she took her rifle and went off in the opposite direction to practise shooting. Mzekala had told them that in two weeks they would leave the mountains and return to their own country, driving their herds before them. But the weather suddenly changed. A cold wind got up, there was thunder in the night, and next morning there was a light sprinkle of snow.

163

A council was called, and the unanimous decision was to pack up and leave at once, as if the winter came as early as it threatened, it would be a serious matter getting the sheep through snow out of the high mountain. Frenzied activity followed. Pack saddles were brought out, fitted and mended; all the carpets on the sakls rolled up, cooking pots fitted in each other and put in netting bags, trusses of hay piled up. By the early morning of the third day, the trek began with the departure of the herds of sheep and goats with the mounted shepherds and their dogs, and a certain number of pack animals loaded with trusses of hay. Early next morning the women and children left, with a guard of the older men and all the pack animals. Only the younger men and horse-boys who were to round up and follow with the herds of horses remained. Valeri and Tamar were asked to go with these because they could be useful. Their pack-pony had gone with Mzekala. After she had gone, they had no interpreter. Mirza also had gone with the men guarding the women. The sakls were left swept and bare, the smokehole of the roof covered, and the entrance closely shut up against drifting snow. So it would remain until the Turkomans returned the following summer. Getting the herds of horses to leave the prairie was a long and difficult task. All the men and boys were wanted. Time and again the herd was brought to where they would have to leave the prairie and funnel out along the track going down through the forest. Time and again one or two of the stallions would break away, and a stream of wild-eyed horses after them. Then followed a wild chase. Tamar and Valeri, being well mounted, often found themselves in the lead, heading off a racing band. Valeri had the satisfaction of being able to show that even if he could not play polo, he could beat most of them in a straight race and that his seat was as firm as any. Once Tamar found herself in the middle of the herd, all galloping madly and swerving as the outlying herdsmen with their long whips closed in. There was the drumbeat of hoofs, an occasional scream from one of the stallions, a sea of tossing manes, tails all stretched out straight behind them, wicked glances all about her. One sorrel came sidling in towards her with its lips drawn back and gums showing, ready to bite, but she lashed out with her knout catching it round the muzzle and it changed direction. Then, while they were galloping at top speed, the leaders wheeled and rushed back in a solid phalanx of horseflesh. It was only the agility of her mare that saved her from their being knocked over together.

At last the herdsmen got the herd bottled up in the corner in a solid mass, from which the leaders dashed on to and down the track, kicking and squealing and cannoning into each other impatiently, until the whole herd funnelled out and dashed down the track at a wild gallop. Luckily all the women and children with the pack-horses were by this time several hours ahead, or there would have been disaster. The next problem was for some of the herdsmen to get ahead of the herd, but this was impossible until they were out of the high mountains and the track widened. By then it was almost dark, the sun had set over Ararat, and the wildest of the horses were tired. There was a full moon and it was very cold. They kept on, hour after hour, through the night until the lights of the women's and children's encampment shone across the river. They rode up, fell off their horses exhausted, leaving the younger women to unsaddle them and water and feed them and tie them up, while they drank some hot tea, ate a little kasha and fell asleep. The great herd of horses was left to look after itself. Tamar was dead beat, and it needed all her resolution not to ask to be allowed to go with Mzekala next morning, when the women and pack-animals moved off, soon after dawn. But next day it was easy enough jogging along. The herd was a mile down the river where there was good grazing. They did not start until the sun was high and the air was warm and they had all had a good breakfast that the women had left for them. There was no trouble with the herd. The horses streamed along quietly, with boy outriders on each side and a party of men in front and behind. When they came to a village, the inhabitants had shut themselves in their houses and looked out from cracks in fear at the wild unknown mountain men who brought their flocks and herds through their lands in early summer, and again in autumn. Before evening, the Turkomans were facing the chief difficulty of their march – the town of Tabriz. When the herd reached the bazaar, Tamar who had been one of the boys riding alongside it, hung back and waited till the last of the horses had passed and a band of twenty armed men, riding four abreast, brought up the rear. Valeri was among them and Tamar signalled to him. When he pulled up beside her, she asked: 'Have you any money? Could we buy a cake of soap?'

This was their undoing. The backs of the Turkoman rearguard were disappearing in the distance, and the next moment police officers were threatening them with drawn pistols. Both of them had their rifles slung. Valeri's sabre was packed away on the pony in Mzekala's care. Had Valeri been alone, he would probably have made a dash for it, but he had to think of Tamar. So they made no resistance and were taken off to the police station. There they were separated. Valeri was put in a cell by himself and Tamar taken at once to the chief of police for interrogation.

He addressed her in broken Russian, but as she did not know a word of that language he might as well – indeed better – have addressed her in Persian. Her lack of understanding was taken as insolence, particularly as she tried to smile and look cheerful.

At an order she was thrown on the ground, her hands tied behind her back and her knees and ankles bound. Then her riding boots were pulled off and she was bastinadoed: that is beaten on the soles of her feet. After every half-dozen or more strokes the man who was beating her paused, and the chief of police asked her a question in Russian. She could only reply in screams, curses and entreaties in Georgian, and in the few words of Persian she had picked up from Mustapha Sasun and his wife. She did not afterwards remember how long this scene of torture lasted: it seemed for ever. Nor did she remember how it ended.

When she came to herself she was lying on a plank in a small cell and the pain in her feet was appalling. They were bleeding and had swollen to a monstrous size. She lay there for two days.

Valeri and Tamar first met as they were about to be taken to the court. He looked down and saw a little hunched up creature crawling towards him like an ape, with its hands taking as much of the weight off its feet as possible. At first he did not recognise this broken, shuffling object. Then he saw it was Tamar, her rosy face grey, her short hair matted and filthy. She looked up at him sideways and her blue eyes held the expression of a trapped wolf. Valeri broke away from the policeman holding his arm and ran to her. Only then did he see her distorted swollen feet which left prints of blood and pus wherever they touched the ground. The policeman, who had drawn his pistol, returned it to its holster as Valeri bent and picked her up and held her in his arms. She gave him an unexpected smile, her first for three days. With Valeri carrying her, they came to the courthouse. There the policeman dragged her out of his arms.

'Valeri, you will ruin us. Have pity on me and accept everything,' wailed Tamar, for he had been about to hit the policeman, but at her cry he submitted and was handcuffed, and Tamar was handcuffed too, for it was a police regulation that all prisoners should be handcuffed in court. But the policeman was a kindly man and took pity, so he lifted Tamar up, putting one leg over each of Valeri's shoulders so that she was sitting astride high up, holding on with her handcuffed hands by his hair and her bleeding feet hanging down to his waist. Like that they went into the courthouse. The clerk of the court was sitting in an outer room. He looked up with interest when this strange couple were brought in. Then he motioned to the police guarding them, and they were brought in front of him. He addressed Valeri in Russian. Valeri could understand and talk a little Russian and was able to say: 'I'm not Russian. I'm Georgian.'

'Can you speak Georgian?'

'It's my language.'

The clerk said something in Persian and a man at the back of the court came forward. 'I'm the interpreter,' he said in Georgian.

'I am Prince Valeri, Son of the Falcon.'

'You are accused of being a Russian spy who got into the town on the heels of the Turkomans.'

'I am a Georgian, not a Russian.'

'Even if you are a Georgian – and you certainly speak the language all right – you might be a Russian spy.'

'I am Prince Valeri, Son of the Falcon, and the Russians are my enemies, who are invading my country.'

'Can you prove it? Do you know anybody in this town?'

Valeri was silent. He could prove nothing.

Suddenly Tamar cried out in a desperate voice: 'We know Mustapha Sasun, the silversmith.' The interpreter said something to the clerk of the court, and the clerk spoke to a policeman.

Then the interpreter said, not unkindly, 'We have heard of such a man. If he is in the town we will fetch him, if he wishes to come. Now you will go into the court with the other accused. I will come with you, as I shall be wanted.'

The court was full, and on a sofa sat a small man with the yellowest skin and the most vindictive expression that Tamar had ever seen. The accused were crowded in the back half of the room. Luckily Valeri's explanation to the interpreter had led to their being the last of the accused. This meant that there was a little longer for Mustapha Sasun to be found and fetched. Nevertheless the judge worked through the cases before him with terrifying speed. One by one, the accused were brought forward, and a policeman explained the charge.

'That man Ibrahim is accused of striking a tax-collector.'

The judge spoke and the interpreter whispered: 'He says it is treason and that there is no defence. The man is to be beheaded.'

The accused was dragged out mumbling and another man pushed forward.

'He is a thief who stole a donkey. He says it was dark and he mistook it for his own.'

'The judge says: have his ears cropped.'

'This man is a servant who was taken in adultery with his master's daughter.'

'The judge says he is to be impaled.'

At this sentence, a woman in the court screamed out.

'She says she will marry him and that her father agrees.'

'The judge says that he cannot alter the law. The punishment for rape by a servant is impaling. If it was not rape, she is guilty and her punishment is death by hanging. As she accused him, the judge gives her the benefit of the doubt.'

'If the idiot woman hadn't accused him, nobody would have known,' said Tamar.

'Fortunately women feel differently about this sort of thing,' said the interpreter, shocked.

'This man was caught passing false money.'

'Nail him through the ears to the notice board outside the police station.'

So the cases went on, but after a little the interpreter stopped whispering, for he was a kindly man and he noticed that Valeri was becoming angrier after each of the sentences, and he knew that it always went hard with an accused if he were angry.

Finally Valeri and Tamar were brought forward, and charged by the police with being Russian spies.

'He denies the charge and has sent for a witness to identify him,' said the interpreter.

The judge asked something, and from behind them they heard the voice of Mustapha Sasun.

'The judge is asking if he can identify you,' said the interpreter. Sasun came forward and looked very carefully at Valeri and Tamar. Then he spoke to the judge.

'He says that he cannot be sure about the boy. It was two years ago and the boy may have grown, but that the man is Prince Valeri, Son of the Falcon. He is saying also that he lived for nearly three months in your father's aoul, and that your father sheltered him from the Russians.

'The judge is telling the clerk to make out a firman which will protect the Georgian Prince wherever he wishes to travel in the Persian empire.'

They left the court, Valeri carrying Tamar in his arms, following Mustapha Sasun through the town, but noticing nothing – not the latticework doors, the heavily barred windows and the gables of the houses jutting out over their heads – not the throng of turbaned and tarbushed Persians, Kurds, Turkomans, Tatars, with a sprinkling of Afghans, Armenians, Turks and Arabs. For Valeri walked in a delirium of anger, indignation and longing for revenge, which blinded him. Tamar was also blind, for not only was she half-dead with pain and exhaustion, but she had a migraine and had shut her eyes against the alternating brilliant sunshine and shade in the alleys through which Mustapha led them. So they came to the silversmith's house, where his wife greeted them with cries of recognition, welcome, and then horror as she saw Tamar's feet.

'You'll be a girl now, while you stay with me,' she declared. Valeri's fury was not allayed when Mustapha, who had been back to the police station, returned with the two horses, but with the news that the police had confiscated the Martini rifles and Valeri's pistol.

'I shall drag the fellow who has stolen them before the judge,' Valeri exclaimed, and he was on the point of going to the police station himself, but was pulled up by Kamela

Sasun saying, 'The sooner you leave this town the safer it will be for all of us!' Then as he stared at her, she went on: 'My husband didn't save you from being tortured and then killed, in order that he and I should be thrown in prison for harbouring a fellow who makes trouble with the police. Off you go, first thing tomorrow. My husband will buy you a gun of some sort, as you may need one on your journey.'

Valeri realised that what Kamela had said was true: that if he stirred up trouble with the police, they were quite likely to revenge themselves upon the silversmith and his wife. Next morning he said good-bye to Tamar and his hosts and rode off leading Tamar's riding horse, which Sasun could not stable or look after, and carrying a cheap sporting gun made in Birmingham, which Mustapha had bought him in the bazaar. Kamela told him that in the spring, after Tamar had completely recovered, she would bring her to rejoin him at the Turkoman camp.

'We can't manage anything before that. Mustapha has too much work on hand in the town. But we'll come as early as we can. Soon after the almonds are in blossom. It will be a pleasant excursion for us.'

With that Valeri had to be content.

His departure was a relief – not only for Mustapha and Kamela but for Tamar. In the morning Mustapha would carry her into the garden where she was able to lie idly on a bench in the shade of the carob tree, listening to the splash of the fountain, the whistle of the mynah bird and the gentle tapping of Mustapha's hammer coming from the little workshop at the end of the garden. Then she would fall asleep until Kamela came out with trays of food and all ate together.

After she had begun to get better and was not perpetually exhausted, she told the silversmith that she would like to watch him at work. He carried her then to his shed, laid her on a bench, propping up her feet and then, paying her no attention, would spend the morning with his watch-maker's glass screwed into his eye, filing, or soldering if he were setting jewels into a brooch, smelting in his little furnace, or tapping with his little hammer if he were inlaying enamel or gold wire, or if he were making a silver bowl. One day Tamar asked him why he was such a happy man.

He seemed surprised. 'Am I a happy man? Well, why not?'

'The world around us is full of cruelty and injustice. The great fight for power and to keep it, and invariably use it to oppress and to interfere with the lives of weaker people. You live surrounded by all this, and you know that at any moment you may be falsely accused, robbed of all your possessions, tortured and put to death. Yet you go on making your lovely jewellery as happily as the swallows who fly in and out to their nests.'

Mustapha looked at her with merry eyes. 'Nothing you could have said could please me more. In a month or two the swallows will have come back from Africa, and I run great risk of thieves because of them. They build their nest on the rafter here, and when they are nesting I cannot lock up my workshop and, you know, I often leave emeralds and rubies lying about, most of which do not belong to me. Luckily swallows are not like magpies and jackdaws which are always on the look-out for something bright and shining. Years ago I missed a silver brooch and, I am sorry to say, I suspected a little girl. I knew it was not an ordinary thief because there had been a heavy gold chain lying beside it on the bench, which was not taken. Two years later I swept the chimney, blocked by a jackdaw's nest, and there was the silver brooch taken as a plaything for the young jackdaws. Now I shoot any magpie or jackdaw that comes into the garden.'

'You have talked about birds, but you haven't told me why you are such a happy man,' said Tamar.

'I did not know I was so happy. I am too busy thinking

all the time of new designs, and variations on the old designs, and of ways of making the jewellery of my imagination, to ask myself if I am happy or not.'

'Do you sometimes reflect that what you are making in this shed will make the eyes of young women sparkle with pleasure and the necklaces and silver belts you make will go on giving delight for hundreds of years after you are dead, because of the perfection of your work?' asked Tamar.

'What a nice thing to have said to me. No, I don't think about people, but about the things themselves and whether I have been able to do what I intended. There is a great art in the juxtaposition of precious stones: pearls and rubies, for example.'

'Are you not terrified of thieves?'

'Not really. It is fate. Like catching an illness. I have been lucky so far.'

'So you are happy because of your work?'

'Yes. I am happy because I can carry out my ideas. Rich men come and ask me to work for them. Jewellers bring me the stones they want to have set – but I only do the work that I want to do. I am a master now. I was unhappy when I was a young man and no one would trust me with the gold and diamonds and rubies which I believed I needed. But I made do with garnets and peridots and smoky quartz, set in tin instead of silver, and soon discerning people were coming and buying my work and saying that my agate brooches were masterpieces. Yes, Tamar, I am happy, and so is any man who can express his ideas in his work and do it in his own way.'

CHAPTER SIX

A few days after Valeri's departure, the Archpriest and Alexander Babashvili went back to the town, and Prince Gurgen was left as the only male living in the inner apartments of the Castle. Under the regiment of women it broke up into components, which had little contact. The Prince and Katerina occupied their bedroom, the Great Hall and the Chapel of Saint Anne, Nina the kitchens and dairies. It was only when Katerina came to issue orders for the day, or when Nina appeared in order to execute them, that they met.

Iriné lived in her room at the bottom of the tower and amused herself by climbing cliffs and precipices where few boys or men would venture their necks. Shorena, living in what had been Valeri's room at the top of the tower, rarely appeared except to carry away food and drink to her eyrie.

Six weeks after Valeri had gone, she went to the little room next to the kitchen where Nina slept and spent the time when she was not working. The door was ajar. She pushed it open and saw the old woman telling her beads.

'May I come in and speak to you?' she asked.

'Yes, dear. I often wonder what you do up there alone all day. If it were not such a climb I would have come to see you.'

'Alone all day – and all night too,' said Shorena.

'So I have noticed.' Nina gave a childish laugh and went on: 'You know I thought you were the sort of woman who cannot live without a lover.'

'I am that sort of woman. But I told Valeri that I would wait for him, and now I believe that I am going to bear him a child.'

174

Nina looked at Shorena very sharply.

'You were to marry Lazar, Ziklauri's son, who murdered my darling Djamlet in the hour of his wedding and who later paid the penalty...'

'Valeri killed Lazar when he was sorry for what he had done and had gone to plant lilies of the valley on the grave. I came with our men to burn the Castle in revenge, because we could not get at Valeri, who was locked up in the monastery. If Ziklauri had bought him from the Archimandrite, I would have tortured him and killed him very slowly. But Ziklauri has always wanted to end the feud and is not a man of blood. Then, after the earthquake, I was taken prisoner, and suddenly Valeri arrived and ordered them to take off our chains and I was given a bath and new clothes by Tamar. It seemed to me then that the opportunity had come for me to kill Valeri.'

'I was afraid of that when he set you all free. It was very rash of him. But he has always done rash things,' said Nina.

'I went with Tamar to the room at the top of the tower, Valeri's room which is mine now, where Tamar had left her things – dresses and jewellery. Valeri was there. He talked to Tamar, and I stood behind her and listened to the man I wanted to kill.'

Nina smiled, visualising the scene. She still counted her beads mechanically. She was enjoying this visit.

'I had never heard a man speak like that. Not even Ziklauri. What he said was beautiful. I saw he was nobler, better, finer, than any man I had known. He was so truthful. I agreed with every word he said, though you would not have agreed. Listening to him and watching him, I fell in love, and that night and the next night I went to his room. He was drunk the first night, and it would have been easy to kill him ... Well, I promised that I would wait for him until he came back. And I shall have a child of his to show him.'

'Are you sure?'

'Yes, I think I am sure.'

175

'Are you sure that it is his?' Nina did not even look at Shorena as she asked this question.

'I have not slept with any other man for three months.'

At these words Nina did look up. 'So you had other lovers besides Lazar?'

Shorena looked at her contemptuously. 'After Lazar's murder I slept with one man after another. But it was no good. It helped at the time. Then I thought I would stop. So I stopped. It is no good ... without ... unless it is all of you at once. Nothing kept back.'

Nina with some difficulty got up out of her chair.

'You came to ask me if I would help you. Of course, I will help you, my dear, when your time comes. I would have helped you whoever the father was. But for Valeri, you understand ... It looks as though I should have my hands full as a midwife in May because Katerina is going to have a baby too.'

'Who is the father?' asked Shorena.

'Her husband, of course,' said Nina.

'Not that divinity student? Babashvili?'

Nina was shocked. 'You ought not to say things like that. No, I could tell next morning it was the Prince. You know, after I made the bed.' Then the old woman chuckled and added: 'Anyway Alexander Babashvili wouldn't have the spunk in him to get a woman with child.' She cackled loudly. 'Pah, what a nasty man! You must go now. It's almost time for the Prince to have that Turkish coffee that he likes so much.'

During the following months, during the pregnancies of his wife and of Shorena, Prince Gurgen's establishment dwindled. The older men, mostly with wives and two of them with children not yet grown up, remained. These were Malik, the baker Souliko, the head stableman Herakli, the old shepherd David, the mason Johann, whose father had been a German colonist killed in an accident, the blacksmith Tamyas and the ploughman Ohota. But the young men and boys disappeared. Irakli, Tengiz, Sumbat, Ramin, Temur and others whom it is not worth naming, quietly vanished. Of them all only the cripple Vakhtang, who could read and write and speak and read Russian, remained.

At first Prince Gurgen was not aware of their desertion, for he kept mostly indoors during the winter, and Malik, whose duty it was to have told him, put off the unpleasant task from day to day and week to week. Perhaps one or two of them might come back. One day, however, the Prince called Malik and suggested a shoot.

'Send all the boys and the more reliable of the children out as beaters under Irakli, and you and I – and, well, as we are short of guns, I think as an exception, we could include the mason and the blacksmith with us in the line and Souliko, if he cares to come.'

These exceptions, of including mere working men among the guns, who by tradition should all have been of noble birth, had been made ever since the death of Djamlet and Valeri's entry into the monastery. It was all wrong, of course, but what else could the Prince do?

'I don't quite know what has happened to the boys. They've gone off somewhere,' Malik confessed uneasily.

'Gone off? Gone off where? And by whose orders, pray?' exclaimed the Prince.

'No one's orders, my Lord. They have just disappeared.'

'Disappeared? I don't understand what you mean!' said the Prince, genuinely puzzled.

Malik said nothing but his looks showed his abject distress.

The Prince continued: 'Are you telling me that we must postpone the shoot because the boys are away without leave?'

'It's because of making peace with Ziklauri,' burst out Malik. 'That is the trouble. While the feud was on, it wasn't safe for them to go to the town. But now peace has been made and they found out they could go wherever they liked. So they have gone off to the town. Some have taken jobs there, I've heard. Others have joined up with the Solutz, and are living in Ziklauri's encampment. They do say that Ramin was taken for the Russian army.'

'Get out! You can't keep discipline,' screamed the Prince.
Then, as Malik made to go, he shouted: 'Wait a minute.
Where are you slinking off to? If any of those lads shows
his face here, take the skin off his back. It's outrageous. If
the Tatars chose to attack us, we would only be half a
dozen men. It needs a dozen to man the defences – fifteen or
twenty, allowing for casualties.'

'I know, my Lord. The young people have no respect, nowa-
days.'

'It's all Valeri's fault. That old fox Ziklauri made a fool of
him. Should have made him swear fealty, if he wanted to
make peace. Valeri treated him as an equal: he's a mere
commoner and a rebel. And just after Saint Anne had saved
us by a miracle and put us on top. We ought to have cut
those five fellows' throats, not feasted them and let them
go.'

The Prince stumped back into his bedroom, and the shoot
was abandoned, although later on Malik organised a less pre-
tentious one of his own, 'to keep the deer out of the field of
winter wheat'.

The question of what the Prince was to do to exert his
authority was discussed by him endlessly with Katerina, who
was almost as much upset by the defections as he was himself.

Her first suggestion, that the Prince should write a letter
to Ziklauri asking for their return, he absolutely refused. It
would be treating the fellow as an equal, which was morally
wrong, and moreover it wouldn't have the slightest effect.
Katerina then proposed that he should write to the Russian
Governor of the town. After all, the Russians had a short
way with runaway serfs, and that is what these boys actually
were, whatever they might fancy. The Governor would
understand that those in authority had to stand by each
other. But though the Prince recognised that the Russian
Governor was far more likely to act than Ziklauri, he felt it
was highly dangerous to draw his attention to the aoul. Then,

someone might tell him about the Persian silversmith, Mustapha Sasun, whom he had harboured not so very long ago. The Governor might send a squadron of Cossacks up the track and demand the Castle's surrender – and send Katerina and him off to St Petersburg. Such things had been happening in the last few years all over Georgia – and not only to the Mohammedan tribes. He was eighty and she was pregnant: it would be a pretty set-out of they had to take refuge in Turkey, like Prince Tcherkess and his people!

A possibility often discussed, finally resolved upon, then postponed indefinitely, was to organise a recruiting campaign. The Russians had been enlisting all the Tcherkessian men who hadn't fled to Turkey and a lot of the Chechens, why should not the Prince do the same – on a much smaller scale, of course?

'It would be far better to have foreign mercenaries, even though one might have to pay them something, than to have back those boys who are now on friendly terms with the Solutz,' said Katerina.

The Prince agreed and declared: 'Under Ziklauri the Solutz were unable to capture the Castle in an act of war, even though they brought a cannon and ladders: now they are corrupting my men. If they came back, who could trust them? Ziklauri would come as a friend with his men, occupy the Castle and take it over. We are safer without those treacherous lads. I would like to get hold of them to take the skin off their backs. But I would never trust them again.'

The desertion of his young men broke the Prince up. He became more and more cautious and stealthy in his movements, and always carried loaded firearms, either on his person or close within reach. He trusted no one: literally no one, except Katerina and Nina and to a large extent Malik. It was because of this distrust, and his fear that some inmate of the Castle might betray him, that Katerina was able to oust Shorena from Valeri's room on the top floor of the tower.

179

'It's madness of us to let one of the Sultzi live up there. She can signal to anyone without our knowing; I dare say that she does signal every night. And you remember that Salomé shot one of the besiegers...'

'Never mention the name of that treacherous little viper...' the Prince broke in.

'Well Tamar then. She shot one of the Sultzi from the tower. This creature could easily shoot one or two of the *defenders* if we were attacked – and there are not so many of us.' So Shorena was sent down to live in a room in the aoul between the bakehouse and the room where the cripple boy lived.

Although not intended as such, it was a kindness. It saved her climbing up and down the stairs during the last stages of her pregnancy, and it led to her making friends with Vakhtang. In his spare time he used to make artificial flies out of all sorts of birds' feathers, and he would bring his tweezers set in a log of wood and his silk threads and feathers, scissors and little hooks, and make them with extraordinary skill, while talking to her. He was a strange boy with large dark eyes and a curious hesitating manner. When Shorena asked him a question, he would wait for so long before answering that she often wondered if he had heard what she had said. But Vakhtang always considered every question in all its aspects, and, if he detected an ambiguity in it, he would amuse himself by giving an answer to its most unlikely meaning.

One day she asked him if he would teach her to read and write.

'It all depends,' said Vakhtang.

'Depends on what?'

'Depends on whether you really want to learn, for one thing.'

'Haven't you got a better reason than that?'

'If you fell in love with the Russian language, you might come to pretend that you were a Russian.'

'You would not like me to become a Russian, then?' asked Shorena.

'I do not want any Georgians to become Russian.'

'But you can read and write the language, and you have remained Georgian.'

'I lived among them as a crippled child,' said Vakhtang quietly.

'Well, what were they like?'

'There are two kinds: slaves and masters.'

'That is the same all over the world,' said Shorena.

'Is it?' asked Vakhtang.

'The Prince here is master – and all the rest of us...' said Shorena.

'The Prince has great faults. But he has a sense of honour. He would not sell any of us, and no Georgian would buy us. He would not welcome that silversmith, Sasun, and then hand him over. And not one amongst us would carry tales about the Prince to the Russian Governor. And though the Sultzi are his bitter enemies, not one of them would do that either.'

'We are of the same blood,' said Shorena.

'But in Russia children betray their parents. The hospital was full of spies. Half the nation are spies. They have no honour,' said Vakhtang.

'So you hate them?' asked Shorena.

'No. But I am glad I am not one. That is why I came back to live here.'

Vakhtang taught Shorena to write a few words, but it turned out that she did not want to learn enough. So she asked: 'Will you teach me to talk Russian instead?' Vakhtang agreed at once and made her learn a great many words and amused himself by weaving them into absurd sentences. She learned quickly, and he proved a good teacher. Spring had come, and on fine days he would make her come with him to the river, holding his rod in one hand and gripping his crutch with the other. One sunny morning after Vakhtang had been fishing for a while, Shorena who was sitting on a rock watching him, called out: 'Come here, Vakhtang.'

He had at that moment hooked a trout and he did not come until he had played and netted it. Then he came and asked why she had called him.

'Valeri's baby kicked me just now. There he has done it again.'

'Let me feel,' said the cripple boy. Shorena took his hand and pressed it to the side of her belly. After a moment the baby kicked again. 'Yes, I felt him. Now you feel here,' and Vakhtang pressed Shorena's hand on to his fishing bag and she felt the trout he had caught leap and wriggle.

'He's just like a fish in a bag, isn't he?' And they both laughed.

Another day Vakhtang said: 'I wonder what colour his eyes will be? You see both Valeri and you have blue eyes, so they are sure to be blue. *Seeniye glahzee*. That's the Russian for blue eyes.' He made her repeat the words, and after that always called the unborn child by that name.

Prince Gurgen never recovered from the shock of being deserted by his young followers. In the spring and early summer his memory began to fail and his speech to become incoherent. Then one morning at the beginning of June, he had a slight stroke, temporarily paralysing the right side of his body.

Katerina, in an advanced state of pregnancy, had taken to sleeping in a room at the bottom of the tower, and it was Nina who discovered the Prince's plight. She told Katerina and called Malik. Katerina insisted that Alexander Babashvili should be fetched from the town. He had married the daughter of a corn chandler and was now a priest. Malik suggested bringing a doctor too, but Katerina pointed out that it was a waste of money. People in the Prince's condition either died, or got well by themselves. Father Alexander's prayers would do more than any physician, and, if letting a little blood were needed, that could be done by the shepherd David who was accustomed to the diseases of animals.

The blacksmith, a thoroughly reliable man, who would not be tempted by the fleshpots of the town, or likely to desert to Ziklauri, as his two sons had been killed the year before in skirmishes with the Solutz, was sent off on a cob well up to his weight, leading a mule on which Father Alexander could ride to the Castle.

Before his arrival Shorena was taken with pangs of labour. Nina, who was experienced in such matters, gave her a pad of linen to bite on and hung a towel from the head of her bed to which she could cling at the worst moments. The waters broke early, and the pains were acute and prolonged. However, after eight hours' labour, Shorena was delivered of a fine baby weighing about twelve pounds. The length of her labour was possibly affected by the fact that Katerina had also taken to her bed and was constantly demanding Nina's attendance upon her.

Shorena's baby had scarcely been wiped and washed and the cord tied up – Vakhtang was asked for a strand of silkworm gut to tie it with, and came in and tied the knot, when Katerina began uttering piercing shrieks and shortly afterwards was delivered, with little difficulty, of a puny infant half the weight of Shorena's and of the opposite gender. After washing it and putting it back with its mother, Nina went back to Shorena's room. The child Eteri who had been put to watch at Prince Gurgen's couch, came rushing in crying: 'The Prince is dying, but he can speak.'

Nina at that moment was holding Shorena's infant in her arms. Still holding him, she ran to the Prince's bedside. To her astonishment he was conscious and asked: 'Is that a boy or a girl?'

'A boy,' replied Nina.

'Then I die happy,' said the Prince. However he showed no signs of immediate death, but raised himself on his elbow, and mumbled out instructions – of the utmost importance.

At that moment Father Alexander entered the room raising

his hand in benediction. But the deathbed scene he had come for was transformed already. A powerful cry from the baby in Nina's arms indicated that he was the most important person present.

'My new-born son. The heir of the Sons of the Falcon. I name him Leonidas after the greatest Captain of Antiquity,' said Prince Gurgen and fell back exhausted on his bed.

Leaving Father Alexander with the Prince, Nina left the room, and finding Katerina in a happy sleep, removed her child and substituted the young Leonidas.

'What's this?' Shorena demanded an hour later, holding up Katerina's wizened daughter.

Vakhtang was silent. Then he said: 'Half an hour ago everyone was summoned into the yard to hear Nina announce that the Son of the Falcon, Prince Gurgen, is the father of a legitimate male child, whom he proclaims his heir to inherit the Princedom and the Castle.'

'Wasn't my baby a boy?' demanded Shorena.

'I would not like to say. Not at the moment, you know,' replied Vakhtang with his gentle, but somehow serious, smile.'

'And this poor little mite?' asked Shorena.

'Rather dark, isn't she? But quite a family likeness.'

'What shall I do?' asked Shorena desperately.

'I think the little creature wants the breast,' said Vakhtang. And then when Shorena had persuaded it to suck, the cripple boy bent over and said with emphasis:

'You must do nothing, but wait and see how things turn out. It might be the best way.'

'What do you mean?' asked Shorena.

'If anything has happened to Valeri.' He said no more, but Shorena understood.

A christening can take place anywhere, and that of the boy Leonidas took place in the Prince's bedroom. The question of godparents was a difficulty. In the absence of any suitable man of noble birth, Malik, a lapsed Moslem who had never been either christened or confirmed, was chosen as godfather. Nina asked if she might be the godmother, but the Prince indignantly refused her, little knowing that she had already done as much for the boy as any godmother in a fairy tale. The Prince ordered that Iriné, a woman of the noblest blood, though illegitimate, should be her half-brother's sponsor. She carried out the functions allotted to her perfectly, but wound up the proceedings with the words: 'When our Saint Anne performs miracles, she doesn't do things by halves.'

Christenings in the Georgian and Russian Orthodox churches present features unknown in the occident. Hair is clipped from the infant's head and floated in water and afterwards ceremonially burned. Magic plays a more prominent part than in the West, and every possible incantation accompanied the removal of original sin from young Leonidas. Compared with that, the christening of the female infant, called Serapita, for whom Nina and Vakhtang stood as godparents, might be described as ' a lick and a promise'.

The health of Prince Gurgen rallied during the summer months, and on fine evenings he would walk out into the yard and sometimes through the gateway and take a few steps down towards the river. In early September a horseman drew up at the aoul. It was a young Russian officer in uniform who, having dismounted, presented Katerina who went to meet him with a card on which was engraved:

'Lieutenant Mihail Semyonitch Arbatsky
3rd Regiment Imperial Artillery.'

He bowed, kissed Katerina's hand and explained that he was an officer doing his military service, stationed in the Caucasus, that he had an enthusiasm for Georgia, the Georgians, and everything Georgian – 'the most ancient and most noble of the people in the domains of His Imperial Majesty' – that he was writing a book about Georgia, its history, legends and noble families.

It turned out that he had been to see Ziklauri, who had told him that Prince Gurgen was the head of the Sons of the Falcon and that he possessed at his Castle the famous wonder-working icon of Saint Anne.

The Prince appeared, and as the Princess had to attend to her son, Vakhtang was called as interpreter. The officer's questions and his eager enthusiasm delighted the Prince. Nina brought in vodka, caviare and pickled cucumbers, and over this refreshment, the Prince recounted the miracles of Saint Anne: the siege of the Tatars over a hundred years before with the besiegers and their horses swept away in a flood when the garrison was down to its last bag of powder and the last crumb of mouldy bread. 'I've made sure that will never happen again,' said the Prince with quiet self-satisfaction. Then he related the miracle that happened only last year, when followers of Ziklauri fled as an earthquake shook the rocks and split the rock wall holding the waters of the lake, so that all but a few of the scoundrels were swept away and drowned. After a last swallow of vodka, the two men rose to look at Saint Anne herself. They stood for a time in silence with bowed heads and the Prince was about to give an account of how the young Saint and Martyr, his five-year-old son Vasso, had given his life to save Saint Anne from falling into the hands of 'the men of our blood' under Ziklauri – and that they were standing before his shrine – when the Prince noticed that the silver rattle which was one of its most precious relics was missing.

'Nina where is the rattle?' bellowed the Prince.

The old woman flushed. 'You must ask the mistress, my Lord.'

But when Katerina appeared, she seemed very much surprised. 'The rattle? I didn't even know that there was one!'

The Prince stern and dignified, but shaky, said no more. But before Lieutenant Arbatsky left he said that their visitor must see his son Leonidas – the heir of the Sons of the Falcon. They went to the nursery – and suddenly the Prince hit his wife in the face, shouting out, 'Disobedient, lying slut. How dare you commit sacrilege.' For there, dangling over the baby's head from a pink ribbon, was the Holy Relic of Vasso, Son of the Falcon, Saint and Martyr. But the strain had been too great, and as the Prince tried to strike his wife again, he tottered and would have fallen if Lieutenant Arbatsky had not caught him. Five minutes later, Prince Gurgen, Son of the Falcon, was dead of apoplexy.

His funeral took place in the town, the service being conducted by his father-in-law the Archpriest, assisted by the Reverend Father Alexander. The occasion was chiefly remarkable because the cemetery was packed with mourners. All the surviving men of the Sultzi, headed by Ziklauri, attended, as well as the Russian Governor of the town, many Russian officers and a large number of the townspeople. Prince Gurgen had become a legend, and it was not so much his corpse, but the end of an era, that they had come to see buried and many of them to mourn.

As the service concluded Iriné remarked : 'No goat for the Archpriest, this time,' which only a few of those present understood. But although so many who had never seen the Prince attended, there were few of the humbler members of his household. Malik was there naturally, as he had been in charge of bringing the coffin to the town, but Nina had stayed at the Castle in charge of Leonidas and could not attend. Shorena felt no wish to, and had Serapita to look after. Of the workers not engaged in taking the coffin to the cemetery only Souliko the baker chose to go. After the service he got drunk in the town, and at the Castle they ate stale bread for a week until he was back at work.

The baby Serapita had been ailing since her birth – unable, apparently, to retain or digest what she swallowed, she vomited after every meal until she was mere skin and bone, but somehow went on from week to week and month to month. She died a fortnight after the Prince's funeral.

Unlike her father, Serapita was shovelled into the earth

with little ceremony. The goats were absent that day, and there was no ecclesiastic to mistake one of them for Satan. The burial service was read by Vakhtang. Katerina did not attend, and her absence did much to alienate Nina from her mistress. The old woman was slowly sinking into a state of religious melancholia. She had become increasingly aware of the sins for which she would soon receive a just punishment. She had little hope that Saint Anne would intervene on her behalf.

The Princess, as Katerina correctly insisted that everyone should call her, decided to get rid of all the old retainers of the household and install a dozen families of the new German colonists. However, while Avetis Gulerian was engaged in the complicated negotiations for their employment – some were to be paid, while others were to be sharecroppers working the fields – events which were to upset these plans were moving fast.

After the death and burial of Serapita, the Princess ordered Shorena to appear before her. When she came in, she asked: 'Oh, what is it, Princess?'

'While your child was ill, I thought it kinder to allow you to remain, but now that it's dead, you must be going.'

'Going? Where to?' asked Shorena.

'That's your business not mine, you silly woman,' replied the Princess.

'I promised Prince Valeri that I should wait here until his return. I shall keep that promise.'

'You will do nothing of the kind,' screamed the Princess.

'Besides – I think it right to stay with my son, Leonidas,' said Shorena.

'Are you mad?'

'Several people know the truth. Look, he has blue eyes.'

Shorena left the Princess in a state of terror and turmoil. She decided that night that at all costs she must get rid of the Sultzi woman before the Germans arrived. It would be disastrous if she were to start spreading stories among them.

Nina was also dangerous and rapidly becoming useless. Then, somehow, Iriné must be taken care of. She too must go before the Germans came. She was always saying things. The Princess brooded over the problem for several days and came to believe that the only way left at this late date was poison. If there were a general outbreak of poisoning it would seem less peculiar than if Shorena alone were singled out. The trouble was that the Princess knew so little about poisons!

However, in walking round the aoul walls she discovered a straggling bush of woody nightshade. She had been told as a child that its red berries were deadly poison, so she picked a pocketful of them. Two days afterwards she ordered a dish of roast duck with cranberry sauce.

The Princess dined alone, as befitted a widow in full-mourning living among her inferiors. After her dinner had been brought to her and she had finished with it, the main dish was carried out for the others to partake of it. The girl Eteri, who had brought the duck, stood in front of her waiting.

'What are you waiting for? I may want to take some more. I will ring when you can remove it,' said the Princess. Then, when she was alone, she helped herself liberally to the cranberry sauce and mixed two spoonfuls of the squashed-up nightshade berries with what remained. Soon afterwards she rang the bell, and the girl, who helped Nina in the kitchen, came in and carried out the tray. Shorena and Iriné were waiting in the kitchen. They helped themselves and carried their plates away. Nina was fasting that day. 'Help yourself, dearie,' she said to the girl, who was looking with longing eyes at the food of the Great People.

The cranberry sauce tasted so unpleasant that Shorena spat out her first mouthful. Iriné swallowed some of it without noticing how nasty it was, and then left it, but the girl in the kitchen finished up all that remained. That night Nina was called by the girl's mother: her Eteri was dying, she had terrible stomach pains. It is possible that the child would have died if Nina had not given her an emetic and had her kept warm with hot-water bottles, and made her drink a quart of warm milk. She was ill for two days and then recovered completely. Iriné complained that she had severe pains and had been sick in the night. Shorena, she and Nina talked about the poisoning all the next morning and decided it was the cranberry sauce. Nina examined what was left on Shorena's plate and picked out two nightshade berries.

It was clear to both women that the Princess was mad. She had tried, very ineffectively, to poison them all and had nearly succeeded with the innocent child Eteri in the kitchen. And Shorena remembered Ziklauri saying in her hearing: 'Once a poisoner, always a poisoner.' That meant that unless she were stopped the Princess would try again.

The only way out was for her to kill Katerina and to get in first. If she were to do it, it had better be immediately, and without consulting, or discussing it with anyone.

Shorena waited until Katerina had gone to the privy in the yard. Then she went in to the Prince's apartment and took one of his pistols. It was, as she expected, still loaded, but she drew the charge and loaded it again and put a new percussion cap upon the nipple. Then, when Nina had gone out for the evening milking of the goats – she would take longer now that Eteri was not there to help her – Shorena went to the Princess's room, knocked at the door and walked in.

Katerina looked at her in astonishment, terror and dismay. She could not be coming to accuse her!

Then Shorena said: 'I have come to ask you to help me.'

Then, as Katerina stared at the sheer insolence of the woman she most feared and hated expecting her to help her, Shorena went on: 'I am going to do something very wicked and I must leave a confession. But I cannot read or write. Will you, Princess, write down my confession for me?'

'What do you intend to do?'

'I am going to destroy myself. Valeri will never return. I cannot live here, and I have nowhere to go. But I cannot do it unless I leave a confession, so that people should understand and forgive me – and it is for Valeri too, if ever he comes back.'

Katerina looked at the crushed figure before her, her heavy mouth, hidden eyes, despair written all over her, and she felt the sudden excitement, the thrill which is like faintness, that the hunter feels when the deer that he has been waiting for steps out of the forest into range, and turns broadside on, exposing the heart as the target.

'Well, if you wish. It will do you good to confess.'

For a moment she busied herself finding a quill and paper and ink that had not dried in the pot. At last all was ready, and Shorena began : ' "Confession of Shorena, woman of the Solutz, living at the aoul of the Sons of the Falcon." That is the first line. Leave a gap and begin again : "I beg forgiveness. I am mad. I am going to destroy myself because I am a danger to others and they know this. I am a danger to the child. God forgive me." '

As Katerina finished writing, she looked up, expecting a final sentence. Shorena pulled the pistol from under her skirt and shot her in the ear at point-blank range. She dropped the pistol by the body, took a pair of scissors out of her pocket, and cut the top line off the paper. She put the sheet of paper back on the table. Then, as she was leaving the room, she put the strip with the top line on it into her mouth and had chewed it up and swallowed it by the time she was back in her little room in the yard. She lay down on her bed sighed deeply and said aloud, 'I've got a headache.' Five minutes later she was asleep, and she was sound asleep when Nina rushed into her room twenty minutes later.

Everyone in the Castle rejoiced discreetly at the Princess's death. Malik tried to spell out the note left by the dead woman, and Vakhtang read it aloud to the assembled company. It was clearly in her handwriting, and everyone realised its importance as providing a simple explanation of her death. The story of the cranberry sauce which had nearly poisoned Eteri showed that the Princess was mad.

'I wonder why she cut off the top of the sheet of paper?' said Iriné after looking at it, but nobody was interested in such a silly question.

Important complications were to follow Katerina's death, but all the old retainers breathed a sigh of relief. They would not be turned away at the ends of their lives with nowhere to go. There would be no Germans coming now that the Princess was dead.

The widow Tara was certain that Katerina had not committed suicide, for she knew that she was incapable of feeling guilty of being a danger to others, or minding if she were. She could not give this reason to the Archpriest, though he ought to have known it himself. It had to be camouflaged.

'It's not in character. She was so courageous,' she said.

'I know, I know. But what about that extraordinary note? It is in her handwriting, I can swear to that. Besides they are all illiterates at the Castle, except for a cripple boy.'

'Whatever the evidence, I will never believe it. She was murdered, the poor darling.'

'That story about the cranberry sauce being poisoned is very peculiar. That cannot be true,' mused the Archpriest.

The widow Tara saw nothing odd in that, though she could never have admitted it. She remembered that when she and the Archpriest first became such close friends, Katerina, then a lively little girl of twelve, had played a practical joke on her on the First of April – an Easter Egg that had made her very unwell for a week. But that was best forgotten.

So she pressed the tips of her fingers together in an attitude of infinite wisdom and put out the tip of her little pink tongue before she said: 'Depend upon it, one of those who says she was poisoned is the criminal.'

Intuition, however, is not evidence.

'Murdered. Yes, it is almost certain that my child was murdered. I warned her that it was madness to marry that old ruffian. Of course, she managed him very well, and while he was alive she was safe enough.'

'That's more than some of his other wives were,' said the widow. Such considerations would lead them nowhere. She must be practical.

'What are you going to do about darling little Leonidas?' That, of course, was the question, and Father Alexander and the Archpriest had already discussed it. The Archpriest favoured carrying out Katerina's plans: getting rid of all the workmen and retainers – one of whom was probably the murderer – and introducing a small colony of honest Germans and of then appointing Father Alexander as the guardian of Leonidas and supreme authority at the Castle. This plan did not appeal to Father Alexander, who was looking forward to rapid promotion in the Church. He was only twenty-four years old, and when Leonidas came of age he would be thrown out of his job at forty-six – with no position of authority, or even prospect of employment, for the rest of his life. Moreover the job of supreme authority at the aoul was no sinecure. He had managed to teach himself French – now he would have to learn German and, supposing something unpleasant were to happen, if the Russians were to withdraw – they were now holding the peace – he would be at the mercy of the Solutz. In any case the aoul was at the end of nowhere. It would be all right for some old fellow, caught out in a scandal, but was a ridiculous place for a rising young man. So he was determined not to accept the position of custodian of the Castle, but he had to refuse without offending the Archpriest, whose help would be valuable and whose enmity fatal to his career. He therefore stressed the danger of the Solutz. Ziklauri was probably thinking of taking possession of the aoul, now undefended, in the name of the majority of the Sons of the Falcon. And the Russians might easily accept such a claim.

'Unfortunately I am no Cardinal Richelieu. I am totally inexperienced in war and the management of arms. I should be quite unsuitable and inadequate to the task.' Father Alexander had just clandestinely devoured *Les Trois Mousquetaires*. He then put forward his own suggestion. The Archpriest should ask the advice of the Russian Governor of the town. 'Whether we like it or not – and none of us would choose it – the Russians rule our country. They are very anxious to win over our nobility, and, for that reason, many of the scions of our Princely families have been sent to St Petersburg. I am certain that the Governor would be delighted if he were offered the opportunity to undertake the education of your grandson. He would provide a private tutor for Leonidas, send him to St Petersburg, and after the education of a Russian nobleman in the Corps of Pages – he might easily become a favourite of the Tsar and become the leading nobleman in Georgia.'

The Archpriest was both fascinated and horrified at the idea. 'It is because of your devotion to the material interests of my family that you suggest this, Alexey. But there are difficulties. As you know I am a strong Georgian patriot and hate to see the occupation of my country, even by such enlightened invaders as the Russians. After what we suffered from the Persians they are indeed angels.... But I am a Georgian patriot, and though I would not let that stand in the way of his receiving the best possible education, I should hate my grandson to return a foreigner, a man neither Russian or Georgian, to find his inheritance usurped by others. The problem now is not the darling child's education. That can be left until he is six or seven. It is the management of the estate and the preservation of the property. The chief danger is that the Solutz may claim it and seize it. That is the disaster most to be feared. But the Russians might put in a military garrison if the aoul were left empty and the estate neglected, and that would be almost as bad. If only you would undertake the task! But a premature appeal to the Governor would be fatal. We do not want to remind him of the existence of the aoul of the Sons of the Falcon.

No, Prince Gurgen was right when he forbade Katerina to appeal to the Governor after those young scoundrels deserted him and went over to Ziklauri. And I do the same.'

These discussions had occupied weeks. October passed, and the extreme urgency that the Archpriest had felt at the time of his daughter's death changed to a feeling that it would be fatal to do the wrong thing. Little Leonidas would be safe enough in the hands of dear old Nina, and the Solutz would not have postponed an attack in September or October, in order to attack in winter when the track was often impassable. Malik had earlier sent reassuring messages about the harvest, which had been good and gathered in excellent condition. Iriné had asked for soap and caramels to be sent. Such a message might have annoyed him if it had not shown that there was very little amiss at the Castle. He would certainly send his grandson some sugar plums for Christmas, if nothing had been settled before.

Both Nina and Iriné shared the widow Tara's doubts about the suicide of the Princess. 'Not like her, was it?' said Iriné.

'But, you see, it wasn't her choice,' replied Nina.

Iriné opened her eyes wide and her mouth wider. 'Do you mean someone made her do it?' she asked.

'Indeed I do. She was under orders from Saint Anne.'

'Saint Anne?' asked Iriné with a shade of disappointment.

'Our blessed guardian, Saint Anne, couldn't let her go on like that, poisoning little girls. She intervened to save us all.'

'Well, if Saint Anne got Katerina to shoot herself, it is the best thing she has done so far, by a long chalk. I don't count the earthquake, because I'm not sure that she did it.'

'Hush, my dear. That's not the way to talk.'

Iriné's own view which she kept to herself (though as everyone believed that she was crazy she knew that it didn't much matter what her views were), was that the strip of paper cut off the top of Katerina's confession would have shed some light on the matter. Luckily, however, all had turned out for the best.

CHAPTER SEVEN

The sixty parasangs between the town of Tabriz and the valleys where the Turkomans spend the winter months were a no-man's land inhabited by the poorest of the poor – peasant cultivators whose entire wealth consisted of a water buffalo and a primitive plough. Their miserable huts were thinly scattered, usually beside a swamp. It was a district in which fever and disease were endemic, but as the traveller from Lake Van in Turkey had to pass that way, it was infested by roaming bandits. Thus it was by no means a safe country through which to travel for a man carrying a small bag of jewels and accompanied only by his wife and a young and pretty girl. Mustapha was accustomed to travel among robbers, and his solution was not to carry any precious metal and only to work with silver belonging to his clients. On such journeys he disguised himself as a knife-grinder. But to the wild men whom they would meet, Tamar's body would be as precious as though it were made of silver, her lips rubies and her eyes sapphires.

How could her attractions be disguised so that she could travel safely through that land of bandits?

'Not as a boy,' said Kamela. 'Many of those ruffians would prefer a boy to a girl.'

'We must try and paint her face so as to make her ugly,' said Mustapha.

'I doubt if you would succeed. Her beauty is so great that it would shine through any dirt and rags. The only way is for her to pose as an idiot. Oddly enough, though men hate women to show the least sign of intelligence, they are seldom attracted by idiots.' Then, turning to Tamar, she said: 'You must practise drooling, my dear.'

The three of them set out on a fine day in February, on foot, with Mustapha's equipment packed on one donkey and all their possessions on a second. Mustapha was a knife-grinder, his wife had a basket with cards of buttons and packets of needles, and Tamar was their idiot daughter, wearing dirty ragged clothes, buttoned up wrong, and smelling of urine, her hair tangled and filthy. They were stopped several times by bandits who wanted their daggers sharpened. On the last occasion, looking back along the road by which they had come, Mustapha saw a cloud of dust travelling towards them. He halted and led his donkeys off the road so that the hurrying horsemen should have a clear passage. When they came abreast, they reined up sharply, and a jovial fellow, who seemed to be their leader, called out: 'So I've found you at last! I have come four parasangs out of my way to get my sword sharpened!' Mustapha unpacked his grindstone and sharpened the sword carefully, putting the last touches with a Turkey stone, while Tamar stood idly by, with the saliva dribbling out of the corner of her mouth, a victim of the evil eye. None of the bandits would have paid her the least attention if she had not taken the initiative and sidled up to the handsomest of the young men and, after staring up into his face for a long time, plucked him by the sleeve. 'Get away you foul creature,' cried the young man jumping away from her.

'Don't pay any attention. It's a curse on us,' said Mustapha. Kamela came forward and led Tamar away.'

'I had to do something. I was running dry of spit,' whispered Tamar.

When he had sharpened the sword and all their knives and daggers, which took him two hours, Mustapha looked humorously at the leader.

'Ha! Ha! I know what you want. You want to be paid. What a joke,' cried the jovial fellow. 'We're bandits. Now that our knives are so sharp we might as well cut your throats with them. But perhaps you will come in useful another time – so I'll give you a silver dollar instead. Have you ever had one of them before, my fellow?' And mounting their horses, the bandits galloped back the way that they had come.

Next day they had reached the first of the Turkoman villages from which they were directed where to find Mirza and Mzekala.

Valeri had traversed the same stretch of paludine country three months earlier. On the way he had encountered only one adventure. He had ridden through an encampment of bandits, surprising them as much as they surprised him. One of the men had jumped up from the camp fire, seized a musket and fired a shot at him. Valeri was riding at a canter and the shot was from the side, with the result that the bullet whistled past a foot behind Valeri's head. He spurred his mare, and Tamar's led horse bolted ahead of him. A second shot which followed by the time the bandit had reloaded his piece, came when he was already out of range. There was the sound of horses following him at a gallop, but when he pulled up, half a parasang further on, he saw that the pursuit had been abandoned.

He reached the villages of the Turkomans not long afterwards. When he rode up to the sakl, he thought that Mirza was not too pleased to see him. Mirza and Mzekala had had the pack-pony with them. Tamar's colt, Valeri and Tamar's fine clothes, the famous sabre; these and the tent and pots and pans were a profitable recompense for the hospitality of many weeks. Now Valeri had unexpectedly returned and would claim his possessions and perhaps settle down to live at their expense once more.

However, once they had exchanged the first words, it turned out that Valeri had a story to tell – and an exciting story pays for many gallons of koumiss and messes of kasha.

Mirza listened fascinated as Mzekala, translating, described the torture of Tamar by the police, and of their timely rescue by the silversmith.

By the time Mzekala had finished, a new audience had gathered, and she was obliged to tell it all over again. Among these listeners was a dark young man of short stature and a dark handsome girl. Mirza had left the sakl, and in moving to make way for him, as he re-entered carrying a carpet in his arms, the girl blundered against Valeri. He realised that it was done on purpose, for she pinched his thigh, then making him excuses he could not understand and giving him an inviting smile. As Valeri did not feel too sure that he was a welcome guest, he told Mzekala that he would put up his tent and sleep in it, to which she agreed with alacrity.

A few days later he saw the girl who had pinched his thigh guarding a flock of sheep. He pulled up, dismounted and a moment later she was in his arms. Before they parted he whispered words he had carefully rehearsed.

'Come to my tent tonight.'

'I shall be late – after they are asleep. My brother would kill you, if he found out.' Words he did not completely understand.

After that Zaidate came for several nights. They made love in silence, in the dark, and she never stayed long and was obviously afraid of being discovered.

For Valeri the danger was part of the excitement and the pleasure. He liked the uncertainty and the fact that she should come to his tent and seek him out and not he her brought Shorena vividly back to his mind. And having no language in common made it more exciting.

Two weeks later Mzekala said to him: 'What is this I hear about your marrying one of our girls?'

'I know nothing about it,' said Valeri.

'Well, Mahood has been saying that you are wanting to marry his sister Zaidate.'

'I don't know where he got that idea.'

But to his astonishment, that evening Mzekala called him and said: 'The village matchmaker has come to arrange about your marriage with Zaidate.'

Valeri looked up and there, squatting by the fire, was an ancient hag.

'What am I to tell her?' asked Mzekala.

'Tell her that I have no intention of marrying the girl. And that I don't know why anybody should think I had.'

The old woman flung up her arms and went off into a flood of indignant invective and Valeri went back to practising the art of writing Russian, which he was in danger of forgeting.

That night it was brilliant moonlight. It was perhaps the extreme brilliance of the moon which kept Valeri awake, but it was also anger with himself and a vague indignation with Zaidate also. Why, he asked himself, should she imagine that because they had made love for eight nights and enjoyed it, that he, or she, for that matter, would be happy living their whole lives together? He was a foreigner, and how could he be expected to settle down and become a nomadic tribesman, a horse breeder or a shepherd? And surely if she had got the idea into her head, she would have done better to come and talk to Mzekala herself, instead of spreading the rumour round the village and employing a matchmaker? He was much more in love – or anyhow liked her better – with Shorena. But would he want to marry her? They could be happy together without marriage. And, as he was no longer a Christian, it would be dishonest to go before a priest and go through a ceremony which meant nothing to him and which he disliked, hating many of the words in the service? Valeri was honest enough to admit that this argument, a rather feeble one, could not apply to a Moslem girl. He had been truthful enough in his answer to the matchmaker, but was he being really honest as regards Shorena?

As Valeri asked himself these disturbing questions and told himself it was his fault for responding to the girl's advances, he saw a shadow obscuring the brilliant moonlight at the mouth of the little tent. It was a human being: it could only be Zaidate. He lay still and saw that she was on all fours, and something she was holding gleamed brightly in the moonlight. She was holding a knife.

Valeri shut his eyes for a moment and remained perfectly still. Then, as he looked under his half-closed lids, he saw the entrance of the tent grow dark as the body of Zaidate filled it. He felt her half shuffle and half glide into the tent until her body was alongside his. Then he opened his eyes wide and, as she raised her right arm, he caught her wrist in his left hand and with a violent twist of his body, accidentally giving Zaidate a blow in the breast with his right elbow, he smashed her right hand with the dagger down into the spot of ground where he had been lying. Zaidate gave a cry of pain. But, turning his back on her, he twisted her right arm with his left hand and then took the dagger from her with his right. Then he turned back towards her. Both Valeri and Zaidate were shocked and exhausted. Both had much to say to each other, but no language in which to say it. Suddenly Zaidate made a gesture. She lay on her back and bared her breasts, as though inviting the hand that held the dagger to strike between them.

Valeri pushed his hand under the edge of the tent and thrust the dagger deep into the earth outside. Then he turned to Zaidate and kissed her. Soon afterwards it was another kind of dagger that he drove into her body.

Zaidate went away, but Valeri lay awake for the rest of that night. By morning he was in a strange delirium and shaking with fever – malaria that he had caught in the marshes beside the road from Tabriz, where he had camped for a night. He lay like that all day, but in the evening Mzekala put her head into the little tent and asked: 'Why haven't we seen you all day?'

Valeri raised his head and apparently the sight of his face was a sufficient answer, for she said: 'I'll make up a couch for you in the sakl. You're ill.' Later Mirza came and very tenderly supported him and led him to the couch Mzekala had prepared. Valeri was delirious that night, and Mirza sat up with him, sponging his face with a cold wet cloth. After midnight he dozed off, and Mirza, half asleep, thought he heard something moving in the night. He went out and walked over to Valeri's tent. There was a shadowy figure kneeling in the entrance. Mirza saw that it was Zaidate.

'What are you doing here? Valeri is ill.'

'I came to tell him that if he won't marry me I am ruined and my brother will kill him. Why isn't he here?'

'He is ill. Very ill,' said Mirza.

The next day Valeri was awake and conscious, lying in the sakl. He had taken no food – only drinks of water. His surroundings were unreal and his memories confused. Mzekala came and looked at him. 'There are two men outside, Kerriman and Mahood, the brothers of Zaidate. Kerriman has a gun, and I think that he has come to kill you.'

'How funny of him. Ask him to wait while I dress and I'll come and talk to him,' said Valeri.

'I told him you were very ill, but he doesn't think that matters,' said Mzekala.

Valeri tried to get on his feet from the floor, but lost his balance and fell down again.

'Tell him I'll fight a duel with him with sabres on horseback,' said Valeri. He lay down again and became unconscious, unaware of the long discussion that went on at the mouth of the sakl, a discussion in which Mzekala played a leading role.

Duels, fought on points of honour, were unknown among the Turkomans, and it took Mzekala some time to explain the underlying idea. About the details she was vague and had to confess ignorance. However the novelty of it appealed to Kerriman, who became enthusiastic.

'Well, look after him until he's fit. And don't let him run away. We'll have it on the polo ground.'

Two days later Valeri's temperature was down, but he felt rather groggy when, after several cups of strong coffee that Mzekala made for him, he girded on his sabre, mounted his mare and accompanied by Mirza, rode off to meet Kerriman on the polo field.

Kerriman was riding a small polo pony. It was agreed that they should each wait at the opposite ends of the ground until Mirza dropped a handkerchief and the duel should then start.

Valeri could not have chosen a form of combat in which he was at a greater disadvantage. Kerriman was a skilled polo player and was riding a clever and responsible pony. Valeri's mare, though much swifter, was untrained in stopping short and making rapid starts and swerves. Valeri might have been cut down several times if Kerriman had not been afraid of his longer reach and advantage in height. Several times he swerved past, pulled round short and attacked from the rear. To the spectators, who were skilled falconers to a man, it was like watching a peregrine attacking a crane. On one occasion Valeri only escaped because he dug in his spurs and his mare gave a great leap forward. He was then ignominiously chased by Kerriman until his mare had outdistanced the pony. He pulled up to face him, and after that adopted a defensive tactic, keeping his mare standing and turning her this way and that so as to try and face the sudden darts made at him. Kerriman, however, did not expose himself, and the duel was becoming ludicrous, when Kerriman drew off for about twenty yards and suddenly came at him at a full gallop as though he had at last summoned up his courage to put all to the touch. Valeri sat on his mare quietly waiting for the inevitable clash.

But suddenly, when only two lengths or less away, Kerriman pulled his pony violently over to Valeri's near side, at the same time changing his sabre to his left hand, and slashing at him as he came alongside and past. Valeri, taken by surprise, threw up his left arm, holding the reins, to protect

203

his head and received a terrific blow which half-severed his forearm half-way between the wrist and the elbow. The point of Kerriman's sabre then inflicted a scratch on the haunch of Valeri's mare. She bolted. If he had lost his seat, Kerriman would have ridden up to him and cut off his head with great satisfaction. Luckily he kept it and his mare having a start and being much the swifter and more powerful of the two animals, soon put a good distance between him and his pursuer.

It is next to impossible for a man riding a bolting horse to sheathe a sabre with one hand, particularly if his useless left arm is spurting blood like a fountain. It is also next to impossible to bring a bolting horse under control while holding a sabre in the only hand available to get hold of the reins. Valeri therefore dropped his sabre, managed to grab the reins, and brought his mare under control, after which he galloped back at top speed to Mirza's sakl, where he fell unconscious, after dismounting.

Kerriman and Mirza arrived shortly afterwards to find Mzekala winding a piece of string as tight as she could above Valeri's left elbow. When Kerriman informed her that he had come to cut off his head, she cursed him roundly, told him that the duel was over, and that he had better give Mirza a hand in carrying Valeri to his couch. After inspecting his victim with delight, Kerriman did his best to help. Then, on his way home, he stopped to pick up the sabre, which he appropriated as the spoils of war.

Mirza sent for an old man who had served in the Persian army during the invasion of Turkestan and, having had the luck to be wounded in the foot, had often watched a surgeon at his trade. He made a very skilful amputation of the forearm at the elbow joint, tying up the main arteries and sewing up the skin round the stump with catgut. The operation was long and extremely painful, and his patient fainted during the course of it.

Among the spectators was Kerriman, who remarked with

satisfaction after the operation had been completed: 'He'll never be able to put both arms round a girl again.'

The wound did not go seriously septic, and in two months, that is by the time that Mustapha Sasun and his wife reached the village with Tamar, it was completely healed.

Mustapha did not make the mistake of accepting Mirza's hospitality, which had been stretched to breaking point by Valeri's operation and convalescence. He also told Tamar that she had better sleep in Valeri's little tent and continue to take her meals with them. She soon realised that the sooner Valeri and she set off to find her mother's people in Turkey the better.

The meeting between Valeri and Tamar was unfortunate. Her first emotions of sympathy and horror on discovering that he had lost his arm were so violent that she rushed to him and threw her arms about his neck. She had forgotten that she was a disgusting object, and Valeri's recoil from her was something that she never forgave or forgot. He was only anxious that she should go to the bathhouse and change into clean clothes and showed no delight at being reunited with her. Then her first emotions were qualified when she found out that he had lost his arm as a result of a duel because he had refused to marry the girl he had seduced.

Ever since they had left the aoul together, Tamar had been growing more critical of Valeri and building up an un-acknowledged resentment against him. At the moment of joy at meeting, this was swept away. But his reception of her, the idiotic duel in which he had made such a poor showing, and the reasons for the duel, brought all her past grievances against him back and increased them tenfold. Her mind was full of them as she took her steam bath and put on her boy's clothes, in which she intended to make the rest of the journey. Thus when she appeared, looking fresh and radiant, and Valeri was ready to receive her love and sympathy, she felt a cold and critical hostility. Even stronger than her anger with him for having got himself into this mess, was an instinctive desire to conceal her feelings from Mzekala and Kamela. In this she was not successful. She had not tried to conceal her anxiety and dismay on hearing of Valeri's injury – but her manner had changed abruptly when Mzekala had explained how it had come about.

'You must not be so angry with him. That girl, Zaidate, threw herself at his head. It was she who came to his tent in the middle of the night. She was entirely to blame. You see she was trying to save herself by making him marry her after her brothers found out.'

'I am not interested in the details. I just think that he is a hopeless character,' said Tamar. It was what she had meant not to say, and felt angry with herself.

Mzekala said no more in Valeri's defence, but she reflected: 'She means hopeless as regards herself. And the odd thing is that he has never seemed to be attracted by that girl, who is far more beautiful than any of the girls here. And she was in love with him, too, when they first arrived at our summer camp.'

But if Tamar's meeting with Valeri had been upsetting to them both, there was mutual joy in her meeting with Byron. Soon after her arrival she asked Mirza about the colt. 'I have fenced him in, so the older stallions should not attack him. I groom him every day and ride him two or three times a week.'

When Byron saw Tamar approaching the corral in which he was shut up, he pricked up his ears, whinnied with delight and galloped to meet her. She saw that he was in splendid condition, as he threw back his head again and again and nuzzled her.

'Put a bridle on him and then give me a leg-up,' said Tamar. Then she rode him bareback round and round the corral.

That evening Tamar asked Valeri when he would be ready to leave. 'I am ready. There's only one thing that's keeping me. I want to get back my sabre.'

The mention of the sabre was like a red rag to a bull – Tamar being the bull.

'Surely Kerriman has won it and has a right to it,' she said.

'Well, I am asking Mustapha to see him and try to buy it back, without mentioning that he is acting for me.'

'That seems to me contemptible,' said Tamar.

Valeri turned pale with anger at her insult. 'It was my grandfather's,' he said.

'Well, it was an unfortunate inheritance. It was your vanity about your sabre that led you to suggest a duel on horseback. And because of your vanity you got your arm cut off by a much better horseman. You would have bled to death but for Mzekala.' Valeri was silent, and Tamar went on ruthlessly: 'But you haven't got the money to buy it back, even though you are ready to stoop to doing so.'

'We had better not discuss it further,' said Valeri.

Much to Tamar's surprise, Mustapha was able to buy the sabre back for about a quarter of its real value, and he accepted Valeri's promise to pay him when he could. When this was settled, they were ready to go.

But on the morning they were leaving Tamar took Mirza aside and when they rejoined the others it was clear that she had made him very happy. He said a few words to Mzekala and she cried out:

'Tamar has given us Byron.'

This act of generosity produced mixed feelings in Valeri. He felt wounded that she should have given away his gift to her – a gift which had grown into so magnificent an animal. He suspected that she had given the stallion to Mirza as a reward for all that he and Mzekala had done in looking after him, when he was wounded, and he felt ashamed that Tamar should have made such a splendid gift, when he had given them nothing. Against these feelings was one of relief that they would not have the young stallion with them on the road, bothering them, when he, with only one arm, was not well equipped to deal with complications.

'He's the finest stallion the Turkomans have got, and Mirza

207

is going to breed from him,' said Tamar. That was the real reason why she had given Mirza the animal, and made up for what was a great sacrifice. After such a return for their hospitality, there was an outburst of cordiality. Mzekala loaded them with halva, apricot and peach cheese and rose-petal sweetmeats, to which Mirza added a smoked leg of lamb.

'Promise to come back soon,' cried Mzekala, and Mirza smiled, all friendship. Kamela was less hypocritical.

'I'm not inviting you to return to Tabriz. I'm inviting ourselves to the aoul. We'll be coming to stay for a long, long visit.' Then she took Tamar in her arms and kissed her again and again.

'It's years since I've kissed such a pretty boy as you are. I feel quite excited by it. Mustapha will have a time of it soothing me down tonight. Well, take care of yourself, my darling. Keep out of the hands of the Turkish police.'

Valeri had wrapped up his precious sabre, and it was packed on the pony wrapped up in the tent. He knew that he could not control his mare and use it. Mustapha had bought each of them a pair of horse pistols, and the holsters were strapped on their saddles. Valeri could, if need be, hook the reins over the pommel of his saddle, fire a pistol and then pick up the reins again. Tamar was more adequately armed, for she had Valeri's Birmingham gun, which was useless to a one-armed man, and since Valeri had refused to lend her his sabre, she had bought herself a Turkish yata-ghan. Mzekala gave them each a drink of koumiss, and they set off with much waving of farewells.

They rode for two hours in silence. Then Valeri said: 'You think I was contemptible to buy my sabre back. But I'm glad I got it. Cheap, too. Do you think I ought to have paid more?'

'I think you ought to have given it, and anything valuable you have got, to Mzekala and Mirza. They cared for you and saved your life.'

'They saved my life, I suppose. But they did not love me really,' said Valeri.

'You should not expect the impossible,' said Tamar.

They rode in silence after that, and when they stopped to eat and to breathe their horses, they ate in silence. They rode on till nearly dark, then dismounted. Tamar unsaddled and hobbled the horses, unpacked the pony, all in silence. Neither would be the first to speak to the other. Valeri was in despair. His new one-handed helplessness made him dependent on Tamar and added to his misery. She had said that it was impossible for anyone to love him and obviously it was true. He had always been confident that she did love him and admire him: what blindness! And now he could not saddle a horse and even found mounting one difficult.

If she would not speak, neither would he. But he helped her humbly to put up the tent and then went to collect wood for the fire. That night they lay side by side in the tent in silence. After a time Valeri heard from her breathing that Tamar was asleep. One of his troubles was that it was at night, when he was lying awake, that his arm was painful.

During his weeks of convalescence he had planned what his life was going to be. He would study: he would be a scholar. Go to Alexandria perhaps. In a library the loss of his arm would not matter. If only he could find Brother Foma! If only Foma were alive!

The thought of his friend, his *kounak*, changed his mood of despair. For Foma had loved him and had trusted him, and after one look in his eyes had understood what he was feeling. The difference between Foma and Tamar was that Foma wanted to understand him and was able to do so; Tamar wanted him to be the man she had imagined and to do the things that such a man would do.

Next morning he slept long, and Tamar woke him with a fire burning and a kettle boiling and tea made. She caught the horses and while he held them, she saddled them. Two hands are needed to pull girths really tight. They had packed up the tent and the pots and pans, only speaking when necessary about the work in hand, when Tamar asked: 'Why didn't you marry the girl?'

Valeri was taken aback. Zaidate had been far from his thoughts. 'Well, I don't think that she would have fitted into my life. We can only say the simplest things to each other. Actually we never spoke because she was so afraid of being discovered. I don't want to be a nomadic shepherd, or a horse-breeder.'

'But you thought you had found the Golden Age and wanted to live with the Turkomans for ever a few months ago.'

'That was just an interlude. What I really want is to become a scholar, to read books, to find out what other men have thought and why,' said Valeri.

'You said all that before we set out. But you didn't give a thought to it all this summer. All you wanted then was to play polo – and then, as soon as I was out of the way, to get some girl to come to your tent. Just as with Shorena, that Sultzi woman.'

'If a girl who attracts me wants me to make love to her, I don't refuse. If her brother wants to fight me, I don't refuse. That seems elementary to me,' said Valeri.

This made Tamar furious. It showed that Valeri was so vain that the woman had to propose to him, not he to her. That there was no question of love in his sexual feelings, only vanity. However she swallowed down her anger and asked: 'Why did you fight that duel – and such a silly one, with sabres on horseback? You knew he was a magnificent horseman.'

'I was lying in a fever when Kerriman came to the sakl with a gun wanting to murder me. I could have got out of the sakl the back way, and coming on him unexpectedly, have murdered him before he got his shot in. But it seemed to me that a duel would be fairer than trying to surprise each other. I chose sabres because my pistol had been stolen by the police in Tabriz. And I suggested fighting mounted because I knew that Kerriman was a fine horseman, and on foot my greater height and longer reach would have given me the advantage,' said Valeri patiently.

'You make it sound awfully fine and noble. But I don't think it was. It seems to me that having that girl, whom you weren't the least bit in love with, and then risking your life fighting about her, and choosing to fight mounted because Kerriman was a better horseman, was all due to your vanity: vanity run mad.'

'I would call it a sense of honour,' said Valeri. There was a silence and then he added: 'I suppose it is two names for the same thing. It is honour to me, looking at it from the inside, and it is vanity run mad to you, seeing it from the outside.'

Tamar had no more to say. Her anger was gone. She still felt that Valeri was hopeless, but he was himself. She knew that in his life there would be many more 'interludes', but there was a desire for honesty, a belief in truth, that she respected. And courage.

CHAPTER EIGHT

Their quarrel was over and it would never be renewed. But it had changed their relationship. For the future neither would ever imagine that there might one day be physical love between them. Up till the quarrel they had, as it were, been holding hands; the result of it was that they had let go. In future when Valeri's name was mentioned, Tamar would smile and speak warmly and affectionately of him, but always with the unspoken qualification that she knew him, his character and defects, better than anyone else could do. When Tamar's name was mentioned, Valeri would become enthusiastic: 'A darling, really a wonderful creature. She was like my sister. Much more than my own sisters.'

But there would never, in what he said, be that undercurrent of regret with which a man speaks of a woman for whom he has felt physical passion. And, underlying the affection, was a tacit assumption that the other was incapable of passionate love – of the real thing.

They rode through stony, hilly country, then over a plain that grew more fertile as they rode on towards a belt of hills. There were arable fields, green with winter rye and wheat, and fields just sprouting with new sown barley, and then, as they rode on, everywhere there was water. The road they followed wound upwards. There were vineyards on the slope of the hill, and between the vineyards and the cliff of the hill, were orchards of apricot and peach and plum in blossom, pears with buds breaking, and apple and quince to come. There were gardens and the sound of water

– and a man singing in the fields. Then, when they had pulled round a sharp corner in the road, they saw above them the aoul, a little fortified hill town, and chickens running, and geese holding up their beaks, and ducklings following their mother in single file. Valeri, who was in front, pulled up and waited for Tamar to come alongside. They looked at each other smiling: each delighted they had found a beauty that they could share and, by a common appreciation, cement their uneasy peace.

Although they had passed several of the inhabitants, men and women working in the orchards and gardens, no one had done more than look up at them and then go back to their occupations. Though the men all carried rifles slung on their backs, there had been no challenge from armed sentries, no rush out of savage dogs, no gaping crowd of children. Everyone was busily occupied, everyone at peace and confident of being secure. It was not until they had ridden right up into the middle of the main street and pulled up to look where they should go, that a man, crossing the road, altered direction and came up to them. Like most of the Circassians, he spoke good Georgian. Valeri explained who he was and the purpose of their journey.

'Follow me. Prince Ardigheb will be delighted. I heard his friend talking about you.'

'Ardigheb is what the Circassians call themselves. Tcherkessev is the Russian name,' said Valeri. The man walked ahead of them and took them, not to a castle or a palace, but to a cottage which was actually smaller than the ones on each side of it. It was where Prince Ardigheb lived – but an old woman who came to the door said that he was away, but would be back next morning.

'I'll take you to the guest house. There are those Russians there – but there'll be room for you.'

Tamar felt rather deflated by the Prince's absence and the casualness of their reception, and was wondering if she should ask where her mother's relatives were living and ask to be taken to their house, when there was a shout from Valeri – a shout of joy! 'My *kounak*!' He had stepped into the living-room of the guest house and there, sitting in front of the fire, twisting his retreating forelock and reading a book, was Brother Foma. At Valeri's excited cry, he pushed up his spectacles, and then rushed at him, kissed him, took him by both hands, jumped for joy, yelled at him, kissed him again and then, catching sight of Tamar, rushed up to her and kissed her: one, two, three. He then exclaimed: 'Oh, what joy! Oh, how delightful! Introduce me to the young lady!' A moment later he was calling: 'Lenotchka, come quick. My dearest friend, my *kounak*, Prince Valeri has arrived.' A woman, no bigger than a child, but thin and exquisitely formed, with yellow hair and grey eyes and a whimsical amused expression on her long face, came in to the room. 'This is Prince Valeri ... his sister Tamar ... allow me to present my wife: Elena Ivanovna ... Well, they are tired. We've no vodka, let's give them some wine...'

All was happiness, laughter, bustle and confusion.

That evening the two friends had to explain how they came to be there and all the events that had happened since their parting in the monastery. Brother Foma told how, when the Archimandrite wanted to get him out of the way, he had ordered him to go on a visit to the Armenian monastery of Echmiadzin to inspect the famous illuminated manuscripts.

'But as I am not any longer interested in illuminated manuscripts I didn't go there. Particularly as I suspected that that Turkish bastard had asked that I should be kept there a prisoner for life. No, I went to Constantinople and got myself a job as the tutor to the young son of Ibrahim Pasha. Lenotchka here is a Russian dancer. She had been sold to Ibrahim by her protector, who was hard up. We met and fell in love. A romantic and hazardous escape from the Pasha's harem followed, and here we are, though we are going to move on shortly in case the Pasha catches up with us.'

'There was a good deal more to it than: "So here we are," ' said Elena.

'Well, it's your story, and you must tell it them – but not tonight because I want to know what Valeri plans to do next.'

They talked, drank and slept late; and Valeri had only just woken up, to wonder if he must get up because the sun was high and sunshine pouring in at the window, when there was a cry: 'Still in bed you sluggards! And I've ridden six parasangs since breakfast and was looking forward to a cup of coffee.'

Valeri got to his feet and, looking through the window, saw a small alert man of between forty and fifty, dressed in a peasant's shirt and smart well-cut English riding breeches and top boots. He had a thick shock of fair hair beginning to go grey brushed straight back from his forehead and covering his ears, merry brown eyes and a thick curly beard that spread like a fan over his chest.

'Jason Ardigheb – at your service,' he called out to Valeri at the window.

'Prince Valeri, Son of the Falcon,' replied Valeri, and for the first time in his life felt embarrassed by his title – for this was Prince Ardigheb or Tcherkessev, as the Russians called him, who had apparently discarded his.

'Oh, that's exciting! Have you news of my cousins, Anastasia who married your father, and her little sister Tamar?'

Valeri was telling him that Anastasia was dead, and that Tamar was in the next room, when she put her head out and Valeri went back to dress.

By the time he had come down they had disappeared, the Prince having forgotten the cup of coffee he had been hoping for, and Tamar dispensing with breakfast. They were gone for the whole day, not reappearing until the sun was near setting, and Valeri and Foma were sitting drinking glasses of wine and nibbling a bit of goat cheese, and Lenotchka a raki.

During the day, Valeri had been so occupied in listening to Foma and discussing whether he should abandon his plan of going to study in Alexandria, and, if so, what they should do together, that he hardly noticed Tamar's absence. When, at the midday meal, Lenotchka wondered where Tamar could have got to and added that of course she would be all right if she was with Jason, she watched him closely and was surprised that he showed no sign of jealousy, but replied: 'Well, she has always thought of herself as a Circassian girl, and I know she is absolutely thrilled to be among her own people and her cousin, the Prince, will have a lot to tell her.'

Valeri turned from this subject of slight importance to discuss Foma's plans for going to St Petersburg in the country of what Valeri felt were his enemies.

Tamar and Jason arrived just as Lenotchka was saying that the evening meal was ready. They did not attempt to account for their long absence, or seem abashed. On the contrary, Jason was glowing with geniality, and Tamar did not hide her adoration for her new-found cousin. She was longing to touch him, and, when a drop of the *shchee* – cabbage soup – fell on Jason's beard, Tamar jumped up, fetched a napkin and wiped it away, at the same time running her hand over the top of his head and stroking his shock of hair. It was obvious to Lenotchka, watching her, that she had fallen in love with Jason at first sight, and, from his smiles and occasional glances, that he was aware of her feeling and reciprocated it.

After the meal Jason brought in an armful of vine prunings and then oak logs and lit a fire which blazed up the stone chimney, and they sat round it, sipping raki and talking. Foma explained that Valeri had wanted to go to Alexandria and study comparative religions and that he had been dissuading him from it.

'I agree, of course, with Valeri that the Church – not only

the Christian Church but all the Churches – are a racket, and a particularly nasty racket because they are organisations designed by dupes to dupe others and to batten on both the superstitious fears and the generous impulses of kindness, goodness and human brotherhood, and not only to exploit them but to render them subservient to the cruel and wicked governors of this world. "Render to Caesar that which is Caesar's" is as vile a piece of advice as can be imagined, because it postulates the view that there is a dichotomy between the material and the spiritual. Actually there is not.' Foma paused after this and then added: 'But I don't want to convert anyone. There are some people who are unhappy unless they bolster themselves up with a belief in a future life, just as Jason here could not live without believing that science and reason are going to overcome man's stupidity and cruelty in the future.'

Jason grinned, showing a set of gleaming white strong teeth and said: 'It all depends on our numbers. We are like the lemmings, which are peaceful little animals until their population increases beyond the safe limit, and then they go mad and try and invade and devour the earth and end up by destroying themselves and perishing by millions. In my opinion mankind is unfitted to live in groups of more than a hundred or two persons. I am an example. My title is Prince of the Circassians. Imagine for a moment that I was their autocratic Prince. Should I be better off, would they? I should not be here, a free man talking to free men. No, I should fancy myself a Napoleon on Elba, I should be enslaved by circumstances and no happier than the slaves I ruled over. The Russians, our enemies and neighbours, are actual serfs, who until six years ago could be bought and sold by their masters. Even now that they are called free they are slaves. Even if they had a revolution like the French, they would always be slaves. The reason is that there are too many of them. The French and the English are not much better off. They are the slaves of their numbers, herded in great cities, working in factories. They are seeds sown so thickly that there is no room for any of the plants to grow to their full stature.'

'All the civilisations of the past...' began Valeri. But Jason interrupted him: 'Quite so. All the civilisations of the past, and I may add of the present, depended on slave labour of one kind or another. A community enslaves itself as soon as it contains more men than can know each other personally; in fact, when it ceases to be a collection of individuals and becomes a community. That is because the men of big communities cease to respect each other's individuality and impose themselves and their ideas upon their fellows. They aim, if not to be the wolves, at any rate to be the shepherd dogs, of those whom they regard as sheep.'

At this Foma turned on Jason and said: 'What you don't realise is the paradox that you can live in a big city as though it were a desert – without knowing any of your neighbours. The hundreds who live in the same street might as well not exist. You see only your friends and the people you love and pass by all the others without even looking at them. That is the advantage of the great city over the small town. So long as you wear the same kind of hat as other people and don't attract the attention of the police, you can be an individual and perfectly free. And the great cities have libraries, museums, theatres, you can hear learned men lecture...'

'I could not live in a town like that. I like seeing flowers and trees. I like fishing and hunting ... I am a man...' Valeri burst out, but Foma interrupted: 'Yes. I know. You are Prince Valeri, and life for you is the excitement of being seduced by savage girls and fighting their brothers and feeling that you are a fine fellow.'

Valeri looked at his friend furiously, but Lenotchka broke in: 'To hear Foma talk, you would think that he was a celibate saint who had kept his nose between the pages of a dictionary all his life. He is crazy – the rash things he does – worse than Valeri, I am sure. And as for passing unnoticed because he wears the same sort of hat! He never wears the same sort of hat. He only escaped in Constantinople because everyone thought he was mad, and Mohammedans respect lunatics and are kind to them.'

'That's how I escaped being raped by the bandits,' said Tamar.

'While in Europe the unfortunate lunatics are shut up and, if they are violent, beaten by their keepers,' said Jason. There was a silence, and then he went on: 'That's what the shepherd dogs do for their sheep. I'm not sure that they don't cause more misery and unhappiness than the wolves. I would say that all organised government, like all organised religion, is inevitably bad and an enemy of the individual. Far better live surrounded by bandits like Busrawi Ali, my Kurdish neighbour, whom I am proud to call my friend.'

Foma waved his hands at Jason in an ecstasy of amusement. 'To hear you talk about that bloodstained old ruffian! You know...' and Foma turned to Valeri and Tamar. 'You know that this aoul we are living in was occupied by Armenians fifteen years ago. Armenians built it and lived here for centuries. Then Busrawi Ali and his delightful Kurds came and massacred them all, men, women and children. But Kurds won't live in stone houses, so when our princely friend, Jason, led his people into Turkey, he was able to put them into this empty aoul, thanks to Busrawi Ali taking a liking to him.'

'Don't talk such rot. It's a purely business relationship. I've leased the aoul and the surrounding fields for a hundred years, at a rent of twenty sheep a year,' said Jason.

'He wouldn't have leased it to anyone else in the wide world. And aren't you rather naïve, Jason to believe that the Kurds will keep to any agreement?'

'No. You see they are nomads and are only our close neighbours for four months of the year. So we don't get on their nerves too much. Then Busrawi and I have agreed on a set of rules.'

'Do tell us,' said Tamar.

'First not to raid each other as we live too close for that to be comfortable. Then the Armenians traded with the Kurds and sold things on credit. That led to bad debts and bitter feelings, and finally to the Kurds liquidating their debts by massacring their creditors. The difference in religion was only an excuse. So we have forbidden all buying and selling and barter between our tribes. We have also forbidden attendance at each other's dances and ceremonies. For it is at dances that the young men draw their knives.'

'What happens if a party of young men come and break the rules?' asked Lenotchka.

'That hasn't happened yet.'

'Don't the young Kurds come after your girls? I know I should,' said Valeri.

'Yes, they do. And the old Kurds too. It's not a one-way traffic, as one of our boys has married a Kurdish girl and gone to live with her family.'

'We have here what Jason claims to be an ideal state: three hundred people who know each other and live practically without a ruler, without a permanent council, in a state of ideal anarchy. But what happens if one of your children had great talent? If he showed signs of being a philosopher, a scientist, a poet, painter, writer or musician? What hope would he have of developing his talent in this individualistic, ignorant paradise of Jason's?' Foma paused and, as there was a silence, went on: 'A young genius if he is to fulfil himself, must somehow get himself to St Petersburg, or Paris, or London or Vienna. That is where this paradise of anarchism fails.'

There was a long silence. Jason seemed about to speak, but thought better of it. Foma continued: 'It is because the really civilised places are few: Paris, Weimar, Vienna, London, that I think it is better to acquiesce and pass as a Frenchman, Englishman, Austrian or Russian, than to live in a primitive paradise on the sufferance of a bloodstained Kurd.'

'You began by telling us that "Render to Caesar that which is Caesar's" was as vile a piece of advice as could be imagined, and then, half an hour later, after two glasses of raki, you end up by giving us that advice yourself,' said Tamar unexpectedly.

'I agree with Tamar,' said Valeri. 'If you are ready to acquiesce in the autocratic rule of a despot over a nation of slaves, if you acquiesce in a police state that employs torture, if you acquiesce in a Church which exploits the fears and the generous impulses of mankind in order to gain power, if you acquiesce in injustice and oppression, you acquiesce in telling lies, and cease to be a moral being. What hope is there for the future unless someone has the courage to stand up and tell the truth?'

Jason nodded his approval, stroked his beard but kept silent.

'The hope lies in progress. Education leads to tolerance. Civilised man will no longer wish to conquer other peoples and to oppress his own,' said Foma.

'So you are prepared to wait until you have a Tsar who doesn't believe that the ends justify the means?' asked Valeri.

'That is until the cows come home,' put in Tamar.

'We all hope for progress. We all believe in education. But if we look at history we see that progress has come from a few exceptional individuals: from Voltaire who stood up against the Catholic Church and the injustice meted out to the Calas in France, by Galileo and Columbus, by Franklin and Jefferson – those are the men who have changed the world, because they were not ready to acquiesce. I led my people into Turkey because they were not willing to submit to the Russians. I would not have chosen Turkey, but there was nowhere else, and it was better than Persia,' said Jason.

'Quite right,' said Tamar, with memories of the bastinado.

Then she added: 'I wish you would tell us about it. I was little more than a child when it happened, and Anastasia would never talk to me about it. And I don't expect Lenotchka knows any more than I do.'

Lenotchka nodded, and Jason began: 'The beauty of my people and the beauty of my country has been our ruin. You all know that Circassian women are famous throughout the world for their beauty ever since Jason, after whom I am named, led the Argonauts to our country and carried off Medea, a Circassian woman, and the Golden Fleece. Because of our girls' beauty our villages were always being raided by Tatars and Turkish slavers, trying to carry them off to sell in Stamboul and Teheran slave markets. Some came quite honestly seeking a girl in marriage, like Tamar's father, but we have always had to guard ourselves on two fronts. On the north the Russians trying to steal our lands, on the south, slavers trying to kidnap our wives and daughters. On all the borders of our country we had lookout platforms with a sentry watching. And at night we had dogs to attack strangers and to give the alarm. We have always carried arms: a man ploughing a field will have his rifle slung on his back. We have always been a warlike people who raided the tribes near us, who raided us back again. But with the Russians it has been different. They did not fight for honour or glory, or to steal horses or sheep, but in order to exterminate all who lived in the mountains. We are all lumped together as Tatars by them. They paid ten roubles for the head of any mountaineer. After it had been cut off, rolled in the dust and carried about in a sack, one head looked very like another. The head of an Armenian selling honey cakes fetched as much as that of one of Shamyl's warriors, and was easier to obtain. So no one was safe under Russian rule.

'Instead of improving their own country, the Russians have always tried to annex the lands of their neighbours. They tried to enslave the Finns without much success, they have taken Poland, Lithuania, Latvia, the Ukraine, the lands of the Kirghiz and Bashkirs and all the tribes of primitive people in Siberia – and now those of all the peoples of the Caucasus.

'They neglect their own country and maltreat their own people. The only part of their empire in which they have built roads is the Caucasus – but there only for military purposes. When they invaded our mountains, we fought back, and we held them off for fifty years, defending our country against the whole Russian army for five years after Shamyl had surrendered. Finally they conquered us and drove us out of our rich farmlands and fertile valleys – the most beautiful country in the world, inhabited, and I say it with no false shame, by the most beautiful race in the world. Six hundred thousand Circassians were driven out of their aouls in the mountains down to the seashore. Every Circassian has the right to be heard at our councils. We held meetings, and the great majority voted to emigrate. The Turks said they would send ships and that we could take refuge in Turkey. But the ships took months to come, and thousands of our people died of plague and famine. My wife, who nursed them, caught the infection and died: my son was taken to be educated in Russia. But I, and other impatient leaders, took thousands of our people overland, marching through the mountains into Turkey. I saw it was only possible to go in small parties: the smaller the group, the less we disturbed the people we were coming to live among. The tiny group here – there are not more than three hundred of us – are mostly my own personal people, relatives of mine and our servants and their descendants. There are much larger groups in other parts of Turkey, some in the Balkans, and all the way down through Syria and even Palestine. But as a people we Circassians no longer exist. The Russians who drove us out of our farms and orchards and villages in the mountains have tried to colonise them with peasants. But coming from their illimitable plains, they are unhappy and fall ill. They imagine themselves beset by demons, and more than half of them have died or run away. The most fertile and beautiful mountain slopes are fast going back to a wilderness where wild boars replace cattle, and wolves sheep.'

'Have you any hope of regaining your country?' asked Valeri.

'Many of our people believe that, with the help of the Turks in a war between Russia and Turkey, we shall one day go back. I doubt it. There are too many Russians. I think we must not delude ourselves. But it is impossible to forget certain injuries. And the only way in order to avoid war – in which we should be beaten – and which falls most cruelly upon the innocent and brings disease and famine in its train, is for an individual to carry out a symbolic act of vengeance which will enable simple and suffering members of the tribe to feel that their wrongs have not gone unpunished and so allow them to forget the past and look forward.'

'Are you advocating assassination?' asked Foma.

'Yes I am. It is necessary for simple people to feel that evil does not go unpunished. And by the assassination of a single man you satisfy their need in the most economical way and ensure that one of the guilty is punished. Whereas in a war the innocent suffer, the guilty escape and abominations are multiplied.'

'I killed the boy who had murdered my brother without guessing that he had repented. I can never forgive myself for that, although his father was able to forgive me. Beware lest the same thing happen to you,' said Valeri.

'You believe that the end justifies the means: in doing evil that good may come. In that case you are morally the same as the Russian General who drove the people out of your country and herded them together to die of plague and famine,' said Foma.

'I don't think killing a monster is evil,' said Jason.

224

'Don't you believe that mankind is capable of moral progress?' asked Foma.

'Not really. I believe that the great mass of mankind will remain the same. The ways of life and the accepted beliefs will vary from place to place and century to century. But basically mankind will always be much the same. There will be less liberty and more oppression in large countries than in the smaller ones. But in all of them you will find occasional individuals and groups of friends who for some reason rise above the mass and who can change the thoughts and attitudes of their fellows. Just as a few men who lived in ancient Athens still influence us and set a standard of tolerance and civilisation.'

'I think such men will influence mankind to throw off the inheritance of hatred bred by divisions of race and religion and by greed, *in order to understand*,' said Valeri.

'Such men are arising in Russia today,' said Foma.

'It is because *I want to understand* and my little group of followers here to *understand* that I welcome a Russian who is no longer an enemy, because he is an intellectual and an example of the new man who wants above all things to understand,' said Jason.

'Thank you,' said Lenotchka. 'You have a gift for saying nice things.'

Valeri broke in upon this exchange of compliments with: 'The most important thing since the French Revolution is the emergence of the scientist who, without *a priori* beliefs, discovers the truth by experiment. Scientists are the men who will change the world; not heroes like Shamyl; not fanatical Moslems or brutal Russian Generals. They will show us the truth.'

'Still more the writers and artists who soften our hearts and enable us to understand our enemies,' said Foma.

Jason agreed and said: 'I have changed my feelings about Russians since reading a book by a Russian called Dostoevsky: *Crime and Punishment*, it was published two or three years ago, and I found it in the saddle bag of a Russian officer whom I killed when I went on a raid back to our country.'

'What effect did it have on you?' asked Foma.

'It made me resolve not to revenge upon the innocent what we have suffered from the heartless and the inhuman – to try to live in the future.' As he said this Jason turned to Tamar and took her hand. 'You will help me there.' His eyes filled with tears, and he could not go on.

'Now we had better say good-night,' said Tamar.

'Thank you very much for telling us what you have,' said Lenotchka. The lovers went out into the night, and Tamar did not return.

They were not seen again until they came to the guest house next day for a late lunch. Tamar was wearing the splendid dress of Anastasia's which she had brought with her, with an amber necklace and a silver belt with her dagger, and three rings that Mustapha Sasun had given her. Jason was wearing a long, white, waisted, woollen Circassian coat called a chokha by the Georgians, with pockets on the chest for silver cartridge cases, which he was wearing over a dark red silk shirt. On his head was a tall white Circassian papakha with a blue top and silver braid. From his silver belt hung a big Circassian dagger or kinjal, nearly two feet long with an ivory handle and a silver sheath – on his legs topboots of green morocco leather.

The sight of the pair in such grand clothes astonished Valeri, but Lenotchka did not seem surprised when Jason said: 'Congratulate us. We were married this morning. Old Busrawi was our witness and gave Tamar that gold head-band and told her to preserve it as untarnished as the honour of her husband. Luckily gold does not tarnish easily.'

'I know that most of your people are Moslems, but I thought that you were a Christian, Jason,' said Foma.

'That sort of thing doesn't matter to me. My people here

226

are Moslems in theory, but the older ones still worship Shible, the God of Thunder and of Justice, Tleps the God of Fire and Seosseres the God of Water. We don't have an Imam of our own, so we make use of the one living with our neighbours.'

This sudden wedding was the cause of much rejoicing in the aoul, and all who were not bedridden came that evening to the market place to wish their Prince well and to dance, or watch the dancing.

Valeri, Foma and Lenotchka came too, and Jason asked Lenotchka to give a solo dance. This was a mistake. In the first place the market place was uneven with bumps and hollows in its beaten earth floor, and Lenotchka's style of dancing needed a smooth and polished surface. Then her performance was toe dancing, whereas the Circassian dances were fierce and vigorous or languorous and sexual.

Moreover Lenotchka was one of their enemies: one of the hated Russians because of whom they had lost everything; because of whom most families had lost a husband, lover or brother. Many of them found it impossible to understand why the Prince had allowed two Russians to stay in that splendid house which he had refused to take as his palace but had reserved as a guest house. The two Russians were almost certainly spies sent by the Tsar. The man had been overheard arguing that they would have done better to stay under Russian rule.

While Jason stayed dancing with Tamar and then with one or two of the women, all went well. But after he and Tamar had said good-night, and while Foma and Lenotchka lingered watching the dances, lit up by a great fire, a woman came up to Lenotchka and threw a glass of wine in her face and then spat at her. This assault was so unexpected that Lenotchka stood for a moment dumbfounded. Then a woman who was dancing the leezginka drew her dagger and came dancing up to her with the bare knife in her hand. Lenotchka turned and ran, amid hoots of laughter. Foma ran after her, and when Valeri followed a few minutes later, he found her crying hysterically while Foma tried unavailingly to comfort her.

But if the Circassian women disliked having Lenotchka among them, they adored Tamar. She was, they all said, the right girl for Prince Ardigheb. The older people could remember Tamar's father and mother, and many could remember Anastasia too. Tamar was half Circassian, and her father had been a gentle, honest man. There was nothing of the hated Russian about her, or about the one-armed Prince who had brought her to find her mother's people. It showed what a fine girl she was to make such a long and dangerous journey. They all felt it was a pity that Tamar's uncles should have quarrelled with Prince Jason and that they had treated him as a fool under whose leadership they were at the mercy of the Kurds, and so had packed up and gone down into Syria. Marrying a pretty girl who looked every inch a Circassian would make him settle down and have more sense than he had sometimes shown.

Such were the reactions of Prince Jason's people to his marriage.

After endless discussions, Foma and Lenotchka had agreed to return with Valeri to the Castle. If they were to travel in Russia, or in Europe, Valeri would need money. A one-armed man cannot easily find work and support himself, and if there were three of them they would need more than if he were alone. What they would do after visiting the Castle would depend upon what they found when they got there. Before they left, however, Tamyas, the saddler in the little town, constructed an artificial arm for Valeri. It was made of a sleeve of very thick boiled leather which laced on to his upper arm and was strapped round his shoulders and across his chest, with a ball and socket joint at the elbow and ending at the wrist in a block of wood into which various tools could be screwed: a hook, a pusher for food, and a snaphook to which all sorts of things with a ring in them could be fastened.

After the wedding dances, Valeri sat up with Foma and Lenotchka at the guest house, and any of the Circassians who had overheard the conversation would have been confirmed in his suspicion of Russian spies.

Foma began with: 'Jason is a crazy fellow. The idea of subjecting oneself to Turkish rule in order to avoid that of Alexander II! Out of the frying pan into the fire! I don't defend our autocrat, but Russia is a country bursting with ideas and with new talent, whereas Turkey is a dead country, and one finds nothing but apathy in it from one end to the other.'

'I think that Jason thinks it safer for his people just because of that apathy. Under Russian rule they would soon be absorbed: in Turkey they will remain themselves. There's no danger of their children growing up to be little Turks,' said Valeri.

'But what hope can there be for an island or two of a few hundred Tcherkesses in the morass of the Ottoman Empire? What future? What culture? Whereas Russia is bursting with young genius, as you will discover when you have taught yourself to read Russian fluently. There is Pushkin, who was killed in a duel even sillier than the one you fought. He was a magnificent poet and he wrote short stories as well. Then there's Lermontov who wrote charming love poetry and died when he was twenty-seven. And there's a man called Gogol who is very funny and original. An aristocrat called Tolstoy writes with extraordinary force. Russia is bursting with talent, and anything may happen there. An Englishman once wrote that fifty years of Europe was better than a hundred years of China. I would say fifty years of Russia was worth five hundred of Turkey. Yes, Jason is crazy, and I hope his dear friend Busrawi Ali doesn't cut his throat and massacre all his people.'

'Somehow I think that his sincerity and his idealism will protect him,' said Valeri.

'Or the rifles all his men carry everywhere,' said Foma.

'Weren't you astonished at Tamar suddenly marrying him?' asked Lenotchka.

'No, not at all. It was wonderful to see them fall in love at first sight like that,' said Valeri.

They said good-night, and suddenly it occurred to Valeri that he ought to give a wedding present and immediately decided to give Jason his sabre. He was unconscious of the fact, or had forgotten, that Tamar had hated the sabre which was the symbol of the vanity which had led him to neglect her and to expose himself. Next morning, feeling that it would be intolerably mean to go back on his generous impulse, but already regretting it, he took the sabre and went round to the Prince's cottage.

'Come in, come right in,' shouted Jason in answer to his knock on the door. They had just finished breakfast, and Tamar was sitting on Jason's knee with her arm round his shoulders and made no effort to spring away. Seeing them so intimate embarrassed Valeri, but he could not have explained why.

He unwrapped the sabre and told the Prince that it was a wedding present and that it had been made a century before by the most famous swordsmith in Damascus. Tamar got off his knee and Jason drew the sabre and they examined the inscription on the blade.

'I shall treasure it because of you, but I hope I shall never use it, as I don't look forward to war, so I shall hang it up on the wall over the fireplace,' said Jason. This irritated Valeri, because a sabre is made for battle and not to decorate a room. But his irritation was allayed when Tamar rushed at him impulsively and kissed him again and again saying: 'You should not have given Jason that because it is an heirloom in your family – but it is like you to be generous. You know, whatever I said, I never doubted that.' Then she kissed him again, and Valeri felt that it had been well given.

Half an hour after Valeri had returned to the guest house, Jason arrived running.

'Busrawi had just sent warning that a detachment of Turkish police on mules are coming up the valley – no doubt to arrest Foma and Lenotchka. You must be off at once. No time to pack. I've given orders for the horses to be saddled. Foma can ride Tamar's mare and Lenotchka a pony. Come on all of you. Tamyas will go with you the first five parasangs to see you on the right road.'

Valeri had not unpacked his tent and bags of camping gear and was able with Tamyas's help to load them on the pack-pony. Foma and Lenotchka had to leave most of their possessions behind. Foma taking nothing but a saddle bag of books and his spectacles. Lenotchka filled a bag with clothes. None of them thought of food. Chivvied by Jason, they set off with Tamyas on a road towards the mountains due north, for they planned to strike down towards the Black Sea, avoiding crossing into Persia – and then through the Russian-occupied parts of the Caucasus to the town and back to the Castle. They would not be safe until they had crossed the Russian frontier over fifty parasangs to the north, and they would have to avoid towns and villages and get past the frontier post, if there was one. In the middle of the afternoon they halted. Tamyas changed to Tamar's mare, which he was taking back, and Foma mounted the little Kurdish pony that he had been riding. From there on they were on their own, taking the least frequented tracks through the wildest mountainous country. Foma was oblivious of his surroundings and talked incessantly of Russian literature and the Russian language. Valeri was occupied in picking out the path to follow, judging his position from the sun, and with his mind occupied in finding fodder for the horses and water at their next camping place, did not listen. Lenotchka was silent. They had not had time to pack food, but Valeri was anxious to get as far as possible before going to a town or village where, if the Turkish police were pursuing, they would leave clues. From his camping equipment they had tea and sugar. Lenotchka had brought a bottle of raki and

Tamyas a bear's ham which he left with them. They had no bread and no cheese. For three days of travel they lived on sweetened tea and a few slices of raw bear's ham, cut as thin as possible with Valeri's dagger. Foma talked incessantly. Lenotchka was silent, smiling and always with a helping hand for Valeri.

The last shreds of ham had been cut off the bone when Valeri said: 'We are running out of sugar, and we cannot keep alive on tea.'

'I will make soup out of the bone. I think there are a few wild plants I can boil up with it,' said Lenotchka. Thin and wiry, young and beautiful, her quiet courage was a surprise to Valeri. So was her devotion to Foma, for whom he felt the deepest admiration, but whose sweaty hands and complexion pitted with blackheads had always filled him with physical repulsion. It was a marvel to him, as it is to most handsome young men, that women can fall in love and feel physical passion for ugly and unhealthy men and for the old. Foma, twenty years older, was feeling the strain before either of them. He sweated profusely, staggered after dismounting and tossed and moaned in his sleep. Next morning they swallowed Lenotchka's soup with relish, though it was very salty. But they could not go on without food. That morning as they rode round an escarpment of the mountain, they saw a few horses in the foothills below them. Where there were horses, there might be men.

'I'll go down and see if I can find someone and buy food,' said Valeri.

'Let me go. They are less likely to harm a woman,' said Lenotchka.

'We'll both go. Then if we say we have a sick friend on the mountain, they may be generous,' said Valeri.

Soon after they began the descent they came in sight of some round Tatar huts, half burrows in the ground. They met an old Tatar shepherd, who took them to one of the burrows, a windowless hut, deeply sunk into the earth from which a dirty and unkempt woman emerged. They spoke of their sick friend and the woman gave them a bag of millet, a round loaf of bread and a bag of apricots. While they were thanking her and trying to get her to accept payment which she refused, a richly dressed man came up and hearing they had a friend sick on the mountain, gave them a bag of dried milk, leban, and a piece of raw camel. He also refused payment.

He could talk Georgian, and Valeri asked him if he had ever been past the aoul of the Sons of the Falcon.

'My grandfather was drowned at that place,' replied the Tatar, and a fierce glint came into his eyes.

'Next time you are passing, come to the door and ask for Prince Valeri, and I will make a feast for you and your followers,' said Valeri.

'You are a brave fellow to tell me who you are. Where did you happen to lose your arm?' asked the Tatar.

'I left it with one of the Turkomen,' said Valeri grinning.

The Tatar nodded. 'Well go now, in the name of God and His Prophet, Son of the Falcon.'

'Why did you tell him who you were, when we were both at his mercy?' asked Lenotchka as they rode away with their provisions.

'I would like to repay him for his generosity to us and the only chance would be when he brought a caravan past the Castle,' said Valeri.

'And if you are not there when he comes?' asked Lenotchka.

'I shall leave orders.' Then, noticing a sceptical smile on her face, he said huffily: 'My orders are obeyed.'

The dried milk saved Foma, who would not have been able to digest stringy camel meat or apricots, but who ate a bowl of hot leban and water with rye bread crumbled into it and revived at once.

They waited all the next day on the mountainside for Foma to be well enough to continue. During the afternoon the Tatar chief rode up to have a look at them. He was carrying a long gun and pulled up his pony thirty yards away. Apparently what he saw satisfied him, for he dismounted and walked to them.

'I have brought some opium for your sick friend, it will help his stomach,' he said, and handed Lenotchka a lump as big as a goose's egg.

'I'll have a roast sheep for you and your friends when you come,' said Valeri. 'And we'll make peace.'

'That's as may be,' replied the Tatar chieftain. He walked back to his pony, mounted, and rode away down the mountain. A small bit of the opium and a diet of bread and reconstituted milk cured Foma rapidly, and they were glad to proceed, as they all felt that the Tatars might repent of their friendship. After leaving the hillside above the Tatar burrows, Valeri tried again and again to find a track which would take them across the frontier over the mountains and that was passable by a man riding on a horse. It was impossible. The mountainside became too steep, and the loose stones and screes too dangerous. Slowly and inevitably they were forced down into the valley. Having failed to find a track on the eastern side, they tried the western, and that proved as bad. A track would lead them up to a shoulder of the mountain and then disappear among immense boulders, above which the cliffs from which they had crumbled rose sheer. Three times they tried to get out of the defile to cross by the mountains, but each time they were forced back into it, and with each attempt they and the horses became more exhausted. There was nothing for it but either to abandon the horses and risk crossing the mountain on foot, or to go to the frontier post and attempt to pass it by night, or in the early hours before first light, without being detected. If they abandoned their horses, they would be helpless when they had got across, as they had not enough money to buy others and there were some two or three hundred miles of wild country to traverse. Moreover they did not know whether

234

it was in fact possible to find a track which would take them across on foot.

They went on down the road and camped well out of sight of it. Next morning, in the darkness before the first light, they would make their attempt. If they woke up the guards, they would mount their horses and ride back to the Tatar camp, and try somewhere else, if it were possible. It was a dark night, and there was a strong and very cold north wind blowing, a wind which might help to hide the noise they were bound to make, but which made them shiver and their fingers numb. Valeri and Foma dismounted when they were two hundred paces from the barrier, leaving Lenotchka mounted and holding all the horses. When they had opened the barrier, she was to come through at a sharp trot, and Valeri and Foma were each to catch the bridle of his horse from her, mount and gallop after her as fast as they could.

The two men crept up to the barrier noiselessly and began examining it by touch. It was fastened at one end with a chain and padlock, but at the other it swung on hinges. In the dim light, Valeri could see that if they could lift it off the pins of the hinges they could open it. But the gate was too heavy for their united efforts. There was, however, a flagstaff with the Turkish flag fluttering beside it, and they were able to rock the pole of the flagstaff to and fro until they were able to pull it out of the ground. Valeri then put one end of the flagstaff under the bottom rail of the barrier and while he levered it up, Foma held the barrier steady and then when the hinges were clear of the pins, pulled it away while Valeri lowered it. They dragged it open with a lot of scraping noise and then when they had got it nearly wide open, Valeri tripped and the barrier fell with a crash. He immediately gave the signal – an owl's hoot – and Lenotchka beat the horses into a trot and came up as the frontier post came alive: a bell rang, lights showed, and, as Valeri and Foma caught the reins of their horses and began to scramble on to them, men came running down the steps.

Lenotchka was well ahead, Foma had got into some trouble with his pony which was spinning round away from him. Then came shots, shouts, and then more shots. When they had ridden four hundred paces Lenotchka and Valeri pulled up to wait for Foma, but, to their horror, his pony dashed past them riderless. Valeri slid off his mare.

'I'll go back and see if I can see anything. You ride on to the Russian barrier and wait for me there with the horses.'

'No. I'll wait here.'

'No. It's you that Ibrahim Pasha wants to capture. I want to know that you are on the safe side of the frontier. The Turks aren't interested in me. Take my mare with you and I'll follow on foot.'

While Lenotchka reluctantly rode on, Valeri walked back, keeping close to the side of the track. Dawn had broken, but the defile through the mountains was in shadow. It was a cold grey mist. When Valeri came in sight of the Turkish barrier, he could see men moving about and even make out one of them running up the wooden steps into the office. There was no sign of Foma. If he had been killed or wounded by one of the shots, which Valeri thought the most likely explanation of his riderless pony, the frontier guards had already removed the body. There was absolutely nowhere – no shrubs, or bushes or ditch, where Foma could have dragged himself if wounded and be lying hidden. Whether dead or alive, he must be in the hands of the Turkish guard. Valeri thought that there was no point in getting arrested if Foma were dead, and he turned and walked the two versts to the Russian post. There it might be possible to hire some local man, who was known to the Turks, to go to their frontier post on some excuse and find out if Foma was alive. Lenotchka had arrived and was waiting for the Russian Lieutenant to wake up, have his breakfast and see her. Valeri saw to the horses and joined her. After three hours they were summoned to the office of a lean youngish Lieutenant in a white tunic and wearing a heavy moustache.

Valeri introduced himself and Lenotchka, and the officer, without getting up or offering to shake hands, barked out: 'One of these ten-a-penny Georgian Princes. Well, when your luggage has been examined, you can cut along. As for you, my lady, you'll have to wait. You have no passport. That's usual. Ladies who leave Constantinople always mislay their passports – yellow ones, nine times out of ten.'

Valeri controlled himself at this outrageous insult – for in Russia only prostitutes have yellow passports – and said nothing. Lenotchka spoke of Foma. Would the Lieutenant send a man to ask what had happened to him?

'Certainly not. The Turks were quite right to shoot him. The only surprising thing is that they should have hit him. I shall congratulate Yussuf Khan on his men's shooting when I next meet him.' Then, turning to Valeri, he said: 'I don't want you hanging about here. I'll give you a native's *laisser-passer*. Wait outside.' Then as Valeri and Lenotchka were about to leave the room, the Lieutenant said to her: 'You stay. I've some questions to ask you. And anyway you'll have to stay in custody until they've checked your story and issued a new passport.'

Foma Ilyitch caught the rein of his pony, pulled it to a halt, got his foot in the stirrup, swung his body up, and the stirrup leather broke. He fell on his back half under the pony's head. It was a severe bump for a man in his forties. But Foma had kept hold of the reins and he rolled over, under the pony's head, got up, put his right foot in the other stirrup and swung into the saddle, successfully this time. He got his pony into a gallop almost at once. Then came a volley of shots which made his pony go all the faster. A few seconds later came a single shot and the pony jumped sideways, to the left and Foma, with only one stirrup, lost his seat and fell heavily into the road.

He was half stunned. Two small stones were stuck in his forehead, his shoulder seemed dislocated and his hands cut

and bleeding. He struggled to his feet, and the blood that had
been held back by his eyebrows began to trickle over into
the corner of one eye and down the side of his nose and
into his mouth. Foma was unaware of the blood and barely
aware of the pain and the shock. His whole being was con-
centrated on the part he had to play. He did not seek con-
cealment, but stood swaying in the middle of the road. Then
he began to stagger back towards the Turkish post. The
guards might have shot him as he came, looming out of the
mist. But he limped and wavered in his walk and his waver-
ing progress excited their curiosity. They could kill him
later, but they would question him first. When he reached
the guards he stared at them without speaking. Then he
bowed and made the sign of the cross and muttered a blessing in Russian. Suddenly he turned fiercely on the corporal
and said: 'Why do you let them knock an old man down?'
The corporal made him repeat himself. He was puzzled. 'What
are you?' he asked.

'A pilgrim: I'm going to Jerusalem. They knocked me
down. Why do you let them ride so fast? No time to get
out of the way.'

'Take him and wash that blood off him and bandage
him up. The Lieutenant will want to get his story out of him,'
said the Corporal and Foma was led into an outhouse where
his wounds were washed. Two hours later he was telling his
story to the Turkish officer, with the Corporal interpreting.
Foma said he had lived in a monastery and was now on a
pilgrimage. He had not the money to take ship from Batum.
He was cross-questioned about the monastery and gave so
many details that his story was accepted.

He could not be sure how many men there were on
horses: four or five maybe – but they came galloping out of
the darkness and knocked him over. He kept repeating that it
ought not to have been allowed. Finally the Turkish officer
took pity on him as he seemed holy and crazy, and told
him he was sending him back into Georgia as there was a

Tatar encampment down the valley and that they would cut his throat. He must begin his pilgrimage over again and cross the frontier much further west, where there were villages and inhabitants. Otherwise he would die in the desert, or get his throat cut by Tatars or Kurds. The Turks gave him a cup of coffee and then sent him back to Russia.

As Valeri went into the yard he saw Foma walking into it. He was limping and there was a bandage round his forehead, but he was alive and had escaped from the Turks.

Valeri just had time to tell him that the Lieutenant intended to detain Lenotchka, but that he had been told to clear off, before a guard came up and told Foma to step into the waiting room. Luckily the guards were fresh from Russia and did not know Georgian, so that Valeri and Foma were able to talk freely for the few minutes before Valeri was given his *laisser-passer* and ordered to go on down the road into Russian-occupied Caucasus.

Valeri told Foma that he would say that all the horses were his and that he would wait with them at the first suitable place he could find down the road. He would be watching it during daylight hours, keeping a look out for Lenotchka and him. If they could manage to get permission to go for a walk, they might escape. They were more likely to be allowed some freedom if they had no horses.

Valeri had scarcely had time to put forward this plan and had not heard Foma's story, when he was called out of the room, given a paper and told to leave at once if he didn't want to be sent back to Turkey. Foma's success with the Turks was his undoing when he came in front of the Russian Lieutenant. For he stuck to his story of being a pilgrim – but this time making his way back to Russia. The Lieutenant who had at first looked bored at the sight of the bandaged vagabond, suddenly smacked his hands together and looked at him with an impudent smile.

'I have been told to look out for you. You're to be sent back to your monastery. We know all about you, Mr Pilgrim. And the woman your companion is wanted in Turkey. A common prostitute and a thief.'

Then turning to the guard who had brought Foma in, he said: 'Put the chains on his legs while transport is getting ready to take him down to headquarters.'

The period of waiting was only a few hours, but Foma, who had kept his nerve with the Turks, collapsed. He was prostrated by despair which took the physical form of a violent headache and nausea. The injuries he had made so light of became almost unbearably painful, and he had double vision.

Lenotchka, however, bribed her gaoler to allow her to speak to him out of the window, after he had already been handcuffed and with leg chains put on him and had been led out and put in the tarantass in which he was to be driven to the nearest prison. As the guards knew Russian, she called out to him in French. He looked up, and by shutting one eye was able to focus her in the window which was quite close to where his carriage was waiting. 'I am so happy you are alive. My life hasn't been wasted since I met you. Now it is finished. This vile type wants to send me back to Ibrahim. But I am not going. That Tatar gave us enough ... and now I am going to swallow it. Don't be afraid for me. Death is kind.'

The gaoler came and took her by the arm. Then as he turned towards the door, she opened her hand revealing a piece of opium as big as a duck's egg.

'Just one moment please,' she said to the gaoler and then cut off a lump of opium with her pocket knife and swallowed it.

'Prostchaite,' (farewell for ever) she called out and swallowed another lump. Foma looked at her out of his one eye and said nothing.

'Come along lady,' cried the gaoler.

The driver of the tarantass whipped up his horse, and the guard who was to take Foma jumped in beside him.

'Funny you being a monk and having a good-looker like that, who loves you,' said the driver.

Valeri had ridden off driving the three ponies in front of him and looking vainly for a cleft in the mountains where he might camp and conceal them and himself until Lenotchka and Foma escaped, or were released. In this way he came down to a straggling collection of huts, among which was a grander building of two storeys, with a courtyard and stables, which was a posting station. He drove his ponies into the yard, dismounted and decided to stay there openly.

Lenotchka was the only one of them with any money: Valeri hoped he would not be asked to pay until she had arrived.

After the week of starvation since he had left the Circassians, Valeri was happy to have two cooked meals a day and a bed to sleep upon, though there were fleas in it. But his first request was for a bath, and a few hours later he was told that it had been heated and was ready for him.

He had never, he thought, enjoyed such luxury. After the first room of hot steam, he lay on a stone slab and the old woman who was the attendant on bathdays, not more than once a week or fortnight, rubbed him down and great rolls of black dirt came off him. Then she threw pails of cold water over him, and after that he went into the steam for a second time and beat himself with birch twigs and then was sluiced down for a second time.

The frontier guards lived in the village when they were off duty and occasionally came in to the inn for a drink, and to play cards together. Valeri wondered how he could get in touch with one of them – but there were always two or three of them together – and he thought it better not to approach them. He spent the day in his room, looking out on the road, or exercising his mare and the ponies. At night he slept badly, lying between waking and sleep and wondering what wild scheme he could devise to rescue his friends. Never had the loss of his arm seemed more of a handicap: for a one-armed man is instantly recognisable. What hope was there of his being able to impersonate a Russian General, coming to inspect the frontier post? Even if he could obtain the uniform, his Georgian accent and his lack of an arm would instantly identify him. Valeri was not used to being helpless – but during these days of waiting, he realised the despair and rage that consumes those who are at the mercy of the powerful. There was no one to whom he could talk, no plan that he could devise, no outlet for his pent-up bile and fury. For the first two or three days, the fact of being able to eat and rest was a relief. But by the fourth he was almost mad with frustration. On the fifth day, when he came into the inn from the stables, one of the frontier guards came up and asked him:

'Are you staying here for long?'

'I am waiting for my friends. There was some question of passports,' said Valeri.

'I wondered if it was that. They've been gone four days,' said the guard. Then as Valeri gazed, unable to believe what he heard, the man went on: 'The man was put in leg chains and was driven to headquarters in a carriage the day you came here.' Valeri suddenly realised that it must have been while he was having his bath.

'Was the woman with him?' he asked.

'No. She was sent back into Turkey.'

'But she was a Russian,' said Valeri.

'It seems the Turks were after her. There was a price on her head. Our Lieutenant would sell his own sister for money. He's a real Tchinovnik, a dirty swine.'

Valeri sought out the innkeeper, sold him the two riding ponies to pay his bill, and after buying provisions for the journey, set off to ride to his aoul.

CHAPTER NINE

The sudden death of Prince Gurgen, followed by the suicide of the Princess, made a deep impression upon Lieutenant Mihail Semyonitch Arbatsky. He felt that he had participated in a tragedy as lurid as any that he had met in the translations of Monk Lewis, William Godwin, or Mrs Radcliffe. As he had ambitions as an author, he immediately began writing a romance to be called *The Curse of the Falcon*. He was entirely carried away by this ambition, and, as he found that service life in barracks in Tiflis interfered with his writing, he decided to sacrifice his career for art – sent in his resignation and planned to go and live at the Castle – in order to get the real local colour that he needed.

Before doing so, however, he made a call on the Archpriest. He condoled with him on his tragic loss and mentioned that he had been present at Prince Gurgen's deathbed. He did not however, speak of the Prince having struck the Princess, or reveal that the cause of the fit of fury which resulted in the Prince's death was a child's rattle. He suppressed this, not out of tact, because it would give the Archpriest pain, but because he had already suppressed the memory – which did not suit the style of tragedy which he was writing.

Lieutenant Arbatsky, in his white tunic, with his epaulettes, sabre and polished boots, yet obviously a polite young intellectual, deeply imbued with a love of Georgia, made a most agreeable impression on the Archpriest, who inquired where his visitor was staying and insisted that he should immediately leave the inn and come to stay in his house. Then, when Arbatsky had left to fetch his horse, his servant and his portmanteau, the old man hurried round to tell the widow Tara about his visitor.

'Just the man we want for Leonidas,' she exclaimed.

'What? I don't follow,' said the Archpriest.

'You were quite right not to consult that fine gentleman our Governor. But this young man seems just what we want as a tutor for the little boy.'

The Archpriest was astonished. 'Leonidas is not yet two years old,' he said.

The widow gave a ripple of silvery laughter.

'Well, that is rather young for lessons, I admit. I am running ahead. But if this young man goes to the Castle, I should encourage him to stay.'

'He asked if I thought he might stay for two months ... he wants to write some sort of romance.'

'Quite so. But if he could be persuaded to stay, he would perhaps act as a lightning conductor.'

'Whatever do you mean?'

'If he were permanently installed in the aoul, the Russians would be satisfied and they would not strike it. That's what I mean.'

The Archpriest called her a fanciful little Puss and, on her insistence, promised to bring Lieutenant Arbatsky round for a cup of tea the following afternoon.

Next morning the Lieutenant rode over to the encampment of the Solutz and asked if he could see Ziklauri. He was kept waiting for half an hour while Ziklauri shaved, put on a clean shirt and a new pair of top boots. It was important, he felt, to meet these damned Russian officers on equal terms as far as appearances went. Arbatsky, however, scarcely noticed the delay, as Ziklauri's daughter came and flirted with him – a marvellous bit of local colour for his romance!

When this was interrupted and Naida went off pouting, Arbatsky found himself in the presence of a well set-up man of fifty, whose hair was beginning to grow grey over the temples and who was looking at him with shrewd blue eyes. Arbatsky had to do the talking, but his remarks seemed to make no impression. He said that he loved Georgia and its peoples. He said that he was writing a book about them. He said that he had visited the aoul of the Sons of the Falcon and that he had been present at the death of Prince Gurgen. He said that he had been horrified by the suicide of the Princess. He said that, with the encouragement of the Archpriest, he intended to revisit the Castle and spend a few weeks there.

Finally Arbatsky said: 'I have come to ask you what hope is there of reconciling the two halves of the clan of Sons of the Falcon and ending the feud?'

Ziklauri's expression did not change as he replied: 'There is no feud. I am at peace with Prince Valeri.'

The mention of Valeri was totally unexpected.

'Do you mean the son who became a monk?' asked Arbatsky.

'Yes, I mean the heir to Prince Gurgen and head of the clan.'

'I thought he had disappeared and was presumed dead,' said Arbatsky.

'Have you any reason to presume it?'

'No. I understood that he had not been heard of since he left and is not expected to return,' said Arbatsky, who was feeling out of his depth.

'I think that he is likely to take up his inheritance very shortly,' said Ziklauri.

'I had understood from the Archpriest that the baby, Leonidas, is the heir.'

For the first time Ziklauri's expression changed and he laughed. 'I should not leave Prince Valeri out of account. He is a brave man and an intelligent man, and brave men who are intelligent live longest.'

'Why, are you expecting him to return soon?' asked Arbatsky.

'He went on a journey that might last two years. It is now nearly two years since he went.'

'If you knew that Prince Valeri were dead, would you take possession of the aoul in the name of the younger branch?' asked Arbatsky.

'Certainly not. I was, without knowing it, partly responsible for the death of the child Vasso. I would not do anything that might endanger the baby Leonidas.'

'How could you endanger him?' asked Arbatsky.

'There is the icon of Saint Anne watching. Vasso was murdered for her sake. Leonidas might also be sacrificed to her. I would not risk that child's life for any aoul. So there, Mr Russian Lieutenant, you have the truth.'

Arbatsky came away from his interview with Ziklauri very impressed. He would have liked to see more of the man. And then he would like to renew his acquaintance with his daughter, Naida. He imagined her all fire: yielding herself at one moment and turning to bite like a wild animal at the next. There would be a niche for her in his romance. But the chief thing was that, when he went to the aoul, he must be prepared for the return of Prince Valeri.

Widow Tara crooked her little finger elegantly as she poured out tea. Conversation was stilted and polite. Arbatsky did not mention having visited the encampment of the Solutz, or Prince Valeri's name. When the Archpriest said: 'Well we really must be going,' the widow said: 'Run along, my old friend. I have one or two things to say to this young man in private. Two's company, you know.'

The Archpriest raised his eyebrows, murmured, 'God bless me,' and toddled off. The widow Tara waited until he was out of her garden. Then she put out the tip of her pretty tongue, smiled sweetly and putting the tips of her fingers together, said with an air of great wisdom: 'You are taking a risk, young man, in going to the Castle. Many people have died there.'

Lieutenant Arbatsky was thrilled. 'Tell me more,' he murmured.

'I cannot stop you going, because you are a brave young man, a soldier accustomed to danger. But while you are at the aoul, I would like you to ask yourself many questions. How did Vasso die? Why did his mother throw herself off the tower? But most especially ask yourself: How did Katerina die? But ask *yourself* these questions. Whatever you do, do not let a hint of them escape you to the women at the Castle.'

'What about Saint Anne?' asked Arbatsky, feeling greatly daring. The widow Tara crossed herself three times and murmured a few words of prayer. 'Her least of all,' she whispered.

Next morning Lieutenant Arbatsky set off for the aoul, with his servant riding behind him leading a mule loaded with a comfortable mattress and his portmanteau full of clean shirts and bottles of scent and half a dozen cakes of toilet soap scented with Parma violets.

He reached the Castle in the late afternoon. As he came in sight of it, he saw goats scampering down to the ford from the yard and by the time that he had reached it they were climbing the hill above. The goats were the only sign of life, for he and his servant rode through the open gate into the yard without seeing a human being, or being challenged by so much as a barking dog.

Arbatsky dismounted and knocked with the knob of his riding whip on the half-open front door. After an interval he knocked again, and suddenly Iriné made her appearance, fresh, smiling and charmingly dressed.

'So you've come back Lieutenant! How delightful!' she exclaimed and taking him by the hand led him into the hall.

'You must be tired. I'll get you some tea – but you would prefer vodka? And your servant – isn't he called Stiva? He must have a drink. We can find a room for him next to yours

– the Castle is so empty now. And Herakli will look after the horses.'

'I did not see anybody as I rode up,' said Arbatsky.

'The men are all out doing some great work in one of the fields. I expect Nina is in the dairy.'

Arbatsky gazed at her, as she talked without any shyness. He had no idea that she was such a beautiful, tall and attractive woman.

'You must make me talk Russian while you are here. *Pozhaloosta*. I've been learning it. *Otchen krasseeviye yezik*,' (a very beautiful language) she said.

She left him and he wandered about the empty hall and looked into the chapel, where the little heap of Vasso's toys, swept and dusted, were still piled up in front of the altar and Saint Anne was looking at him with her pale blue eyes, lit up by the flame that was always burning. Before Iriné came back he could hear Stiva and Herakli talking in the yard, the mule was being unloaded and then led away after the horses to the stables.

Iriné brought in the samovar and tea things and they drank tea out of glasses with birchbark holders like Russians, and ate red currants preserved whole in jelly, and Iriné poured him out a glass of vodka. By the time he had drunk his second cup of tea, Shorena wandered in with Leonidas. She seemed in no way surprised to see him. Then old Nina came in, followed by Stiva carrying his master's portmanteau up to the room in the tower where they were putting him, and coming down immediately to carry up the mattress. Everything was peaceful and quiet. The baby Leonidas did not cry, but looked at him inquisitively with his deep blue eyes and then tottered up to him and allowed himself to be picked up and sat on his knee while the three women watched attentive and silent. Lieutenant Arbatsky had never imagined that the Castle which had seen sieges, earthquakes, tumults, suicides and sudden deaths could be a place of such peace. A place also in which he felt at home and

248

welcome. The fortnight that followed was the happiest of his life.

In the morning he would sometimes make a pretence of writing his story; then he would find Iriné and they would spend the day sometimes riding horses, but more often on foot, going up the river to where the lake was slowly reforming, or climbing crags and precipices. Iriné had no fear of heights and would pick out a way easy enough for Arbatsky and then, lying beside him on a narrow ledge, would laugh and tease him and practise her pidgin Russian.

A week after his arrival, he asked her to marry him.

'Not unless you are crazy, because, you know, they all say that I am a crazy woman. Everyone except you knows that,' she replied. When he took her in his arms and kissed her, she laughed and said: 'Russian Officer seduces girl in Caucasus. Asks to be posted to Archangel.'

She would not go to his room at night, or allow him to come to hers. 'I am not going to take advantage of you, my dear man. You'll come to your senses presently,' and again she laughed, and when he had turned away in anger she pounced on him, kissed him, and crying out, '*Spokonye notch,*' ran up to her room on the floor above. Arbatsky wished his nights were less restful. Though often he lay awake, listening to the rush of the river and the song of the nightingale-thrush, and wondering, supposing Iriné agreed to marry him, where would they live and how the marriage would turn out.

One day Arbatsky overheard Shorena saying to Nina rather sharply: 'We'll leave that until Valeri comes back, if you don't mind.'

He intercepted her soon afterwards and asked: 'Have you any idea when Prince Valeri will return to the Castle?'

Shorena looked at him savagely, baring her teeth, and snarled: 'It won't be long now, Mr Russian Officer.'

Arbatsky stood in front of her, barring her way, as she tried to pass. 'I went to see your kinsman Ziklauri before coming here. He told me that he expected Prince Valeri back very shortly.'

Shorena's whole expression changed to one of eager curiosity.

'So you saw Ziklauri! How is that good man? He had not any definite news of Valeri, I suppose?'

'I don't think so. Only that he had expected him to be gone for two years and the time is nearly up.'

Shorena went off with a happier expression on her face than Arbatsky had seen since his arrival. Later in the day she came up and asked: 'Did you see either of the girls? Salomé and Elisso? I heard that Salomé had a boy. He would be Ziklauri's grandson.' Shorena was not in the least interested in Salomé or Elisso, but she wanted to show that she was not quite such a savage as she had revealed.

The man who rode at walking pace towards the Castle was wearing a long Circassian coat open to the midriff which revealed that he was not wearing a shirt. On his legs was a pair of coarse linen trousers which had originally been made of striped blue and white material, but were stained with all the different coloured soils between Trebizond and Elizetapol. On his feet were a pair of woven birchbark lapti held on with crossgartering of twine. The lines of his face were ingrained with dirt, and his little yellow beard and moustache were clotted with dust and spittle. He was one-armed, and the left sleeve of his coat hung empty. He carried no weapons except a kinjal. He wore no hat, and his fair hair was matted with filth and hung to his shoulders. The animal he was riding was in as bad shape as he was himself. Between each of her ribs there were deep sunken grooves, and she occasionally stumbled with fatigue as she picked her way along the stony track. Her rider occasionally asked himself why he should be returning at all to face the fury of his old father and, far worse, the contempt of his father's young wife. What hateful changes would that woman have made?

It was possible that the old man, or if he were too impotent, some priest or monk, had given her a child. He would not have come back at all; he might even at the last moment turn away, except for a fierce and sardonic curiosity to know the worst. No, that was not entirely true. For, when he analysed his feelings, which he was apt to do, he knew that the weakness of the flesh counted for much. He would endure Katerina's contempt for the sake of a bath and clean clothes for himself and a bed of straw and a feed of oats for his darling mare – all that was left him in the world.

'It will be humble pie, very humble pie, but at least it will be pie,' he admitted. 'Pride is a luxury I have long forgotten.'

Yet some of his recent actions had been dictated by pride. He knew that if he had visited the Solutz encampment, Ziklauri would have welcomed him and that his sisters, Salomé and Elisso would have given him a clean shirt and decent clothes in which to return home. But, owing to his pride, he had purposely avoided them and had ridden round the outskirts of the town, though it is doubtful if any one in it would have recognised this wild one-armed beggar on his famished horse as Prince Valeri, Son of the Falcon.

There was no one to be seen near the aoul. His mare, knowing she was near home, made renewed efforts and climbed the steep slope up from the ford inspired by memories of her stable. The Castle seemed deserted, as Valeri rode through the open gateway, under which no carcases of sheep were hanging, into the yard. At the sound of hoofs on the cobbles, Herakli came limping out as Valeri dismounted.

'Oh, what have you done to her?' the old man exclaimed, but his indignation was forgotten, as he looked at the wretched figure of his master.

Valeri burst into sobs at the reproach of the old horse-keeper, but he swallowed them down.

'Look after her, Herakli. She is very weak with famine. Don't let her gorge herself, whatever you do. Bran mash, bran mash, bran mash,' he repeated and, with his face streaming with tears and his shoulders shaking, he turned from the old man and the mare, and walked to the open door of the hall. He waited to master himself. There was no one. He stepped in. A moment later Shorena appeared. She stared for a moment, then ran to him, threw her arms round him and kissed him again and again and again, and clung to him. He had not recognised her until her arms were about him and her face pressed to his, and, at her reception, he cried out aloud: 'Oh, oh, oh! Oh, no, you mustn't. I'm so filthy. How can you kiss me like this?'

They were both weeping. After a little Valeri made an effort and said: 'I must see my father, darling.'

Shorena was astonished. 'Don't you know? He's dead. He's been dead for ages.'

It took a little time for him to understand this. Then he asked: 'And Katerina? Is she here – or has she gone back to the town?'

'Oh, she's dead too, thank God.'

This took him less time to realise – but it did not occur to him that he had come into his inheritance.

'I must have a bath and some clean clothes,' he said at last. Luckily the bath house was heated and Shorena followed him into it and said: 'I'll give you your bath, darling.' And then: 'I see you know nothing, and I've got a great deal to tell you. All the mix up about Leonidas, too.' And she had to hold him and kiss him again.

When Nina woke up from her nap, she found Herakli in the kitchen making some hot bran mash and putting a little beer with it, and he told her that Lord Valeri had come back. She heard voices in the bath house and knocked and Shorena called through the door that she was to bring a clean shirt and clean clothes for Valeri. But Nina knocked on the door again, saying: 'Will you just speak to me, so I can hear your voice, my precious?'

'Yes, Nina I am happy to be back. I'll be out in a little while.'

The old woman hobbled off, thinking: 'I forgot to call him My Lord. But he won't mind.' She fetched a shirt and a pair of cotton drawers, which had been lying scented with herbs, and some socks, and then a pair of velvet trousers, a silk jacket, a dressing gown and a pair of Persian slippers, since he was not likely to want to go out riding again that day, and she handed them in to Shorena, through clouds of steam. Then she hurried off as fast as she could to tell Natiella to catch a couple of pullets and wring their necks and pluck them, because there would not be enough other-wise for supper. Then she started to make pastry for piroshki for the soup. Valeri did not, however, put on his fine clean clothes that evening, for on going into the hot room a second time, he fainted. Shorena flung open the bath house door and gave a cry for help. Iriné and Lieutenant Arbatsky had just ridden into the yard, and they ran at once to her. Nina came too, with her hands covered in flour. Shorena had been splashing Valeri with cold water and he regained conscious-ness as Arbatsky and she carried him into the hall, just in time for him to hear Iriné say: 'Mary Magdalen discovered washing our Saviour.'

Nina was making ineffective attempts to cover his genitals with a towel, and murmured: 'The darling looks like Christ being taken down from the Cross,' and then drew her breath in horror, at the sight of the stump of his arm, and ex-claimed: 'Oh, his poor arm! It's lucky it's his left.'

'So it is. How very appropriate. He killed Lazar with a left-handed blow. If thine hand offend thee, cut it off,' said Iriné. At this Valeri laughed, and felt better. Iriné had how-ever one more shaft to fire off, for she turned to Arbatsky and said: 'Since the search for wisdom has brought Valeri to this condition, I hope you will stick to a life of folly,' and Valeri laughed again. It made him feel that he had got home, but he was feeling very weak.

Shorena was soon feeding him with spoonfuls of the egg soup for which the piroshki had been intended. It was the *avgolemono* of the Greeks, except that at the Castle they put a handful of their home-grown barley into the chicken broth, instead of rice.

After swallowing a bowl of it, Valeri fell asleep.

Lieutenant Arbatsky and Iriné did full justice to the soup and piroshki, to the trout fried in butter and the creamed chicken that Nina had prepared for her master, and Shorena also ate her share, as violent emotions make one hungry.

Such was Prince Valeri's return to his inheritance.

During the short time that Shorena had been scrubbing Valeri in the bath house she had told him a great deal of what had occurred during his absence, but she had not described the death of Katerina – only the finding of the body and the message written in her hand.

Valeri remained rather feeble for a week and he was very emotional, several times bursting into tears, so Shorena never did tell him how she had shot Katerina. It was unnecessary to relive that terrible moment – and everything had turned out for the best. Valeri was well enough, however, to dress and to see Malik. The old man had gone bald, and his moustache had grown grey and hung down in long points like a Tatar's.

When he saw Valeri's empty sleeve he said: 'Who did that? And what did he get for it?'

Then he shook his head mournfully when Valeri replied: 'He was one of the Turkomans and a better horseman than I was. He got my sabre. But I got it back and gave it to Prince Tcherkess as a wedding present, when he married Tamar.' He did not tell Malik that Prince Tcherkess called himself Jason and that he had hung the sabre on his wall and had said that he would not use it, because he knew such newfangled notions would depress the old man. However, he added: 'Prince Tcherkess is a great friend of Busrawi Ali.'

'Better a friend than an enemy. All the same he ought to look out,' said Malik. Then he looked at Valeri and smiled: 'I always thought that girl, Tamar, was going to marry you.

Well, we old fellows will be glad to see you back and taking over the reins.'

Malik had never been known to speak of his past, and Valeri was astonished when the old man lingered by the door of the bedroom and pulled his long moustache and looked at Valeri with a glint in his eye and said: 'Busrawi would have put me in a pit full of bugs if he had caught me. I had his youngest wife – had her three nights running while he was away, when I was a young fellow. Then I had to clear out.'

Valeri was well enough to have dinner in the hall with Shorena, Iriné and Arbatsky that night and was in for another surprise when Iriné said: 'This fellow, Mihail Semyonitch, is crazier than I am. He loves everything Georgian and he wants to marry me. He thinks he ought to ask your permission as the head of the clan. Do you give it?'

Valeri laughed. 'As long as you are satisfied, my dear sister. That is what matters.'

'*Otchen harashaw* ... I announce our engagement then,' said Iriné.

After the kissings and congratulations were over, Arbatsky said: 'Now Prince Valeri has taken up his inheritance I don't suppose little Leonidas will be taken off to St Petersburg.' Valeri asked for an explanation and Arbatsky said: 'The official policy in the Caucasus is to take the young heirs to the Princedoms and heads of clans to be brought up as Russians in Russia. But, of course, Prince, as you are likely to marry and to have a son, Leonidas would not succeed you, since he's your younger brother. So I feel sure that they won't take him.'

Valeri looked at Shorena and shook his head slightly. She said nothing, and not long afterwards Valeri and she got up and said good-night.

Neither of them wished to change their relationship. As Valeri no longer called himself a Christian it would have been repugnant to him to go through the ceremony of marriage in a church. And when he mentioned marriage, Shorena was against it on account of Leonidas, who would not inherit the Castle if she and Valeri were to have a legitimate son.

'Let him grow up thinking that he is your brother; the relationship of two brothers is often happier than that of son and father. Let us leave it as it is. Nina will never confess her action, and the only other person who knows the truth is Vakhtang who can be trusted never to reveal it.'

Shorena's fierce physical love for Valeri was exactly what he wanted. They slept in the big room that had been that of Prince Gurgen and his four wives. Valeri rearranged the furniture, changed the rugs on the walls and put away his father's personal armament of sabres, swords, daggers, guns and pistols.

Shorena and he were untroubled by ghosts. She never thought of Katerina whom she had murdered so cleverly in the adjoining room. Valeri often thought of Anastasia, but never when he was in bed with Shorena.

Before his father's death Valeri had promised himself that when authority came to him, he would burn or banish the icon of Saint Anne. But one day, soon after his return, he saw old Nina on her knees in prayer before it, and he realised that it would be as cruel as one of his father's worst acts to rob the old woman of the image and to shake her belief in his own salvation. He hated that pale-eyed piece of painted wood almost as much as though the miniature were a living embodiment of evil. He hated her for two reasons: it was because of her that his brother, a child he loved, had been murdered, and because of that murder that he had lost Anastasia, the only woman he would love completely, without any selfish reservation. She had been his first love as a boy. He had felt for her a love purer and more intense than any which could come afterwards, and she had destroyed herself because of the result of a quarrel over that piece of painted wood.

He hated the icon because it was a cause of cruelty. But if he went into the chapel and pulled Saint Anne out of her frame and threw her on the fire, he would be putting old Nina, who had loved him and brought him up as a child, in torture. So Saint Anne looked out from under her lamp at the little heap of Vasso's toys, including his silver rattle, piled up before her.

Nina's strength was failing. She still rose before dawn and forced herself to go to the dairy. But it was Natiella and a child Eteri, who milked the goats and carried in the birch-bark buckets, and it was Natiella with a happy smile lighting up her broad face, and her bare feet leaving her footprints on the flagstones after scrubbing them, who did the work. One morning Nina did not appear at the dairy, and Natiella found her lying on her pallet bed, gasping and holding her side.

She complained of the cold, and the girl lit a little charcoal brazier and brought it into the room. Afterwards Nina drank a cup of tea and later in the day managed to get out of bed, but she had to be lifted back into it, as she was too weak to sit on a chair. When Shorena went to see her she asked if as a great favour Prince Valeri would allow Saint Anne to come to her room as she was not strong enough to go to the chapel. Shorena went to Valeri and he took the little panel out of its great silver setting and carried it to the old woman's bedside, not guessing that she would have far rather have prayed to her in all her glory and that, out of her frame, Saint Anne had painful associations. Nina refused to take the icon in her hands. They were too gnarled and steeped in years of sinning to touch the Holy Mother of the Virgin. So Valeri propped the little picture on a chair so that the old woman could gaze at it without making the effort of lifting her head, which drooped forward with her chin on her chest.

She murmured something about her sins and asked that the child should be brought also, and Valeri and Shorena carried him in, asleep in his cot. Then she asked them to forgive her. They both thought she must be thinking of having changed the babies. All that Valeri could think of to say was: 'I love you. I have always loved you.'

It was not really true. He had feared, admired, respected Nina, and finally had pitied her, but he had never loved her. But it was doubtful whether she heard. She was breathing, but when he came a moment later with a handkerchief to wipe her mouth, he saw that her breathing had stopped.

No, Valeri had never loved Nina, but his eyes filled with tears as he looked at her, realising the misery of old age and the meaningless progression of human life. The skinny, withered worn-out old corpse had once been a little child like his son lying there asleep. And one day, if he lived long enough, Leonidas would be like Nina, his skin loose and wrinkled over his withered muscles and brittle bones, and his heart, and all the rest of his body, worn-out and good for nothing but the grave. That realisation, which comes rarely to strong and healthy active men, made Valeri weep tears of angry pity.

He brushed them away and, turning, caught sight of Saint Anne gazing with her light blue eyes at Nina. She seemed to have a slight simper. All Valeri's hatred and secret fear of the icon burst out in rage, and he picked up the painted bit of wood.

'But for you, Vasso would be alive now. How many other murders have been committed because of you? How many hundreds of evil deeds have you inspired through all the long centuries? Well, your reign is over!' Valeri exclaimed, looking at her with hatred; and he put the little panel on to the brazier which heated the old woman's room.

Nothing happened. The icon lay unharmed on the bed of glowing charcoal. Saint Anne stared with her slight simper of superiority and triumphant complacency at Valeri, and he stared back.

He was appalled. A cold shiver shook him. His skin was gooseflesh, and he began to sweat. He was actually witnessing a miracle. Then, at last, a deep yellow flame curled up from the charcoal, the paint of the face cracked and began curling also. A flame laid hold of it that was for a few seconds a vivid green and then crimson, and suddenly with a crackle the icon was blazing. Valeri had scarcely time to recover from his absurd fear when there was a loud pop, almost an explosion, and a shower of sparks flew from the brazier in all directions. The largest of them shot right across the room and fell on to the cot where Leonidas was asleep. Valeri saw it fall beside the head of his sleeping son and tried with his one arm to snatch the child up, making a clumsy job of it and then held him pressed against his chest. He was shaking all over and making inarticulate noises of panic terror. Leonidas gave a little wail.

At that moment Shorena came back into the room. She gave one look at Nina, then turned to the child.

'Let me have him,' she said quietly, and, taking Leonidas, she put him back into his cot, noticing that a small black hole had been burned in the cotton quilt. The room was full of the smell of burning, but penetrating it was the sickening smell of fear. Shorena had smelt it once before in her life, coming from one of the prisoners with whom she had been locked up after the earthquake.

She turned to Valeri, who was still shaking uncontrollably. It was the only time in her life that she was ever to see him show fear. She put her strong arms round his shoulders, then, picking up the handkerchief, she wiped the sweat off his face.

'What's the matter with you, darling?' she asked.

'I have burned Saint Anne. First she would not burn, and then at the end she exploded and shot a shower of fire trying to set light to the child in his cot. She was trying to kill him like Vasso.'

Shorena laughed, and her laughter was so unforced and so healthy that Valeri's fear left him.

'So she was spiteful to the end and succeeded in frightening you,' said Shorena, still laughing.

'I know it sounds silly ... but it was terrifying. It was awful.'

'It must have been to put you into such a state, since you don't believe in all that nonsense. But it's over now. So help me carry the cot out of this room. It stinks, and it can't be good for him to breathe air like this. I must say you didn't lose much time in getting rid of Saint Anne.'

Valeri was on the point of saying: 'I hope that I have got rid of her,' but he stopped himself. He had made himself ridiculous enough as it was. But he was still rather frightened.

Nina was buried in the little graveyard across the river. Valeri threw the ashes of the icon into the grave before it was filled in. The goats that Nina had tended so long were the most numerous of those present, and when the other mourners had gone they assembled to sniff the raw earth and drop their pellets upon it.

CHAPTER TEN

Ziklauri had gone to the bazaar to buy camphor and was surprised when a tall monk, whom he knew by sight as the Bursar of the monastery, crooked his finger at him and then went into an inner room of the merchant's where they were both shopping and looked at him over his shoulder, before he disappeared behind the Baluchi carpets which served as a door. Ziklauri followed the monk and found himself alone with a strongly built old man with an anxious expression.

'I've heard a rumour that Prince Valeri, Son of the Falcon may be back at the aoul and I want a message taken to him in secret. His friend Foma Ilyitch was sent back to the monastery from the Turkish frontier by the Russians. I don't know if they had a legal right to do it, or not. The Archimandrite has him locked in a cell and he is being scourged every day. I don't think he'll live long under the treatment, and I thought Prince Valeri might be able to do something about it. Will you take the message? You realise I am putting myself in grave danger in telling you this?' Ziklauri nodded, and, after the monk had left the room, he asked the price of a copper lamp and started to bargain for it, although he had no intention of buying it – and he went on and on, pointing out defects in the lamp for some time after the monk had made his purchase and left the bazaar. Hagystiarchos had many spies.

Next day Ziklauri rode up to the aoul taking Salomé and her husband and baby with him so as to make carrying the message into a family party. He took Valeri aside, told him what the Bursar had said and added: 'If you wouldn't mind parting with the icon of Saint Anne, I am sure the Archimandrite would exchange Foma for her.'

Valeri gazed at him in horror.

'But I've burned her. I burned her just after old Nina's death, so that she should do no more evil in the world ... and now she has made me do the worst thing of all ... she has made me sacrifice my *kounak*. I couldn't guess...'

Ziklauri gazed at Valeri with horror. 'You did very wrong to burn an icon ... any icon ... but Saint Anne had worked miracles. You have committed a mortal sin. It looks as though she were having her revenge ... and at the expense of Brother Foma.' He was very much shocked and hardly spoke to Valeri for the rest of the day.

'I shall have to think of some other way to save him. Thank you for bringing the message.' They went back and joined the others.

Salomé was exactly what Valeri and Iriné had remembered, except that she laughed louder and was more downright than ever.

'Never thought to set foot in this hell-hole again, but it seems that blood is thicker than vinegar.... just think of Iriné finding a husband at her age! Most girls would have given up hope long ago. Enough to make a cat laugh.'

Later, when she was introduced to Mihail Semyonitch: 'My God, but you look smart in that uniform! Quite the gent. Don't think me rude, but I'd rather be married to a horse coper like my husband than have to spend the afternoons presiding over a samovar! I warn you, you'll have a wife who will startle St Petersburg when she opens her mouth. It will be a scream. I wish I could be there to hear her sometimes.' Then she flung her arms round Iriné when she came back into the room and said: 'Congratulations old girl. I've just been giving Mihail the low down on what to expect.'

Ziklauri and his party stayed the night and enjoyed their visit. Immediately after their departure, Valeri called a council.

It consisted of Shorena, Malik, Vakhtang, who Shorena said was the most trustworthy and intelligent of them all, and Iriné and Arbatsky, whom Valeri included because he was a Russian and could tell them what reprisals the Russians were likely to take if they broke into the monastery and rescued Foma by force. They sat in a silent circle, Malik tugging his moustache and shaking his head uneasily, as Valeri put forward his plan of getting the Bursar to leave a door unlocked and a rescue by armed men at night.

Iriné interrupted him. 'I've a much better plan, Valeri. Yours is daft. If you leave it to me, you'll have your friend here the day after tomorrow. Come into the next room and I'll explain.'

Valeri followed her reluctantly. When he returned he said: 'Iriné's plan is worth trying. If it fails we will go ahead with mine – even if it means our all taking refuge with the Turkomans afterwards.'

'You're incorrigible Valeri. Losing one arm would be enough for anyone else,' said Iriné. Then turning to Arbatsky she said: 'Get Natiella to wash and iron your best tunic at once. You have to look respectable, and we've no time to lose.'

Next morning Lieutenant Arbatsky, in full uniform with Iriné dressed in a green riding habit that Katerina had had made in Tiflis by a Russian dressmaker only three years before, and with Stiva leading a saddled pony, rode down the track by the river. They turned aside to the monastery before entering the town, and, while Iriné waited at a little distance, Lieutenant Arbatsky and Stiva rode up, and Arbatsky ordered his man to knock and say that his master demanded an immediate interview with the Archimandrite. Only after the porter returned, did he dismount, threw the reins to Stiva and followed the porter to the cell of the Archimandrite, with his regulation sabre clanking on the stone floor. On entering the building, he crossed himself devoutly, dipped one finger in the stoup of Holy Water, but kept his plumed shako on his head, a sign that he was on official business.

When he entered the Archimandrite's cell, he scarcely looked at him and said: 'I have been sent by the Governor, most Holy Father, to ask you to hand over immediately a Russian scholar...' (Here Arbatsky paused and looked at a small piece of paper tucked into the opening of his left-hand glove.) 'Ah yes, the scholar, Foma Ilyitch Iribanov, to me, for interrogation.'

Arbatsky had not looked at the Archimandrite while he spoke. Then he lifted his eyes, looked at him arrogantly, took a step backwards and taking a handkerchief out of the sleeve of his dolman, held it ostentatiously to his nose.

Hagystiarchos sat motionless, saying nothing. At intervals he passed a greenish tongue between his hairy lips.

'Oh, by the way, I was forgetting,' said Arbatsky in a tone of insufferable condescension. 'Here is a letter from the Governor: you may wish to read it.' And he passed him a paper sealed with blue wax and a double-headed eagle. The Archimandrite took it but did not break the seal or look at it. He could not read Russian cursive script. Arbatsky tapped his boots impatiently with his riding whip and jingled his spurs. The Archimandrite rang a bell, and a young monk came in. 'Bring Brother Foma here,' he ordered.

'It's most unfortunate ... the health of Brother Foma ... He's in a poor way....' But Arbatsky was not even pretending to listen. He tapped his boots again and then turning his back on the Archimandrite, stood on tiptoe to look at his reflection in the silver surround of the ivory crucifix with the golden figure of Christ. When he had caught a glimpse of himself, he set his shako straight. The Archimandrite was silent. Foma was brought into the doorway of the cell, supported by two monks. Arbatsky did not give him a glance. 'Do you want me to sign for him?' he asked. He had to repeat the question, but the Archimandrite still seemed unable to understand it.

'I had better sign. It's more regular,' and, taking a pencil out of his breast pocket and tearing a leaf out of a small notebook, he scrawled: 'Received Brother Foma Ilyitch in bad shape,' and added incomprehensible initials. Then, giving a sign to the monks to carry or drag Foma ahead of him, he gave the Archimandrite a perfunctory salute and strutted out.

Iriné's plan was in jeopardy when it became obvious that Foma was in no condition to sit on a horse unaided, after he had been lifted on to one.

'Fetch a carriage from the inn, Stiva,' ordered Arbatsky. Then, turning his back on Foma and the two monks, he began talking to Iriné who presently slapped him playfully with one of her riding gloves.

Foma suddenly created an unexpected diversion. He fell on his knees and then on his face, crying out: 'Mercy, Barina, mercy, I beg you mercy.' Iriné stepped away from him, giving him a contemptuous glance and he began to crawl towards her crying out: 'Pity, pity, pity!' This scene was so horrible that it affected all their subsequent relations. It filled Iriné with profound, unforgettable disgust and Foma with shame which could not be lived down. Arbatsky, who was holding the horses while Stiva was fetching the carriage, flicked at Foma with his riding whip, at which the crowd which had gathered to watch, murmured. Then Arbatsky helped Iriné to mount and swung into the saddle himself. They walked their horses up and down in front of the monastery, without ever looking at Foma, for half an hour while the crowd grew larger and murmured whenever Arbatsky had his back to it and then fell silent when he walked his horse towards it. At last, and none too soon, Stiva returned with a coachman driving a tarantass.

'Get in with him, Stiva. I'll lead the ponies,' said Arbatsky. Then he shouted: 'To headquarters,' and they set off. But where to go? No wheeled vehicle could proceed far along the track to the Castle. 'Tell him to drive to the Solutz encampment,' said Iriné, directly the crowd had been left behind. They drove there at top speed.

Ziklauri came out to greet them, and their troubles were over. His first action was to tell one of his men to take the coachman to his house, give him vodka, get him drunk and incapable and not to allow him to go back to the town on any pretext. Then he dispatched another man to borrow a hooded litter carried by two mules, harnessed head to tail, of the kind used by respectable Mohammedan women travelling in the mountains. Some Persian merchants, who were neighbours, had one.

Before dark they were on their way with two of Ziklauri's boys carrying torches when they were out of sight of the town. Shortly before dawn they arrived at the aoul.

It was three days before the Archimandrite discovered that he had been tricked, but even then he could not understand it. The idea of a hoax was incomprehensible: he believed that the Russian Governor, or some rival of the Governor's perhaps, had carried off Foma and would not return him. Whoever was behind it, it was just a lie – a denial of responsibility. Hagystiarchos had not left the monastery for five years, but on this occasion he knew that he must make his position felt, and he went to the Governor in person to complain. He sat down in front of the Governor and told him once, he told him twice, he told him three times, that a young officer in full uniform, wearing his shako and not just a forage cap – he knew the difference – had come, had demanded one of his monks, then undergoing penance, and had taken him away. At the third telling, he produced the sealed authority given him by Arbatsky.

The Russian put out his hand, and Hagystiarchos reluctantly handed it over, with the seal unbroken. The governor produced a handkerchief, wiped his fingers, broke the seal and read the message dictated by Iriné to Vakhtang.

'I, the Archimandrite Hagystiarchos, hereby hand over Foma Ilyitch Iribanov who has been held by me in illegal detention, to a representative of Prince Valeri, Son of the Falcon, who requires his services as tutor to his brother Leonidas.

'(Signed) Hagystiarchos.'

It took the Governor a full hour to discover all the details of what had occurred. He read and re-read the purported authority. Finally he dismissed the Archimandrite with roars of laughter and rushed round to the Club, where all the Russian officials were playing vint at four o'clock in the afternoon, and described the joke played on the Archimandrite and read and re-read the 'authority' amid roars of laughter from all assembled.

'All the same this young man will have to be disciplined,' he concluded.

'Gogol! Pure Gogol,' said one of the younger officers.

Hagystiarchos went back to his cell, utterly baffled and mystified and convinced that the Russians were all liars and in league against him, and he determined to have his revenge one day when it could not be pinned down on him.

Two days after the Archimandrite's visit, Arbatsky rode down to town, wearing fatigue uniform from which he had removed all badges of rank, and called upon the Governor.

He was kept waiting for an hour and a half. When he was admitted he removed his cap.

'Come to put yourself under arrest, you young rascal,' was the greeting he received. 'You'll be court-martialled. That dignitary of the Church, the Archimandrite, is howling for your blood.' And the Governor allowed himself a chuckle.

'With great respect, your Excellency, I must point out that I am a civilian.'

'What do you mean?'

'Your Excellency, I resigned my commission, and my resignation was accepted ten days ago.' And Arbatsky held out an official paper. The Governor looked through it and handed it back.

'What are you doing, then, in uniform?'

'It's my wretched tailor, McAdam of Petersburg. He hasn't sent me a coat in which I could present myself before you, your Excellency.'

McAdam was the most fashionable tailor in Russia, and the Governor was impressed.

'Well, it looks as though the court-martial was off. Ha-ha! I can just see the Archimandrite's face when he hears that. But you've made a lot of trouble for me.'

'I have one request to make of your Excellency. I am marrying the sister of Prince Valeri, Son of the Falcon, next week. Will you honour me and my bride by attending the wedding?'

'You impertinent puppy! You know I can't do that without getting in wrong with the Church. Otherwise ... it would be a pleasure. So you are forming quite a little colony of Russians up there at the Castle. All loyal subjects of His Imperial Majesty?'

'I think my marriage is sufficient proof of that, your Excellency.'

'Keep an eye on our interests up there, and let me know if there's any Turkish or Persian infiltration.'

'You can rely on me, your Excellency.'

The marriage of Mihail Semyonitch Arbatsky to Iriné took place at the new Russian Orthodox church in the town. Valeri gave his sister away, Salomé and Elisso, with their husbands and friends from the Solutz encampment, were present, and so were a dozen or more officers from the bridegroom's former regiment and the garrison in the town. Foma was not well enough to go, and Shorena stayed at the Castle to look after Leonidas. Gulerian, who realised that the 'mountainy people' were moving with the times (and there was profit to be made from them) gave a terrific wedding reception at his own expense, with gallons of wine, buckets of vodka, mounds of caviare, little pies filled with sweet-breads and cocks' combs, pickled cucumbers, wood mush-rooms of all sorts, followed by a dinner, for the selected guests, of a haunch of venison with honey sauce and a brace of sucking pigs stuffed with buckwheat.

Naturally these proceedings did not go unnoticed in the town. Father Alexander was jealous of the newly-established Russian Orthodox church, which was attended by the Governor, all the Russian tchinovniks and by the Russian military, and he kept a watchful eye on its activities. When it came to his ears that the illegitimate daughter of old Prince Gurgen, who had replied to his proposal of marriage by rudely questioning his virility, that this crazy girl, possessed by demons, was being married to the rich young Russian who had abducted a monk from the monastery and was going unpunished for it – chiefly because he employed McAdam as his tailor – the priest was taken ill with rage and spite. What made it particularly galling, and also demanded diplomacy, was that the Archpriest and the widow Tara had both received invitations and had happily gorged themselves at the wedding feast. Whereas Father Alexander had been pointedly omitted. But then the Archpriest, in spite of his protestations that he was a Georgian patriot, always liked Russians and had taken a fancy (or at any rate the widow Tara had) to Arbatsky.

Father Alexander would have refused to go to the wedding, after having been insulted in such a scandalous and obscene manner by Iriné. But his refusal would have been a consolation. He was determined on revenge: but his hand must not be seen in it. He spent a sleepless night, continually waking up his placid wife and getting up and drinking dill water for indigestion, but it made him no better. Everyone in the town knew that the young fellow, who had given himself airs as an author, had escaped being court-martialled by cleverly resigning his commission before his escapade. But why should young Russian puppies, even if civilians, be

269

allowed to insult the Georgian church with impunity? Just because his coats were cut by a Scottish tailor!

Next morning he drafted a letter addressed to the Russian Minister of the Interior, complaining of the infamous behaviour of Mihail Semyonitch Arbatsky, giving full details, which he then took to the Archimandrite to sign.

Hagystiarchos looked at his visitor with suspicion. Father Alexander had long, carefully tended fingernails; his beard had been recently washed and trimmed and was parted in the middle. He smelt, not only of incense as every priest must do, but of soap. And his flowing black robes made of the most expensive alpaca, had recently been ironed, so that the creases were still visible. His appearance told against him. Then, what motive had this worldly young ecclesiastic, with whom the Archimandrite had nothing in common, for trying to help in getting that insolent young Russian officer punished? Hagystiarchos knew that he had made a fool of himself by handing the Governor that paper unread. Perhaps getting him to sign his name to a letter was another trick? There might be a plot to replace him as Archimandrite by some fellow who kowtowed to the Russians and went in for book-learning! So he sat silent and motionless and gave no sign as Father Alexander expatiated on his plan.

It was only when he spoke of Valeri's sudden return and how it had upset the prospects of little Leonidas inheriting the Castle. Of how he himself had almost been appointed the child's guardian by the Archpriest, his grandfather, and then went on to talk of the suspicions attaching to Katerina's mysterious suicide – in which Iriné was very possibly involved, that the Archimandrite saw daylight. The letter about Arbatsky was the beginning of a long campaign. As he listened Father Alexander made it clearer.

'So long as this Russian puppy, Arbatsky, is living at the aoul, particularly now he is Prince Valeri's brother-in-law, the Governor and the District Commander will take no action. He is their spy, and they will be guided by whatever he

270

says. But if he should get into disgrace, who knows? Prince Valeri is known to have liberal ideas...'

So the Archimandrite signed the letter, which Father Alexander sent off by express that evening to St Petersburg.

After the wedding reception given by Gulerian, Iriné and her husband spent a restless and uncomfortable night as Ziklauri's guests in the encampment of the Sultzi. Arbatsky was quite tipsy; Iriné had wrapped herself up like a mummy in a nightdress and dressing gown and turned her back on him. When, with the feeling that it was his duty to consummate the marriage, Arbatsky approached and tried to unwrap her, she resisted strongly and said, quite loud, not in a whisper: 'For God's sake, let me alone. Otherwise I shall start screaming and wake up all the dogs.'

Next morning she was all sweetness and honey, and they enjoyed the ride back to the aoul. Shorena put the bridal pair at the top of the tower which had been Valeri's and afterwards hers.

That night Iriné made a great effort to control her revulsion against physical contact with her husband. She loved Mihail, or she thought she loved him, but a man's body was strange and unpleasant to her, and his excitement and emotion had the effect of making her hostile and critical. The process of making love, which she had known all about almost as long as she could remember, seemed disgusting when she was faced with having to take part in it. She lay still, rigid with repulsion, and forced herself to say nothing. Arbatsky, although given no encouragement, broke her hymen. It hurt her a great deal and she bled so profusely that he became frightened by what he had done and withdrew before having an orgasm. His anxiety and fears for her only increased her hostility. Finally she said: 'Well you've got what you wanted. Let me alone now until the pain is over.' But as he was unsatisfied, all Arbatsky's instincts forbade his letting her alone.

On subsequent nights their efforts were not much better.

271

Iriné remained frigid and complained that Mihail was hurting her. He felt guilty, angry and frustrated.

Without telling each other, each of them sought outside advice. Arbatsky consulted Foma Ilyitch who told him that it might help if he made no further efforts at copulation for a week. Iriné consulted Shorena, who told her to get drunk and to encourage Arbatsky to do whatever he liked with her and she would find herself enjoying it. Both followed their instructions and the results were self-defeating.

Iriné got thoroughly tipsy and Mihail resisted the desire to take advantage of his opportunity, thus incurring a hysterical contempt. At the time when there was the best chance of Iriné responding, Arbatsky refrained from all attempts to copulate, and then her monthly periods started, and lasted for nearly a week. Finally she took pity on him and used her hand.

At the end of the first month of marriage, they had reached a see-saw relationship. Iriné did all she could to avoid normal physical relations and then, feeling shame and pity, did all she could to make up for coldness which left Arbatsky puzzled and angry at her inconsistency. But, in an odd way, these unhappy exchanges bound them together. Each of them was aware that the other was suffering – and mutual suffering can tie as tight a knot as joy. One day, as they returned from a climb round one of the crags up the river, they saw a Russian Cossack's horse tied up in the yard. The man had brought an official letter for Arbatsky. It read:

'MINISTRY OF THE INTERIOR
'Mihail Semyonitch Arbatsky, retired lieutenant of 3rd Regiment of Artillery, is to report to the investigating magistrate's court for Colonial Affairs, Bielostroy Ulitza, St Petersburg, within 30 days of this summons.

'(Signed) Vyazhnitsky.'

Mihail Arbatsky left the following morning for St Petersburg and would not hear of his wife accompanying him.

Soon after Foma had been brought to the Castle, Valeri described how he had burned the icon of Saint Anne immediately after Nina's death, and how he had been terrified because at first she would not burn, and then she exploded in a shower of sparks, one of which had shot across the room and fallen on to the cot where Leonidas was asleep.

'I thought she was trying to kill him, as she killed Vasso. I did not know it was possible to feel such fear. I had never experienced it before,' he explained.

'That doesn't surprise me. You only burned it because you secretly believe that a piece of wood can have evil, magical properties. It is a great disappointment to me that I shall never see that icon. It sounds so interesting and may have been a beautiful painting. It is very wrong to destroy any work of art. Those pale blue eyes don't sound Byzantine. It might conceivably have been painted by a Norman from Sicily, and the halo added later, and the little picture turned into an icon. Thanks to your vandalism we shall never know.'

'Well, I burned her, and I am glad I did.'

'You see, you believe that she had magical properties.'

'And why not? You believe that a picture can inspire you with good emotions. So why shouldn't Saint Anne have inspired abominable ones?'

Foma laughed. 'I think I know why. But it would mean a lecture on aesthetics, and I'm not up to rational discussion at present. I'll tell you another day.' Suddenly his eyes gleamed and he asked mischievously: 'Who are you putting in her frame? Jeremy Bentham?'

It took three months for the epidermis stretching from the nape of Foma's neck to the backs of his knees, which had been removed by the monastic flagellations he had endured, to renew itself. But the loss of Lenotchka was a wound which did not heal, and changed him permanently. When Valeri had first met him in the monastery, his *kounak*

273

had faced the follies, lies and tyrannies of the powerful with a bubbling defiant gaiety and irreverence. After Lenotchka's loss there was an implacable cold anger against the rulers of the world. No longer was there talk of acquiescence, or of a belief that education and progress would transform governments and abolish cruelty, or that art, literature and science would be sufficient to civilise mankind. When, before Lenotchka's death there had been talk of a Russian war with Turkey, to liberate Bulgaria, Foma had spoken like a Russian patriot. But after it he would say: 'Let them put their own house in order first. They have abolished the buying and selling of human beings like cattle, but withhold the land and let them starve. Let them get rid of their tyrant, and of the tchinovnik jacks-in-office who do his work, and set our own people free before we talk about crusades to liberate the Bulgarians.'

And if Valeri spoke of the beneficial changes that a war might bring with it, he would say: 'It's not the Sultan of Turkey, or the Tsar of Russia who will suffer, but the common soldiers who butcher each other and the simple people who have the misfortune to live on the battlefield.'

A year later they were sitting round the table in the hall drinking little cups of coffee, and for some reason Shorena started a conversation by asking Foma how he proposed to teach Leonidas to be a good man; for she secretly did not believe in the ideas of good and bad and all the theories that he and Valeri would sometimes discuss.

'You can't teach positive goodness. So I hope to teach Leonidas, or any child, the things to avoid. Just as you teach him not to fall into the fire, or eat poisonous berries. One can bring him up so that he is unlikely to want to be a priest, or a tchinovnik. A soldier is always more attractive to a child, of course, but one can try. I can bring him up so that he will not be like his grandfather, or his father, or like me. One can try and teach him not to want to manage other people's lives. That is more difficult with girls, I believe.

And just as boys, at a certain age, want to be soldiers, so later on they want to be revolutionaries, and it needs a lot of skill to head them off from that,' said Foma.

'Why do you want to prevent them being revolutionists?' asked Shorena.

'Because it involves the same thing as religion: the belief that the ends justify the means. And they don't. And even if they did, which I deny, no revolutionist has ever achieved the ends for which he started his revolution. But, as I said, you cannot teach positive good. You can only set him on the road if you have models that he will want to follow. And that brings me to a proposal I want to put before you.'

But here Iriné interrupted him: 'Before you go on to that, may I ask whether you agree with me that everyone's positive good is different and individual, and as much part of their make-up as the colour of their eyes or hair? I believe that you could no more hope to be good by imitating a man whom you thought was good, than you could make yourself beautiful by dyeing your hair the same shade as a famous beauty. Both the goodness and the beauty would turn out to be false and unnatural. And unless they are innate they don't exist.'

'I don't agree,' said Valeri. 'My extremely brief acquaintance with two men has influenced my opinions and, from that, my behaviour. I don't refer to Foma, but to Ziklauri and to Jason Ardigheb, or Prince Tcherkessev, as you call him. I don't imitate them consciously, but their values, higher than mine, influence me all the time. I agree therefore with Foma, that a boy or a young man needs models.'

'That was the justification of homosexual love among the Greeks, put forward by Socrates,' said Foma.

'Will all the models you are choosing for my son to imitate, have to be queers?' asked Shorena. They all laughed at that.

'You are proposing real men, aren't you? Because if they are just heroes out of history books, you will infringe the first principle of education, which is not telling lies,' said Valeri.

'Actually my proposal is not simply for the sake of Leonidas, but for all of us. Valeri is an admirable, even a heroic figure,' and Foma looked mischievously at his old friend. 'He can impersonate Nelson with his one arm, just as I can play at being a mute inglorious Voltaire – but the truth is that we and our ideas are both getting stale. We develop mental habits. You may notice that the ladies do not listen so attentively as they used to do. What I am saying is that we need new blood.'

'Where do you intend to find it?' asked Iriné.

'All over the world. I think that the Prince here,' and Foma bowed to Valeri, 'should invite poets, writers, painters, philosophers from all over the world: Russians like Turgenev, Germans like Heine, Frenchmen like De Nerval, the man who translated Goethe into French, Englishmen like that young writer Dickens, Italians like the revolutionary Mazzini, to meet here, and that he should keep open house for the intellects of Europe.'

'Do you suppose that our autocrat, and his secret police will approve of a gathering consisting of English liberals, Russian writers and French, German and Italian revolutionists meeting on the frontier of his empire?' asked Iriné.

'Some of them might get here by way of Constantinople, or from India and Afghanistan and the uplands of Persia,' said Shorena. She got up saying, 'I must go and find Leonidas. It's time for his tea,' and left them.

'The idea of a caravan of philosophers, traversing Asia to visit us here is fascinating,' said Iriné laughing. Even Valeri, who did not like making fun of Shorena's simplicities, joined in.

'At first we shall have to be content with Russian writers and poets. They will think the aoul romantic, and Georgia and the peoples of the Caucasus will inspire them to great original works,' said Foma.

'I suppose we can try inviting one or two,' said Valeri.

'If you succeed, the Castle will become famous in literature as a centre of art and culture,' said Foma.

Shorena ran back into the hall and, as they looked up, cried out: 'The Russians.' Leonidas trailed after her.

'Sojers, sojers, gee-gees, gee-gees,' he said blissfully, but they had risen from the table and were running into the yard to look.

Through the gateway they saw that there were twenty or thirty Cossacks by the ford. Some were already dismounted. A line of others was still arriving along the track with baggage mules. They had chosen the field of standing wheat in which to make their encampment. Some of them had taken off their jackets and were busy putting up tents, the sound of mallets driving in wooden pegs was distinct. Others were putting up a picket line for their horses; still others were carrying buckets of water from the river. Amid all the disorder it was obvious that there was a common plan, and that each man was going about his allotted task.

The inhabitants of the Castle watched in silence, until Iriné suddenly said: 'Here are Foma's Russian poets who will show their love of Georgia by raping Natiella, and roasting our lambs on their camp fires.' They were still watching in silence, when a young officer rode up and dismounted.

'Who is in charge here?' he asked roughly.

'I am Prince Valeri, Son of the Falcon. Allow me to introduce Madame Iriné Gurgenevna Arbatskaya and my friend Foma Ilyitch Iribanov,' said Valeri.

The officer's manner changed abruptly at the Russian names.

'Lieutenant Lvov Sergeitch Timoshenko,' he said, clicking his heels and bowing to Iriné.

'What exactly are you wanting?' asked Valeri.

'You realise I have no option but to perform a disagreeable duty, Prince. I am in command of the advance guard – a squadron of Cossacks. Tonight I shall only require four rooms – three bedrooms; one for myself and two for my two ensigns, and a downstairs room as an office. We shall need to requisition hay, oats, straw and a few sheep and to have the use of your bakehouse tomorrow. But in the course of the next week, a supply base will be established here with a permanent garrison and we shall take over all the buildings in the aoul.'

'Including the Castle?' asked Valeri.

'Including the Castle.'

'Do you ever have any trouble with the inhabitants?' asked Iriné. Addressed by a Russian lady, the officer thought it incumbent on him to reply in French.

'*Nous avons eu quelques scenès, plus ou moins comiques, avec les indigènes,*' he replied.

'*Le pouvoir de mettre les paysans dehors de leurs chaumières et les princes de leurs châteaux doit faire rigoler un homme d'esprit comme le vôtre,*' said Foma blandly.

To their surprise the officer blushed scarlet and bit his lip.

'It is my duty to make a short survey,' he stammered.

'Would you mind taking your compatriot round the Castle, Foma?' said Valeri in Georgian.

CHAPTER ELEVEN

While Foma took Lieutenant Timoshenko over the Castle and intimidated him by insisting on talking fluent French, Valeri went out and found Malik in the yard looking through the gateway at the Cossacks. He told him that the Russians were taking over the aoul. He added that resistance was out of the question, and that he was going to call a meeting of the men to ask them to decide what they would prefer to do.

Then, without ever having thought about it, he found himself saying that he intended to leave Georgia and Russia with Shorena and Leonidas, and travel to Switzerland and Italy. He was going to advise his men to join the encampment of the Sulutz under Ziklauri.

Malik, without taking his eyes off the Cossacks, listened carefully and said at last: 'I shall go back to my own people. Busrawi will have forgotten me by now, or have forgotten he was going to kill me by slow death.'

'Will you go by Tabriz?' asked Valeri.

'I might very well,' replied Malik.

'Mustapha Sasun promised to pay me a long visit. I want to send him and his wife a warning message and pay him what I owe him for buying back my sabre.'

Malik gave a little smile, and in it Valeri could read the old man's approval for his having remembered his friend's safety at such a time. Until that moment Malik had shown him a contemptuous reserve. Valeri knew that he was perfectly aware that resistance to the Russian Empire was futile. Nevertheless he would have dearly liked to have shot

279

half a dozen of the intruders – beginning with the young puppy who was choosing the most comfortable bedroom in the Castle. In the old days, when the Old Prince kept sentries out, they could have held up the Russians, coming along the mule-track in single file, almost indefinitely. That was one reason perhaps why they had left Prince Gurgen alone. Those days were over, and Malik regretted them. Valeri had one order to give before the meeting, an order which he knew Malik would find disagreeable, unless it were explained.

But before he gave the order he said: 'I've got two rugs: a Persian and a Baluchi that I remember Mustapha admired very much. Could you find room to take them to him? And if there is one you would like...'

Malik smiled again. 'I think I shall get out tonight, before they send men upstream and block my escape route. But I'll take the carpets and pick out a prayer mat for myself. I shall have to start praying again and bumping my forehead towards Mecca.... What's the order?'

'Collect all the firearms. I don't want some fool shooting someone. That's just what the Russians are hoping for. It would be their excuse to cut off the heads of the men, collecting the ten roubles bounty for the head of every mountaineer, rape the women and expropriate the aoul without compensation. I shall have all the arms packed in cases and taken down and given to Ziklauri. Guns may be useful at some future time.'

At the meeting, the men said that they would all leave the aoul and join the Solutz encampment, if Ziklauri would accept them – a decision which was confirmed when he arrived himself, having come along to say that all who did not want to stay under Russian military rule would be welcome among the Solutz.

There was one exception. The cripple boy Vakhtang said that he would stay on at the Castle for a little while, as he had things to tidy up and thought he might be useful.

Some of the men looked at him and muttered among themselves.

'So he was a Russian spy all along,' was a phrase that Valeri caught and which puzzled him.

To Shorena, her friend's decision was a shock. She took him aside and said: 'You as good as told me that you hated the Russians. Why should you stay?'

'Do you remember that I said that Georgians have a sense of honour?'

'Yes, and that you said also that Russians...'

'Don't quote my words against me. Ever...'

Shorena opened her beautiful eyes wide, and said no more.

It was after this exchange that Valeri raised the question of Leonidas. He had always disliked the fiction that the child was his younger brother and not his son. But he had not been able to get round the argument that Leonidas would not inherit the aoul if he were declared the illegitimate child of Shorena and himself. But now that the aoul was being expropriated by the Russian Army – why not tell the truth about Leonidas? He put this enthusiastically to Shorena and was a good deal surprised when she replied: 'I am not at all sure that it would be a good thing. But before you make up your mind I wish you would discuss it with Vakhtang.' Valeri was flabbergasted. To discuss his private affairs with one of his retainers was something that he had never done and would find extremely difficult.

'What on earth has Vakhtang got to do with it?' he asked angrily.

'Be yourself and not a bad copy of your father,' said Shorena.

'I had no intention of being that. But why Vakhtang?'

'Because he is the most intelligent person here. And because he is the only person, now that Nina and Katerina are dead, besides ourselves, who knows the truth about Leonidas.'

'How did that come about?' asked Valeri suspiciously.

'Nina called him in to tie the cord with a bit of silkworm gut a few minutes before Katerina's baby was born.'

So Prince Valeri went cap in hand to discuss the future of his son's parentage, and his position in the family tree of the Sons of the Falcon, with his crippled servitor, whom Shorena thought more intelligent than himself.

He found him leaning on his crutch watching the Cossacks.

'Shorena wanted me to come and discuss a rather private matter.' Vakhtang was immediately all politeness and attention. But he did not appear honoured or surprised.

'Now that I am losing the Castle, I don't see why we should keep up this absurd pretence that Leonidas is my brother and not my son ... Shorena wanted to know your opinion, if you have one on a subject that does not concern you, before I took a decision.'

'What does she really want herself? Isn't that really more important than the opinion of a complete outsider?' said Vakhtang.

'Of course. But she is his mother and must want him to be recognised as her son, however willing she is to sacrifice herself for the boy's material welfare,' said Valeri.

'You say she must. I asked you what does she really want. I think that you should find that out.'

'Of course. But when the Castle is no longer ours for Leonidas to inherit, what does legitimacy matter? There is only the title of Prince, and that means nothing to me.'

'If it is all that he can inherit, it may mean more to him.'

'What I object to is that our relationship will be all wrong. He will think of me as an elder brother and Shorena simply as my mistress.'

'Is it the authority of a father that you want?'

'No. Not the authority. The relationship.'

'The relationship of an elder and a younger brother is sometimes happier than that of father and son.'

'But you are leaving Shorena's feelings out of account,' exclaimed Valeri.

'I thought that I had suggested that you should find out what they are and be guided by them,' said Vakhtang quietly.

This was too much for Prince Valeri to endure. He nodded, and said: 'Thanks a lot Vakhtang. Of course you are forbidden to divulge a word of this conversation.'

'Your order is unnecessary, my Lord Prince, Son of the Falcon,' said Vakhtang bowing.

Valeri did not pursue the matter further, or discuss it again with Shorena, and Leonidas grew up to be his younger half-brother and, in the absence of a legitimate son, the heir to the title and whatever property went with it. Though his principles prevented him from admitting it, for several years Prince Valeri secretly resented the fact that he had been forced to discuss his private affairs with an inferior.

Iriné announced that she would leave to join her husband on his estate and had arranged to go next morning with a young Russian ensign who was taking a dispatch back to the town.

'Mihail writes me such touching letters. Listen to this: "My own little Pear" – Now I ask you, was there ever anybody less like a pear than I am? An unripe quince possibly – but a pear!

' "My own little Pear. I think of you every day and all night. The fact that we have been unhappy means that great happiness is in store for us. It was the mountains that had always shut you in, that cast their shadow over our marriage. Here in the great spaces of Mother Russia, among the luxuriant fields of the black earth, we shall listen to the nightingales, smell the limes and wander in the forests with our love for each other stimulated by picking wood mushrooms..." You see Mihail is turning into a poet. Foma Ilyitch will give us lectures about him one of these days. And yet, you know, I bet you he is living happily, sleeping with one of his serf girls. I shall do my best to show him that I don't mind, but

283

Mihail is so conventional that it will shock him to the core unless I make jealous scenes...'

She left next morning looking very elegant in Katerina's old riding habit.

Valeri told Foma that he planned to go and live abroad in Italy or Switzerland, with Shorena and Leonidas, and invited him to come as the child's tutor. To his surprise Foma declined.

'I think you will be happier without Russian attendants. Our national feelings are stronger than we realise. In any case if you engage a French tutor for the little boy, he will acquire a better accent than he would from me.'

Valeri felt wounded by his *kounak*'s refusal. It showed, he thought, that Foma could not rise above national prejudice. When he spoke of this later on to Shorena, she said with some tact: 'Foma was thinking of me. And you know he is right.'

This cheered Valeri up.

'But what do you intend to do, *kounak*, friend of my heart?' he asked, and Foma replied: 'I have long wished to investigate that curious sect, the Molokani, who took refuge in the Caucasus fifty years ago. They pretend to live like the primitive Christians, but I shall see for myself. You see my trouble is that I still believe in God, but think that religion leads everyone else, except myself, to be a liar and a hypocrite. It is a sort of curse.'

'Well, when you are tired of living on sour milk and being self-righteous, you can come and join us in Italy,' said Valeri.

A month later he realised that it was a relief not to have Foma with them. He was able to start thinking for himself. He would discard God and religion and substitute the ethic of honour and truth.

Soon after Iriné and her escort had left the Castle, taking Foma with them, Ziklauri set off with all the men, most of the ponies and baggage animals with all the guns, pistols, sabres and daggers loaded upon them.

Valeri, Shorena and Leonidas, with Natiella as nursemaid, were the last to leave the Castle. They were given lodging by Avetis Gulerian, who was unexpectedly friendly and generous. Next morning they watched two hundred Russian troops with mules and camels, loaded with mountain guns and the vast equipment of an army battalion, set out for the aoul from the main square of the town.

Valeri hired a coach and they drove to Batum, where they got passage to Naples on an English boat. It was thus some months before they heard what occurred at the Castle after their departure.

General Ivanov, commanding the Russian army in the south-east of the Caucasus, accompanied by Colonel Averoff, with their aides and staff officers, paid a visit of inspection to the new fort and advanced post on the frontier.

Great preparations were made. The General arrived feeling exhausted after the long ride, fatiguing to a man of his girth and weight. However, after a good night's rest, he rose delighted by being deep in the mountains. He was feeling fresh and was enchanted by all he saw. The inspections of the troops were most gratifying. A team of artillerymen unloaded, assembled and fired rounds from a mountain gun, which they then immediately took to pieces and packed up with its trail and ammunition boxes on six mules, in twenty-three minutes, by his staff officer's watch.

'That would winkle out any rebellious Tatars that Johnny Turk sends us over the border,' said the General laughing.

Later he inspected the horse lines, watched a cavalry charge over the field that had been sown with poppies, looked in at the men's quarters and tasted their cabbage soup. Like everything that day, it was excellent.

As the sun was setting, the General with twenty-three officers, no less than eleven being of field rank, sat down to a splendid dinner in the Great Hall. There was a new icon in the niche in the chapel and portraits of the Emperor Alexander II and his consort on the walls.

They had a delicious borshch with sour cream, sturgeon with lemon sauce, roast sucking pig, roast lamb and a superb cassata ice as fine as you could hope for in Naples. Vodka of course, and the very best Georgian wine and a dozen bottles of French champagne for the senior officers.

The meal lasted three hours, and the General was beginning to nod sleepily and one of the majors was telling the old chestnut about the two Jews who shared the same mistress who had twins, one of whom died at birth: Moses broke the news to Ikey: 'Rebecca has had twins but it is so sad, mine has...' But at that moment there was a blinding flash and a stupendous roar, and the Castle and its occupants shot into the night sky. Showers of stone fell among the tents and marquees, many falling into the river. The sentries on guard were deafened and almost blinded by the flames that shot into the sky like an erupting volcano.

Nothing of the Castle, which had withstood sieges and an earthquake, was left standing, except the tower, which was reduced to a ruin. Next morning there was no trace of the convivial party of officers, except one epaulette with the badge of major.

In the investigation which followed, the blacksmith who had gone to the encampment of the Solutz, gave evidence that there were thirty barrels of gunpowder in the inner cellar, part of a provision laid in by Prince Gurgen in case of a long siege, such as that of the Tatars more than a hundred years ago.

The disaster seemed to have been an accident if, as surmised, one of the Russian orderlies had tapped a barrel, thinking it contained wine, while carrying a naked light. The old smith swore that no one in the Castle knew about this magazine except himself and Malik – and he had been gone a month.

It seemed that it was an accident. There were, however, other views. Among the Solutz the explosion was universally attributed to the icon of Saint Anne. The same thought occurred to Iriné, who sent Valeri a postcard which he found waiting for him in Rome:

'Have just heard of the terrible disaster at the aoul. Saint Anne seems to have taken her revenge. It was rash to instal a rival icon.'

Five years later, when Prince Valeri and Shorena were living in Geneva, they were invited to meet a fellow Georgian, a patriot and refugee from Russian rule, who was living at the house of a noted Russian political exile.

Valeri was reluctant to go. He did not like the mixture of Russian anarchist and exile, and of a self-styled Georgian patriot. He was perhaps influenced by the fact that by that time he was drawing a small pension from the Russian Government. Shorena, however, insisted.

'It would be lovely to meet someone who can talk our own language. I'm going, even if you stay and look after Leonidas.' So, reluctantly, Valeri accompanied her.

The self-styled Georgian patriot was Vakhtang. Shorena had a few words in private with him, while Valeri was talking to their host.

'So it was you,' she said.

'I might have asked you the same question once, but I refrained,' said Vakhtang.

Shorena said no more.

After they got home, Valeri and Shorena had a short conversation.

'Do you feel that getting rid of all those Russians was worth the destruction of the Castle – knowing that it was unlikely you would ever get possession of it again?' she asked.

'What do you mean, darling? I think that it was appalling. The only comfort is to know that it was an accident.'

At these words Shorena looked at Valeri with surprise and some amusement.

'I could never be happy if I thought it had been blown up intentionally. I have come to agree with Foma that violence

287

is always wrong. That's why I didn't want to go to see Bakunin tonight.'

'All the same don't you feel that it was natural justice that those officers should have been killed as they were feasting in the Castle that they had stolen from you?' asked Shorena.

Valeri shook his head.

'You only feel that because of your natural indignation, and also because of your innocence and lack of experience. You don't know the agony of having killed another human being. I shall never forgive myself when I think of Lazar.'

Shorena looked at him with a smile blended of love and pity.

'I'm glad you killed Lazar. Otherwise we shouldn't be together, and Leonidas wouldn't exist.'

Valeri was baffled. 'Darling if I believed in God, I would say, as I used to: "Thy ways are inscrutable." Foma thought that I said that because I was afraid to think. But I don't know that thinking gets one anywhere in a case like this.'

'What a confession! Well you must admit that it has worked out well in the end – murders, earthquakes, explosions were all for the best. Now come to bed,' said Shorena.

THE END